ALL IN THE FAMILY

Maxine Thompson

Melanie Schuster

Janice Sims

Dreams Books
Dreams Publishing Company
www.dreamspublishing.com

Dreams Publishing Company
Post Office Box 4731
Rocky Mount, North Carolina 27803
www.DreamsPublishing.com

Dreams Titles are available at special quantity discounts for bulk purchases for sales promotion, premiums, fund-raising, educational, or institutional use. Special book excerpts or customized printings can also be created to fit specific needs. For details, write to:

Dreams Publishing Company, Post Office Box 4731, Rocky Mount, North Carolina 27803; Attention: Special Sales.

Cover Designed by Nicki Angela

ISBN 0-9770936-6-2

Library of Congress Control Number (LCCN): 2006930341

1. Family & Relationships – Love & Romance
2. African American Women – Fiction
3. Interpersonal Relationships

First Dreams Books Printing: April 2007
10 9 8 7 6 5 4 3 2 1

Manufactured in the United States of America

Contents

SUMMER OF SALVATION

Maxine Thompson

DEDICATION

This story is dedicated to the memory of my late mother, Artie Mae Vann, whose wise words come back to guide me all the time now.

Also, I'd like to dedicate this to my sisters, Nancy and Sonya Vann and to my daughters, Michelle Burroughs and Tamaira Johnson.

ONE

RESEDA, CALIFORNIA

August 3, 2007

Dear Debra,

I know I'm the last on your list when it comes to priorities, being as you're this big Hollywood casting director and all, and being as you haven't been home in over 4 years, but I'm speaking to you as your mother.

Life is short, and I don't know how much time I have left to live, but I know there is one thing that is true. You're going to miss your dear mother when I'm dead and gone.

So with this in mind, I'm inviting you and your new husband Juan to come visit me for the family reunion. It will be held on August 17, 2007.

I know I sent you the invitation back in March, but I just want to remind you.

Not being one to pick a bone, but I must say this. I'm sure Juan is a nice man, but I can't understand how you've been married 4 years and have never brought him home, but I want to meet him. I don't care if he is Mexican. I still haven't gotten over how you eloped, but so much for that.

Anyhow, I know you and I have had our differences in the past, but I want you to know I love all of you girls the same.

I'm writing to remind you that I plan on having all your sisters come home for this family reunion on August 17, 2007. Your daddy and I look forward to meeting Juan and seeing you both together. I expect you to be there!

Love,
Momma

P.S. You know we are not getting any younger. Your daddy's arthritis is still flaring up. I might have to take him to an acupuncturist.
    You better be there!

"Eee-wwwwooo-ee!" Letting out a hiss of anger, which came deep from within her solar plexus, Debra Johnson-Soto flung the letter across the room as though it were a Frisbee while she continued speed-walking on her treadmill. A health buff, Debra refused to miss a beat as she did her daily five-mile trek on her personal gym. She had her iPod, attached to her ear, with Beyoncé's "Keep Giving Your Love to Me" bumping in her ears, but her mother's letter upset her so, she couldn't even concentrate on the music. A red wave circled the family room and made the walls swell.

Even 2000 miles away, her mother had the ability to infuriate her.

The letter read like a directive from your boss—no, a black mother-guilt missile. One meant to shoot her straight through the heart. How dare she pull that mother-rank card on her! She pushed the pause button, stepped off the treadmill, stalked over to the leather playpen sofa, and took her fist and punched one of the forest green tossed pillows. Without missing a beat, she climbed back on the treadmill, pushed the button, and re-started her steady pace.

"Que paso, Mamacita?" Juan looked up from his Sunday Spanish newspaper. He retrieved the letter off the floor and put it on the credenza, which stood in the corner.

It was Sunday afternoon and Debra and her husband Juan were lounging in the family room of their home in Reseda, which was their favorite Sunday pastime. Juan was chilling from his growing business as a landscaper at some of Beverly Hills' most prestigious mansions, and she was having downtime from her job as a Hollywood casting agent, as well as her new burgeoning side business as an independent film producer.

"I can't believe she came at me with the big guns."

"What do you mean?"

Juan had just finished pressing 200 pounds on his workbench, and then settled down with his newspaper. Debra, having completed her five-mile-trek, wrapped the towel around her neck and climbed off the treadmill.

"Mother's guilt. She knows she's not going to die. She's too ornery to die," Debra hissed through her nostrils, and then leaped off the treadmill. She thought of how healthy her mother was at fifty-nine. She still walked five miles to town to do her grocery shopping at the Piggly Wiggly Market.

"Don't say that about your mother. What's really the matter, Mami? I see ain't no sense in catching you in this mood. Are you PMS-ing again?"

"Naw, I'm not PMS-ing. I'm just sick of her."

Debra cringed. If Juan thought the Tasmanian devil could come out of her at that time of the month, he really didn't know about the fear lurking in her mind. She looked away nervously, twisting her wedding band on her left ring finger.

Debra spoke with finality. "I ain't going, so she can just do what she got to do." Debra thought of the last family reunion fiasco, as she called it. She and Candace had gotten into a fight over the "heir property"—including a pearl necklace heirloom, which belonged to her grandmother—that her paternal grandparents, Moses and Beulah Johnson, had bequeathed. To Debra, her mother seemed to have taken Candace's side, which reminded her of the old days, and she had stormed out and sworn she'd never return. How come they couldn't be a normal family?

"Now you know how you say you don't make any major decisions before or during that time of the month?"

Debra set her chin and, from habit, watched Juan retreat. After they made up following arguments, Juan often told her he knew that when her chin poked out, she was beyond being reasoned with. The same thing about this situation. Plain and simple, she did not want to go home for the family reunion. She remembered the last one, four years ago, which had turned into a disaster for her. She had flown out in a huff on the third day, and hadn't been back to Mason Corners since. It was during that period she'd met Juan and they'd eloped on a motorcycle trip to Las Vegas after a six-week whirlwind courtship. It had been lust at first sight, and Juan's muscular, toned body still had the ability to excite her and make her liver quiver.

At the time when they'd met, she'd felt lonely, alienated from her family, and tired of being single. Talking about serendipity, Juan was a bronze Adonis, dripped in golden sunshine, muscles rippling like a river torrent as he worked in her garden. Although he was not the type of man she would normally date, she was mesmerized by his presence. Up until then, she would only date professional, educated men with careers equivalent to her own. But not only had Juan proven to be an exciting date, even better, Juan had turned out to be a wonderful husband who gave her everything that was missing in her life.

"Calm down, Mami. Don't let something like this mess up your day." Juan began massaging her shoulders. That's what she loved about Juan. So laid back. He was totally the opposite of her multitasking, Type A-driven personality.

But why did her mother have the ability to reduce her to the bad child, the middle sister again? No matter that she'd received Oscar nominations for some of the African American and Latina actors she'd cast in different roles; no matter that she had come to one of the hardest towns in which to crack the code in and made it as an African American casting director; no matter that she had walked the red carpet of the Oscar Awards in 2002 when Halle Berry, Sidney Poitier, and Denzel had received their Oscars, her mother could still make her feel like she was nothing. A frisson of anger rippled up her back and wound its way up into her wrinkled brow.

For a moment, contradictory emotions of hurt, rage, and hate—yes hate— for her mother flared like a crimson tide in her bosom. When she came out of the wave, she found her fists clenched and nail prints in the palms of her hands.

"She always does this. I wonder if she wrote her precious Candace."

"Do I hear a little bit of sibling rivalry?"

"No, I love my sister, but my mother always made a difference in Candace. That was her firstborn who could do no wrong." Absently, Debra rubbed the scar on her forehead, a remnant of the fistfights the two sisters had as teenagers. Debra could swear her mother had taken Candace's side even back then.

"Oh, that was her firstborn—you know how it is."

Juan grinned. He was his mother's firstborn and he always felt that they had a more special bond than his five younger siblings.

Debra continued. "She was always so perfect. Each class I took after her, the teachers would try to compare me with her.

"I swore when I grew up, I would move and get as far away as possible from Mason Corners as I could. I got sick of the Bible Belt."

"Didn't you talk to your mother this morning?"

"Yes, and she wanted to know if I was going to church." Debra rolled her eyes upwards in her head.

"You know you can get up early and go to mass with me."

Debra felt a twinge of guilt, but she flipped her wrist in dismissal. "You know I'm Baptist."

Juan laughed. That was a running joke between them now, since Debra hadn't been to church since they were married four years ago. "All right, Mami."

"Why can't my mother be more like your mother?"

"What do you mean?"

"You know—more private? If you want somebody in the family to know your business, just tell my mother. We call her the International Chronicler."

Absentmindedly, she glanced at the oil painting of her father, John known as Jack, her mother, Sara, her three sisters, Candace, Sharon, and Angela, which graced her fireplace. A Sears portrait of Candace, her husband Gregory, Senior, and their three children, Gregory, Jr., age 14, Sarafina, age 12, and Jacquelin, age 9, stood on an easel. She also had old-fashioned sepia-toned photographs of her late grandparents, Moses and Beulah Johnson, who were the parents of seven children, five daughters and two sons, Jack being the youngest son.

Juan smiled. "Oh, you know Mom loves you."

A smile flashed across Debra's face. She never forgot how warm Juan's dumpling-centered, tortilla-rolling mother, Mother Axa, made her feel. Even with her broken English, she communicated love.

"Yes, Mother Axa is good people."

That's why her mother-in-law knew that she was pregnant and she hadn't even told her mother yet. Actually, Mother Axa had looked at her and told her two weeks ago at her sister-in-law Esperanza's baby shower. Debra had poo-pooed the idea. In fact, her period was due that following weekend.

"I dreamed you had a baby girl," she'd said in her heavy Spanish accent. "You're pregnant. I can tell by the gleam in your eye."

True enough, her home pregnancy test had come back positive—to her dismay. Why now? Then, a week later the doctor had confirmed the test. "Mrs. Soto, you're perfectly healthy. You're just going to have a baby."

Debra cringed at the very thought. This was not the time to be having a baby. This was one time she hoped Mother Axa had been her usual discreet self and not told Juan. He was just so 'macho,' there was no way he'd ever understand. She had worked hard to make him accept how liberated she was.

Debra stalked over to her computer, and slammed it on. She signed on to the Internet to look at a Web site that advertised for extras.

Although she typed in a fury, her mind was on something else. Debra decided to evade the issue. She had plans. Big plans to start her own production company and direct her own film. Why did her birth control pills have to fail her now? Not that Juan knew, because she'd pretended to be off the pill anyhow. But he'd never understand how she would want to have an abortion.

Debra paused. She sure hoped he hadn't noticed that she had missed her period. He seemed to know her cycle better than her.

How could she tell her husband, whom she loved dearly, that she was a snap of a finger away from contemplating—no, truth be told, actually planning—an abortion? Her mentor, Camille Dixon, had already found her a private clinic in Beverly Hills. How could she tell him that her career meant more right now than a baby? How could she tell Juan she had mixed feelings about starting a family at this point in her career? In fact, she had been trying to get into producing, had just found the right script, and was trying to do a low-budget film. This was worse than last year when she had to tell him she had re-financed her house—without his knowledge. Why couldn't she be content with the simple things like Juan? How could she hide this from Juan? And, if her pregnancy came to his attention, could she fake a miscarriage?

She hated to think about the abortion she'd already scheduled for that coming Friday.

That Sunday when Reverend Stokes made the altar call in church, Sara, feeling the pull of mother radar, went straight forward and fell to her knees.

She prayed, "Lord, I want all my girls to come home. I know in my heart, they need me more than when they were little. Something is wrong; I feel it in my spirit. I worked hard to make them independent, but even though they are, I don't think any of them are happy. I also dreamed about fish. I wonder who's pregnant."

TWO

*D*id you go to church today, Debra?"
    "MOTHER!"
    "Don't MOTHER me. You know I didn't bring you up to be a heathen."
    "Juan goes to mass and he doesn't mind me going to the Baptist church."
    "I thought you had already joined the one I see on T.V sometimes—what's his name? Reverend Price's church?"
    "Well, I've been too busy to go to church."
    "On Judgment Day, what are you going to say when the good Lord looks at you?"
    Debra's spirit quaked. If only her mother knew she was contemplating an abortion. All her church teaching about 'Thou shall not kill' had taken a back seat to her worry about getting her film made.
    "Did you get my letter about the family reunion?"
    "Yes."
    "I'm expecting you to be there."
    Debra didn't answer.

Debra picked up the phone and called Sharon, her 32-year-old sister who produced a talk show in New York. Of her three sisters, she and Sharon were the closest. Unfortunately, she got Sharon's answering machine. She started to call Candace, but changed her mind. Although they had made up since the fight at the family reunion, their relationship was still strained. And Angela, the baby, was out of the question. She was too big of a dilettante who couldn't seem to find herself or what career she wanted. So who could she discuss her dilemma with?

Debra had an idea. She picked up the phone and tried to call her co-producer, mentor and advisor, Camille Dixon. Camille, who was in her early fifties, had never married or had children. As far as Debra was concerned, Camille had the perfect life. She lived in a huge mansion in Bel Air near Mulholland Drive, overlooking the city's basin. She drove the latest model of Mercedes and even owned a Rolls Royce. She had a long-term relationship with Marlon Dean, one of the powerbrokers at a top cinema studio in Hollywood, and from what Debra could see, she didn't want a marriage, she just loved dating him, so her life was complete. Once again, though, Debra got an answering machine. Technology. She decided to email Sharon.

As she typed out her e-mail, she thought of Camille and smiled. She was blessed to have Camille as a mentor. As a single African American woman, Camille was the most successful of any of the people she'd met in the film industry so far, and she felt lucky that Camille had taken her under her wings. Camille was the only person who knew she was pregnant—in fact, she'd provided the private doctor's phone number for the abortion.

"Kids just mess up your creativity and your flow," she said. "You can have a baby anytime—but opportunity only knocks once. As a black person, when you get a window of opportunity, you've got to jump. That's our problem—we don't plan anything, not even our deaths. That's why everybody has to scramble around when June Bug dies to pay for the burial, but I'm not going out like that."

Camille had even intimated that she would put Debra in her living trust, if they continued working together.

After she signed off from the Internet, Debra started working on a letter of proposal for the investors in her film.

"Hey, how about us going down to the beach?" Juan interrupted Debra's train of thought. "We can grab something to eat at Gladstone's." As an afterthought, he added, "Why don't you wear that cute little number I like?"

He was talking about Debra's ragged edge, French Vanilla silk, georgette tie-back dress with pin tucks.

Debra heaved a deep sigh. "You sure you want to go somewhere? I got so much work to do, I don't know…"

"Come on. Enjoy life. Let's go down to the Santa Monica Pier. Why don't you take a break?"

Reluctantly, Debra agreed, and then cut off her laptop.

"I guess I'll be up all night, trying to get this proposal done. Don't say I've never done anything for you."

Juan grinned and pinched her behind. "Weekends are for us."

Actually, Debra had wanted to see the movie, "What the Bleep Do We Know?" which was about the power of quantum physics, the power of intention, but she decided to let that go.

Suddenly she felt Juan's warm hands rubbing her back. Juan believed in family, hard work, country. A second-generation American, he believed in the American Dream, believed in coming to America and pulling yourself up by your bootstraps, believed hard work was the great equalizer. He was a good man, a sensuous man.

In contrast, Debra was the kind of woman who looked all-the-way business in the office, who could lift her eyes in a way that belied a smoldering temper, but she was a hellcat in the bedroom. Oddly, she took that same steely determination to get hers into the boardroom. She had a 'bring-it-on' attitude when she was negotiating for clients, and everyone vied to be on her list.

From the time she was a little girl and saw how Gordon Parks directed "Shaft," she'd known she wanted to make movies. During college, she wanted to be the next Julie Dash—who could get over the awe-inspiring cinematography of "Daughters of the Dust"—by any means necessary, even if it meant—meant her marriage. If she had to risk everything she had like Melvin Van Pebbles, did with "Sweet Back," similar to Michael Morrison, "Fahrenheit 9-11," she wanted to polarize people and have an avant-garde film, which made people talk; like the movie, "Crash." She wanted to bring the issues she and Juan, as an interracial couple, had faced to the big screen as well.

෨ Oෆ

The freeways were packed with Angelinos doing their Sunday thing, going surfing, to the beach, to The Getty's Museum, to the La Brea Tar Pits, to the African American Museum. Debra watched the palm tree fronds sway gently in the wind outside their moving car.

After they traveled down the back-to-back traffic on the 101 Ventura Freeway East, to the 405 San Diego Freeway South from their home in Reseda, California, instead of Juan taking the Santa Monica Freeway West, he turned on the 10 Interstate East, heading towards San Bernadino

"Where are we headed? The ocean is west," Debra commented when she saw Juan get in the right lane, then switch over to the left, to travel east on the San Bernadino Freeway instead of take the fork going west on the Santa Monica Freeway.

"Oh, I need to stop by Mama's house," Juan said, pointing his index finger east in an off-handed manner.

"All right." Debra didn't give it a thought. They often visited Mother Axa on the spur of the moment.

Juan took the interchange, which led into the San Bernardino Freeway, then exited on Eastern Ave near County General Hospital. Once off the ramp, they traveled up César Chávez Boulevard and it was like entering Little Mexico. The land of taco stands, burritos, chile rellenos, women selling tamales from the street corners, the colorful graffiti wall murals, the tattoos, the sombreros, and what Debra dreaded the most, the local gang, the Cholos.

Her East Angelino in-laws were such a colorful bunch, Debra even felt an affinity for the Latino community and saw a lot of similarities between the nearly all Black community she'd been raised in. Over their four-year marriage, she'd learned some "Spanglais," as she called it. She had even come to understand the plight of the immigrant, the undocumented, and the illegal Spanish Americans, which was really becoming a hot button politically as of late.

When they pulled up to the turquoise stucco, terra cotta, tiled-roofed house in East L.A., somehow the house looked different. Today something was unusual. No grandbabies hung off the porch, no button-eyed, amber-faces with shiny sable-colored ponytails swinging down their backs, as they played jump rope. Absently, Debra looked for the rainbow of nutmeg, cardamom, and turmeric children. For some reason, Mother Axa's house seemed quiet, subdued, but Debra didn't give it a thought.

Instead, Debra was thinking about her meeting with producers on Thursday for her new film, "Summer of Salvation." To this end, she'd even joined an entertainment-networking group that was devoted to developing more diversity in the industry. A fairly unknown writer had provided her production company, Johnson-Soto, with an original, fresh screenplay. It was the story of a Black traveling evangelist, Jonah, who tricked people into thinking he did healings. He had an experience where an ancestor, who was a former slave, began to visit him in his sleep and prick his conscience. Meantime, he met a Chicano woman, Cecelia, and they fell in love. Debra knew Hollywood wouldn't be interested in magical realism since they were more interested in negative image portrayals of Blacks and Latinos, but she wanted to do something about her southern upbringing and had finally found the best screenplay.

As the producer/director, her movie would even be informed by the love she'd shared with Juan. She planned to use a fractured plotline, using parallel past and present scenes of this couple's descendants, detailing fights in the different L.A. prisons between the African American and Latino inmates as a backdrop. She was sick of the movies portraying black people gangbanging, pimping and whoring and that seemed to sell out the race. How come no one wanted to do a love story about blacks or even Mexican Americans? That's why she wanted to do an independent film—for the creative control.

ဆဂ

As soon as Juan used his key and opened the door, the dark house lit up.

"Surprise! Happy anniversary!" a crowd of people yelled out. Debra gasped and put her hand over her mouth. Hot tears sprung to her eyes.

"What?" Then she remembered. She'd forgotten her fourth anniversary. "Juan, you big sneak," she said, playfully thumping him on the shoulder. "How did you pull this off without me knowing?"

"You were hard to fool, but Rebecca and everyone helped me."

Rebecca placed her index and thumb in a circle sign to Juan and he gave her a nod.

Everyone laughed and clapped while inside, Debra felt so awful. How did she forget her anniversary? How could she be such a horrible wife? What did she do to deserve such a good husband as Juan? Eyes scanning the room, she saw young and old and in-between. She even took in the latest newborns of the family. The whole family believed in partying together. She even saw friends and enemies.

Mother Axa, Juan's three sisters, Esperanza, Xochilt and Guadalupe, whom everyone called Lupe, and his brother Javier, were present. Everyone, with the exception of his youngest brother, Hector, known as Loco, who was a local gang member, was present. The room, decorated in turquoise and pink streamers and balloons, seemed transformed to a Cinco de Mayo celebration. Everything had a Latin American flair. Red and green St. Jude candles graced the fireplaces. The sound of a mariachi band floated in from the backyard.

Mother Axa came forth and hugged her. "Hola, Mija. So good to see you."

Debra felt Mother Axa's rough hands on her, the sound of her rosary gently ting-a-ling-ing up against Debra's chest. Her mother-in-law's hands were worn from sewing in the garment district for years as she raised her six children after her husband's premature death from emphysema at the age of thirty-five. "I made your chicken mole and your chutney," she whispered as she kissed Debra's cheek. Debra kissed her slightly wrinkled cheek back with genuine warmth.

Everyone took turns hugging Debra and Juan. "Debra and Juan, we love you."

Javier said in his heavy accent, "I wish you and Juan many more, Debra. You're a good woman."

"Thank you, Javier. That means a lot."

Juan took Debra by the hand. "Come on, Ma." Debra's eyes took in a crowd of Juan's family, relatives, and more than a dozen actors, of all ethnic persuasions, whom she'd gotten parts for on TV recently.

Suddenly the party traveled to the backyard. A group of Spanish rappers, were rapping in what Debra called "Spanglais." The sound of reggaeton and hip-hop rivaled with the rhythms of salsa and mariachis.

Everywhere she looked, she saw clients she had worked with in the past or was still working with.

Debra turned to Juan. "How did you get all these addresses?"

"I looked in your planner and in your phone book."

Debra gave him a strange look, but didn't say anything. Juan knew how she valued her privacy, and he generally respected her wishes, but she guessed it was all right in this instance.

All of Debra's clients kissed her first, then waited for her to introduce Juan. Although Debra wasn't the star or the celebrity, she was the star maker, the dream holder and the dream maker. So in the actor's world, she was the female version of "the Man." In her way, she had the it, the wit and the grit factor. And although everyone knew talent counted in Hollywood, Debra knew the real truth of the matter—relationships counted the most.

She saw and waved at Rebecca Wang, the Chinese actress, whom she'd cast in the part of a new soap opera series, and her Black boyfriend, Ralph, who was a former child star who resembled Todd Bridges. She and Rebecca had a somewhat loose friendship, as well. She also saw Lexi Garner, who was one of her co-producers of "SOS," as they had started calling their film project. She saw both Black and white actors who hadn't worked in years, so she knew they were there to see if they could get parts. She looked on, watched the plastic "smooches" on both cheeks, heard the proverbial, "Let's do lunch," and witnessed the exchange of business cards.

Another actor, Joseph K., who was a Brad Pitt look-alike, called out, "Hey, Debra. I went on that audition. Got the part. Good lookin' out." He pumped his fist in the "you go" sign.

Another actor, Gideon, had just gotten out the much-clichéd Hollywood rehab for his cocaine addiction and he was looking fresh and clean. "One day at a time," he mouthed to Debra, who gave him the thumbs up.

Absently, she looked around for Camille, but didn't see her. Inside, she was secretly relieved. She knew Camille would have wanted to throw the party at a top Melrose restaurant or on Rodeo Drive.

Debra jumped with a start when the music roared up and Juan's youngest sister, Xochilt, age 25, with Indian-style, waist-length hair, hiked up the hem of her red lacy Spanish-styled dress and did that Latin move where they made that guttural sound in their throat and swiveled and wiggled and shook their hips. The more she gyrated sensuously, the more her husband, Jorge, moved up on her. Everyone stood around, clapping and cheering the young couple on. Although Xochilt now had two children, she looked about fifteen years old, with her trim figure.

Juan's second oldest sister, Guadalupe, age 32, was an ob-gyn doctor, who was suffering through her first pregnancy, which was considered a late pregnancy by her family's childbearing standards. She held her hand on her stomach with a solicitous, silent pride. Her husband, Wayne Miller, a white real estate investor, stood nearby, looking uncomfortable. Juan's oldest sister, Esperanza, age 37, who was the mother of seven, was doing her mother hen, hosting thing.

Debra tried to hide how lousy she felt. What had she done to deserve such a thoughtful husband as Juan? Debra thought, here she'd forgotten their anniversary between trying to get her film produced, meetings with producers, deciding whether to go from film to DVD or trying to go the route of the almost extinct theater.

The party fell into an easy casual rhythm. Everyone stood around eating chips, salsa and guacamole. The men drank Cervantes beer and the women tended to drink the punch.

Spices such as cayenne, tandoori, cardamom, cloves, cinnamon, bay leaves, coriander, mustard seeds and whole red chilies wafted in the air. The food was spicy, but Debra knew it to be delicious, yet for some reason, she had no appetite.

When they got ready to eat at the round tables set around the back yard, her Chinese friend Rebecca proposed a toast. "We bless the nicest couple we've ever known. May you have many more years to come." Rebecca lifted her long-stemmed glass.

Debra was the only one not to sip her champagne. Just the thought made her queasy.

For a moment, Debra wished her party had been given in Beverly Hills at a nice hotel, but she immediately felt ashamed of herself. At least Juan's family was down-to-earth and made everyone feel comfortable.

Her thoughts were interrupted by Esperanza.

"Come on, Juan and Debra. Do your stuff!" she called out, after the toast.

Debra shook her head, but everyone stood around and cheered them on.

"Go Debra, go Juan, go Debra, go Juan," they chanted.

Anyone who knew the couple knew that Juan and Debra could dance the Salsa like no one else; this was a dance Juan had taught Debra on their first date. They were so in sync with each other; their dancing looked like a well-orchestrated adagio.

The couple finally relented and Juan took Debra in his arms and right away she felt that warm-fuzzy feeling she always got when they danced together. When they finished, everyone blew their fingers as if to say "too hot."

As she tried to sit down, Debra saw the ground move up toward her and the crowd of people swirling around her.

Mother Axa offered her a sliced up mango with lemon and red pepper, which usually was Debra's favorite treat. But, to her surprise, she became so nauseated, she couldn't stand the sight of it as rivers of water ran through her mouth. "Me seinto enfermo," she told Juan (*I feel sick.*).

"What's the matter?'

"I don't know, but I feel like I'm going to be sick."

Juan helped her to the bathroom, where she retched and retched until her stomach felt empty. The next thing she knew she felt dizzy and passed out. When she came to, Juan and her mother-in-law were standing over her and she was lying on her mother-in-law's old-fashioned quilt. Juan had a white towel that he wiped her mouth with. Guadalupe had her stethoscope around her neck as if she'd taken Debra's pulse.

Debra looked around. Where was she? The last thing Debra remembered was biting the mango's stringy sweetness, and then becoming so nauseated her vomit scorched the back of her throat, and having to be rushed to the bathroom.

"Como te seinte?" (*How do you feel?*) Juan said. He often slipped into Spanish when he was speaking in comforting tones.

"Me siento bien," (*I feel all right.*) Debra replied.

"Seems like we're going to get a visit from a little birdie in about eight months," Mother Axa said in a conspiratorial tone. How could Mama Axa figure things out with those old-fashioned instincts? Oh, Lord, she'd told Juan what she suspected. Debra wanted to curl up and die inside.

"I think you have a little bundle on the way, too," Guadalupe conceded. "Might have low progesterone count. Have your doctor check you for that."

Oh, no. Juan's excitement was so palpable, Debra could feel it. He *was* happy. No, ecstatic, to be more exact. Debra lay there, too stunned to believe it. If only Juan knew how she didn't want a baby right now. She hated now that he'd found out about the pregnancy. Now this was going to be more difficult. Well, now this meant she'd have to fake a miscarriage.

"You mean I'm going to be a father? I can't believe it. This is wonderful, Mamacita." Juan reached down and kissed her. "Oh, Debra, a bambino. I'm so proud. I can't thank you enough. You're having my baby—our baby."

Now, if only this was a different time, a different place. She just didn't want a baby right now.

"Yes." Debra gave a wan smile. She hoped she could hide the horror she felt underneath. What a horrible place to be. She felt worse than a pregnant high school teen. She had dreams and plans and a baby would only disrupt this. Her movie *was* her baby.

Before she could cover up her frustration, the air was pierced by POP, POP, POP.

Everyone began shouting. "Que paso? What is it?"

Debra climbed out the bed and followed Juan, Mother Axa, and Esperanza to the living room. Esperanza's husband rushed in the bedroom and told her to stay in the room.

Debra noticed that most of the partygoers had gone home by this time, but those who were left hit the floor. Debra had forgotten about drive-bys in East Los Angeles. That's why she had moved out of South L.A. to the valley.

Glass shattered. The sound of people hitting the floor and even people outside running filled the air. The noise of metal hitting metals and cars crashing in the front split the air.

Mother Axa let out a scream.

"Que paso?"

Unexpectedly, Hector broke through the door, running at breakneck speed.

"Hector, Mijo, what's the matter?" Mother Axa said.

Juan grabbed his younger brother by the shoulders. "What happened, Hector?"

"It's those niggas from the Rolling Sixties again." Sheepishly, he glanced over at Debra. "I'm sorry, sis-in-law."

Hector, flailing his tattooed arms around, covered only by a sleeveless vest, which was opened to his navel, pulled his greased brush cut hair in frustration. "It was those Crips," he said, "Excuse me, Debra. I didn't mean no harm."

Juan's voice became stern. "Hector, didn't I tell you not to bring this mess around Mama's house?"

"Hey, Homes, I couldn't help it. Don't forget, the name is Loco."

"Look, man, you're still my baby brother. Stop calling yourself crazy. You're not crazy. What happened to my little brother? I don't want to see you get hurt."

Mother Axa crossed her heart with her rosary and began fingering the beads. "Come and eat, Son."

"I'm not hungry, Ma. I've got to go get back with my homes. My boy Alberto been hit. I gotta get down to County General."

Juan spoke to Hector in a stern voice. "Aren't you supposed to report to your probation officer Monday? I told you, you can work for me. I'm licensed and can show proof." Hector had just completed a bid at Chino Prison.

"Man, that's chump change."

"It's a decent living. If you don't get a job, you'll get locked up again."

"Man, look around you. Mother Axa has worked hard all her life and she has nothing to show for it. Nada."

"Don't you ever say that. She has the love and respect of her children and her community. Money isn't everything. All money is not good money."

"But Diablo says that America uses us Mexicans like slave labor. You working stiffs are the chumps."

Debra had heard that Diablo was a local drug dealer who was influencing all the young Cholos and he was reported to be one of the heads of the Mexican mafia.

Juan's voice rose. "I've told you to stop listening to Diablo. He is nothing but the devil. You used to listen to me—what happened to you?"

"Life, big brother. Life." Hector looked over at Debra and, for a moment, she felt ashamed. She knew that since her marriage to Juan, he hadn't been able to act as a surrogate father to his baby brother who was 15 years younger. Hector had been a baby when his father died twenty years ago, so Juan had taken on the role of the man of the family.

"Hector, you're my baby brother and I don't want to see anything bad happen to you. I love you. These fools in the street are just using you."

"Do you want me to be a leaf blower the rest of my life like you?"

Without warning, Juan slapped Hector with a wide, opened hand. The smack resounded throughout the room.

Mother Axa gasped, pulling her rosary to her lips. For a moment, Hector looked shocked as he held the side of his face. Afraid, Debra looked on. Suddenly, looking into her young brother-in-law's eyes, she felt the same danger as if she was looking into the eyes of a killer, the same emptiness as if she was looking at a trapped cougar. The room fell silent. Before Hector could say another word, Juan grabbed him by his collar and through clenched teeth growled, "Don't you ever talk to me like that in your life again. Do you hear me? Don't talk like that in front of my wife or in front of my mother— our mother. What I'm doing is making an honest living—unlike that Diablo.

"What is it going to take to get through to you? Do you want to get shot like Alberto, or even worse, killed?"

Hector snatched away from Juan. "You better be glad you're my brother. Anyhow, I've got to go get with my homes."

"Don't go back out there tonight, Hector," Mother Axa cried.

Hector ignored his mother, then pulled out what looked like over a thousand dollars in twenties. "Later for that chump change. Here, Mom, take this money."

Mother Axa threw the money back at Hector as though he had spit on her. "I don't want this money—never!"

Hector slowly picked the money off the floor and stared at his mother. The room was quiet with pain, apprehension, tension. Without warning, Hector ran into his bedroom, came out with a 9-millimeter gun, which he brandished and waved wildly towards Juan. Debra felt her heart leap into her throat. She stood frozen, her feet glued to the floor.

Mother Axa stepped between them. "So you're going to kill your brother now? What has happened to you, my muchacho?"

Hector paused, and then looked Juan in the eye. "This is not about you, Juan. We're not going to stand for what happened to Alberto. We're gonna smoke some of these fools." He glared at his oldest brother, turned away from him, then ran out as swiftly as he had come in the house.

🐲🬃🐳

Afterward, Juan and Debra drove home in silence. Debra didn't want to say anything. Years ago, she'd learned that blood was thicker than mud. It seemed even more so in Juan's family. Perhaps that's why she got along so well with his family, because she kept her opinions to herself.

From what Juan had told her, he had never banged, but the gangs had always respected him. It broke his heart that his younger brother had gotten caught up in the tidal wave of gangbanging and drug dealing, and Debra felt that Juan blamed himself. Hector already had done an eighteen-month stint in Chino, and was on probation. Debra understood Juan's concern about his baby brother, but she would never understand this machismo code of honor.

THREE

*O*n the Thursday after the anniversary party, Debra drove the 101 Freeway from a power-schmooze-fest breakfast with some of the most influential women in Hollywood—the powerbrokers in Tinseltown. Camille had arranged the meeting for her to meet producers, investors, and agents, and once again, she was happy to know Camille. Women and Improved Images in Film was a multi-cultural group that was women-centered. The group was devoted to improving the images of Blacks and Latinos in Hollywood. Many deals had been brokered here, and Debra felt that much closer to making her film.

Debra was tired of the movies portraying African Americans and Latinos as thugs, gangsters, pimps, killers, ballers, and wannabe ballers. The subtext of her film, "Summer of Salvation," would deal with the interracial relationship, which took place when African Americans and Latinas helped settle Los Angeles and lived in relative peace and harmony. In a later scene she would bring it up to how their grandchildren would be fighting one another in the prisons and how polarized the two groups would become against each other. This would capitalize on the same old divide and conquer theme. Debra wanted to do a movie similar to "Crash," but with the edginess of a Quentin Tarantino flick.

She had the convertible top down on her 1975 souped up, antique Corvette, with the wind whipping through her short haircut. As she drove home, Debra hummed dreamily. She could just see herself on the cusp of being powerful. She could see people coming to her as the make-it-happen person; as the new Hollywood player, the new female media mogul. She could already visualize her film credits rolling. She wondered if she could get Denzel for the male lead? Or even Sanaa Lathan?

Suddenly, she wished she wasn't married. Then she could be free and wouldn't have had to refinance her house last year without Juan's permission. Yes, she could be like Camille and just date and have a "friend," and she could devote more time to her career. Most of all, she wouldn't have to be faced with a pregnancy that she had to hide from her husband or even have to hide the abortion. She could just go get one, simple as that.

When she saw Juan's Hummer in the driveway, she was still so excited about the possibility of getting distributors for her film; she sprinted into their two-story Mediterranean house. Today her peach stucco home trimmed with soft azure never looked more inviting.

"Bay, where are you?" she called from the marbled foyer.

He didn't answer, but she heard him stirring about upstairs in their bedroom. She couldn't wait to tell Juan her good news. For a moment, her excitement overshadowed the darkness about getting the abortion the next day. She decided she wouldn't think about that right now. Her mind was made up. She had to do what she had to do.

When she climbed the stairs, she saw Juan sitting at his desk in their bedroom, his back to her, the room darkened.

"Why is the room dark, Juan?"

Juan didn't answer. Debra cut on the light.

"Baby, I've got good news."

"Hmmph."

"Oh, you won't believe what happened today? I—" Debra stopped in mid-sentence. This wasn't like Juan. Her joys were usually his, but now his coldness was so palpable Debra felt a ripple of trepidation race up her spine. "What's the matter with you?"

"What do you mean—what's the matter with me?"

"Why are you acting so cold?"

"So you've got good news for me." Oddly, there was a note of hope in Juan's dry voice, but Debra was baffled by it.

"I just thought you would be happy for me."

Juan turned to her and dropped his hands on both sides as if they were too heavy for his muscular shoulders to hold. "Tell me this, Debra? What kind of hold does Hollywood have on you?"

"What are you talking about?" Debra couldn't believe her ears or her eyes. Juan's face had transmogrified into a mask of anger like she'd never seen in him before.

"Just tell me, what is so great about your work? I make good money."

"I'm just trying to improve the image of Black and Latina people. Why can't you understand that?"

"No, that's not all I'm talking about. You mean you're so interested in Black and brown people but you don't care about one life?"

"What do you mean?" Debra's heart plunged. Her antenna went up. "What are you talking about?"

Juan sounded colder than Debra had ever heard him talk. "How could you, Debra?"

"What?"

"Stop lying to me. Where have you been, Debra?"

"I told you I went to the networking breakfast."

"Don't play me stupid. I saw the number in your planner. I've asked around. I've got more connections than you think I have. Is that where you were planning to go—or have you already gone? What did you plan to tell me, that you had a miscarriage?"

Debra began to stammer. "I—I—I…" How had Juan found out?

"You what? You did or you didn't. I can't believe you."

"Juan, please listen. Try to understand. You know I'm trying to get my production company off the ground. Anyhow, what were you doing in my personal things?"

"You know I've never gone through your purse or anything. I did this to invite the people for your party."

"Well, that still doesn't give you the right to—"

Juan interrupted Debra. "You took a vow to honor our marriage, but have you? First, you lied and took the pill and didn't tell me. Then, you still get pregnant. Now you've gotten rid of my baby. How could you?"

"Juan, this is just not the right time to be having a baby. We don't have the money to have a baby. I had planned to save up enough to stay home for a few years after I have one."

"What has money got to do with it?"

"It's got everything to do with it. Don't you see? We as black and brown people never plan our lives. We don't plan for death or for birth."

"Oh, I see you've been talking to Camille. I told you that woman was a snake and I can't stand her. But what is the problem? Isn't it my baby—our baby?"

"How could you even say that?" Debra slapped him before she knew it.

Juan held his face but didn't say anything. He kept his one hand clenched.

"I don't know what you do with all these big time producers? I've heard about all those wild Hollywood parties and wife swapping?"

"Juan, you can go, too—"

"I don't want to go to those parties with you."

"Well, speaking of race, I find it's mighty funny that you didn't say anything when Hector called me out of my name. Don't you know your baby will be considered the 'N' word if it comes out of me? Are you Mexicans the new white people here in L.A.?"

"Debra, any baby that is mine I would want. This is—was going to be my first baby. Unlike most of the men I know, I don't have babies spread from here to there with different baby mamas. You know I don't care if it is purple, red or green. That is—if you haven't already aborted it."

"Well, I haven't had the abortion."

"Oh, you mean you haven't had it—yet."

"Juan, I was just so confused. I'm not sure. Don't you see what our child would have to face—not only the white world but racism from both the Mexican and the black community?"

"If you loved me, that wouldn't make any difference to you."

Before she could get her words out, Juan had gripped her shoulders. "Debra, how could you think like that? You're a married woman, not some high school student. I swear you're the most hardheaded woman I've ever known. I've never hit a woman before, but I swear, I could—"

His voice faltered, then he dropped his grip on her. "I'm leaving you. I can't take anymore of this madness. You know I'm Catholic and I thought you were raised a Christian, but I don't know now."

For a moment, Debra was too shocked to speak. When she found her voice, she pleaded, "Juan, don't leave." Hands outstretched, she crumpled down to her knees in tears.

"Debra, two of us can't wear the pants in this relationship."

For a minute, Debra decided to man-up and try to use reverse psychology on Juan. "Stop all that macho talk, Juan. If you want to be such a man, why didn't you hit your brother when he called me out my name? But when he makes fun of you, then you go off."

"Well, why haven't you taken me to meet your parents if our race doesn't matter?"

"That had nothing to do with you."

"It has everything to do with me. I talked to your mother and father and they said they were looking forward to meeting me.

"What would you not sell your soul for, Debra?"

"What do you mean by that?"

"I know my name wasn't on the house until last year, but you didn't put me on it until you wanted to re-finance it and needed my signature for the loan. You've been on the pill for the longest, thinking I didn't know you were on it. You missed them when we went up to Santa Barbara last month, so there. I'm not as gullible as you think.

"Now, as if that wasn't bad enough, you plan on getting rid of our baby without asking me how I feel about it. How can you get rid of our baby? A gift from God? I thought I knew you, Debra, but I guess I don't. Don't I matter? Am I just a sex partner for you?"

"Juan, you know I love you, baby."

"Don't ever come out of the pocket with me."

Juan stood up, walked over to his walk-in closet and in one continuous motion, snatched out a suitcase and began throwing clothes in it haphazardly. Shocked, Debra looked on. She couldn't believe it. He snapped the suitcase shut with an air of finality.

"What are you doing?" Debra's eyes widened in disbelief.

"I'm outta here." He began muttering in Spanish and Debra couldn't believe it. Juan sounded like Ricky Ricardo in an old "I Love Lucy" re-run.

"Where are you going? We've never been apart since we got married?" In an instant, Debra's eyes filled with so many tears she could hardly see.

Juan didn't answer.

Debra heard the coldness in each of his footsteps as he stomped down the stairs. From the front window, she could hear the roar of his engine rev up, then the screech of his tire wheels as they spun the gravel in their circular driveway.

ജറയ

That night, Debra boohooed and wailed all night. She didn't know what to do. Now, what had started out as the best day of her life had turned to a nightmare. For the first time in her marriage, she'd slept in an empty bed without Juan and she didn't like it. Not one bit. Not at all.

She thought of Roe vs. Wade. Wasn't it a woman's right to choose? But her answer that came to her in her spirit was hollow.

She didn't know what upset her more. That he knew she had planned an abortion, or that he would even hint she'd been with another man was unthinkable. She hadn't even been tempted to look at another man since she'd been with Juan, he filled her soul so....

Now she understood what a Pyrrhic victory was. It was a victory gained at too great of a cost. She might be able to make her movie, but she'd lost Juan in the process. Is this what she wanted? She missed Juan already. Who could she call? Most of her friends lived in Mason Corners and they had grown apart over the past eight years. Her closest friend, Beneatha, whose mother named her after a character in the movie, "Raisin in the Sun," and she hadn't talked in eight years. Bennie. Oh, if only she'd kept in touch with good old Bennie, she'd know how to say the right words to make everything all right.

Although she and Rebecca were close, she was not close enough to discuss this dilemma. She was too proud to call Camille and tell her Juan had found out about the planned abortion. Camille would tell her to go ahead and go through with it anyway. But now she wasn't sure what she wanted to do. She looked at the bronze-framed picture on her nightstand with the picture of her and Juan at the State Fair and broke down into a fresh wave of tears.

As her sobs slowly subsided, something dawned on her. At the pit of her stomach, she was afraid. Afraid Juan would never return. Afraid if she got rid of his baby, she'd have nothing left of their four-year marriage, their torrid love affair.

The next morning, Debra called the doctor's office and told them she had to change the date to a later one.

"Don't wait too long," the nurse advised.

The next thing she did was something she'd sworn she wouldn't do. She picked up the phone and called the airlines. Suddenly she wanted to go home and see her parents—especially her mother, Sara, even though she wouldn't admit it to herself. She made reservations to go home to Mason Corners that night on the redeye. Although she grabbed her laptop, she didn't want to work. She just wanted to go home.

FOUR

O *n the redeye that night, unable to sleep, inky indigo clouds swirling*
outside her half-mast shaded window, Debra thought back to her first
date when Juan invited her to a salsa bar in East Los Angeles, right
after they'd just left Aunt Kizzy's Soul Food Restaurant in Marina Del Rey.

"Aren't you full yet?" Debra lifted her eyebrow.

"No, this is to go dancing, my little one." Juan had laughed and tilted his
head to the side, looking down at Debra who stood a foot shorter than him.
"Salsa is a form of Latin dancing. This is not salsa, the food."

"Oh, do you always just jump up and do things on the spur of the
moment?" Debra stared at Juan strangely, like he was breaking up her
schedule.

"Why not? I like spontaneity," Juan replied offhandedly. "Besides, I hardly
can get out with my business."

Debra knew she could be a bit regimented, something that her previous
boyfriend Lance complained about, but she liked life to have some order.
That's why she couldn't stand her new Hollywood life. It was all messy and
unpredictable. She didn't know what was going to happen from day to day. If
her clients were going to get the parts or not. But one thing she knew for sure
was that it wasn't talent that counted, but relationships. To that end she did
her share of schmoozing and networking. She'd become a member of several
organizations for women in film.

When they arrived at the bar, at first Debra was embarrassed at how
explicitly sexual the dancing was. The air even smelled of sex, and it
reminded her of the odor of exotic dancers at the strip bars.

"Is this what they call dirty dancing, Juan?" Debra asked.

"No, this is what's called salsa dancing. Loosen up, Debra. Just go with the flow."

At first, Debra felt ashamed to get on the dance floor, with all the humping, grinding, bumping couples, some of whom were of the same sex. The music had that wild Latin mambo beat, and the crowd went wild over "Mama Kyelele," by Ricardo Lemvo and later, "Qui Qui Qui Qui," by Andy Montañez.

But the more Debra twirled and the more Juan rubbed up against her from behind, the more she flung her hair, the more aroused she became and the less self-conscious and inhibited. Juan dipped her, swirled her, and turned her around. Debra liked how they did what she considered the old back-it-up dance, the African fertility dance and every other movement that came to them. They even did the cuddle and sweetheart position and for the first time they kissed, in front of everybody, right there in the middle of the dance floor.

Debra fell into his rhythm and swayed in time with Juan.

For a moment, Debra forgot her anger and depression and just enjoyed the moment. They didn't have clubs like these back in Mason Corners. Talk about a turn on.

This was when Debra started really getting into Juan. He told her he liked the way she held her hands like an Egyptian dancer and how she stayed in rhythm with the music, even when she did unpredictable moves. Debra liked the way he moved gracefully and with sophistication.

Debra smiled at the memory. Absently, she twisted her wedding ring. Oh, how would she be able to live without Juan? Would he ever be able to forgive her or had she gone too far? She knew from how he took care of his nieces and nephews how much he loved children. Now, she knew what a broken heart felt like. Although she had her laptop with her, she didn't pop it open and work on any of her notes. All of a sudden, her movie didn't feel quite so important.

ಬಃಛ

As soon as her plane landed, Debra popped open her cell phone and speed dialed Juan's phone number, but, unfortunately, she got his voice mail. She knew he generally kept it on for customers, so he was purposely not answering the call when he saw her number. Tears dampened her eyes again, but she didn't know what to do. Her eyes were swollen and looked as if she had laundry bags hanging beneath them from crying all day and night. She reached in her purse and pulled out her shades. She didn't want her mother to know things weren't right between her and Juan. She wanted to play this off.

Debra rented a Toyota Camry at the Hertz car rental section of the small airport, then drove herself into town.

ജ❁ങ

Mason Corners, South Carolina. Population 3768. Looked just like she remembered, but everything appeared smaller than she recalled. Home. A place where everyone spoke to one another in molasses-throated drawls. Where the oppressive heat, the humidity, made pregnant women want to curl up and cry.

After passing the farm area outside of the airport, she drove through the part people called "Up Town." She pulled over and stepped out her car to examine the town. *Boring*, was the word that resonated in her head. Nothing much ever happened here in Mason Corners and nothing ever would, as far as she was concerned.

Main Street still held its two-story courthouse, which sat adjacent to the park with General Lee on horseback, his sword pointing skyward. The same Piggly Wiggly Market and a Winn Dixie Market stood on the corner. Main Street still only had the two street lights at both ends of the ten block radius.

A few new antique shops had been built. The only updated store was a video store. What she noted was that there were still no fast food restaurants, so people still went to Diane's Café if they didn't want to cook.

The public library, which Debra frequented as a child stood on the self-same corner, but it looked much smaller than she remembered.

Debra pulled her car over just so she could walk around. It was Saturday morning around eight A.M. The shops weren't opened yet.

The first person she saw was Miss Lit, pushing her wobbly grocery cart down Main Street. Some things never changed. She looked older; her graying hair more straggly, but her skin was still as taut as a smooth young peach. Upon closer examination, her tattered-looking, earth-brown outfit was clean.

"Hi. You one of those Johnson girls, ain't you?"

"Yes, ma'am." Debra tried to remember her down-home manners. She consciously reminded herself to slow her speech pattern to match that of the denizens.

Without the slightest warning, it began to rain while the sun was shining.

"The devil's beating his wife," Miss Lit mumbled as she continued pushing her cart and humming under her breath.

"Sure thing, Miss Lit," Debra agreed. She couldn't help but think how quirky the people of Mason Corners were. Once again, she was glad she left this crazy town.

As she sashayed down the street, not even worrying about the rain since she wore a perm on her short haircut, the next person she saw was Sheriff Lucas, who was once what Momma called, "Hell on wheels," before he met and married his wife Maggie. She taught at Mason Corners' high school. Throughout Debra's childhood, he'd always stopped by and dropped gifts off for her. Her mother had told her that he was like a godfather, but she'd never questioned it. He had just been an avuncular, warm presence throughout her childhood.

"What you doing home, Miss Debra?"

"I'm here for the family reunion, Sheriff Lucas."

"Well, it's good seeing you... I heard you got married. Where's your husband? Any babies yet?"

Debra wilted inside, but managed to keep her composure; both good-natured questions felt like shark attacks. She straightened her face and tried to sound like she wasn't telling a lie. "He'll be here next week." She didn't answer the other question. Babies? She didn't know what to say to that.

FIVE

When Debra saw the farm, she'd never realized how beautiful her parents' home was. The farm sat on top of a small grassy knoll. A tea-colored stream, where she and her father used to go fishing, meandered along the bottom of the hill. Everything still looked the same except she didn't see the Freedom Tree, the old oak tree which stood near the stream, that her great-great grandparents, Josiah and Easter Johnson, had first planted when they were emancipated from slavery, and somehow were able to get their "Forty Acres and a Mule" through the Freedman's Bureau, but everything else looked the same. She wondered what had happened to her "old friend" when she saw a stump where the tree had once stood so proudly. This had been her favorite tree to climb when she was a wily, young tomboy growing up.

Wine-stained apple orchards and grape vines saddled one side of the farm. Her mother's beautiful roses graced the front yard and a ruby-throated hummingbird fluttered over one of the yellow roses. The sounds of nightingales cascaded from the meadow behind the russet-colored barn. The old family cemetery lot sat to the south of the farm, where generations of the descendants of the Josiah and Easter had been buried. The redolent scent of jasmine and wisteria wafted on the air. Underneath that was the smell of water in the rich earth her father was fortunate to own.

The old-fashioned verandah to the rambling ranch house still had the same old wooden swing on it. It looked like it had been recently painted a bright cherry red. Sprawled across the swing were Candace's three children, Gregory, Sarafina, and Jacquelin.

"Hey, Auntie," Jacquelin jumped up and hugged her. "What did you bring me?"

Sarafina gave her little sister a glare of disgust. "Stop begging, Jacquelin. You're such a baby."

"I'm not a baby." Jacquelin pouted.

"Hi, Aunt Deb." Greg, Jr. stood up, arms outstretched.

"Hi, Gregory, Sarafina, and Jacquelin. You guys, come over here and give your auntie a hug." Debra tried to hide her feelings and attempted a smile as she and her two nieces and one nephew gave each other a group hug. "You guys are getting so big. I'm sorry I didn't bring you anything, but I'll pick you up something before I leave."

When Debra swung open the screen door, which was typically unlocked whether the grandchildren were visiting or not, the house still had the sound of Andrae Crouch's "My Tribute: To God Be the Glory," floating over their thirty-year old stereo. Momma was a staunch Baptist and she loved her gospel music. The smells of turnip greens floated on the air.

The same ceramic what-knots decorated the étagère in the living room, a wall full of family portraits of three generations of Johnsons at different ages graced one wall, and a sense of the past washed over Debra as soon as she trudged into the room and placed her suitcases in the floor. The plastic covered, flowered damask sofa and love seat sat in the same place. The same throw rugs that Angela had tripped on and broken her ankle when she was about six. The same old-fashioned floor model TV where Debra had cracked her tooth, when she and Candace had been wrestling over who would watch what TV show back in the eighties. She recalled that the fight was over a rerun of "Good Times" versus the newer Black show "What's Happening?"

Without warning, Sara, apron around her rotund waist, sashayed out of the kitchen, speaking over her shoulders to Jack, who was obviously still in the kitchen. "Jack, Bay, we're going to have to pick up two more barrels for the barbecue. You know Robert think he can do better with that little pit he got, but I want you to do all the meat this year."

Before speaking, Debra drank in her mother's appearance. As usual she wore long sleeves though it was over one hundred degrees. Debra guessed her mother wore long sleeves to hide her big ham-hock upper arms. She was still 'bright-skinned' as Debra often heard her Aunt Ruth say. Sara had gained about twenty more pounds, was even "thicker," as her father used to say as if she was a luscious steak, and looking as formidable as ever. Her father never acted like her mother was robust; he acted like her weight was a sign of their prosperity. "A man don't want a bag of bones," he would say. In her late fifties, Sara was still considered a good-looking woman. In Debra's Hollywood thin consciousness, her mother at a size 16 was considered "fat."

When her mother saw Debra, she gasped, and put her hand over her heart. "Baby, what are you doing here?" Sara asked. "Jack, Honey, Debra's here."

Debra heaved a sigh of disbelief. "Didn't you ask—no, tell me to come to the family reunion?"

"Debra, it's too early. It starts next week." Sara reached down and hugged her, a look of absent-minded concern written over her face. "What are you doing wearing sunglasses in the house? For Christ's sake, it's still morning."

Debra didn't want her mother to see how red her eyes were from crying so she just acted as if she didn't hear that question.

"Well, I guess I'll be here to help you. Why are Candace's kids here?"

"Me and your daddy went down to get them so Candace and Gregory could spend some time together. We've had them a few weeks. Where's your husband?" Sara gave Debra a pointed look.

"He had to work. He'll be here for the family reunion though."

Sara gave her a strange look, but didn't say anything.

"Hey, baby girl," her father interrupted her mother before she could give Debra the third-degree and for that, Debra was grateful. Her father, a deep Espresso-color, in his early sixties, was still muscular and trim from working on the farm. Wearing his usual uniform of denim coveralls, he kept his habitual piece of straw twitching up and down in the corner of his mouth. Years ago, he used to smoke a pipe, but since he'd quit, he used the straw to keep his usually laconic mouth moving up and down in a silent tic-like movement.

When Debra gazed up at her handsome, graying father, Jack, she felt a catch in her throat, and almost felt like crying. Although his shoulders still held the memory of his muscles, he had aged in the past four years, and for the first time in her life, didn't seem as omnipotent. Other than Juan, no man had ever measured up to her father.

"Hi, Daddy." She couldn't help it; she'd always been a Daddy's girl. She fondly recalled riding on his tractor side by side with him when she was a little girl. She was the only sister who had liked working the land with her father. The other girls used to complain and grumble when they had to work in the garden. "We ain't Kunta Kinte, Momma."

Debra and her father had often fished in the stream, and he would tell her the family history regarding The Freedom Tree, a story she loved to hear over and over. How his great-great grandparents had planted the tree after slavery and promised that all their generations would sit under the shade of their own tree as free people. Debra had always secretly felt like she was her father's favorite.

"Daddy, what happened to the Freedom Tree?"

"Had to chop it down this spring. Got diseased."

"Oh, no."

"Yep." Jack had always been a hardworking, quiet man. Debra knew he was through talking for the day.

After all the pleasantries had been said, her father took her Louis Vuitton suitcases to her old bedroom she'd shared with Candace until her big sister kicked her out for being a pig. Everything in here was like a shrine. The same twin beds, the same lilac curtains, and the old scarred desk. Once inside her room, Debra tried to reach Juan on her cell phone again. This time she didn't leave a message.

Before Debra could get settled in, her mother rushed in the room.

"I need you to come with me," her mother said, grabbing her hand. "I'm going to the hospital to see Versie Lee"

"What's wrong with Miss Versie Lee?" Debra asked when they climbed into her mother's old-fashioned Ford, flatbed truck. Miss Versie Lee had been Sara's best friend since childhood. The local midwife, she'd delivered most of the people Debra knew, including Sara's children. Miss Versie Lee was now a widow, but had never had children of her own. Sara and Versie Lee had gotten married around the same time and had been there for each other through their marriages, Sara's childbirths, their parents' deaths, and their friends' deaths.

"She's got lung cancer."

"And—"

"It's not good."

"Why didn't you tell me she was so sick?"

"One day we were shopping, the next day, the doctor told her she had lung cancer."

"When?"

"Just five months ago."

"But she never smoked."

"I know, but these things happen. She's put up a fine fight, but I think it won't be long...."

☙🙛

When they arrived at Mason Corners' one and only hospital, Mason Medical Center, Debra was shocked when she saw Miss Versie Lee. Her fingers resembled puffy sausages and the right side of her body was swollen like bread dough.

"I just saw her three days ago," Sara whispered, "and she's swollen up almost twice her size."

Miss Versie Lee was sleeping peacefully, a railroad of tubes ran in and out her arms, and a tracheotomy for oxygen went into her neck. "Well, at least they've taken those horrible tubes out her mouth. That had to be painful," Sara commented under her breath.

Sara took her friend's hand and began to rub it. "Versie, we getting ready for the family reunion and I want you to be able to come. Debra's here. She got here early. You remember my second born?"

"Can she hear you, Momma?"

Sara never answered Debra. Almost imperceptibly, Versie Lee's eyes began to flutter, then open. They had a vacant, glazed look and she had a funny-sounding rattle in her chest, but she attempted a weak smile.

"Versie, remember when we was girls together? I'll never forget how we met at church. You won the Bible-verse reciting contest."

Versie nodded her head and mouthed, "I still can beat you."

Sara laughed with a soft clucking sound of her dentures. "I know you can. You were always the best. You know you've had a good life. You delivered almost half the county. You were a good midwife, a good wife, and a good friend."

"Where's my baby?" Versie Lee's words were clear, her eyes wide open.

Debra was shocked. What baby?

Sara patted her friend's hand. "Versie Lee, your baby is fine."

Tears started rolling down Versie Lee's face.

"What baby? Is she hallucinating?" Debra asked sotto voce.

Sara whispered back to Debra, "Years ago she lost her only daughter when she was a baby. She and Jeb were never able to have children after that."

"Oh, I didn't know that." Debra wondered how many other things she didn't know.

Her mother continued to talk to Versie Lee in a low, soothing tone. "Versie, it's nothing you did or didn't do. This could've easily been me, but it's not my time. It could've just as well been you here holding my hand."

Versie flashed a weak smile. "Sara, I'm not afraid. I'm going home."

"Yes, you're coming home…soon.…Versie, you know you've been a good friend to me. You gave me so much love; I don't know what I would have done without you."

Versie seemed to be delirious. "I never lost a baby for other people."

"That's right, you even delivered breech births and C-sections by yourself. We need to go back to having midwives, the truth be told. I know I owe you my life."

Versie continued to murmur through parched lips. "My mother was a midwife, too. She taught me the trade when I wasn't but a girl myself."

Sara took the lotion from the side table, and rubbed Versie's hands in an up and down scrubbing motion. "Versie, you've always loved and cared about people. You loved with your whole heart. I am so grateful to have had you for a friend. I've always appreciated your love. You've been a forgiving person, too. I love you, Versie Lee."

Versie Lee never answered. She drifted back to sleep, a smile of contentment settled on her face.

"She's heavily medicated," the nurse whose badge identified her as Nurse Laura Bradford said as she came into the room.

Sara turned to the nurse and spoke in a low voice, "Laura, how is she?"

Nurse Laura paused. "She's needing more and more oxygen, and she's less able to breathe on her own, but today, she seemed to be doing better. It's just a matter of time. We don't expect her to live more than a week or two."

"Well, make sure you keep her comfortable," Sara said. "I don't want her to suffer."

When they left, Debra looked at her mother and saw her eyes were damp with tears. She wanted to reach out and touch her, but her mother had always been so strong. Now her mother and her best friend were making the walk down Miss Versie Lee's final corner.

"I guess, it's just the circle of life," Sara said, quietly as they walked down the hospital corridor. "Versie has given me power of attorney for when she can't speak for herself."

SIX

*W*hen they drove home from the hospital, neither mother nor daughter spoke. Open fields, a few Bosco cows, dogwoods and moss-covered Spanish oaks sped past the traveling car's window.

Debra thought about the upcoming family reunion and all the preparations Sara would put into it. For the first time in the twenty-minute drive, she spoke. "Mother, what do you want me to do to help?"

"Well, your daddy and maybe your uncle Robert, is going to do the barbecuing. We've got your Aunt Debra in charge of games. We have the picnic, talent night, fashion show and the banquet dinner. The hotel is going to provide the food for that. Your dad and I are going to have a fish fry next Thursday. Of course, we're having church on the last day so everyone can get prayed up for traveling mercies."

"How many people you expecting?"

"About two hundred, plus your husband. When did you say he was getting in?"

"I don't know. Maybe Thursday or Friday next week."

Her mother eyed her suspiciously, and then continued. "Anyhow, folks will be getting in town starting next Wednesday. We've divide up who will stay with who. We have some new bed and breakfast hotels in town. You know Beneatha and her husband own one now."

"What? I've got to call Bennie."

"Well, I see you've lost touch with everyone." Although it was a comment, it felt like a barb to Debra. "You know she's pregnant."

Debra cleared her throat and ignored her mother's remark. "Again?"

"She only has three children—girls. They want a boy this time."

"Well, what is she going to do? Have a half-dozen until she gets one? Didn't she just have a baby last year?"

"With this new ultrasound equipment, I understand she's having a boy. I wanted a boy, but the Lord never gave me one, but I'm satisfied with my four girls."

Debra changed the subject. "Well, it sounds like you have everything together for the reunion. I see Candace has even set up a Web site. You know, I can help with the videotaping of the reunion."

Sara didn't answer. As she made a sharp left onto the country road, her tone changed like afternoon sun to evening shade. "Tell me, Missy. Why haven't you been home in four years nor invited us to visit you and your new husband?"

"Moooother, I have a busy life. I have a film I'm trying to make. Why didn't you and Daddy fly out to see me?"

"You know your daddy doesn't like to fly, especially since 9-11. Besides, you never invited us." Sara hissed through her narrow nostrils. Making a left turn off Main Street, she headed out to the farm. "Well, I got a daughter that hates me. Lordy, mercy on me."

Debra was flabbergasted. Flabbergasted to the point she couldn't respond right away. Sara needed to quit, she thought to herself.

Finally, she found the words to answer. "What are you saying? You know I don't hate you."

"That's all right. But I know one thing. Looking at poor Versie Lee, I've learned just as much from watching her make her transition as from her life. When it comes down to it, it don't matter who was famous, who made a film, it all depends on who you loved and not who loved you. I love you anyway."

Debra thought Sara sounded strange, but she didn't interrupt.

"Poor black people, we don't plan our lives nor our deaths. But Versie Lee left a living trust. She's leaving everything to me and to my children."

Debra was surprised. That's what Camille always said—that black people never planned anything, including their deaths. Her mother drove home the rest of the way, not speaking.

When they pulled up in the gravel driveway, Debra turned to something brighter. "Momma, can I have some of your fried chicken and black-eyed peas? And can you make me some of your homemade ice cream?"

Her mother paused. "Sure."

Debra smiled, feeling like a child again. She hadn't realized how much she missed her mother's cooking.

ಬಂಡ

Later that afternoon, Debra sat down with her parents at the dinner table of fried chicken, oxtails, black-eyed peas, cornbread and turnip greens. A pitcher of lemonade sat in the middle of the table and her mother's customary vase was filled with seasonal flowers—this time she had fuchsia-colored daisies with yellow disks. Candace's children had gone to town to visit their friends.

After they bowed their heads and said grace, Debra took her first bite of food and felt like she had died and gone to Heaven. Her mother could still cook fried chicken like no one else. She also salivated, knowing her mother had made some homemade ice cream for her, even if it was with her electric ice cream maker.

Sara cleared her throat. "Debra, have you talked to Angela? Sharon will fly in with her new boyfriend, Simon Freeman, on Wednesday night."

"No, I haven't heard from Angela in a while." Debra frowned. She really didn't care for her younger sister and her wishy-washiness.

"Have you talked to Candace?"

Debra was quiet for a moment. She knew her mother wanted her and Candace to be close—in fact, she wanted all of her daughters to be close to one another. "Not lately."

A strange look flitted across Sara's face.

⁞⁞

Later that evening, the wall phone in the kitchen rang. Turning off a pot, Sara, feet swollen, swung around from the old-fashioned six-eyelet, ebony-colored stove, and handed the phone to Debra. "It's Candace," she said, casting Debra a pointed look.

Debra sighed, twisted her mouth to the side in a smirk, and then took the phone. "Hey, Candace. How are you?'

"Where are you?'

"I'm here."

"Here where?"

"At Momma an' nem's house." Debra enjoyed slipping into the speech of her youth.

"Okay. I'll see you when I come to the family reunion. I can't wait to get back up there to go antiquing."

"Are you serious?"

"Believe it or not, Mason Corners has some of the best antiques in the country. People come from miles around."

Given the fact that Candace would drive 300 miles from Charleston, South Carolina, Debra decided she needed to check out the antique stores herself.

"Where are the children?" Candace asked. "I kind of miss them."

"They've each gone to see their friends. Go on and enjoy this break while Momma and Daddy have them."

"Where's hubby?"

"Oh, he'll be along later this week. He got tied up at work. You know how it is."

Candace sounded so friendly, Debra wondered if she could tell Candace about her pregnancy, her quagmire, her separation from Juan, her indecision about her pregnancy, but she changed her mind.

"Have you been to see Papa and Big Mama's graves?" Candace's voice suddenly took on that 'bring-it-on' lilt. "We used money from the Family Reunion Fund and bought new headstones for all of the ancestors going back to Papa Josiah and Big Mama Easter."

Debra took a deep breath. Why did Candace have to go there and bring up the fight from 2002? The fight had been over the dividing of the heir property between the grandchildren and her father's family, but it hadn't even been worth it because two of the paternal aunts still had the timberland property and the farmland, in fact, everything, tied up in probate. "Have they settled yet?"

"No, we're still in probate. Aunt Beatrice and Uncle Knee Breeze, and Aunt Esther can't agree. They feel because they didn't have children they should get a larger portion."

Uncle Knee Breeze was Aunt Beatrice's husband.

Once again, Debra thought about how country her sister was—just like Momma—and she was glad she'd moved away. Only Sharon lived up to her standards by being in New York, and Debra couldn't wait until she got there.

"How's Angela?"

"She's doing okay. Had a little problem, but I wired her the money to make it to the family reunion."

Debra couldn't take anymore of her sister's self-righteous, Captain Save-a-Chick complex. "Why are you always pulling Angela out of jams?"

Candace paused, and then hissed in the phone, "After all, she *is* our sister."

"No, she's a space cadet," Debra snapped. "And it seems like you're always enabling her. That's why she can't stand on her own two feet."

"Stop using all this white psychobabble on me. I know you think you're so all-that because you live in Hollywood, but this is the truth. We've got to help each other in family. You need to stop being so critical of your family."

"Well, you taking care of everybody so much you'll wind up looking older than Momma."

"Well, that might be, but the family knows my husband and I know where my husband is. And he loves me. But your husband? No one's ever even met him. You've been married four years and we don't even know if you even have a husband."

"You're just jealous because I have an exciting life. I'm doing things you never even dreamed of. I'm meeting exciting people that you see in the movies and in the magazines and on the news. Candace, you're just straight out country."

"Debra, you're too pathetic for words. You always thought you were uppity and more than who you are. Money isn't everything. I've got a good sane, balanced life down here. I make a good living. What are you trying to hide?"

"Candace, you always did hate that I finished college and moved away from this hick town and you have stayed here and gotten buried alive. Look at you. You're old before your time."

Candace raised her voice. "Listen, Debra, I don't have to take these insults. I'll see you at the family reunion next week. Give Mom and Dad my love."

Debra slammed the old-fashioned phone down on the receiver.

Sara, who was at the kitchen table peeling potatoes, stood up, knife poised in the air in one hand, her other one outstretched in a pleading manner. "Debra, don't be like this. I want you two to be there for each other when I'm dead and gone. I thought you all would have each other."

Debra spun on her heels, stalked out the door, the screen door slamming behind her and bouncing on its hinges.

SEVEN

T *hat night, Sara's soul couldn't rest.* She didn't feel good about Candace and Debra's argument. Although there was a six-year age difference, those girls had argued since Debra could talk. This time, she didn't want to be accused of taking sides. And anyhow, what was Debra doing home so early—without her husband? Maybe what Candace had hinted to her earlier that summer was true. Maybe Debra wasn't married to Juan. After all, she'd never seen a wedding invitation. She'd already felt something wasn't right—in fact, she didn't think Debra even had planned to come to the family reunion. She'd heard her reluctance over the phone. So why had she come home so early? What was this about?

After she heard Jack dozing peacefully, she lumbered out of the bed. She went to Debra's room where she was sleeping soundly. Something was wrong, but she couldn't put her finger on it. She did what she did when the girls were teenagers. She went inside of Debra's Prada purse and found Juan's business card, which had his cell phone number on it. She tiptoed into the kitchen and called him at his cell phone when she couldn't get him at home or on his business line since it was earlier in Los Angeles. She wondered why he hadn't called Debra on her phone line all day and that bothered her, too.

"Hello, Juan. This is Sara Johnson."

"Hello, Mother Johnson. How are you?"

"Fine. I just called to see when are you coming to the family reunion? Debra is hemming and hawing when I ask her when you're going to get here."

Juan paused for the longest. Finally he spoke up. "No, Ma'am. I won't be there."

"Why, may I ask? You know I was looking forward to meeting you."

Juan took another deep breath and the line went silent.

"Juan, are you there?" Sara asked.

Finally Juan spoke up. "Ma'am. I don't know how to tell you this, but we're separated."

"What? When? Debra said you were coming in on Thursday or Friday."

"Well, I won't be coming at all."

"I talked to Debra on Sunday and she talked like you guys were getting along fine. Plus, she called me Monday and told me you threw her a surprise fourth anniversary party. What happened?"

"It's a long story, Ma'am."

"I've got plenty of time." Sara waited for what felt like hours, but was actually minutes.

Taking a deep breath, in words that sounded like choked up tears, Juan spoke up. "Did she tell you she's had an abortion? I'm Catholic, Mrs. Johnson, and I just can't live with the thought of her getting rid of my baby—our baby."

"Juan, I didn't even know she was pregnant. I'm going to talk to her. I will call you back."

When she hung up, Sara wondered how she had missed this. She knew she'd dreamed fish, but she thought it might be wild Angela, her baby. Never in a million years she'd thought it would be Debra. But why not? She'd almost lost her life twice with Debra. It wouldn't be surprising if Debra would finally be the death of her, after all.

෫෭൵ഌ

Sara shook Debra shoulders until she got her to wake up. "Debra, we need to talk."

Debra yawned and shook her head drowsily. "Momma, what is it now?"

"I talked to Juan."

"And?"

"He told me you've had an abortion. Is this true? Why did you go and get rid of my grandbaby?"

"No, I haven't had it—yet."

"What do you mean yet? Are you still pregnant?"

"Anyhow, how did you get Juan's business number?"

"I found it in your purse."

"You have no right to go in my purse. I'm not some little teenager again."

"I'm your mother and as long as you're under my roof, I can seek and search where I want."

Debra thought back and shook her head. There was no chance of having a Columbine High School bombing when she was growing up, her mother had kept such close tabs on her four girls. She guarded her four daughters like they were prized pumpkins at the fair.

"Well..." Debra was at a loss for what to say.

"Now don't change the subject, Missy. Tell me. Is this why Juan didn't come to the family reunion? You've had an abortion?"

"No, Mother. I'm still pregnant, but..."

"But what? You're a married woman. Even if you were a teenager, I wouldn't have approved of an abortion."

"It's a woman's right to decide what to do with her body."

"Horse puckey. God's law says 'Thou shall not kill.' Don't you love your husband?"

"I love him with all my heart, but I don't think he'll ever forgive me."

"He will—if you have his baby."

"I don't want a baby right now. I'm trying to make my film. This is just not a good time to have a baby."

"It's never a good time to have a baby. Babies never come at the opportune time."

Feeling like she did when her mother caught her in a lie when she was a teenager, Debra broke down in tears and found herself blubbering. "Anyhow, you ain't never cared about me. I don't want to have a child and feel the same way you felt about me my whole life."

"How dare you say that? I carried you for nine months during one of the worst years your father ever had on this farm. In fact, we almost lost the farm that year with me having such a difficult pregnancy with you. But did I get rid of you?"

"Well, that was a different time."

"What do you mean that was a different time?"

"Momma, abortion was dangerous back then. You could've risked your life. It's not that dangerous now."

"No, it's not just that. It's because I loved you from the time you were conceived, even if it wasn't a good time to have a baby. I loved your father and I could never get rid of his baby."

"Momma, I don't know what to do. Juan found out before I could get the abortion, so I canceled it—for now."

"Don't you see that is a sign from God? Juan sounds like a good man who doesn't want you to get rid of your baby."

"I don't want a baby right now."

"Well, with you being thirty-five, it's not guaranteed you'll get pregnant again. Look at poor Versie. She lost a baby to crib death and was never able to get pregnant after that. I'm glad I had you—even though the circumstances weren't good."

Miffed, Debra lashed out at Sara. "That's not the same as loving the person I became. You always acted like you loved the other three more than me."

Sara hissed in anger, "I've always loved you. You've always pushed me away and preferred to be with your father. Don't you know how proud I've been of you all these years? Your ambition, your creativity?"

"Momma, didn't you want anything for yourself? You pushed us to be independent, but you gave up your whole life for us. I just don't want to wind up like you."

Sara dropped her shoulders and shook her head. "I guess I don't know you anymore. I thought I raised you to be a Christian and now I just don't know."

Her mother spun on her heel, shambled out of the room, shoulders slumped, head tucked in.

Debra looked at her mother's life and she could cry. How could her mother have lived such a life—all wrapped up in her children and her husband's life? No, Debra wasn't ready to relinquish her freedom yet. She didn't care what her mother said. She didn't want to have the baby. She couldn't have this baby. Oh, the vagaries of the heart.

That was the first time Debra had ever realized something.

"Momma's getting old."

Debra went back to sleep. She dreamed about Juan. In her dream they already had a baby. Although she couldn't see the baby, or its sex, she and Juan both looked happy.

EIGHT

*W*hen *she woke up the next morning, Debra found the Bible near her bed.* Sara must have left it, she thought, but she didn't need no bible. Her mind was made up. She turned her head away from it, then leaped out the bed, stretching like a feline cat.

When she entered the kitchen, she found her father, pouring a cup of coffee.

"Where's Momma? Church?"

"No, she went to the hospital to see about Versie Lee. Sounds like she took a turn for the worse last night. They'll be having revival all week, so, just depending on what's going on, she'll probably go later tonight."

"Don't Momma ever get any rest?"

"You know your mother. Besides, your mother owes Versie Lee her life…and yours."

"I didn't know that. What happened?"

Daddy, who was usually taciturn, stopped talking. The piece of straw he kept in the corner of his mouth continued to twitch. He turned on his heel, left out of the house, and Debra knew from past experience he was through talking for the day.

ഓദ്ധ

After her father went back out to the fields to work, Debra clicked open her cell phone and punched in Juan's cell phone number. Once again, she didn't get an answer. Next she tried his office. When he answered, she said, "Juan, we need to talk."

The phone clicked in her ear. Debra took her top lip and bit the corner of her bottom lip, to keep the sobs from escaping. After a few gulps and swallows to keep from letting out her disappointment, she pulled herself together. She didn't want her father to see her crying if he should come back in the house.

She decided to call Camille on her cell phone. Once again, she got the answering machine.

To pass time, Debra perused through the old family albums. Pictures of Easter Sundays gone by where she and her sisters were dressed in wide, frilly chintz, taffeta and voile dresses, all sewn by Sara's hands. Growing up, the family had gone to church every Sunday and perhaps that was why Debra didn't care for church now. To her surprise, she found all her old school papers and awards that her mother must have kept. Then she found an old-fashioned film reel that she'd done of an old family reunion when she was a girl. Big Mama and Papa Johnson really looked young on the film, although they were about in their late sixties. She decided to take the film into town and have it put on DVD to surprise her mother.

Before she left for town, Debra went down to the family graveyard. She remembered when she was a girl, how she used to be afraid of the all the old tombstones, which looked as if they were faces with eyes. She looked at the newly replaced headstone of Josiah and Easter Johnson. Both had lived until the 1900's and were buried side by side. She went down the line of each couple until she got to her grandparents, Moses and Beulah Johnson.

She noticed none of the couples had been divorced until this last two generations. Now here in her generation there were more divorces and never-married people than ever. Debra shuddered. She guessed she would wind up a divorcée also. Running her hand over the smooth cement, her heart crumpled into macadam of grief for Juan.

Suddenly two doves broke out; wings flapping, then they cooed and landed on a tree branch together. Debra shook her head. Even doves had a mate.

NINE

A fter Debra dropped the old-fashioned reel off at the video store, she picked up the phone and called directory assistance to get Bennie's phone number. She'd lost it, and had never programmed it into her cell phone.

When she got the answering machine it said, "Hello, you've reached the Harriet Tubman Bread and Breakfast, the original underground railroad home of Todd and Elizabeth Tyler. If you would like to make a reservation, you can call us, or you can look us up on the World Wide Web. Also, you can Google us." The message gave out the phone number, the Web site URL, and the bricks-and-mortar address that was out on Old Hickory Road. Debra decided not to leave a message and to just drive out to see if Bennie was at home.

Once again, she dialed the three different numbers for her husband—Juan's phone number at home, his office phone number, and his cell phone, but at all three numbers, she got the answering machine or voice mail. Boy, she reflected, how happy she had been when she'd made their home answering message. "You've reached the Soto residence. Juan and Debra are not home. Please leave us a message." There were almost a sing-song, 'I've-been sexed-up-and-I'm-happy' chime in her voice. She guessed she'd have to change her message when she made it back to L.A., She didn't even want to think about it right now.

When she arrived at the Harriet Tubman Bed and Breakfast, she saw two houses on the lot, a white framed, old-fashioned breadbox colonial, and the back house a smaller version of it. Debra *loved* Bennie's house. It looked so inviting. Impatiens and geraniums spilling out of flower boxes on the window ledges. Red, yellow and white calla lilies stood proudly in old-fashioned wood tubs on each side of her porch. Debra heaved a sigh, then lifted and dropped the brass knocker on the Kelly green double door and waited.

Finally, the door opened and Debra's mouth almost flew open when she saw Beneatha. At first she tried to hide her shock; Beneatha was absolutely, positively humongous. Forget the press talking about "glowing, radiant," pregnant women. Her friend Bennie gave pregnancy a bad name. She looked like she would burst at the seams and there was no way she could see her feet. Her stomach stuck out like a basketball up under a pointed tent. Bennie had a dark pregnancy mask on her face and her feet were swollen as large as two baked bread loaves. Attached to her hip was what looked like about a one-year old little girl with Afro puffs and a sidelong shy smile.

"Hey, Bennie."

"Hey."

She couldn't fool Bennie, though. "Don't stand there gawking. You act like you never saw a pregnant woman before."

The truth was Debra had never been around when Beneatha had her three daughters. She had moved to California around the time Bennie got pregnant with her first child so she wasn't prepared to see how Bennie's features had distended, how her nose had spread from what seemed like one end of her face to the other, how her face and neck skin had turned tar black. She looked strange with her brownish-tan arms.

Although Debra had felt critical of her friend, when she saw her holding her little girl in her arms, something inside of her stirred. Did she want a baby? Maybe someday, but not now.

Immediately Bennie turned her back towards Debra as though she was angry.

Debra didn't know whether to go in or whether to stay out. When she heard Bennie say in a nonchalant manner, "Come on in and close the door. You're letting the air conditioning out," she followed Bennie inside.

"Bennie, your little girl is adorable," Debra said, cooing at the little girl who peeked over her mother's shoulder. "What's her name?"

"Deigan." Bennie's words were terse, to the point.

"What a beautiful name. I'm glad you didn't give her one of those ghetto fabulous names like Shaniqua, Takisha, you know."

"No, my other girls are named Arianna and Toni." Bennie sounded defensive. She didn't respond or laugh as they used to do together. Instead, with her hand pushed into her back, she waddled through mahogany French doors into a hardwood floor living room with a stone-faced fireplace on the center wall. She put her baby down on the antique settee, then slowly, uncomfortably, eased herself into a Queen Anne chair.

"So, what do you want, Debra? I haven't heard from you in eight years, then you waltz in here like nothing has happened."

Debra paused for a minute, stunned by Bennie's brutal bluntness. She'd forgotten how straightforward people from the south could be, particularly after L.A.'s brand of insincerity.

"Well, Bennie, I've been busy, but I'm here now. You know our family reunion is coming up this weekend."

"Yes, some of your relatives are scheduled to stay here. We have 24-hour staff, but only the cook is here today. I've had the house cleaned for your folks when they get in town."

Debra, changing the subject, looked around the room. "Your bed and breakfast is gorgeous. Who decorated it for you?"

Bennie seemed to soften a bit and some of the tension eased up between the two lifelong friends. "You know your brother-in-law built the back house. Candace decorated some of the rooms. My husband and I did a lot of the renovations and decorating on this house though."

Debra had forgotten that Candace was an interior decorator and her husband, Greg, a builder. "Well, you could open up an interior design business."

"I'm thinking about it when I finally get back to work," Bennie said, a light shining in her eye. "I guess I have enjoyed refurbishing this house. The white family's descendants who owned this house have even come and left some of their original books for the library, so this is part-museum, part local historical landmark to our town."

"Can I see the house? I'll carry the baby," Debra said, picking up little Deigan. "Where's Aiden?"

Bennie had gotten married nearly ten years ago, a few years after college, to her high school sweetheart, Aiden.

Bennie struggled to get up from her chair. "He's in Raleigh at a business convention. The baby's not due for another three weeks, so I'm fine."

"Good. Are you feeling all right?" Debra was afraid Bennie's back would break she walked with such an arch in it.

"Well, I was placed on bed rest with this baby since I was six weeks but what's the use? They even kicked me out of prayer dance at church. Boy, was I disappointed. But I haven't been able to stay in the bed either. What can you do with a growing family?"

"You want to have more?" Debra's tone was incredulous.

"At least one more. Now that I'll have a boy, I'd like to try for one more so he won't be by himself. I know the girls are going to spoil him rotten."

Debra thought to herself, "You must be crazy."

"What do you plan to name him?"

"Benjamin, after Aiden's father."

"That's a good sturdy name. I like it, too."

As Bennie showed Debra around the house, she loosened up and seemed more friendly. Arianna and Toni were at school and their grandmother was to pick them up.

Debra couldn't believe how warm and cozy the house was. Decked out with beautiful wall paintings, old ceramic water pitchers, old-fashioned calico wallpaper, hardwood floors, and lace window treatments, each room held an assortment of old-fashioned handmade, throw quilts, rocking chairs and other memorabilia. Each of the five bedrooms were filled with antiques, wood vanities, mahogany sideboards and old-fashioned dressers with round mirrors. Debra figured she'd bought much of the furnishings on Main Street. No television defiled any room in the house. Each room possessed a solemn hush, a blessedness that Debra hadn't felt in a long time. It felt like she was back in the nineteenth century.

"This place has such a sense of serenity," Debra commented. "It feels like a convent."

"It's because of the ancestors," Bennie explained. "This was a runaway shelter for the slaves. That's why I named the rooms after my ancestors." She pointed to the doorjambs over each room where there was a bronze plaque, identifying the rooms. "This room is Grandma Lucille's room."

"This room is Grandma Ethel's room."

"This room is named after great-Grandma Virginia."

Each room had soothing lilac, persimmon, sky blue, sunshine yellow paint on the walls.

She could see how a runaway slave could feel like they had reached a sanctuary here.

When they went to the back house, right away Debra noticed the difference. In the front house, everything was immaculate and put in place.

In this house, finger prints, skates, books, and balls lay in disarray in the living room floor. She felt like the house was sticky and cloy before she even sat down and she even had to move a toy to sit down. Cereal was spilled on the living room floor and the empty cereal box was strewn in the floor. Debra was so glad she had a cleaning lady—Miss Maria—come to her house daily and her house was always in order.

"Girl, I'm so sick of talking to these kids. Please excuse this place. Deigan spilled the whole box of cereal on the floor this morning and I didn't even have the strength to sweep it up."

"Don't worry," Debra flagged her hand as if it didn't bother her, but the clutter did bother her. *Chalk this up as another reason you're not ready for a baby*, she thought to herself. Debra couldn't stand disorder or clutter. And she definitely didn't want to lose her five-foot four, 120 pound figure.

"I hate I'm missing revival. I can't wait to have this baby. I'm tired of being pregnant."

Debra wanted to say, "Then why would you even want to go through this mess again?" She couldn't even imagine Aiden wanting to make love to Bennie. Once again, she felt adamant that she wanted to have the abortion. No way was she going to look like Bennie. Bennie used to be a nice-looking, honey-skinned sister with a cute waistline. She was the one of the most sought-after girls when they attended Clark University in Atlanta, but she had always remained loyal to Aiden, who had gone to Southern University. Now, her education and her looks had all been ruined by this pack of crumb snatchers, as far as Debra was concerned.

When Deigan began to whine, Bennie calmly took her, hooked her up under her armpit, and began to breastfeed her. She didn't seem like the old modest Bennie. She didn't even try to cover up her breast with a diaper. And anyhow, who even breastfed anymore?

Debra was shocked at how large and saggy Bennie's breast looked. No way was she going to have her 'puppies' as she called them, heading south at this age. And didn't that child have a mouth full of teeth? Debra looked on in horror, fascination and disgust. How could Bennie do this so openly? But when she saw the look of contentment and the smacking sound Deigan made, she felt the strangest twinge in her uterus. She dismissed the thought. No, she didn't have a maternal bone in her body. How could she be a mother?

"Debra, could you go to the kitchen and get a vanilla milkshake out of the 'fridge? I have craved this junk every since I got pregnant. I had Aiden stock up on them for me before he went out of town."

"What does a craving feel like?" Debra wondered why she was so curious.

"It's like you can't be satisfied until you eat what you crave and need. This baby loves calcium."

After Debra returned from the kitchen with the tall milk shake, she saw Bennie standing up, still nursing the baby who had a suction cup grip on her with her arm around Bennie's back. Deigan's eyes were closed and she was peacefully falling asleep. What shocked Debra was the wet spot that covered the front and back of Bennie's maternity dress. On the floor a puddle of water was growing.

"What's the matter with you, Bennie? Are you peeing on yourself? What happened?"

"Fool, my water broke."

"Oh, Lord, you're kidding."

"No, I'm not."

"Well, girl, I'm like Prissy. Miss Scarlett, I don't know how to birth no baby."

"Real cute, Deb. I don't expect you to deliver me. Just help me get to the hospital. My back's been hurting for the last three months and last night was no different. I didn't think it was time though. My girls are at school and my mom is supposed to pick them up, but she went shopping today, so I'll have to take Deigan with us until we get there."

Bennie remained so calm; it scared Debra, who panicked. She asked frantically, "Where's your suit case? What do we do? You sure it won't be delivered in my car?'

After that everything happened in such a blur that Debra couldn't remember how she got Bennie in the car, the baby in the car seat, and drove the five miles to Mason Corners' hospital.

When they arrived, Debra carried Deigan, still sleeping in her car seat.

By then, Bennie was moaning and puffing and blowing. "Call my mother and tell her to come get Deigan and call Aiden, so he can try to get here. Tell them both I'm in labor."

The hospital staff ran and put Bennie in a wheelchair, then rolled her into the birthing room.

Debra's hands trembled as she called Bennie's mother and relayed the information. Bennie's mother, Mrs. Carrington, said she would call Aiden.

Debra had planned to sit in the waiting room with Deigan who continued to sleep peacefully in the car seat, when a nurse came out the birthing room.

"Put on this gown."

"I wasn't ready to be her coach."

"Well, her coach is out of town; she says you're her best friend and she wants you to stay with her."

"Who's going to watch her baby?"

"I will, don't worry. All her babies were born here and I know Little Miss Deigan. I was here when she was born. You're going to do great."

Debra could feel her teeth grinding, but she went in, scrubbed her hands and put on the green hospital gown.

"Don't push yet," Nurse Nora said.

Finally the doctor, Dr. Long Chang, showed up.

"One more big push," he said, jumping in position. "We see the baby's head. He's a big one."

Debra couldn't believe her eyes as little Benjamin's bloody, slippery head emerged from the birth canal. Finally Benjamin plopped out like a fish out of water, bright crimson red, screaming and hollering at the top of his new lungs.

The strangest feeling washed over Debra as she looked on in amazement.

Once the baby was totally disengaged from Bennie's body, the cord still pulsating, Doctor Long Chang handed Debra the scissors. "What's this for?" Debra asked, dumbfounded.

"Cut here," Dr. Long Chang ordered in broken English after he tied the cord in two places.

Debra hesitated for a moment. What should she do? Then she took a deep breath and just hurried and snipped the cord.

Nurse Nora put Benjamin on Bennie's stomach, and Debra couldn't believe that after all that pain, Bennie was shedding tears of joy; as if she had already forgotten the bloody agony she'd been through.

Even Debra had to admit, she'd never witnessed anything more beautiful than this. She stood staring, amazed at what she'd just seen. She couldn't get over the perfect little baby she saw who immediately started to root for his mother's breast. The nurse stopped him from sucking and took him away to wash, clean and weigh him. When Nurse Nora brought the baby back, swaddled tightly in a receiving blanket, she announced, "Nine pounds, seven ounces."

"Wow," Debra said.

The nurse handed the baby to Bennie, who started breastfeeding him.

"Boy, Benjamin. You've got a good appetite for a newborn," Bennie commented as her son sucked greedily. Slowly, Bennie unwrapped the blanket and examined his toes and his fingers. She checked his whole body and looked relieved that he was healthy. She ran her hand over him. "Thank you, Lord," she said quietly as she kissed his round head.

When the baby appeared to be satiated, Bennie asked Debra, "Would you like to hold him?" She wrapped the blanket back around the baby.

"I'm not sure. He's so little. I might drop him."

"No, you won't. Just hold his head like a football and cradle him in your arms."

Debra held her arms out, and felt the strangest emotional attachment to little Benjamin. For the first time, she was beginning to doubt her decision as to whether or not she should have an abortion. She couldn't remember any time she held a newborn like this.

Suddenly Benjamin's eyes opened and he stared right at Debra as if he'd waited for this moment since he was conceived. Debra's heart melted. "Bennie, he is beautiful."

"Will you be his godmother?" Bennie gazed at her as if she didn't know what to expect.

"Sure." Debra couldn't think of anything more that she wanted to be in the world.

Before she left the hospital, Mrs. Carrington, Aiden, and Debra's two daughters, Arianna and Toni, had showed up. The nurse even allowed Deigan to lay in bed with Bennie and Benjamin. Debra felt a little twinge of jealousy as she looked on, yet, at the same time, she was happy for Bennie.

Most of all, Debra was glad she'd been there to drive Bennie to the hospital. Now, for the first time in years, she felt like she'd been there for her friend. Without a doubt, this would help re-cement their friendship. The only melancholy she felt was when she saw Aiden and Bennie kissing as they cuddled Benjamin between both arms.

She really missed Juan.

TEN

*W*hen *she made it back to her mother's house, everyone was asleep.* Debra was so exhausted, she fell into a deep sleep, the best one she'd had all week.

The next morning Debra told her mother what had happened and how she had witnessed Bennie's baby's birth, then she went into her bedroom to gather her thoughts. This was a hard thing to wrap her mind around, seeing this baby born. It wouldn't have been so bad in and of itself, but seeing the love between Aiden and Bennie, she felt something strange stir in her. Aiden gazed at Bennie with eyes that sparkled with love. He didn't seem to notice her big saggy stomach or her pendulous breasts, but he just saw the woman he loved and whom he was building a family and a life with.

Debra slowly felt her resolve weakening as she studied the old-fashioned lilac print wallpaper. How come life wasn't as simple when she was growing up in Mason Corners? Why did she want to make her film so much? Why did her pregnancy have to come at such an inopportune time?

She really wanted to talk to Camille to help assure her that she was making the right choice. She tried her cell phone number again, to no avail. Where was Camille? She hadn't talked to her in two weeks. She needed Camille to assure her that she needed to have the abortion. "Look, that thing doesn't have a heartbeat yet. Go ahead and get rid of it. You need to get on with your film."

Her ringing cell phone interrupted Debra's thoughts. As she fumbled through her purse to find it, she briskly answered. It was an Unknown I.D. on her phone and secretly, she hoped it was Juan on the phone.

Heart thumping, she held her breath. "Hello, this is Debra."

Her heart dropped in disappointment when she realized it wasn't Juan. At the same time, she couldn't quite recognize the voice on the other end, although it sounded slightly familiar. The caller I.D. listed the call as out of the area.

"They're trying to kill me. Get me out of here. They're crazy. I saw this director and I cried, because they saw me in a straight jacket. I don't want them to see me like this…" The voice broke into sobs.

Debra listened intently and suddenly realized it was Camille. Her voice was several octaves higher than normal, shooting out a rapid staccato of words.

"Camille? Is that you? Please slow down. I can hardly understand you. Camille, take a deep breath."

"I could get raped."

"Calm down. What's going on? I've been trying to reach you."

There was silence and erratic breathing before Camille finally spoke. "Debra, I'm in the hospital. I've been here for two weeks, I think."

"Were you in an accident?

"No, nothing like that. It's Marlon. They say I tried to kill him."

Debra couldn't believe her ears. "What! What happened? "

"I gave him the best ten years of my life. I should have killed him. Even though I said I didn't want marriage and kids, I just didn't want him to feel that I was too emotionally needy." Once again her voice went into the high octave and her diction speeded up.

Debra could hardly understand her. "Camille, slow down. I'm listening."

"Don't you understand he's making a mistake? I've got to save him from this young bimbo who only wants his money. He's going to marry her. He hardly knows her. Is he crazy?

"She's even got him to stop answering my calls. She's holding him hostage at his place—I know she is. He'd never do this on his own. He loves me."

Debra interrupted, "Who is she? Start from the beginning."

Debra went and sat down on her old twin bed. She felt like she was sitting in a psychiatrist chair.

"Okay." Camille took a deep breath. "Two weeks ago Marlon asked me to meet him for lunch at Spago's. He said he had something important to tell me and I could tell by the excitement in his voice that it was going to be big. Debra, I thought this was the day all my dreams were coming true. My life was finally going to be complete."

"And what happened next?"

"So I canceled all my appointments, had the masseuse come to my house, got a facial, got my hair done and a manicure and a pedicure. Girl, I was looking good if I must say so myself.

"My intuition told me that he was going to ask me to marry him."

"Why did you think that, Camille?"

"Well, the last time we made love it was so special." She began to gush in a baby-sounding voice. "We both felt sheer ecstasy as we snuggled in between my Egyptian sheets. Marlon had laughed and said if he could bottle it and sell it, he'd really be rich."

Suddenly her voice went into a nasty tone. "I made him. I bought all his clothes so he could have a suitable image. I'm the one who decorated his house and imported his furniture from Italy. I'm the reason he made it in Hollywood. I gave him my contacts, which built his business. I did this, because I assumed, when he was ready, we would get married."

Shocked, Debra was silent for a moment. "But I thought you didn't want to get married?"

Camille didn't answer Debra's question. She just rambled on. "When I arrived at Spago's, he was already there. He looked so handsome, wearing the last Armani suit I had bought him. Anyhow, I tried to be cool and nonchalant and wait for him to start. We chatted briefly and when he said, 'I've got to tell you something,' I felt all quivery inside. *He's finally going to ask me to marry him*, I thought.

"First, he started with, how much he's always loved me and enjoyed our friendship. 'Camille, you know we've known each other a long time. I have always enjoyed your friendship and your business mind. It never ceases to amaze me, the business deals you're able to put together. You're like my alter-ego. You think like a man when it comes to business. I've always admired that trait in you. You've been my best friend. In bed you throw off all stops. Making love has always been a bonus with you. I've always been able to tell you anything.

"'Anyhow, I've been thinking about my life. About six months ago, one night after dinner, I got chest pains really bad. The restaurant called 911 and rushed me to the emergency room. I was in so much pain, I thought I was going to die. It made me think, what do I really want in my life? If I die today I have no family, or children to leave all my hard work and assets to. So I've decided to get married.'

Camille paused for a moment. "So I held my breath in anticipation. I couldn't wait for his proposal. But when he opened his mouth, I couldn't believe the next words that came out. He told me he'd met someone about six months ago with whom he'd become friends.

"I didn't know where he was going with it, so I said, "'And?'"

"He went on to say, 'She's beautiful and smart. She reminds me of a younger you. I think you'll really like her. She wants to have children and so do I. She's in her early thirties but very mature. So I've asked her to marry me and she's said yes. I wanted you to be the first to know. Her name is Anastasia.'

"Debra, suddenly I saw red. I knew this heifer was white. After that all I remember was his mouth going up and down and turning into a big maw that was eating up my wasted years. I must have blacked out. When I came to, I was in the mental hospital. They told me I tried to stab him to death.

"And the funny thing is I had wanted children. And even more ironic was the fact that I had an abortion by him when I was 43 because he said he didn't want no children. Then I ended up hemorrhaging and then I had to have an emergency hysterectomy. And now I can't have any children. When I was younger, I had put off children because I always thought I had plenty of time."

Debra didn't know what to say, she was so outdone. Camille continued. "Can you do a three-way on your cell phone and call him so I can talk some sense into him? I know that that bimbo is holding him hostage. If you call him I'll be calm and not scream in the phone this time."

A female voice interrupted Camille. "Camille, get off the phone. It's time for your meds and your group therapy."

Camille whispered in the phone, "I'll call you back."

Stunned, Debra held her cell phone in her hand without clicking it off. She didn't know what to think. What was the world coming to?

Here, she had thought Camille had the perfect life. She had a powerful boyfriend who Debra thought adored her. Neither one of them wanted to get married so they both lived separately in their large fabulous mansions, and both had booming businesses. Debra had always assumed if either of them decided to get married, Marlon would marry Camille. Whatever happened to loyalty for all the years Camille had invested in Marlon?

It seemed like the perfect life for an independent woman, which is what Debra had always envied in Camille. Now to find Camille wanted just what most women wanted—a husband and a family. How well had she ever known Camille?

Debra sat on her bed and shook her head.

ELEVEN

*G*irl, come help me snap these beans." Debra gazed up and saw her mother, arms akimbo, standing in the bedroom's doorjamb. Debra almost didn't want to help her mother because she knew her mother would be talking smack.

She heaved a sigh and stood up. "Yes, ma'am."

When she made it to the kitchen, her mother handed her a bowl of fresh green beans from her garden. Debra hadn't seen such green-looking string beans since she moved to Los Angeles. The smell of the earth and the aroma of the vegetables gave her a sense of rootedness, which made her feel a little less shell-shocked. What was the world coming to? she thought, reflecting over Camille's nervous breakdown. Here she'd thought Camille had it all together, was the Rock of Gibraltar.

When Debra sat down on the red swing next to her mother, the two did not speak for a while. But Debra felt a strange sense of comfort. The sound of the snapping beans, the creaking swing, and the smell of jasmine floated around the two women. This reminded Debra of so many evenings from her childhood where all the sisters would sit around their mother and snap beans.

Finally, Sara spoke up, as if she'd been having this conversation in her mind. "Debra, don't you see that's another sign from God? The fact that you would help your friend deliver her baby? It reminds me of Versie and me when you were born."

A faraway look settled in her mother's eyes.

"Mother, are you listening? Did you hear me?"

Shaking her head, Sara snapped back to attention.

"Listen, Mother. I'm not a midwife now. I was just her coach. Don't go reading more into it than it was. It is what it is."

"But you and Bennie will always be close now. Believe me. There's going to be a special blood bond between you until you or she dies."

Debra grunted. "Yes, that was some bloody mess. I don't see how you went through it four times. And I sure don't see how Bennie keeps going through it. Got the nerve to be talking about having another one. I don't want to go through it once."

Debra changed the subject. "How's Versie Lee doing?"

"Versie Lee pulled though and is okay for now. They say she even flat-lined, but she came back. But it's just a matter of time."

Her mother paused and Debra held her breath. She knew her mother was working her way up to letting the boom down on her.

"Debra, I have to say this. Didn't you say how good Juan was to you and even how good his family has been to you? You know I've so looked forward to meeting Juan so we could make up to him for how good he's been to you".

"Yes, but I think you need to stay out of this."

"Well, I'm your mother and I wouldn't tell you nothing wrong. You need to apologize to your husband, but you need to keep your baby even if he doesn't come back.

"You don't know who this child could turn out to be. He could be the one to discover the cure for AIDS."

"Mother, let's don't talk about this right now." Debra's mind was already spinning, first with seeing Bennie's baby born and then, next, she was still blown out the water behind Camille's mental hospital episode.

Her mother persisted. "When is the best time to talk about it? You're having problems now. Then what is a mother for if I can't tell you anything?

"I'm grown. I think I can handle my own problems."

"Well, from the outside looking in, it looks like you're making a mess of your life. I don't want you to get rid of my grandbaby."

"Well, it's not for you to decide. It's a women's right to do what she wants with her body. I'm not going to be barefoot and pregnant like you stayed all your young years. Didn't you ever want to do something with your life?"

"I did. I raised four independent young women, and you the most ungrateful of all of them. And if I had had the same attitude, you wouldn't be here talking smart-mouthed to your mother."

Debra broke down and started sobbing, "You never did like me. You've always made a difference between me and Candace." She hated feeling so vulnerable. This pregnancy mess had all her feelings burbling right underneath the surface. She used to never cry; now she'd been crying every day. Especially since Juan walked out on her.

Sara just stared at Debra with the strangest look.

Out of nowhere, her father burst through the screen door and appeared on the front porch. "Debra, let's take a walk." He took Debra by her elbow and led her down the flagstone path towards the stream. It reminded her of when she was a little girl and she and her mother would have arguments where her father would take her aside and comfort her. They left Sara sitting on the porch, just staring at them.

ଓୠ

"Let's go down by the stream." Her father's straw twitched in the corner of his mouth as if he was in deep contemplation.

They walked in silence as Debra's tears slowly subsided. When they got to the Freedom Tree, her father stopped walking.

"What happened to the Freedom Tree?" she asked. It held so many childhood memories; it was like a part of her had died with that tree.

"It's a long story, but all I can say is that it died when all this fighting started over Momma and Daddy's land. It's a funny thing. That tree has seen blood from unfair lynchings that didn't destroy it, but it seems like the backbiting and fighting within the family has had a worse effect. It seemed to die for no reason."

"That's too bad."

"Do you remember the story I told you about the Freedom Tree when you were a little girl?

"Yes, I remember how each ring represented a generation of Johnsons'."

Her father nodded his head up and down. "That's right. Well, the tree had seven rings when it died. I hope that's not a sign that this will be the dying out of the Johnsons—especially with me having all girls.

"And through all those generations, slavery, poverty and all, there was nothing more important than our children, because that meant that our race would continue on. Somehow, even back in slavery, the Johnsons' children never got sold away, so Josiah had made a promise to keep this land in the family. But now it's tied up in the white man's court and could be lost through taxes, lawyer fees and probate expenses."

Debra couldn't believe it. Her father had never talked this deeply about what was in his heart. She realized she really didn't know her father and how much he loved the family and the land. "That's too bad about Big Mama and Papa's land."

"Debra, life isn't always easy and marriage really isn't easy. Your mother and I have been married almost forty-two years and it hasn't always been peaches and cream. We didn't have expectations of what the other person had to be or had to do, but we were committed to each other and to our family and to raising our children together.

"Your mother and I grew up together, and in the process, we became whole people.

"Your mother and I have been watching you, and you haven't been yourself since you been home. Your mother has been praying every night for you. She's so worried about you and the choices that you're making."

"Why?" Debra snapped. "She doesn't care about me. She loves Candace the most and the others."

Her father's tone went from gentle to firm. He'd never raised his voice at Debra before, but he did now. "Don't you ever say your mother doesn't love you! She almost lost her life when you were born, trying to save you."

"What do you mean? She never told me that."

Her father paused, the straw still twitching in the corner of his mouth. "There are rooms of experience that we don't even want to go in or that we don't even want to try to fathom. What your mother went through was unthinkable. Debra, have you ever seen the cuts on your mother's stomach and on her forearms?"

"I saw something once when she was dressing, but she covered them up. But she always wears long sleeves."

"Remember when I told you Versie saved you and your mother when you were born?"

"Mother never told me that."

"Well, when you were born you were special."

"Why? Didn't you want a boy?"

"No, not necessarily. I've been happy with the four girls God blessed me with. Anyhow, as long as I live, I'll never forget that day though. I had gone into town for supplies. You weren't due for two more weeks."

"When I got home I found your mother bleeding. She'd been cut up pretty bad.

"This man named Melvin Brown had escaped from that prison down in Shelby Township and he had held your mother hostage. Sara was ironing clothes when he came up from behind her and attacked her.

"Fortunately, or unfortunately, Candace was at school so your mother was in the house alone.

"Obviously your mother fought him back the best she could and he cut her arms as she defended herself, but, as weak as she was, when he turned his back, your mother was able to knock him out with that old-fashioned heavy iron she used to use. She even had him tied up with the clothes line when I got here.

"Your mother was losing so much blood, I thought I was going to lose her and you, too. But your mama remained calm and told me to call Versie Lee. I told Versie what happened and I never heard any gossip about it over the years either. Now that's a friend for you.

"Your mother talked me into not killing the man, while he was still knocked out. I swear I wanted to take my gun and... but your mother was the voice of reason. Could've buried him right on this farm and no one would've ever known..." Her father's voice trailed off. After a while he began speaking again.

"Besides that, I had to tend to Sara. I tied tourniquets on your mother's arm to slow up some of her bleeding until Versie got here.

"Anyhow it seemed like it took Versie an hour to get here, but I'm sure it was just minutes. When she showed up, she came with her black bag. She went right to work.

"After Versie showed up and took over, I went on and called Sheriff Lucas, who came out with his deputy, so the man got re-arrested. The deputy took him back to jail to ship him back to Shelby.

"Anyhow your mother was in such bad shape, we didn't think she'd make it, so Sheriff Lucas stayed behind to help with the delivery. We didn't have health insurance and your mother didn't want to go to the hospital and make another bill. Things were real tight that year. Plus, your mother begged us not to let what had happened get out in the town or at the hospital.

"Versie made poultices, which stopped the bleeding from the cuts, and then she delivered you. She did a C-section right here in the house, right there on the kitchen table, and you were born screaming and hollering. She also used roots and teas to help your mother get her strength back.

"Later, when I asked your mother how did she manage to knock the man out with the iron and tie him up, she told me that she was afraid for her baby's life. She said, 'God must have given me the strength because I thought he was going to kill me and I knew the baby probably wouldn't have survived. And I thought Candace would come home and find us both all bloodied up or he would hurt her or worse.'"

Debra was quiet for a while. Finally she asked what was bothering her. "Did he rape her?"

Her father paused. He nodded without saying a word. Debra had never seen her father cry, but she saw tears glazing his eyes. Suddenly Debra eyes watered up, too. He took a deep swallow, his Adam's apple moving up and down, and then he continued.

"You were even a fighter in the womb. I guess that's why you and your mother always bumped heads. But your mother has always been proud of you. The two of you are so much alike.

"Baby girl, I've been watching you since you've been home. There are parts of your life that you don't know about that have been missing. That's why you came home—to find the truth about your life so that you can be healed—not just for the family reunion. Like the Bible says, 'The truth will set you free.'"

"Oh, Daddy." Debra didn't know what to say.

"When it's all said and done, it's not about appearances. It's about what was true and how you treated one another. That's why Sheriff Lucas always has come by and checked on you through the years."

The two walked back to the house in silence.

TWELVE

*W*hen Debra returned to the house, she saw her mother's bedroom door closed. She figured that Sara wanted to be alone, and she decided not to go speak to her right away. She didn't know what to say anyway; everything was so just so crazy. On an impulse, she decided to do something she hadn't done in a long time—she decided to attend the revival. She didn't tell her mother or her father. She just wanted to be alone.

As Debra dressed for the revival, she thought of Juan. She decided not to wear one of her designer dresses or suits, which made her stand out from the rest of Mason Corners. She dressed as rapidly as possible, not putting on any pantyhose or make-up, her usual attire. She decided on a plain black skirt with a simple white blouse and flat shoes. She called Juan once again and got his answering machine.

She thought about it. *He won't even talk to me. Maybe we really are finished.* The thought of her husband no longer wanting her was too much to bear. As she drove, she blinked, trying to hold back the tears, which threatened to blind her. *He's never ignored me like this. We've never not talked for this length of time. I miss him so much, I can't stand it. He knows I love him. How can he be so stubborn?*

Why? How did we get to this point? I've always told him everything. Well, almost everything. I was going to tell him about the baby. He knew I couldn't have a baby now, when my career is finally taking off. As she rubbed her stomach, she thought, *this maybe all I have left of my husband is our baby. No, he hates me.*

She needed time to think. She caught a glimpse of her eyes in her rearview mirror, and decided to put her sunglasses on to hide her swollen eyes.

She ruminated over her situation as she drove down the country road in her rented Camry.

Something is really wrong with my life, but I can't seem to figure it out. Last week I was on top of the world. Today, I feel like I could crawl into a hole and cover it up.

When she arrived at the church revival, she saw a huge tent set up on the acres behind the church for the overflow of the crowds. There were television cameras, speakers and wires going everywhere, as this was one of the major annual events in Mason Corners. She parked in the already-crowded lot.

She saw many familiar faces and she waved at them. There was Miss Lit, Sheriff Lucas and his wife, Maggie. Sheriff Lucas nodded his head in greeting. He seemed happy to see Debra at the revival.

Debra looked on as people greeted each other with hugs and kisses. Many faces she had not seen since she left Mason Corners and moved to California eight years ago.

Before she knew it, Debra felt the warmth and love of the people surrounding her from the community. She knew she needed to be here; she felt so lost. Unlike in California, she felt at home, instead of always "on call" and "on guard."

She had so many questions in her mind yet she didn't know what the questions should be. She was depleted. How could her life get in such a mess? She bit down on the corner of her lip, fighting back the tears.

She thought about it. *Since I've been home, I've lied to everyone about Juan and our relationship. I never use to lie. What's wrong with me? Why couldn't I just tell the truth? I don't know the truth.*

What was that word she'd learned in college English about Greek Tragedy? Peripeteia. She remembered that it meant everything the hero thought he knew about his life was wrong. In her case, everything she thought she knew about her life was a lie. Even her tumultuous birth had been a lie—a secret. Why hadn't anyone told her? Is this why her relationship with her mother was so fractured?

Debra sat down near the back of the church, trying to blend in and be invisible. Suddenly, the choir broke out singing Kirk Franklin's "Blessing in the Storm."

The choir sang for over an hour, changing the energy of the building. They were excellent singers who changed and lightened up hearts. The holy dancing began and Debra almost could have sworn she was in a nightclub as sisters twirled their full figures around like modern dancers. A few people began testifying. "Thank you, Lord."

Reverend Stokes introduced Reverend Milton, the visiting pastor, from Second Baptist Church in Maryville, South Carolina. Debra remembered him from when she was a teenager. He was well known for not only squeezing the last dime out of the congregation, but he had the gift of prophecy.

Reverend Milton took the pulpit and began his sermon. "As I prayed over this evening's sermon in my sanctuary, I asked God what He wanted me to say to you tonight.

"God has called His special people here tonight. One thing He wants you to know and remember is that God loves you. He always has. Even when you don't love yourself, God loves you. Regardless of what you have done or not done, been or not been, He loves you and you are worthy of love. You belong to God. God is love.

"God has got a message for you tonight. Many of you are here tonight because you have a lot of turmoil in your mind. Some of you did not plan to be here.

"You don't even know why you're here. But you see, your spirit knows God's voice is calling to you.

"Some of you were headed somewhere else and felt the call to be here.

"Some of you are in so much pain that you had nowhere else to go. That problem that has had you pacing the floor at night, that's breaking your heart, God has the answer for you. You thought you could fix it. You've done everything humanly possible to correct it. That health problem the doctor told you they have no known cure for, that child you worry about who's on drugs, or the one you're not even sure where they are, or if they are dead or alive, God can bring them home."

"Yes, Lord." People began to cry. "Thank you, Father."

Reverend Milton wiped his sweaty forehead with a bright white handkerchief. He went on. "Those finances you don't have, and those bills you don't know how you'll get paid, don't worry. God is the supplier. Some of you are worried about losing your homes and your farms. Some of you are worried about your jobs being downsized or about finding a new job. That husband you've been worried about. God put you together and only God can break you apart."

Reverend Milton started dancing around the stage. "It does not matter what it is.

"Ask and the door will be open. Seek and ye shall find. God has got the answer. God's got the cure. God's got the elusive peace of mind you've been trying to obtain.

"God wants you to know He's got the answer and it will come right on time. Some of you have already given up. Some of you have given your problem your best effort, but how about giving it to God?"

The audience began doing the holy dance, lifting their arms in praise, and shouting out, "Hallelujah."

Reverend Milton began to wind down his sermon. "Some of you have given it to God and keep taking it back. Once God starts to work on the problem, do you tell Him, 'I've got this' and take it back because you think you know what God is going to do and can handle it from here? God's got a new thing going on. If you knew the answer, you would not have needed God in the first place. God's got the hook-up—not you.

"The problems we have in the physical world only God can solve in the spiritual world. Then it will manifest correctly in the physical world. Only God can give you perfect peace, regardless of what appears to be going on in your life."

The church broke out in a roar of "Amens," "Preach," "Tell it, Reverend Milton."

Reverend Milton continued. "So many us as Black people live our lives like a checker game. It's over before we even know it. We never plan anything—even our deaths. But people should play their lives like a chess game. Some chess games last for twenty years. We need to start making plans to take care of the next couple of generations so that each generation doesn't have to start at Ground Zero. We need to learn the power of prophesying health and abundance into our lives.

"Therefore, I'd like to make a last call to the altar to renew or join God's fellowship. For those of you who feel God was speaking a message to you tonight, please come to the altar quickly. Don't be shy. Don't think your secret is unknown to others and no one knows. That's a lie the devil is telling you to keep you stuck and in pain. You know who you are. Come down for your healing.

"For those who do not feel they need this, please stay in your seat, and pray for your brothers and sisters who are at the altar. God has a job for each of us."

Without planning what she was going to do, Debra broke from her seat and bum rushed the altar. Something about the way Reverend Milton had used the words for those worrying about their husbands, she knew he was speaking directly to her. She got to the steps, fell on her face and cried, "God, save me. Help me. Where are you, God? I need you now."

Tears gushed down her face, and now she took off her shades and cried openly, shamelessly.

Reverend Milton went from person to person, spending as much time with each one as the Holy Spirit directed. He would then move on to the next person. When he finally got to Debra, she was still lying on the altar, weeping uncontrollably. Reverend Milton asked her to stand up. She did so, her knees buckling, her face flushed with emotion.

"This is what's coming to me through the Spirit. Your husband loves you. He can't imagine his life without you. The baby girl you're carrying said if you'll just have me, I'll never give you any problems and I'll grow up really fast. The business you're trying to start is going to be delayed, but when it takes off, it's going to be more than you ever dreamed possible. And the problems you're having with your mother, they will pass.

"Your mother loved you so much she almost gave her life for you to be born. My child, you are under the grace of God. Whatever you're going through, you're going to make it."

Reverend Milton put his palm on her forehead and assured her he would be praying for her. He moved on to the next person at the altar.

Debra couldn't believe it. How did Reverend Milton even know she was pregnant? Or how did he know her mother almost died when she was born? And he said that I'm having a baby girl, just like Mother Axa did.

As she walked back to her seat, Debra felt like she'd been thrown down in a pit and washed clean.

℠℞

As Debra drove home from the church, she reflected on the revival. Debra had not talked to Juan since she'd arrived in Mason Corners. Once again, she tried to reach her husband on the cell phone. He didn't answer and she decided not to leave another message. She had resolved in her mind that after everything she'd done, he may not come back to her. Tears as rich and full as Niagara Falls rolled down her face.

What if Juan never came back to her? It was too painful to even think about. If only he'd talk to her, she could apologize.

Rain began to fall in thick sheets and it added to her gloom. Yet, as down as she felt, she was so glad she'd gone to the revival service; it had turned out to be a life-changing experience. When he prophesied over her, Reverend Milton had given her pencil-sharp clarity. It was as if her life had flashed before her like a drowning person's—only in the area of her major relationships.

First, she'd lost her connection with God and had turned her back on the Most High. Up until tonight, she had possessed no desire to pray, let alone go to church. How had she lost all the Biblical training she'd been raise with? How could she even be contemplating an abortion?

Next, for the first time of her life, she'd seen with lucidity the relationship she had with her mother, then with Juan and then with her family, which she'd never even bothered to introduce Juan to them. How could she have been so stupid? Juan, his family and her family had all given her nothing but love in the highest order.

All of her adult years, Debra had thought so highly of herself, she had failed to recognize who was the wind beneath her wings. It wasn't just her accomplishments that made her such a snob. It was her circle of who she thought were her influential friends. But what had it come to? Her friend, Camille, who was now locked up in a mental hospital? Camille's powerful boyfriend, Marlon, who after 10 years of a non-committed relationship had abandoned Camille to marry a younger, white woman?

Juan would never do something like that to cause so much pain to another human being, Debra thought. He was so concerned and forgiving, even with his delinquent younger brother, Loco, but she had wanted to blow Loco off as a menace to society.

For the first time, Debra saw a clear picture of herself and it was so ugly, she almost didn't want to view it. Debra had always thought that she would marry a professional man—one who wore a suit and tie to work. Here she was, though, not only married to a man who worked with his hands, she was married to a man of another race.

Worse still, she'd always secretly thought Juan was less than Camille's boyfriend, Marlon, because her husband did landscaping and was not a professional man. But now she thought about it. She'd seen Juan's work, and it was like seeing a little bit of Heaven. Their own yard was emerald green, with the most beautiful landscaping on their block.

Suddenly Debra spoke out loud to the empty car. "My Juan is honest, faithful, and hard working. He lives a Christian lifestyle. It's me who is the questionable one. How could I have been so blind?"

Then she knew in her spirit what the problem had been. Blind ambition. Had her dream of doing a movie been a chimera? Yes, she had been dazzled by the glitz of the exciting L.A. lifestyle, red carpet events, shopping on Rodeo Drive, fancy lunches, and name-dropping of the stars. All this had added to the illusion of her own self-importance.

She couldn't believe some of the unconscious things she'd done to Juan and her mother. How could she have been so insensitive and self-centered when it came to the people she loved, particularly her man, someone whom she vowed to love and honor?

No wonder he won't talk to me. I just didn't know any better.

She thought about it. She'd been so judgmental of Juan because she thought she'd married beneath herself. He was a good man—just like her dad. In fact, he had the same values as her father. *I've been so stupid.*

She'd failed to realize Juan was very comfortable with himself and who he was—also like her soft-spoken father. He never tried to impress others with his self-importance. In fact, he was so secure within himself he had never seemed threatened by how ambitious she was.

A weight lifted off Debra's shoulders as she realized something about herself. Who did she think she was that she could discount her husband, her mother, her sisters, and the people of their town, Mason Corners? Who was she to discount the place she was born as a boring hick town, which actually had given her an emotional base for dealing with the world outside of here? Contrary to everything she'd thought, it was she who had the jaded perspective.

Debra whispered to herself, "God, forgive me."

Tears streamed down her face.

Coming in from church she went straight to her bedroom and plopped onto the bed. She needed to be alone to pray, process what she was feeling, but most of all, she wanted to give gratitude to God for letting her see what she had previously been blind to in her life.

THIRTEEN

*L*ater that night, Debra knocked softly on her mother's bedroom door. "Are you alone, Momma?"

"Yes. Come in."

For the first time, Debra realized how strong the bond between her parents were. Their love had to be strong to have survived racism, poverty and even her mother's rape.

"Momma, I want to apologize. I am so sorry."

Sara opened her arms to her, and Debra fell into her arms and started sobbing, once again a little girl in need of comfort. Her mother patted her back soothingly.

Finally Sara spoke. "A long time ago, I watched this movie called the 'Joy Luck Club.' Although the characters were Chinese, it was about mother and daughter relationships. I wondered why I cried so throughout it, but now I know. It's a shame how we love each other so much and don't know how to show it.

"When one of the mothers in the movie told her daughter her heart was always best quality, it reminded me of my four girls. And I cried all over again because all four of my daughters are best quality. It made me so grateful to God for blessing me with four wonderful daughters that we can both be proud of."

୫୬୯୬

Two nights later, on Wednesday night, Debra heard a soft rapping sound at her bedroom door. She assumed it was Sara or Jack. She was lying in bed reading the Bible and had turned to the Prayer of Jabez, 1 Chronicles 4:10. "You would bless me indeed, and enlarge my territory."

"Come in," she said absently, as she turned the page of her Bible.

For a while there was silence. Then suddenly a voice, Juan's voice, called out softly, "Can I come in?"

In disbelief, Debra bounded from her twin bed. She couldn't believe it. Was she dreaming? Could it be Juan? She sprinted to her bedroom door and flung it open.

As soon as she saw Juan, she leapt into his arms. "Juan, I thought you were through with me."

"Well, I'm here." Juan carried her over to the bed, laid her down on the bed and then sat down next to her.

"I'm so sorry, baby, for the way I've treated you. You are a good man and I've been such a fool. What made you decide to come?"

"Let's just say your mother can be very convincing. She told me—rather she invited me to the family reunion and said they were all looking forward to meeting me. She told me she's seen a change in you since you've been home and that I really needed to come. She told me you're going to have the baby."

Debra had to laugh, but this was one time she was glad Sara had meddled in her 'business.' "Is that the only reason you're here?"

"No, I'm here because I love you. Let's go for a walk so we can talk."

Debra picked up her sweater and they strolled outside. She directed him towards the Freedom Tree—her favorite place.

When they got there, Juan took her by her shoulders and turned her to face him so that she could look him in the eye.

"Debra, I have to tell you this. I was just waiting for my real wife to return, not this selfish, self-centered person who had eased into our life—the one who would kill our baby as if it was not a gift from God wrapped in our love. Mamacita, I've been praying that you would come back to me; not that manipulative person who would sneak and refinance the house and not tell me, and who had planned an abortion.

"But most importantly, the person who treated me as if you're ashamed of me and wouldn't introduce me to your family or important friends. How could I stay married to her? I didn't know her."

"You know my friends. They were at the party."

"Those are people who you get jobs for, not the people who you felt were the most important such as Camille and Marlon."

Debra took a moment to tell Juan what had happened between Camille and Marlon. When she finished, she said, "Juan, I've been such a fool, because you've been there for me, I've always taken you for granted. Can you please forgive me?"

Juan leaned over and kissed her on the lips and Debra knew the answer.

Afterwards, they talked at the Freedom Tree for hours. She even told him that what had happened between Camille and Marlon showed her how their whole relationship had been a façade and how she really didn't know Camille. She apologized again for judging people by what they possessed and who they said they were. Camille had been like a chameleon, making herself shift shapes to blend in with Marlon's life and what she thought he wanted. Whereas Debra realized Juan had been comfortable enough with his manhood to let her be the strong independent woman that she was.

The sun had dipped below the horizon and it began to get cooler. Juan put his arms around her shoulders, and they slowly ambled back to the house.

As they approached the front porch, Juan turned to Debra. He dropped to one knee.

"Debra, I want you to know, these have been the most exciting years of my life, being with you. Will you marry me again with your family present? I want their blessings. Let's renew our vows."

Debra could hardly believe her ears. She was so excited, and relieved that Juan was going to give her another chance, she threw her arms around his neck. "I thought I'd lost you and all I'd have left of you was going to be our baby."

"I love you, Debra. I love your fire and your take-no-prisoners attitude. You're the most exciting woman I've ever met."

"I love you, too, Juan. I promise you I'll be a better person, and a better wife. I understand who you are now. I am blessed to have such a wonderful man as my husband."

Juan took his right hand and put it on her stomach. "I hope our little girl looks just like you."

FOURTEEN

*T*he next two days flew by in a whirlwind of activity. Both of her younger sisters, Angela and Sharon, had shown up on Wednesday night, shortly after Juan arrived. Sharon had even brought a beau, Simon Freeman.

While her father showed Juan around the farm, Debra was able to catch up with her sisters. They each had different memories as to who did what and every memory was as if it had happened to a totally different person in a different family as they each recalled what happened.

Candace and her family arrived on Thursday morning. Although Candace and Debra didn't make up, that first day, they acted cordial to one another. When Candace waltzed into their parents' house, Debra was taken aback at how happy she was to see her sister—fight and all.

"Hey, Hollywood, when did you get those shades? And look how high your eyebrows are arched."

Debra refused to rise to the bait when she saw how catty her sister was acting. "I love your hat." In fact, Candace did look sharp in a purple hat with a plume, which dipped over one eye.

"Look at you. I love that Halle Berry haircut."

She could see Candace was beginning to put on a teeny bit of middle-age spread and beginning to look more and more like Sara. She was the lightest complected of the four sisters, and favored Sara the most. Debra was a tawny sienna, somewhere midway between her mother and father's complexions. For the first time, she was glad she wasn't as light-skinned as Candace because her skin still looked as smooth as it did in her twenties, whereas Candace's was beginning to show a hint of age spots and lines.

Candace used to be fine, the one the guys called out, "brick house" when they saw her walking down Main Street.

"Dang, don't I get a hello or something?" Debra couldn't believe how her sister was eyeballing her so.

Candace reached over to swap a perfunctory hug with Debra. "Give me some love. Where's hubby? I wanted to meet him."

"He's out looking around the farm with Dad." Debra felt relieved to be able to tell the truth this time about Juan's whereabouts.

Next, Candace turned to her mother, and gave her a big hug. She stood back and looked her mother up and down. "Momma, your legs and feet are swollen again. You need to get off your feet."

Sara laughed and shooed Candace's admonitions with a dismissive clucking of her tongue. "I'll be fine."

Candace turned back to Debra. "Debra, you look good."

All this was said in a rush. Debra knew Candace wasn't sincere, but she could feel her look of approbation. Of approval. Debra knew she had a very cosmopolitan look and Candace was taking it in, so she could rush out and buy, get, or do the same thing. Being from L.A., it was a given in her crowd that she received a massage, a facial, a professional hairstyle every week, as well as she worked out at least five days per week. However, Candace warmed up a little when she saw how Debra made over how much her nephew and two nieces, Gregory, Sarafina, and Jacquelin had grown, and how bright and smart they were.

"Mom, Aunt Debra showed us how she shoots her films," Gregory said.

"Mom, look at this dress Aunt Debra bought me." Jacquelin spun around and modeled her yellow chintz dress.

"Mom, can I go visit Aunt Debra next summer? She says I can," Sarafina broke in.

"Candace, these children are taller than me, except for little Jacquelin. They are all brilliant," Debra gushed.

"I know." Candace beamed with motherly pride.

The Friday morning activities opened with cars showing up with license plates from as far as Oregon, Texas, Michigan, New York and Florida. The opening afternoon of the family reunion, they had introductions and "Getting to Know You Night."

Juan met relatives from all the different Johnson clans from around the globe. In the younger generation, there were several interracial marriages. Some were cousins who had been in the service and married women from other parts of the world. Juan fit right in with everyone and he seemed like the perfect host. Juan helped her father fish in the stream, and also helped him fry the fish for the opening night.

By Friday evening, all three of Debra's sisters had given Juan their stamp of approval.

"He's a keeper," Candace said.

Juan not only pitched in and helped the men set up the tents for the picnic, he shot hoops with the teenagers, and pitched horseshoes. Candace's husband, Greg Senior, and Juan hit it off, as they talked about business over a game of dominoes.

The picnic tables, set up in the meadow behind Sara and Jack's farm, were filled with barbecued ribs, chicken, pigs' feet, and goat, macaroni and cheese, potato salad, baked beans, garden grown mustard, turnip and collard greens, green beans, squash, rutabaga pie, sweet potato pie, lemon meringue pie, coconut cake, peach cobbler, watermelon, and homemade ice cream. People ate as much as they wanted, and everyone seemed to have a good time.

Debra was happy to see Reverend Stokes come to the family reunion and he agreed to officiate over the ceremony to renew their vows on Saturday.

"You know Reverend Stokes has stopped having Bible studies and has started having financial enrichment meetings," Candace informed Debra. "Now Mason Corners has more money per capita than some larger cities."

"I'll say," Debra said.

When they had the Talent Show on Friday, Debra entered her film she'd had put on DVD of the 1982 Family Reunion. She was eleven years old when she'd shot the film on a 16 millimeter camera. Everyone laughed until tears rolled down their face over the young people doing the Michael Jackson Moon Walk and break dancing. The only sad moment in the film were the motion picture recreations of Grandpa Moses and Grandma Beulah. It seemed strange to see them still alive, walking around with their canes, spouting words of wisdom.

Even so, to her surprise, Debra won the contest.

"Good," Sara whispered to her. "I'm sick of your cousins with their no-singing selves always winning."

"I love the little girl you were," Juan said, hugging her closely to him as the last of the film rolled on the screen they used up against the barn wall.

Debra wondered, *What happened to her?*

₮℞

On Saturday morning, Candace was helping Debra get dressed to renew her vows in the garden at 10:00 A.M., just before the family reunion picnic day got started. Debra had decided to wear a light powder blue silk dress with sheer sleeves.

"I'm sorry for what I said to you about being country, Candace," Debra said. "The truth is I always thought Momma loved you more because you favored her so."

"Girl, you're nuts," Candace retorted. "Don't you realize that you were always Momma's favorite? I look like her, but you have her fighting spirit. When she talks about you, her chest expands with pride—it always has. That was even before you made it big in Hollywood."

Debra was speechless, but she listened intently.

"You never noticed how Momma always cooked your favorite dinners on Sundays when we were growing up? And the fashion magazines you would bring home and point out what dress you wanted, Momma would sew it for you. As soon as you showed interest in making a movie, Momma and Daddy went out and bought that camera that they couldn't afford so that you could at least feel it was possible. They delayed paying for the feed they needed that year so that you could make your film."

"I didn't know that. How did you know?"

"One night I overheard Mama and Daddy talking on the front porch as they sat on the swing. Dad agreed with Mom that it was important—that as a black child, and particularly as a girl, you needed to feel you could do anything you wanted to do. They redid the budget to make sure you got that camera."

"For real?"

"When you went away to college, Momma was so proud, you would have thought it was her going. They even re-mortgaged the farm to be able to pay for your college."

"How do you know all this?"

"When we were kids, I paid attention because I was the oldest child. And when you went to college, I was a married woman so Momma had begun to confide in me. I even sent money to you in college."

"What?"

"When you graduated Momma and Daddy looked at each other with such love for what they had achieved, which was more than they expected. They were so proud that you were the first in our family to finish college. They thanked God that one of their girls would be able to financially help the others to move up in life.

"But what did you go and do? You moved to Hollywood and never looked back. And when you graduated, they drove all the way to Atlanta for your ceremony and you didn't spend any time with them. You were so busy partying with your friends, that later, Momma told me how they went back to the hotel alone and sat on the edge of the bed, cracking peanuts and looking pitiful."

"I'm so sorry. I really had a lot of things twisted. I guess I've hurt a lot of people. I've been so selfish." She paused. Something had been on her mind and she wanted to ask Candace this since they were being honest with one another. "Do you resent how Momma treated me?"

Candace shook her head. "No, Momma had so much love even coming out her little finger, it was more than enough for all of us. Everything she does is showing love. The cooking, sewing, gardening. Her encouragement on the day-to-day and year-to-year basis. That's what love is about.

"Debra, you've made us all so happy that you're renewing your vows in front of the whole family. That means you want the blessings of your family to be part of your new life."

"Well, do you resent me for how badly I treated you?"

"You're my little sister and I love you. Girl, I used to carry you around when you were a baby and I thought you were mine. And I'm so proud of what you're doing out in Hollywood."

"And I'm so proud of you," Debra said, giving Candace a hug. "I saw Bennie's house and I loved how you decorated her rooms. The ambiance is so warm and soothing. You get such a sense of history there. Maybe I'll have you come to California and decorate my nursery when we get back."

"For real? I'm going to be an auntie? Great!" Candace patted her back, and held the hug a little longer.

Suddenly a rapping sound came at the bedroom door. "Who is it?" Candace called out, breaking out the hug. "It better not be Juan. It's bad luck to see your bride before the wedding."

Debra heard giggles outside the door. "It's y'all little sisters. Can we come in?" two voices chimed together.

Sharon and Angela broke into the room, talking excitedly.

Sharon handed Debra a wide-brimmed straw hat with a blue band. "Debra, you look beautiful! We have Momma's hat, which is perfect for your dress. This is your something borrowed."

Angela handed Debra a garter with a silk blue ribbon running through it. "Here's your something new."

Candace came up to Debra and took a string of off-white pearls off her own neck. "Here's something old."

Debra couldn't believe it. These were Grandma Beulah's pearls that they had fought over at the family reunion four years ago. "Are you sure, Candace?"

Candace gave her a sister-girl look. "You know these are heirlooms and I'm only letting you wear them for the wedding. But this is your something old."

Debra laughed. "All right. Go on and be a player hater. But I still need something blue."

"Your dress is blue," Angela pointed out.
All four sisters broke out in laughter.

EPILOGUE

Reseda, California

*W*e're gathered here together to watch the loving reunion of Juan and Debra Soto,"* Minister Stokes' voice droned on. "They have decided to write their own vows."

Juan gazed deeply into Debra's eyes. "Debra Rene Johnson-Soto, being married to you has been the most fulfilling episode of my life. You make my heart so full. As God is my witness, I'll do everything I can to keep you and my family happy and safe. I'll work hard, and cherish you and be faithful to you all the days of my life. I love you, Mamacita."

"Juan Carlos Soto, I, Debra Johnson-Soto, re-take you to be my beloved husband to honor and cherish. You are the joy of my life. You have all the attributes in you that I've always wanted in a man. Loyal, faithful, loving, truthful and God-fearing. I'll love you and our family always."

The couple stood under a white trellis, decorated with white roses, which arched over their heads. They never took their eyes off one another.

As they watched the film on their flat screened TV, Debra and Juan snuggled on the sectional sofa.

"Mami, you looked so radiant. I never saw you look more beautiful."

"You look pretty handsome yourself. It's funny I had to go home to my roots to understand who you are."

"Our lives are so content now. Everything would be perfect, if it wasn't for..." Juan's voice trailed off.

Without him saying it, Debra knew he meant to say, "If it wasn't for Hector being locked up."

Debra assured Juan, "Well, we have a good attorney working on it. I believe Hector's innocent and justice will prevail."

Juan looked sad for a moment as he considered his youngest brother's plight of being accused of murder, although Hector swore on his father's grave, he never got in the car that night when his gang went to retaliate Alberto's shooting.

Debra decided to change the subject to something lighter.

"Okay, enough already. I'm sick of watching Uncle Knee Breeze do the funky chicken." Debra stood up and reached up to her tape deck and cut the DVD from their August wedding off. Sheriff Lucas had done the footage, but his camera skills had left much to be desired. Although the frames moved up and down, she now had a tape of her and Juan as they renewed their vows. "Okay, Juan, we've seen this tape enough."

"I told you," Juan teased, "you didn't say the part about love, honor and obey. You owe me a dollar." He patted her round stomach. The baby, which she now knew from the sonogram, was a girl, kicked.

"Okay, Papi." Debra smiled and went in her purse to pay the bet. She liked her new life where she'd gotten involved back in the church. For the moment, she had put off shooting her film, but she was rewriting the script to give it a Christian slant when she returned to working on it.

"Oh, you're really going to pay me?"

"Well, you know I'm a liberated woman."

"I wouldn't have it any other way."

ONE YEAR LATER....

Dear Debra,

Never thought your dad would ever fly on a plane, but he surprised me when it was time for the birth of your baby girl. He wanted to be there, and greet Easter just like he's done with his previous grandbabies.

Although we both loved being there in California, and the weather was great, not too humid like here, it's just so expensive out there. How can you afford to raise a family there? Maybe you should move back down here. A lot of young couples are moving back south.

Can you believe it's been a year since Versie Lee died? Lord knows she fought to stay here. I am so glad you and Juan were able to fly in for the funeral. She would have been pleased.

Thank you for the last set of pictures you sent of the baby. Grandbaby Easter is so big. I can tell she's got your fighting spirit.

Juan—he reminds me of your dad. They are so much alike. He hovers over the baby like a mother hen and she has him wrapped around her finger just like you had your daddy. That's how your dad was when all you girls were growing up, too.

Juan loves you both so much. You married well. I don't worry about you being so far away anymore.

Oh, yes, your sister, Candace, is still raving about her visit to California. She said you took her everywhere. She is now the new expert on places to go and what you must see in Los Angeles. She gave us some of the nursery pictures, too. The room looks really nice. I didn't realize Candace was that gifted with interior design. I asked her if she might be interested in doing our living room over. She laughed and said she knows we would not change one memory in our home. She said she's been asking to do the room for over ten years.

I saw Bennie at the grocery store with your godson, Benjamin. Can you believe how time flies? He's walking and talking. He now has a mouthful of teeth. You could hear him all over the store. She said you two e-mail each other often. She told me that you invited her to come and the whole family will be there this summer. She said they hadn't had a vacation since they started the bed and breakfast business. She laughed when she told me her husband said it's a vacation when they have no guests staying there.

You won't believe this, your dad wants to fly out again this winter and spend time with the family, and Juan's family. (I guess we're becoming what they call Jet Setters.)

The Sotos are good people. Daddy said to tell you don't forget to call on this coming Sunday. We always look forward to talking to you, Juan, and the baby.

Love,
Momma and Daddy

WHERE MY HEART IS

Melanie Schuster

Dedication

To my birth sister, Jennifer, for always being there for me.

To all my sister friends, especially Betty, Nicole, Susie, Janice, Dera, Leslie, Gwen and Brenda, the ones I laugh with, pray with, learn with and from.

To the ladies of my book club who have nurtured me, cheered me and kept me going. I love you all.

And as always, to Jamil.

ONE

M *s Johnson, Mr. West is on the line for you."*
Sharon Johnson continued to stare at her computer screen. She was tempted to ignore the voice on her intercom because she was a busy woman and she didn't have a lot of time, or patience, with incompetence. Yes, the receptionist was new, but one of the few things she asked of the woman was to be specific. Sharon always wanted to know exactly who was on the line before she took a call; she was a busy, busy woman. Summoning all the tact she had available at the moment she murmured, "Which Mr. West?"

"Umm, what?" The panicked note in the disembodied voice was expected. The receptionist was new for one thing, and for another, she wasn't Sharon's normal assistant. Her administrative right hand was on maternity leave and Sharon had to make do with floaters like this one from time to time.

This time Sharon glared at the phone. "Which Mr. West, dear? Cornel or Kanye?"

"I, ahh, umm, I don't know." The voice was almost wailing from pure fear.

Sharon rolled her eyes and picked up the phone. She knew very well it was Cornel West because he was scheduled for an appearance on the talk show she produced. Besides, Kanye would have hit her on her cell phone because they had it like that. After a brief conversation with the esteemed scholar, she was in a much better frame of mind. She was never in a bad mood; it would have been inaccurate to describe her as constantly being out of sorts or evil. But Sharon knew how to get what she wanted, when she wanted it and if that meant intimidation through excessive politeness, well, so be it.

She hadn't arrived at her position by being a pushover, that's for sure. She was known for her even disposition, for her diplomacy and her charm, but she was also known as someone not to be messed with. When she was annoyed her voice would descend to a low tone with a honeyed sweetness that would have people shaking in their Prada pumps. The floor director, Chloe Cooper, explained it this way: "If she's being noisy and boisterous, she's okay. If she fusses at you a little, you're fine. But if she gets really still and quiet and starts talking in a real low voice, run. Don't ask any questions, don't hesitate and don't pack a bag, just run for your life. Sometimes that voice is the last thing people hear before they drop dead."

The person Chloe had educated didn't believe her and had in fact, laughed her off. Chloe just smiled and said, "Okay, play if you want to. But when you hear that voice somebody's ass is grass. Don't let it be yours."

Sharon knew she had a reputation for being a dragon lady at times and she didn't care. As long as she got the job done, and done well people could have called her a two-headed heifer from hell. In a perverse way she enjoyed the hype; she would never admit it to a living soul, but it was more attention than she'd ever gotten from her family. Her family was the very reason for her less than perky mood at the moment. *Whoever invented families should have to live with mine*, she thought viciously as she threw the handwritten missive into her desk drawer for what must have been the fifteenth time. *Let them spend a day in the bosom of the Johnson clan and they'd be sorry they ever conceived of the idea of relatives living together until the children were old enough to leave the nest forever.*

She spun idly around in her ergonomically-designed, extremely comfortable and very tasteful desk chair and looked out over the city of Manhattan, shimmering in the heated summer weather. High above the busy streets she stared down at the city she loved. There was nothing like a summer in the city. You either loved New York or it would devour you, simple as that. Luckily, Sharon loved it and thrived on its energy. Energy was something she and the city had in common; she had a never-ending supply. She got up from the desk, picking up her Bluetooth and her Blackberry and headed out into the trenches. When her office door opened, the little floater at the desk in reception flushed beet red and cowered. Sharon flashed her a brilliant and sincere smile and told her to take it easy.

"Nobody is going to remember everything at once, Rachel. In time you'll remember that I like to have the full name of anyone who's calling me, but until then, we'll get through it, no worries. You're doing a good job and in a few weeks you'll have it nailed. I'll be in production, so if anyone needs me you can take a message, have them e-me or call me on my cell. Thanks, Rachel."

As she walked away, the young woman stared after her in awe. That was one of the secrets of Sharon's success. She could be an ice maiden; anyone who crossed her knew that only too well. But she really was a caring, genuine warm person who knew how to treat people. She had too much home training from her mother Sara to do otherwise. She was a powerful combination of sweet li'l southern girl, Ivy League MBA and corporate shark. Chloe had once given her a small glass paperweight engraved with the words "If you don't know, you better ask somebody" because that was the best way to sum Sharon up. That's why she was the hottest producer in town, producing the newly syndicated hottest talk show in the country.

Talk to Me had leapt up the charts, burning up the Nielsen as it did so. Of course, the credit all went to the host Michael Sampson, because of his suave good looks and charm. He was as personable as Oprah, as intense as Montel, had the cutting wit of Bill Maher and the good looks of Tyler Perry or Boris Kodjoe. But he would have been just another face in the crowd if it weren't for Sharon. She made the show happen every day of the week. She was the mover, the shaker, the go-to person, the one who knew where all the bodies were buried. She was the one who got people like Tyler Perry and Boris Kodjoe on the set of the show to bare their souls and promote their projects.

She had, in fact, discovered Michael when she inherited a lame show from her predecessor. Sharon had seen Michael doing the late news and recognized his raw talent and energy. She reformulated the show, recruited Michael and got *busy*. In a relatively short period of time, the buzz was out and the show was making its mark. It went from a late night spot to a daytime throne and now it was in syndication. It was reputed to be TiVo'd more times than any other talk show, even Oprah. In Sharon's opinion, it was due in large part to her public relations genius, Simon Freeman. She worked harder than any producer in town, Michael was extremely well accepted by every demographic and his 'Q' rating was off the charts, but as far as Sharon was concerned, it was Simon who got the party started. She owed him more than she could ever repay him, and she told him so often, something he always brushed aside. He could be as modest as he liked, but Simon Freeman was a major reason for the show's success.

Chloe, the floor director for *Talk to Me*, saw Sharon approaching and flashed her usual dimpled smile. "Sharon, I don't like to brag, but this show is going to be off the chain," she boasted. "Well, yeah, I do like to brag, but shoot, this is gonna be the bomb!"

"You are so right. Getting those two on the same show is a major coup," Sharon said. It was true; today's show featured two feuding glamour girls, little spoiled debutantes who'd been friends since preschool and whose broken friendship had been the stuff of entertainment TV and tabloid gossip for over a year. It would be the first time they'd appeared on the same show to publicly air their differences and it was a win-win situation. "If they hug and cry and kiss and make up, it's good TV. If it turns into a yowling catfight, it's good. It's all good," she grinned.

Chloe was doing her customary warm-up dance, a little shimmy that let off steam and revved her up at the same time. She did it every day before she went out to warm up the studio audience. She looked at Sharon again and added a compliment. "You're lookin' extra hot today. Poor Michael won't be able to stand it," she teased.

Sharon raised an eyebrow and made a little face. "Okay, smartass, you owe me for that. Dinner and whining at my place tonight. Be there or learn the intricacies of the unemployment system in the Empire State," she said with a mock stern expression. It was well-known around the studio that Michael adored Sharon but she treated him like a younger brother. True, he was a few years younger than she, not that much. But she had a strict policy against dating co-workers, so he had no chance in the world with her.

Chloe looked shocked, or tried to. "You wouldn't let me go, you need me," she protested. Then she flashed those dimples again. "Are we talking take out or homemade?" she asked, slyly.

"We're talking baked chicken and dressing with giblet gravy, greens, potato salad and homemade rolls with peach cobbler for dessert, can you handle it?"

A deep male voice answered, "Yes, I certainly can. What time should I be there and what wine should I bring?"

Sharon spun around and gave Simon a bright smile of pure delight. "Be there at eight and what do you mean, bringing wine to a feast like that! You get sweet tea or nothing at all!"

"You're right, what was I thinking? I've been in the big city too long," he agreed. Chloe glanced at the big digital clock on the studio wall and waved them away. "Showtime, folks. See you at eight, Sharon," she added as she headed for the main stage to get the studio audience all psyched up.

Sharon and Simon started walking in the opposite direction, ending up in the main corridor outside the studio. She stopped walking and faced him, so she could tell him again how much she appreciated his hard work. "I still can't believe you pulled this off, Simon. You're amazing."

As usual, he brushed off her sincere words, saying it was nothing. "I just called in a couple of favors. They want to have this meeting and they want publicity so it was a no-brainer," he said with his usual modest aplomb. "Now me, I want some baked chicken and sweet tea," he said firmly. "I know I invited myself and I apologize for that, but you're not going to hold that against me, are you?"

"Of course not. Don't be ridiculous, you're always welcome at my house. See you at eight," she said as they headed in opposite directions.

If she'd looked over her shoulder, Sharon would have seen Simon looking at her with an expression she'd never seen before; not on his face, not on anyone's. He was looking at her with unguarded emotion, with all the love he felt for her. He caught himself just before he made a total fool of himself. It wouldn't do for him to be caught staring at Sharon like a drooling schoolboy, but despite his best efforts to the contrary, that's what he felt like whenever he was around her. He'd been in love with Sharon Johnson for over two years and there wasn't a damned thing he could do about it.

He walked quickly to his office, talking on his cell while he did so. He accomplished a couple of things by doing this. One, he got some business taken care of, and two, it gave him time to stop thinking about Sharon, something that was a near impossibility. When he reached his office he greeted his secretary, told her to hold his calls and closed the door for privacy. He loosened his silk tie and took off his tailored suit coat, hanging it on the mahogany coat tree near the door. Instead of heading for his desk, he sat on the sofa and put his handmade leather briefcase on the low table that faced the couch. He fingered the magnificent smooth leather and gave a wry half smile. The case had been a present from Sharon on his last birthday and he treasured it to a ridiculous extent. He leaned back on the sofa and put one arm across the back and rubbed his forehead with his other hand. *Sharon.* If she had any idea how he felt about her she'd freak out, but the feelings were there, as strong and as true s they'd been since the day he realized this was the woman he'd been looking for all his adult life.

There was nothing about her that he didn't find wonderful. She was beautiful to look at, with rich caramel skin, long, thick curly hair, and adorable features. She had big, wide-set eyes fringed with long lashes, thick eyebrows that were always arched to perfection, and pretty lips, nice and juicy sweet looking, lips he wanted to kiss over and over again. She was tall and slim, but she still had a figure, there were hips and booty and tempting round breasts under those expensive designer clothes that she wore. He knew without even touching her, that she might be slim, but there was a hot, curvy woman there, a woman he was dying to make love to. She was always dressed exquisitely; everything she owned was tasteful and becoming. Sharon had once confided in him that her wardrobe was part of her contract. She was a farm girl, she'd told him, and saw no point in spending *her* money for clothes required by her job. "I was just raised to be thrifty and I can't break the habit. I'll pinch a penny until it's totally unrecognizable as currency," she said with a self-deprecating laugh.

That was another thing he loved about her. Sharon didn't play any games about who she was and where she came from. She was raised on a farm in

South Carolina and had no problems talking about it, unlike the many women he'd met who tried to hide their backgrounds.

Sharon was grounded, funny, talented and smart as hell. She could do the New York Times crossword puzzle in fifteen minutes in *ink*, no less. She was not only smart, she was a true intellectual. Sharon attended lectures and conferences instead of raves and clubs. She did her share of socializing, it was necessary in the line of work she was in. Had to see and be seen to get anywhere in TV, especially in New York. But instead of spending her spare time hunting down the latest P. Diddy soiree or fighting for a front row seat during Fashion Week, Sharon scheduled the least amount of time possible for the hectic New York social scene and spent the rest of it in museums, art galleries and bookstores, the latter being her favorite places.

She was everything he wanted; she was sweet, spicy, feisty and a woman of true substance. And she wouldn't even consider going out with him because she simply refused to date co-workers. If he quit his job, he might have a chance with her, but he didn't even want to contemplate a move like that. He liked his job, he liked his salary and he loved working with Sharon. Between a rock and a hard place, that's where he was. He brooded for a while, and then cheered up. At least he was getting some baked chicken tonight. Life could be worse.

TWO

The buzzer to her apartment went off promptly at eight o'clock, making Sharon look up with a smile. It had to be Simon because he was always prompt and Chloe was always running a few minutes late. Sure enough, the doorman announced that a Mr. Fuller was there to see her and she told him to please send him up. She lived on the seventh floor of a sleek, modern twelve-story building. She stood in her doorway, holding the door open with her hip while she wiped her hands on a dishtowel. In a few minutes he was getting off the elevator, dressed just as casually as she was. In one hand was a bouquet of wildflowers and in the other was a small bag that contained a surprise. She turned her head up for his brief, dry kiss on her cheek, thanking him for his thoughtfulness at the same time.

"Simon, the flowers are beautiful," she said warmly. "You are the most thoughtful man in the world, you really are. And what's in the bag? I told you no wine," she scolded playfully.

"And I didn't bring any," he told her. "This is Haagen-Dazs peaches and cream ice cream to go with the peach cobbler. You want me to put it in the freezer?"

She watched him put the two containers of ice cream in the freezer section of her refrigerator, thinking once again what a handsome man he was. Simon had the kind of looks that didn't announce themselves blatantly, they crept up on the observer like the subtle way a sky turns to molten gold at sunset. Once the colors were seen they were indelibly etched on the soul, never to be forgotten, ever. That's the way it was with Simon.

He was tall, over six feet. He was slim, but his body was perfectly made and he moved with a physical grace a lot of athletes never attained. His skin was smooth and dark and his features were perfect, that's the only way Sharon could describe them. His bone structure was classic and chiseled, his lips were sculpted and sensual and his nose was just the right combination of his African and Native American forebears. His eyes were his best feature, she thought; they were large with just the slightest slant, and his eyelashes were ridiculous. They were so long and curly it was enough to make a woman just throw all her expensive mascara away and scream, "Why bother?" His brows accented his eyes; they were thick and distinctive but not overbearing. He was quite a dish, he really was.

As always, he looked like he'd stepped out of a magazine. He was wearing jeans, and a blue tee shirt with a blue-and-white striped cotton shirt over it and athletic shoes, but he looked fashionable and debonair instead of slovenly. Every item of clothing was immaculately pressed and his hair was cut precisely and perfectly, as was his moustache and goatee. Nothing about him screamed for attention, but every bit of his grooming was as meticulous as though he were about to hit the runway or get ready for his close-up. And he always smelled fantastic, too. He wore something that was light yet compelling and Sharon found herself leaning over to get a good sniff.

Simon looked amused but not startled. "Can I ask what you're doing?"

"I'm trying to get a better smell," she admitted. "You always smell so good. What are you wearing?"

"Soap and water," he answered. "I don't wear cologne. Don't change the subject sister, where's the grub?"

"It's coming. Chloe will be here any minute. Why don't you have a seat in the living room and I'll bring you something to stave off the hunger pangs," she said, playfully.

Simon shook his head, saying "No" with great emphasis. 'I'm not eating anything before we sit down. I plan to gorge myself and I don't want to be full before I start." He laughed at her look of amused surprise. "It's your fault for looking like a runway model and cooking like a country grandma. Nobody told you to throw down like you do."

Sharon flapped the dishtowel at his foolishness. "Well, why don't you put some music on for us, you know where everything is."

No sooner than he entered the living room than the buzzer announced Ms Chloe Cooper. Sharon waited for her in the doorway, but Chloe had run up the stairs instead of taking the elevator. "I figured I needed a little exercise since I'm going to be stuffing my face. Ooh, it smells so good in here, just like my granny's house on Sunday," she said cheerily. "Hey, Simon, what's shakin'?" she greeted him.

"Food's done, just let me put my flowers in water and we can sit down," Sharon said. She reached for a big vase on the top of her cabinet and gasped in surprise when Simon beat her to it. "Thanks, Simon. You all can go wash your hands if you like," she added.

Soon they were seated around the antique dining room table that was Sharon's pride and joy. They joined hands to say grace, rather Simon said grace and they all said amen together. That was another thing Sharon admired about Simon; he was spiritually grounded and never ashamed to show it. He went to church regularly and always bowed his head to say grace, which he did out loud with no embarrassment. *He'll make a wonderful father* she thought dreamily and blinked in shock. *Where did that come from?*

Luckily Chloe started talking, which jerked Sharon back to reality. "Sharon, girl, you amaze me. You walk into work every day looking like Miss High Fashion, you live in this glass box of a building, but your apartment looks like someone else lives here. I would have never expected you to have a place like this, never. It reminds me of my mama's house. I love it here," she sighed.

Chloe was right, if someone didn't know Sharon they would have been stunned at the contrast between her work persona and her home. It was elegantly comfortable, yet homey. Instead of harsh ultra-modern lines she had chosen traditional furnishings that looked like a real home. There were a few antiques placed here and there that gave it an air of timelessness. Her sofa was a regency stripe with matching wing chairs, and there was a sinfully comfortable chaise in front of the sliding glass doors that led to the screened balcony. There were a couple of chintz ottomans that matched the coordinated throw pillows on the sofa and the tables were real mahogany. It wasn't kitschy or overdone, it just looked real, like a person of real taste and substance had put it together.

Sharon smiled, saying she didn't know if that was a compliment or not. "Oh, it is," Chloe assured her. "It's just that you're like two different people. This Sharon is certainly not the Sharon I work with everyday," she said, eying Sharon carefully.

It was true; she did look like someone else when she was at home. Her hair was always in a chignon or French twist at work; now it was unbound and flowed gloriously down her back in a charmingly tousled manner. She had on loose fitting cotton drawstring pants, a short sleeveless top with a flared bottom that showed her toned tummy when she moved suddenly, and her feet were bare. She had washed off every bit of her makeup when she took a shower after coming home because she couldn't stand the feel of summer grime on her skin.

"You don't look like a big time producer now," Chloe said frankly. "You look like a young suburban wife or something."

Sharon raised an arched brow and snorted. "Go ahead and say I look like a rube, it's perfectly true. Y'all forget I grew up bucktoothed and barefoot in the country," she reminded them. "Now please, help yourselves so it doesn't get cold," she urged.

Soon there was utter silence around the table. Sharon had long ago resigned herself to a lack of stimulating dinner conversation; when people put their feet under her table they were transported into a kind of ecstasy where words had no meaning. The chicken was golden brown and succulent, the rolls were divinely buttery and light and the cornbread dressing filled the mouth and the soul with a mélange of flavors that was indescribable. In addition to the greens and potato salad, Sharon had made a cucumber salad she knew Chloe adored. It was sliced cucumbers and shallots marinated in a dressing of sour cream and vinegar and she had to laugh as Chloe's eyes rolled upwards as she tasted it. "Sharon, how in the world do you do it? How can you work all day and come home and cook like this?"

Sharon waved off her praise. "I just love to cook, that's all. All the women in my family are good cooks, even my evil aunts, The Biddies. When I'm bored, I cook. When I'm mad, I cook. When I want to work out a problem at work, I cook. And I cook in quantity, too. The rolls, the dressing and the greens came out of the freezer. All I had to do was make the potato salad, the cucumbers and the chicken. And the gravy, of course, but that took what, five minutes?"

"What do you *do* to it? I've never tasted gravy like that in my life," Chloe said.

Sharon shrugged. "That's just the gravy we make with dressing. Momma always put a chopped hardboiled egg in it with the liver and bits of meat from the neck and I just make it the same way she does, that's all."

Simon had eaten three helpings of everything before he finally stopped. He wiped his mouth with his linen napkin, took a long draught of iced tea and dabbed the moisture away from his lips. "Sharon," he said with a look of utter sincerity, "that was the best meal I've ever had in my life. Will you marry me?"

Chloe screamed and yelled, "Hold him to it! Take him up on it, Sharon, I'll be your witness, he asked of his own volition! You better get him, girl."

Sharon laughed uproariously and rose to begin clearing the table. "Are you ready for dessert or do you want to wait a little?"

Simon rose to assist her. "I can wait if you can. Let me clear the table and I'll serve you ladies, how's that for a deal?"

"Just perfect," Sharon beamed, unaware that Chloe was looking from Simon to Sharon and back again.

Finally Chloe spoke, murmuring, "Sounds good to me, too."

ଚ୨ୠ

After the dishes were cleaned up with the help of her guests, Sharon was relaxing in the living room with the exquisite jazz selected by Simon playing as a perfect backdrop for good conversation. The peach cobbler had been a howling success and Chloe had two helpings. "Just remember, what goes on here, stays here so don't go telling anybody I ate this much at once. It's just so good," she sighed.

Simon was stretched out on the chaise lounge with his eyes closed and a smile of total satisfaction on his face. "The proposal still stands," he said. "I meant what I said, Shay, I've never tasted food that good in my life."

Sharon laughed and said, "It doesn't take much to make you two happy. If you like my cooking why don't you come with me to the mother lode of good food? Our family reunion is next month."

"You mean you're going to Mayberry to commune with the folks? Why haven't you mentioned this before? My vacation is pretty much set, or I'd really consider going," Chloe said.

Sharon made a face. "I haven't said anything about it because I wasn't sure I was going. I'm still not sure," she admitted.

Chloe looked shocked. "But why wouldn't you go? You love going home to Mayberry," she protested.

"You should see the letter my mother sent me. Wait a minute, I'll read it to you," she said, padding out of the room silently on her bare feet. She went to her bedroom and retrieved the letter from her tote bag and returned to the living room where Chloe was waiting anxiously and Simon gave every appearance of being asleep. Walking over to the sofa, she sat on the end opposite Chloe and said, "Listen to this, you'll understand my hesitation."

Dear Sharon,

I'm writing this to let you know that we are hosting the Johnson family reunion this year. Everyone is expected to attend, and that includes you. Over the years our family has grown apart and I've had enough of it. Your sister Candace hasn't been home in three years, Debra hasn't even had the decency to bring her husband home to meet us and Angela is off in Miami doing who knows what with her life.

Your father and I aren't getting any younger and before we leave this earth we want to make sure that the foundation we laid for you girls will last. When all is said and done, when all the sad songs have been sung, all you have left is your family. And it's way past time for this family to start acting like one. The time and place to begin is at the reunion which will be here at the farm from Friday,

August 17th through Sunday the 20th. I will accept no excuses for your absence. This is why I'm letting you know now, in May, so that you can clear that busy schedule of yours.

I'm telling you the same thing I told your sisters; if you don't come to this reunion, don't bother coming home again, not even for my funeral. And I mean that from the bottom of my heart.

Love,
Your mother

Chloe's mouth was open in a perfect 'O' and her eyes were huge when Sharon finished reading the letter. "*Day*-um! Why did your mother go off on you like that?"

Sharon shrugged. "Your guess is as good as mine. I'm not important enough for her to get that mad at," she said with a slight sneer. "Besides, when you wanted me to go with you to Martha's Vineyard this spring I couldn't go because…"

"You went home to Mayberry," Chloe supplied.

"When you wanted me to go skiing last Christmas?"

"You went home to Mayberry," Chloe repeated with a puzzled look.

"I go home twice a year without fail. I'm the one who visits, never forgets a birthday, an anniversary, a christening or anything else, yet I get this," she said, giving the handwritten letter a vicious shake.

Chloe's eyes were full of concern. "Which child are you? Oldest, middle, youngest?"

Sharon made a sad attempt at a smile. "Oh, that's easy. I'm the invisible child. I'm the one nobody sees."

THREE

C *hloe looked so appalled that Sharon hastened to reassure her.* "Oh, I'm exaggerating," she said quickly. "I'm the second oldest and I was just shy and quiet. My sisters were the pretty ones, the bubbly, outgoing ones and I was the mousy little bookworm. Happens in every family," she said airily.

Her friend wasn't buying it, though. "I hate to contradict you, but it shouldn't happen in any family," she said indignantly. "I think you're just trying to play it off now because it sounds like your family treated you badly. I mean, come on now, you go home twice a year. Why in the world would your mother write you a letter like you've been staying away on purpose?"

Sharon shrugged her shoulders. "She probably just forgot who she was writing to. There are four of us, you know."

"So what's your point? I know people who can keep up with more cats than that and not get them confused," she said.

Sharon sighed deeply. She didn't know how to explain her childhood without seeming to be neurotic or self-pitying. She wasn't, not at all, nor was she disloyal. She tried again. "Look, Chloe, I grew up on a working farm, okay? My mother and father both worked the farm and worked hard. There were four of us and each one of us had our own personal dynamic, if you will. There was a lot to keep up with. So if my parents didn't get to every single function for every single child, that was understandable," she said defensively.

Chloe wasn't buying it, though. "So what you're trying not to say is that they missed *your* functions and not your sisters'. You can't kid a kidder, honey. Now what's this about you not being cute? You're a beautiful woman, Sharon, how can you say such a thing?"

This time Sharon laughed out loud. "Honey, when I was a child I was just homely. We were known as the Johnson girls and I was usually referred to as "that" one, because no one could keep our names straight. But if someone said, "You know, that one" it meant *me*. Hold on let me get photographic proof," she said as she prepared to leave the room again.

"While you're doing that I'm just going to get a dab more cucumber salad and just a smidge of dressing," Chloe said slyly. "I can't handle angst on an empty stomach."

Soon they were sitting at the dining room table looking at family pictures. "See? Is my mom a dish or what? Look how fine my daddy is. They still look good, even though she insists on dressing alike when they travel."

Chloe stopped eating. "Girl, no they don't! My parents do that, too! They have these little matching tee shirts and shorts and they stroll around looking like twins or something!"

"Yeah, mine, too. They have matching tee shirts from everywhere they've been, except here. They won't come visit me, for some reason," she said quietly. "Okay, now check this out. Look at those braces and those glasses and tell me I wasn't a horror," she dared Chloe.

"Aww, you were cute! Those great big eyes and those big round glasses, you look adorable!"

Sharon did look like a little doll, even though she was tall and gangly and bespectacled. She made a noncommittal sound at Chloe's compliment and turned the page to show her sisters, the pretty Johnson girls. "Chloe, you can see the difference. They were all gorgeous from birth and I looked like a stick figure with teeth next to them. My aunts used to call me Jackie," she said softly.

"Jackie? What kind of nickname was that?"

"It was short for Jackass because my teeth were so big they said I looked like a mule. It used to hurt my feelings so bad I would cry. Everybody told me to get over it, they were just playing. My aunts are my father's sisters and a meaner bunch of heifers have never roamed the earth. Except for my Aunt Deborah, she's kind of sweet. But it used to really bother me that no one would take up for me and tell those hags to back off. They would always say the same thing, which was "At least she's got good hair." They'd say it right in front of me, too, like I couldn't understand what they were talking about. "Poor little Jackie, she sure is ugly. But at least she got good hair, that's better than nothing."

Chloe was both angry and horrified now. "How in the world could your parents let them get away with that? Why didn't your mama backhand one of the old witches into the middle of next week?"

"Well, in order for her to take offense she would have had to notice their actions, wouldn't she? And since neither she nor my father ever paid me any attention, well, it was just one of those things," she said with a shrug. She pointed at a picture of all four girls one Easter. "Here you go, now take a look at this doozy. Can you pick me out of the group? I'll give you a hint; I'm the one in the back with her head down."

Chloe had stopped listening to her for the moment. Her attention had been caught by a framed family portrait on the wall of the dining room. "Sharon, isn't this your family?"

Sharon groaned, knowing what was coming next. "Yes, it is."

"Well, where are you? You're not in the picture!"

"Oh, that's a funny story, really. We were all dressed up to go have a family picture taken and the photographer was getting us all posed when I had to go to the bathroom. I told Momma I had to go about three times and I know she heard me because she told me where it was. So I went to the ladies room and this was taken while I was there. The photographer had to remind them I didn't make the shot." Sharon laughed as if it were of no importance. "Anyway, when the proofs came back, everyone liked this picture best. My aunts insisted on having this print and went so far as to pay for their own so they wouldn't be stuck with the other one, the one that had me in it. That picture," she said, staring at it, "was in the home of all the Johnson relatives in Mason Corners, South Carolina. It was like I had disappeared or something."

"But I know your mother didn't put it up in her house! Please tell me that thing wasn't on the wall of your living room," Chloe said angrily.

"No, of course not. I keep telling you, my parents are wonderful people. I have a wonderful family. They had a print made with me in it, of course. But," Sharon's voice faded for a moment. "Momma never could find the right frame for it. So it never got hung on the wall at all."

"Oh, you have got to be kidding," Chloe gasped. "That's horrible! I never heard of anything so...so..." she struggled for the right adjective while Sharon shut the photo album with a loud snap.

"Honey, it was a long time ago. Forget it; it doesn't matter in the least. And remember, it made me the woman I am today," Sharon said.

"What do you mean?" Chloe was full of righteous anger on her friend's behalf.

"I decided I had to be the best at everything I did, since I couldn't get any attention. I never got less than an A in any class I ever took, from first grade straight though grad school. I turned into a first class scholar, which got me full scholarships to college and a fellowship for grad school. After I graduated from Howard I had my choice of schools to go to and I picked Harvard. A Harvard MBA goes a long way towards making you forget you were the ugly duckling. I have a great job, great friends and a great apartment. And a great wardrobe, thanks to my ability to negotiate a contract," she added with a huge smile.

"Seriously, I'm fine, Chloe. I don't want you to think ill of my parents or my sisters. It was the way it was and that's all," she said with finality. Hoping to change the subject she added, "If you come in the kitchen with me I'll make you a care package to take home."

As she hoped, Chloe followed her into the kitchen, but the food only distracted her for a moment. "You know what you need to do, girl? You need to walk into that reunion with Kanye or Diddy or somebody. That would show them. Or get Michael to go with you! That would knock their socks off for sure!"

Sharon laughed as she got out some disposable plastic containers. "Chloe, that wouldn't impress my parents in the least. I doubt seriously that they know who Kanye or P. Diddy is in the first place. In the second place, they wouldn't notice; they'd probably think they were some distant cousin or another. And in the third place the only thing that's going to impress them is a husband. And since I'm the official pathetic old maid of the family nobody expects me to bring home a man, ever. Hand me the potato salad, would you?"

Chloe did as she was asked. "So all of your sisters are married?"

"Actually, Angela isn't married yet. There's a guy at home who's crazy about her and she's crazy about him, or so I thought, but then she decided to go to Miami to be a star and left him behind. But there's wedding bells in her near future, trust me," Sharon said, reaching for another container.

"Then you definitely need to go take a man home with you. A really good looking man and tell everybody you're engaged," Chloe said with a conspiratorial gleam in her eye.

"That's called lying, sweetie, and I'm not going there. I haven't come this far in life to stoop to lying to my family. It's just not that deep. I truly don't appreciate the tone of the letter my mother wrote me, but I'm going to the reunion just the same. This way I can go skiing with you this Christmas because this will be my second trip home this year and since it matters so little to them, I won't have to be there at Christmas."

She continued to work, assembling nice carry-out packages for Chloe and Simon. She had no sooner put Simon's into a little shopping bag with handles when his deep voice floated across the room. "Where's mine?"

Sharon laughed. "It's about time you woke up. It's right here. Chloe are you cabbing it home or what?"

"No, I'm hitching a ride with Simon," she said as she stared hard at him, daring him to deny it.

"Okay, good. I'm not trying to run you guys out, or anything. In fact, want to watch a movie before you leave?"

"Girl, I'd love to, but I have a hair appointment first thing in the morning. I'll call you tomorrow," she said as she gave her a tight hug good-bye.

"Everything was wonderful. You're a delightful hostess and my offer still stands," Simon declared as he kissed her cheek."

Sharon laughed at his silliness and walked them to the elevator. She turned to go back into her apartment with an odd sense of relief. At least it was definitely decided. She'd be going to the reunion next month, come hell or high water.

☞☜

Chloe waited until she was seated in Simon's immaculately kept car before opening her mouth. He was just about to put the key in the ignition when she grabbed his wrist. "Look here, Simon, we both know you weren't asleep up there. You heard every word of what we were saying and don't pretend you didn't," she said indignantly.

Simon gently removed her hand and started the car. "Put your seatbelt on, Chloe."

She frowned, but fastened the belt, fussing at him the whole time. "Until this very night I didn't know you were in love with Sharon. I had no idea. The way you men can keep things all bottled up inside just amazes me. Why haven't you done something about it? How long have you felt like this about her? And just when do you plan to do something about it?" she demanded. Her impatience colored every word and made her sound like a small yippy dog.

Simon carefully pulled out into traffic, without speaking. He finally glanced over at Chloe and suggested she slow down. "Take a breath or two, it's good for you," he said with a maddeningly calm smile.

All that did was infuriate Chloe, who gave him a light punch in the upper arm. "You're enough to drive somebody crazy, you know that? You know you're crazy about Sharon. I don't know why I never noticed it before. You love her! And I know good and well you were just playing up there; you weren't asleep and you heard every single word we said. You know how her family treated her and you know she shouldn't be going to this reunion by herself. Now what are you going to do about it, that's what I want to know. What are you going to do?"

To her intense annoyance Simon didn't answer right away. And when he did speak, all he would say was "Chloe, I got this, okay? Don't worry about Sharon, I got this."

And for some reason, calm settled over Chloe. He said it with such self-assurance and such confidence she believed him. Whatever he had in mind was going to work. She looked at him sideways and said "Well, *okay* then," before leaning back to enjoy the ride home in the summer night.

ᏸᎧᎧ

Although he wasn't about to admit it to her, Simon had indeed heard every word of what Sharon had related to Chloe that evening. He had been enjoying the sinful comfort of the chaise lounge and the sublime music while digesting a fabulous meal and yes, it may have looked like he had dropped off to sleep, but nothing could have been further from the truth. He would have considered it extremely rude, for one thing, and for another, the moment Sharon had started talking about the reunion he went on red alert. It was extremely difficult for him to lie perfectly still while he heard Sharon reveal those painful memories. Partly because he admitted there was something rather underhanded about deliberately listening to a private conversation, and partly because what he'd heard had infuriated him as much as it had enlightened him. It was something like being handed the key to a safety deposit box with all her secrets in it.

After dropping Chloe off and making sure she got into her building safely, he returned his car to its rented space in a secured garage and walked the one block to his building. Like Sharon, he lived in a high-rise, but he intended to move into a house in the near future. He'd started the process of refurbishing a brownstone in Harlem, a three-story house with a fenced backyard that he planned to turn into a garden. It was going to be a real home, a place in which he could settle down, marry and raise a large family, that is, if he could find the right woman. Until tonight he had hoped that woman would be Sharon; now it looked like his hopes could become reality.

He used his passkey to enter his building, which was secured but which lacked a doorman like Sharon's. He checked his mail before taking the elevator up to his eighth floor two-bedroom apartment, processing the thoughts that were racing through his head. As soon as he walked in the door, he used the remote to turn on the stereo, and used another to turn on a few lights. He set the bag containing his generous portion of the delicious meal on his immaculate counter and washed his hands carefully before putting everything away. Everything except the peach cobbler, that is. He had to have one more bite before getting ready for bed. His eyes closed in sensual appreciation of the skill it took to put together food that tasted like this. The peaches were transformed from mere fruit into something celestial with the tender crust that literally melted in his mouth and the exact proportions of sugar, cinnamon and nutmeg that blended with the butter to make it an ambrosial treat for the tongue.

Just like Sharon was a treat for his eyes. He couldn't have told her so, but one of the reasons he was so quiet during dinner was because she'd looked so fantastic it was hard for him to stand being in the same room with her. He'd wanted to touch her, to kiss her and fondle her and take her into the bedroom and make love to her over and over again. Operating under that kind of pressure, he knew it was best for him to keep his head down and his mouth full in order to not make a total fool out of himself. After stuffing himself with the meal, which had looked as good as it tasted, he'd taken refuge on the chaise where, as Chloe had correctly guessed, he hadn't gone to sleep. At first he'd been daydreaming, fantasizing that he and Sharon were a couple and that she was about to join him on the chaise where they would lay in each other's arms and talk before they began to undress, kissing and caressing as each piece of clothing hit the floor. Instead he'd learned some very important things about the woman he loved. From the minute she began reading her mother's letter out loud, he knew he'd finally solved the mystery of Sharon Johnson, at least a large part of it.

He finished savoring the bite of cobbler and put it away, singing softly as he went to undress and shower. While the hot water beat down on his head and neck, he felt oddly at peace. He had gained a better understanding of what made Sharon tick and he was profoundly grateful for the knowledge. He'd never approached her in a romantic sense, not because of her dictate that business and pleasure didn't mix, but because her dates had a very short shelf life. True, he wasn't privy to every aspect of her socializing, but during the time he'd known her he'd never seen her with the same man more than twice, She had a reputation for dating a man a couple of times and sending him on his way and now Simon believed he understood why. Growing up without the attention and affection any young girl should have from her family had probably made her wary and uncertain about relationships. Certainly growing up thinking she was unattractive had to play a part in it too, although for the life of him he couldn't see how it was possible that someone as delightful to the eye as Sharon had ever had a homely day. It was obviously propaganda from those idiot relatives of hers that had done a job on her.

He finally stopped scrubbing his body with the rough loofah sponge he preferred and rinsed the suds off thoroughly. When he stepped out of the shower he was smiling widely because he had a plan. This year's Johnson family reunion was going to have a big surprise as part of the festivities, if his idea came to fruition. All he had to do was get Sharon to cooperate and with a little persuasion on his part, he saw no reason why she wouldn't. He walked into the bedroom wearing a towel, which he took off in order to apply an unscented lotion all over his body. He wasn't the one to go strolling out looking like he'd been kicking flour all day; he kept his skin smooth and moisturized to avoid ashiness. And while he applied the lotion he thought of ways he could get his plan into action. He turned back his bedcovers and slid between the cool 1200 thread count sheets. He lay there for a while, enjoying the feel of the ultra-soft sheets against his clean, moist skin, and then he picked up his cell phone.

Sharon's voice answered, saying "Hello?"

"Hello, Shay. I just wanted to tell you thanks again for the dinner. You're an amazing cook and a great hostess," he told her. He could almost feel her blush over the phone.

"Simon, you didn't have to call me to tell me that, you've already thanked me a couple of times," she protested, but Simon was pretty sure she sounded pleased.

"Yes, but I didn't ask you out to lunch tomorrow. It's Saturday and there's an art exhibit in Harlem you'd really like. You busy?"

This time she really did sound pleased. "No, I'm not and I'd love to go. Call me tomorrow?"

"Will do, Shay. Sleep well."

He put his arms behind his head and smiled at the ceiling. Phase one was underway.

FOUR

*S**haron couldn't remember when she'd enjoyed a weekend more.* As promised, Simon called her the next morning and set a time when he would pick her up. He was there promptly at eleven and again, he came bearing flowers. This time it was a big pot of basil, something that not only made her smile, it melted her insides a little. "Simon, this is lovely! How did you know I love basil," she asked as she took a long sniff of the fragrant leaves.

"Because you told me so. We were having lunch at that little place near the studio and you had a chicken salad and bruschetta with pesto and that's when you told me how much you like basil," he replied. "You ready?"

And easy as that, they were on their way to a wonderful afternoon. They went to the exhibit in Harlem, and then spent a couple of hours strolling through the shops in the area. When they were both famished, Simon took her to a pretty little café with sidewalk tables and they had a delicious lunch. While they were eating, Sharon found herself looking at Simon more than usual, staring at him, really. He had to be aware of her scrutiny, but being the gentleman he was he didn't mention it. It was just that she found herself wondering what it would be like to be on a real date with him instead of just hanging out like the friends they were. She felt an odd little chill when she realized where her thoughts were headed. No good would come of that kind of thinking. Simon was her co-worker, therefore a relationship was off-limits. She'd set that rule herself so there was no breaking it. And more to the point, there was her abysmal track record with men.

There was something in Sharon that she couldn't define and didn't want to examine too closely, but whatever it was kept her from forming a deep attachment to any of the men who came her way. She had been dateless all through high school, and for her first couple of years in undergraduate school she had been virtually invisible on campus. When she really started to blossom, somewhere in her junior year, she finally began to go out a little, but she wasn't really comfortable with all the attention she was suddenly receiving from the opposite sex. Men who'd ignored her during her freshman and junior years were suddenly pushing up on her for dates.

One guy was a man with whom her freshman roommate had tried to set her up. He'd taken one look at her and told her roommate, thanks but no thanks. Unfortunately, Sharon had heard him make the remark, followed by the statement that he wasn't that hard up. So it was divine irony when he didn't recognize her as she walked across campus one day and he sprinted to catch up with her, introducing himself and begging her to go out with him. He'd made a lame joke out of it, but he was totally serious, saying he'd take off a limb if she'd go out with him. "And I'm here on a football scholarship so you know I mean what I say," he'd declared. It was sheer curiosity more than anything else, that made Sharon say yes. She allowed him to take her out a few times, and he wined and dined her, and wooed her for a few weeks before she abruptly cut it off. She'd heard the rumors about his inability to stick with one woman, and his declaration that he wasn't getting serious with anyone until he retired from professional football, so she dropped him, quick and clean.

It was the beginning of a habit that was to prove impossible to break. No matter how promising a relationship seemed, no matter how ardent the man was who sought her company, Sharon stayed in control and always broke it off before things got too serious. She used to date the same man for a month or so before finding a reason to dump him; now it was more like a week or two. Sharon made a face, thinking about all the perfectly nice guys she'd left twisting in the wind. It hurt to admit it, but even after all this time she still had the flight syndrome down pat. Leave them before they leave you, because soon as they figure out who you really are, they'll leave for sure. It was a simple, sure-fire way of protecting herself from pain. She wasn't aware of the bleak expression on her face until Simon touched her hand. It felt so warm and comforting that she wanted to cry for some silly reason.

"Are you feeling okay? You look a little sad," he said gently.

"Who, me? Oh, I'm fine," she said. "Really, I am. I was just thinking about something." It was perfectly true; she was thinking, thoughts that had nothing to do with the very sweet man sitting across from her.

Suddenly her cell phone went off, making her jump. She looked at the incoming call on her caller ID and gave Simon an apologetic smile. "It's my mother; I really need to take this."

Sharon answered the call with trepidation, fearing the worst. Her mother never called her, never. Sharon was the one who called home every Sunday; it was never the other way around. "Hello?" She was relieved when her mother's voice came on the line sounding like her usual self.

"Sharon, I'm calling to remind you about the reunion. You are planning to be there, aren't you?"

Her good mood evaporated quickly. Taking a deep breath, she tried to maintain an even tone of voice. "I'm fine, Momma, and you?"

"Oh, I'm sorry, baby. I'm fine, Daddy's fine and so are Candace's kids. They're here for the summer, you know.'

Sharon sighed heavily. "I know they are, Momma. I talked to you and Daddy last Sunday, remember?"

"Hmm? Oh, yes, of course. Now about the reunion. It's next month, you know and you still haven't said if you're coming or not. I think my letter was pretty plain. I meant what I said, Sharon. Are you going to be here?" Her mother sounded unusually uncompromising.

"Momma, about the reunion," she began, only to have the cell phone taken from her hand. She watched in horror as Simon began speaking to her mother.

"Mrs. Johnson, this is Simon Freeman. I'm sorry that Sharon hasn't been able to give you an R.S.V.P., but that's my fault. I wanted to come with her and I had to clear my schedule, so I'm afraid I'm the culprit. I apologize for any inconvenience to you and your family, but I assure you we'll be there."

Sharon's mouth fell open and her head felt like it was about to explode. She tried to take the phone from him but he easily evaded her reaching hand and continued talking.

"Who am I? Again, I have to apologize, Mrs. Johnson. Sharon speaks of you so often that I feel as though I know you. And yes, ma'am, I am Sharon's boyfriend. Well, I'm looking forward to meeting you, too. Yes, ma'am, we'll be there on the 18th. We may arrive before then, if Sharon wants to come early. She's really looking forward to seeing her family."

Sharon was afraid she had slipped into some kind of psychotic episode as Simon continued to chat with her mother. When he finally handed her the phone, she could barely manage to answer her mother's many remarks.

"Well, baby, that was quite a surprise. He sounds like a very nice man, sugar, and we're looking forward to meeting him. We'll see you soon, honey, and you be careful traveling, okay?"

It was a full minute before Sharon could trust herself to speak after the call ended. She looked at Simon with undisguised rage in her eyes. Flames were practically leaping out of her ears, but Simon seemed totally relaxed.

"You're probably a little steamed with me right now," he began.

"A *little*?"

"Okay, you're furious and what I'm going to tell you is going to make you even madder. So why don't you let me take you home and we'll talk about it," he said in his most persuasive tone of voice.

Sharon was so outdone she let him do just that.

⁊⁑

After they returned to her apartment, she finally found her voice. "What in the wide world made you do that? I've known you for over two years and I would have never thought you were capable of something this crazy. Are you deranged in some manner that hasn't come to my attention yet?" She was pacing angrily back and forth with her arms tightly crossed, resembling a hostile cat having a hissy fit. And she wasn't finished, not by a long shot.

"In all the time I've known you you've been kind, considerate and professional. I've always thought you were one of the nicest men I've ever met and now you do this! What is wrong with you?" she yelled.

Simon went to where she was standing and put his hands on her shoulders. It was annoying as hell, but the warmth of his smooth palms was comforting to her and it actually felt really good on her skin, bared by her tank top. "I had a good reason, Shay. If you'll sit down with me, I'll be more than happy to explain it to you."

Once they were seated at opposite ends of her sofa, Sharon kept her arms crossed like a shield against him. She gave him an evil look and said, "All right, Simon, let's see if you can explain yourself. Because if you can't, I never want to see you again outside of a work capacity," she warned him.

To her surprise he agreed. "That's fair enough. You're not going to appreciate this, and I can't blame you. I wasn't asleep last night. When you thought I was taking a nap on the chaise, I was just lying there with my eyes closed."

As the full impact of what he was saying sank in, Sharon could feel hot shame coloring her face.

"Look Shay, I know I should have said something to let you know I overheard you, but I didn't. I couldn't, because what I was hearing affected me too deeply. I heard the letter, it sounded like you're a neglectful daughter when the opposite is the truth. When I heard what you had to deal with as you were growing up, it bothered me. It bothered me a lot, Shay. I have three younger sisters and I know how sensitive young girls are. You shouldn't have been ignored like that. You should have been just as important as anyone else in your family. I want to go with you to your reunion because I want to make sure that you have a good time and that nobody calls you Jackie again," he said quietly.

"Oh Heavenly Father, you heard every word we said," she breathed.

"Pretty much. My mother always said I could hear chinches walking on cotton. My sisters said I was just nosy, but hey, I had to look out for my girls. I learned how to listen a lot because I wanted to know what they were getting into. Both my parents worked and I had to keep an eye out for them."

Sharon covered her eyes with her hands and rocked back and forth, trying vainly to remember every single word she and Chloe had said the night before. She stopped rocking and moved one hand to peer at him. "You heard her say I needed to take somebody with me," she said slowly.

"Yeah, well I'm no Kanye or Diddy," he grinned, "but I'd be more than happy to take you to South Carolina."

"But why did you have to lie to my mother? I've never lied to her in my life," Sharon said fretfully. She used both hands to rake through her hair, still not convinced by his persuasive words.

For the first time, Simon's calm assurance slipped, just for a second. "Because you need a man on your arm. Not some tame friend, or best pal or gay confidante. You need to look like you have a man in your life because unfortunately, that's the only thing that's going to make The Biddies take notice," he said. "Isn't that what you call your aunts?"

Sharon nodded and gave him a sad smile. "It's not just going to impress The Biddies. My mother called me honey, baby and sugar after she talked to you. She hasn't called me names like that since…well, *never*, to tell you the truth." She stared into space for a moment, and then looked into his eyes with an odd look on her face. "Why is it that getting a man or having a man or keeping a man is like the only worthwhile thing a woman can do in this life? Why aren't the things I accomplish enough for my family? I can win an Emmy award and nobody blinks an eye. But let me get a man and whoo-whee, let the good times roll," she said bitterly.

Simon tried to discipline his face but a smile slipped out. Sharon looked so flustered and put out it was just cute. "Well, Shay, why don't you ask them? That's something I think you should do while you're there; get to the bottom of a few things and get a few things off your chest. And I'll be there with you," he said quietly.

Sharon appeared so deep in thought it was doubtful she heard him. Finally she leaned back and looked at him with a pensive expression. "We're never going to pull this off, Simon. We don't know each other well enough to pretend like we're a couple. A Grand Inquisitor from the Spanish Inquisition has nothing on my mother when it comes to interrogating boyfriends. We know virtually nothing about each other," she pointed out. "We'll never convince anyone we're a couple."

This time Simon did manage to hide his smile and answer her with a straight face. "Well, we've got a few weeks to practice. We'll just have to spend a lot of time with each other until it's time to leave."

Sharon stared at him as though she was seeing him for the first time. "That's a good idea, Simon. Do you want to stay for dinner? I cooked an extra chicken yesterday and I was going to make chicken salad," she said in a distracted voice.

"I'd love to, but only if you let me help you make it."

"Okay," she answered in the same slightly dreamy voice.

As she rose to go into the kitchen, Simon let out the smile he'd been holding in. Phase Two was officially underway.

FIVE

*S*imon wasn't a gloater by nature; he was confident, not conceited. But his plan was working better than he'd hoped. In the past few weeks he and Sharon had spent a lot of time together, quality time. They'd gone on dates, shared meals, movies and long walks. Best of all, they had talked. Even when she was out of town, or he was, they talked every night before bed. And as much as he enjoyed her company, Simon liked talking to her the best. He'd come to crave the sound of her voice, it caressed his ear and soothed his soul like no other woman's ever had. The way she laughed, the ease with which they conversed, just the sound of her breathing was enough to set him off. He still hadn't told her how he felt about her because he didn't want to scare her off. Until she really dealt with the issues from her growing up, she wasn't going to be ready to return the love he felt for her. They might be able to have a nice little affair, but that wasn't what he wanted. What he wanted was sitting in the passenger seat next to him as they drove to South Carolina.

When he'd first ambushed her with the idea that he go to the reunion with her, Sharon told him she would pay for their airline tickets. He'd refused at once, because no woman was ever going to pick up his tab for anything. And, as he told her, he didn't get to drive as much as he liked. Driving in the city wasn't particularly enjoyable, and he rarely had the opportunity to take his car out on the road for a real workout. When he'd suggested driving, though, Sharon had looked skeptical.

"With gas costing as much as prime rib, it's not like we're going to save much money. We may as well fly and get there quicker," she said in her practical way.

"That's true, or it would be if I didn't have my Prius. It's a hybrid and it gets great mileage. And besides, it'll be more fun. You can pack us all kinds of food and we can spend some more time together. Look at this as our last study session before the final exam. By the time we get there we'll really feel like a couple and we'll look like one, too."

They'd been sitting on her balcony, surrounded by the big flowering and green plants she grew in pots. There were a couple of comfortable chairs with thick cushions and a small glass-topped table and they were drinking coffee and reading the Sunday New York Times together. She had put down the Arts and Leisure section and given him a serious look. "I still think this is lying. I mean, telling my family that you and I are a couple."

Her sense of honesty was just another thing to love about her, he decided. He reached for her hand across the table and held it for a while, then kissed the back of it. He was pleased to notice tiny goose bumps come up on her slender arm when he did that. "Shay, everything is going to be fine. Don't worry about things so much. Once we get there you'll see it won't be that big a deal, I promise you."

She looked slightly relieved and excused herself to get more coffee. He'd followed her into the apartment, bringing the newspaper with him. He caught up with her in the kitchen and surprised her completely by coming up behind her and wrapping his long arms around her. He held her tightly and told her to trust him. Her body didn't tense up, as he might have expected; instead she relaxed into his embrace and showed no signs of wanting to leave his arms. He turned her around and pulled her closer to him. She'd looked up at him with a little smile on her face. "What are we doing, Simon?"

It was the 'we' that got to him. She didn't ask him what he thought *he* was doing, or why he had his hands on her; she asked what *they* were doing and he was more than happy to answer. "We're holding each other and we're about to kiss. We have to look like we're comfortable with each other, don't we?"

When she nodded and eagerly tilted her head to his, he looked into her trusting eyes and gently stroked her cheek with his fingertips before taking her sweet mouth with his own. Their lips touched softly and their bodies merged closer together as they angled their heads to better sample the delicious experience. He opened his mouth and she responded, inviting his tongue to mate with hers. He'd meant to give her a little kiss, just something to get her used to his touch. But once they connected and the mad sensations started overtaking them, he was lost in the magic. He had to force himself to stop, but even then they stayed close together, their lips touching over and over again, softly yet passionately.

He'd cleared his throat and when he could talk again, he said "I think that went pretty well."

Sharon had licked her lips slowly and sensuously before agreeing with him. "Yes. I think it went very well," she said in a soft, sexy voice he'd never heard before.

After that their dates took on a new dimension; every one of them ended with a long, passionate kiss that drove him straight home to an icy cold shower, sometimes two. He was being driven slowly out of his mind by love as well as lust. If he'd known how much fire burned inside Sharon he'd have gone after her long ago and damn the consequences. The only thing that was keeping him from tearing her clothes off after one of their sizzling lip-locks was the fact that he wanted her mind and her heart, not just her body. When he took her to bed it would be as his mate, not his part-time lover. And if things worked out the way he hoped, he'd be doing that right after they got back to New York. Until then, he exercised a superhuman control and learned to endure cold water and hot dreams.

But it wouldn't be too much longer before all his dreams came true. They were on their way to Mason Corners at last, and Sharon seemed happy. She was relaxed and content and appeared genuinely glad about being with him on the trip. He glanced at her again, just to enjoy the sight of her. She'd had her hair blown out and curled and was wearing it in a ponytail that flowed down her back. She was wearing some very chic looking sunglasses, a crisp white shirt tied at the midriff, a pair of knee length denim shorts and some cute little sandals. She looked fresh and adorably sexy, but best of all, the tension was gone. She was really looking forward to seeing her parents and her sisters.

"Have you ever been to the country, Simon?" she asked.

"You tell me. You're supposed to be an expert on me now," he teased.

She sat up, pressing the index finger of her right hand to her lips. "Let's see. Your family lives in Cleveland, where you were born. You are the oldest of four, your younger sisters are Cecily, Marilyn and Sharice, and your parents are Randolph and Felicia. Your parents are from Alabama and you spent summers down there. You spent a lot of time in Edgewater, a community that's near Birmingham where your great-grandparents lived, so yes, you have been in the country!" She sounded so pleased with herself he asked to go on.

"Okay, let's see. You had a dog named Trouble because he was always in it," she said, thoughtfully. "You were an A-student in high school, you played basketball and football and made All-Conference in both, you went to Ohio University on a full academic scholarship and majored in business, you got a masters degree at Columbia and your sign is Taurus. Your favorite color is blue and your favorite dish is your mama's chicken and dumplings."

"Wrong," he said flatly.

Sharon looked stung. "I am not. You told me your favorite dish was your mama's chicken and dumplings," she said, indignantly.

He took her hand and gave her a lazy grin. "My favorite food is anything you cook," he said.

Sharon burst into laughter and squeezed his hand. "That was good. That was very, very good. Speaking of food, are you hungry? There's a ton of stuff in the cooler and we could stop for a little while so you can stretch your legs," she suggested.

Simon wouldn't have admitted it, but her blithe reply actually stung a little. He wasn't joking when he said anything she cooked was his favorite food. It bothered him just a little that she brushed his comment off as a joke, but he played it off. Pulling over for a while sounded like a good idea, though. They were in Maryland, which was more or less the halfway point of their journey. "That sounds like a plan, Shay. I'll find a nice clean rest area and we can take a break." While he was still mulling over his unexpected hurt from her little joke, he was surprised when she reached over and stroked his arm with her soft, slender hand.

"Simon, I want to thank you again for doing this for me. I can't think of anyone else in the world who would do what you're doing," she said, softly.

He enjoyed the feel of her hand on his arm, but it was his turn to tease her. "I can. Chloe was dying to get in on this," he said dryly and they both laughed.

&OCB

In a little while Simon had found the perfect rest stop, clean, shady and inviting. After using the facilities which were mercifully clean and sanitary, Sharon insisted that Simon stretch out on the blanket she'd brought and relax while she served him the lunch she'd prepared. There was a small cooler in the back seat of the car with bottles of water and lemonade on ice, as well as deliciously ripe fruit. There was also a tin of her delicious oatmeal cookies with dried cherries, walnuts and chunks of milk chocolate. There was also a big cooler in the trunk with freezer packs to keep everything fresh and tasty. Sharon had packed it with two kinds of bread, smoked turkey, sliced tomatoes and lettuce, Simon's favorite mustard, a container of chopped salad and something else she knew he favored, her lemon pound cake. She made a sandwich for him, garnishing his paper plate with kosher dill pickle spears and a portion of salad. She stroked his arm as she called his name and when he sat up, she handed him the plate. She also handed him a bottle of lemonade and a couple of napkins. When he told her she was spoiling him, she could only hope her face didn't reflect the heat that was rising up her neck.

She busied herself making another sandwich. While she wasn't particularly hungry, experience had taught her that Simon could eat at least two. She spread the pumpernickel, his favorite, with Gulden's brown mustard and thought about what he'd said about Chloe wanting to come with her. She most certainly had, but for a totally different reason. She might have wanted to lend Sharon some moral support, but what she really wanted to do was have a front row seat to watch what was going on with Sharon and Simon. She had busted Sharon a couple of weeks earlier. They had been shopping, ostensibly buying a few gifts for her to take to her parents. Chloe had the decency to wait until they'd been seated in their favorite Thai restaurant for lunch before wading knee-deep into her business.

"So when are you going to tell Simon you're in love with him?" she'd asked in a voice that was half mischief and half innocence.

Sharon had just taken a long drink of water and unfortunately she did a classic spit take with the water spewing out in a fine spray. She'd frantically blotted her chin and dabbed the water off her silk T-shirt while glaring at her friend who was laughing with sheer joy. Sharon thought about trying to lie her way out of it but there was no point. Instead her eyes filled with tears. "Chloe, I don't know what to do. You're right; I've fallen for Simon like the proverbial ton of bricks. I'm crazy about him and he's just trying to do me a favor."

Their server appeared with bowls of fragrant Thai noodle soup and glasses of iced chai, thus giving Sharon a momentary reprieve. She was expecting Chloe to have something smart to say, but she was surprised by her response. "There's no reason on earth that you shouldn't love Simon. He's a good man and he really cares about you Sharon. Or should I say Shay?"

Sharon had to take refuge in a sip of chai. Shay was the pet name that Simon called her. She loved it, because it sounded so sweet and intimate and she'd never had a nickname other than the hated Jackie. She didn't know what to say, which was just as well because Chloe was on a roll.

"Listen, chick, I've watched you for years taking perfectly good men and tossing them to the side because you're afraid to let yourself love. You've been programmed to believe that you're somehow not worthy of being loved, thanks to the way you were raised. I'm not saying that your family is awful or anything, hell; my family makes the Addams family look like an episode of The Cosby Show. We put the fun in dysfunctional, honey, but all families do to one extent or another.

"You just sit back and relax and let nature take its course. You go home to Mayberry with Simon by your side and get a few things off your chest.

You'll feel like a new woman. Are you sure I can't come too?" she added, winsomely.

When Sharon assured her that she could not possibly come because she was nervous enough as it was, Chloe sighed deeply. "Oh fine. But take lots of pictures, take videos and take notes. And I'll call the maid of honor," she said firmly as she beckoned their server.

Sharon found herself smiling as she recalled that day. She added tomato and lettuce to the sandwich and sliced it on the diagonal. She held it out to Simon and asked if he was ready for more.

"Of course I am. Why aren't you eating?"

"Hmm? I ate, I ate all those cherries and I had some cheese and crackers and two big whopping cookies," she reminded him.

He took the sandwich from her, thanking her the way he always did. It was a habit she found totally endearing. He not only opened doors for her, and seated her at the table, he stood up when she came into the room and he never, ever failed to thank her for anything she did for him, whether it was giving him a glass of water or fixing him a four-course meal. You just didn't find men with manners like that these days.

"Shay, you're getting quiet on me. We're halfway there, baby, don't get nervous, okay?"

"I'm not nervous," she answered honestly. "Not yet. Now when we hit the state border that might be a different story. But right now, I'm fine."

He finished off the second sandwich and rubbed his flat, hard stomach. "I think there may be some room in here for some of that lemon cake," he said with a hopeful look.

"You think so? Well, let's see," Sharon returned. She cut a large slice and put it on a fresh plate, then went closer to Simon, close enough to feed it to him. He put his arms around her and pulled her into his lap.

"You're going to spoil me, you know that, right?"

Sharon's heart was so full she was afraid she was going to blurt out something that would embarrass them both, but all she said was, "Really? So what are you going to do about it?"

"Spoil you right back," he said, right before taking her lips in a moist, sweet kiss.

As always, a thrill coursed through her body as she gave herself up to the comfort and delight he always gave her. He was right, she was getting nervous but it wasn't just about the reunion. Seeing her family and even confronting her mother about her childhood wasn't nearly as daunting as the thought that when they returned to New York the charade would be over and she and Simon would have no more reason to pretend. They'd go back to be co-workers and casual friends and the thought was more frightening than facing down all of The Biddies at once. They kissed once more and Sharon fed him the rest of the cake.

"Why don't you take a nap while I get all this packed up? I'll wake you up in thirty minutes," she said.

"That's a good idea. That'll give us enough time to get into Mason Corners before dark. Thanks, Shay."

"You're more than welcome, Simon." *You're welcome to my heart, anytime you want it*, she thought, then rolled her eyes. Lovesick was one thing, but maudlin was something else altogether.

SIX

A *s Sharon had predicted, the closer she got to South Carolina, the bigger the knot in her stomach became.* She grew quieter and quieter and as they approached the sign that read Welcome to South Carolina; she felt her insides begin to quiver. She closed her eyes and pretended to be asleep and before she knew it she had drifted off. Suddenly she was awakened by a strong hand on her leg.

"Shay, we're here. I need you to tell me how to get to your parent's house."

She sat up abruptly and tried to push down the sudden feeling of impending doom. "Oh," she said softly. "Well, I guess you should get the dollar tour before we get there. Don't worry, it won't take long," she said with a good attempt at a smile.

"There's the movie theater," she said as she pointed out the window, "and there's Diane's Café. Food is really, really good there," she commented, unaware that her voice was shaking a little. "Lots of antique stores, antiques are really big around here." She continued to point out things of interest until they were heading out of the small, quaint town. Then she issued terse directions that took him directly to her parent's beautifully kept farm. At the first sight of their neat whitewashed fences she had to will herself not to throw up, but she managed. They went up the drive and stopped in front of the big, warmly inviting house. "We're here," she said in a quiet little voice.

She wiped her hands on her shorts and told him to leave everything in the car. "We can come get everything later. Let's just get it over with," she muttered. Before Simon could get around to her side of the car to open her door, it was jerked open by her youngest sister, Angela.

"Well, it's about time you got here! We've been waiting for you all day," Angela exclaimed.

Sharon got out of the car with an odd look on her face, a look that got even odder when Angela gave her a big hug. "It's so good to see you, Sharon. Dang, you look good, girl!"

"Thank you, Angie. So do you," Sharon managed. By now, Simon was standing next to her, his arm firmly around her waist. Angela's eyes lit up with interest as she stared up at Simon's dark good looks. Sharon made the introductions quickly. "Angela, this is Simon Freeman. Simon, this is my youngest sister, Angela."

As Simon was saying "Nice meeting you," Angela ignored his outstretched hand and launched herself at him to give him a big hug, something that annoyed the life out of Sharon. She had to bite her tongue to keep from saying something snippy, especially when Angela showed all her teeth in her prettiest smile.

"It's nice to meet you, too, Simon. Wow," she murmured. "Jackie never brought anybody home before but when she finally gets around to it, mmm-hmm," she said disarmingly.

"Her name is Sharon," Simon said, coolly.

Angela's eyes widened but any further comment was forestalled by Sharon's mother, Sara, coming out of the house at top speed. Sharon couldn't help herself; she ran to her mother without hesitation and put her arms around her. Her eyes closed and she took a deep sniff of the smell that was her mama, a light, sweet, spicy fragrance that was hers alone. It had nothing to do with store-bought perfume, it was just Sara. No one else smelled as good as her mama. She was about to pull away when Sara surprised her by holding her tighter than Sharon could ever remember being held. It was her mother who reluctantly released her, and even then she kept her hands on Sharon's waist.

"Baby, you look so pretty! It's so good to see you," she said warmly. Finally she turned her attention to Simon. "Well, Sharon, aren't you going to introduce me to your young man?"

"Of course, Momma," she said, walking over to Simon and taking his hand. "This is Simon Freeman. Simon, this is my mother, Sara Johnson."

Simon smiled the warm, genuine smile that never failed to melt Sharon's heart. "Mrs. Johnson, it's a pleasure to meet you at last. Thanks for having me; I know what an imposition it must be to have a stranger at your reunion."

Sara shook Simon's hand, looking him over from the top of his professionally cut hair to the very expensive shoes on his feet. "It's nice to meet you, Simon. And please don't feel like a stranger. You're more than welcome here, dear. And thank you for bringing our Sharon home safely," she said, warmly.

It was like having an out-of-body experience, that's the only thing Sharon could relate the experience to. Her father was behaving in the same uncharacteristically affectionate fashion as her mother, and he, too, was heartily glad to meet Simon. The weirdest part of the evening was when her nieces and nephew came out to join the crowd and she could hear Sarafina ask Jacquelin who *that* lady was.

"That's Aunt Sharon," she whispered, loudly.

"Our Aunt Sharon? Was she always pretty like that?" Sarafina asked in the same loud whisper.

"I don't remember. I haven't seen her in a long time," Jacquelin answered.

In a relatively short time their bags were stowed in the house, the coolers were emptied and the leftover food was put away with the exception of the smoked turkey, which Sharon didn't trust by this point; she put it down the garbage disposal. They were seated in the big kitchen because Sara insisted on feeding them. Sara had fixed one of Sharon's favorites, smothered chicken. They had the fork-tender chicken with mashed potatoes, gravy, homemade biscuits, succotash and sliced tomatoes from the garden. In fact, everything they ate had been raised on the farm. While Simon praised her mother's cooking, Sharon tried to ignore the fact that she was being scrutinized.

She had washed her face and hands when they arrived and had released her hair from its ponytail so it flowed over her shoulders and down her back. Long hair was no big deal in the Johnson family; Sara's came down to her waist. But everyone kept complimenting Sharon on her hair and her figure and just everything about her until she was seriously wondering if this was her family or an assortment of pod people left by the mothership. She should ask Angela, she was the sci-fi fiend in the family. As soon as it was politely possible, she excused herself to get showered and unpacked. She showed Simon the room in which he'd be staying, it was a small guestroom as far from Sharon's room as it was possible to be and still be in the same building. She wanted to laugh at the irony, but she was too tired.

"Simon, I hope this room is okay," she said as she showed him the room. "There're fresh towels on the bed and as I recall, the mattress is really comfortable."

She yawned delicately as she went to him and put her arms around his waist, leaning her head against his chest. She smiled sleepily as he returned her embrace, holding her just the way she wanted him to, so close that she could feel his heart beating. "My family thinks you're wonderful," she murmured. She lifted her face up for a kiss, making a soft purr of contentment when he gave her a long and lingering one.

"I think *you're* extraordinary," he said, his voice deep with emotion.

"What a coincidence," she murmured. "That's how I feel about you. Thank you again for coming with me, Simon. You'll never know what this means to me."

"It's my pleasure, Shay. There isn't anything I wouldn't do for you."

₨₧

Sharon wasn't too thrilled to find out she'd be sharing a room with Angela. There were plenty of rooms in the house, so she had fully expected to have a nice double bed all to herself instead of being stuck in a room with twin beds. And with Angela, of all people. It wasn't that she and Angela didn't get along; it was that in many ways Angela had accomplished what Sharon had started out to do. Then she decided that wasn't good enough for her and went traipsing off to Miami to get discovered, something Sharon found laughable, although not because Angela lacked beauty or talent. It was because with one phone call Sharon could have gotten Angela's foot in many doors, all of which would have led to the career of her dreams.

Angela was already in the room, sitting at the vanity watching every move Sharon made. "That's some hunk you've got there," she said.

Sharon didn't know how to respond to a statement like that. Luckily, Angela kept right on talking. "He's not only fine, he's protective. Why did he get so cold when I called you Jackie?"

"Because it's not my name. Never has been, never will be," Sharon answered, brusquely.

"But it was just a nickname; he acted really pissed when I said it."

Sharon tried not to glare at her sister, but she didn't feel like dealing with this right now. "Do you know why I was called Jackie? It was short for jackass because my teeth were so big. I was the only one of us who had to wear braces. It was a hateful name and it was also hurtful," she said, tersely.

"I don't remember you wearing braces. Were your teeth big? I don't remember that," Angela said, thoughtfully.

That did it. "You know, I don't know why Momma put us in here together. I'm going down the hall," Sharon said, crisply. This was the last thing she needed, to be closeted up with her chatterbox sister.

To her surprise, it had been Angela's idea to share a room. "We hardly ever get to talk and I feel like I barely know you," she said almost shyly. "You went off to Howard, and then to Harvard and then to New York and I hardly ever get to see you."

Sharon was taken aback by her sister's words. "You could have come to visit, you know." She busied herself taking her clothes out of her suitcase. Angela surprised her by helping her unpack.

"Yes, I guess I could have at that. I was just so intimidated by you," Angela admitted.

Sharon sat down heavily on the bed. "Intimidated by me how? What in the world for?"

"You were the one with the perfect grades and all the scholarships, who wouldn't be intimidated? And then you went off to the big-time colleges and never looked back. All I did was go to community college and manage the books on the farm," Angela said, derisively.

Sharon curled her legs up on the bed, relishing the feel of the soft mattress. It bore big fluffy pillows and had an old-fashioned chenille bedspread with a handmade quilt folded at the foot. "So what was wrong with working on the farm? That's what I wanted to do."

Angela stopped admiring the silk blouse she was hanging up and turned to stare at Sharon. "Say what?"

"Yep. I wanted to major in agriculture and work with Daddy. All I ever wanted to do was work the farm. I loved it here. I wanted to grow herbs and flowers to sell to florists' shops and restaurants, along with the other crops. I had written up a business plan and everything," Sharon said.

Now it was Angela's turn to sit down. "So why didn't you do it?"

"Because Daddy didn't want me underfoot," she said, bluntly. "When Momma told me I'd be more of a hindrance than a help, I took the scholarship to Howard and changed my plans. So don't complain about working the farm, that was my ideal job."

Angela digested this information for a moment, but pointed out that Sharon had a glamorous career.

"Well, it's interesting, that's for sure. But it's also time-consuming and draining. Dealing with people is always challenging, especially when they think they're all that and a bag of chips," she said with a comical look.

"But you have a real career," Angela persisted. "You pursued your dreams and ended up accomplishing something in life. I've left Mason Corners one time and it was a disaster."

Sharon started searching through her purse for her hairbrush. "What do you mean? That's what you wanted to do, right? You wanted to leave the nest, be on your own and find a great job. Isn't that what happened?"

"No, not exactly," Angela muttered. "There're some pretty awful jobs out there if you aren't prepared for a career."

Sharon was brushing her curtain of hair, twisting it up to keep it dry in the shower. "Angie, how bad could it have been? You make it sound like you were dancing on a pole or something."

"I was."

Sharon gave a short laugh. "Yeah, right. What were you really doing?"

Angela looked away from her sister before answering. "I was an exotic dancer," she said, defiantly. "I took off most of my clothes and I danced for money in front of strange men."

"Why in the hell would you do something like that, Angela? You have an associate's degree and valid job experience, so why in the world did you end up doing that?" Sharon was stunned and her voice reflected it.

"Because I went to Miami trying to get discovered, trying to become a model or a dancer and that's where I ended up. Whoever said to go after your dreams never went to Miami to find them," she said in a lame attempt at humor.

"But Angela, if you wanted a job why didn't you call me? You could have been in the "Golddigger" video, if that's what you wanted to do. I have a lot of connections, Angela. If you were serious about a career in modeling or dancing or whatever, I could have helped you a lot. I can't believe you never picked up a phone to call me." By now Sharon was not only tired; she was totally bewildered by what she was hearing.

Angela gave her a long explanation, something about how she wanted to do it on her own and she didn't want to have to ask for help from anyone. She wanted to prove that she could make it outside of Mason Corners before she admitted that Padraic, the boyfriend she'd left behind was the only man she'd ever love and she had to do it without the help of her sisters. Sharon let her rattle on for a while before taking both of Angela's hand in her own.

"Look, sweetie. I understand the need to be independent. I also understand, to some extent, your desire to experience life away from Padraic. I can understand you wanting to make sure that you were truly committed to him by moving away from him. I guess I can understand that part," she said under her breath. "But here's the thing, when you have family who cares about you, you don't treat them like strangers. Trust me, most of the people in show business had a *whole* bunch of people putting in good words for them, getting them auditions, and calling in favors on their behalf. You use every advantage you can get and if you have a sister who has some good connections, you use them, you dope! Do you think for one minute I'd have refused to help you in any way I could?"

"I guess not," Angela said, slowly.

"Just remember, family is all we have. If they turn their back on you it's their loss, but don't ever turn your back on them. If I ever find out you need something that I could help you with and you were too proud to ask, I'll beat you till the white meat shows, got me?"

"I got you," Angela said and they burst out in simultaneous laughter for the first time in years.

SEVEN

*B*y the time Simon and Sharon showered and changed, they were both exhausted. They put on fresh clothing and made a real effort to have some good family conversation in the living room, but it was a losing battle against the long car trip they'd taken. Sharon tried valiantly to keep up some pleasant chatter, but she ended up sound asleep on Simon's shoulder. It was all good, though, because she'd already made a huge impression on her nieces and nephew. She'd been most enthusiastic when Jacquelin told her she had taken second place in the spelling bee.

"I was the county spelling champion for four years running. It takes a lot of hard work and effort to do that, Jacquelin, I'm very proud of you.

She won Sarafina's heart forever when she told her she had a signed first edition of the first Harry Potter novel, which was one of the child's favorite books. "I met J.K. Rowling at a conference where she was signing books. I'll send it to you when I get back to New York. I love to read. I have over a thousand books," she confided to the awestruck child.

"Wow. Can I come see them sometime?" Sarafina asked, reverently.

"Of course you can. I'd love to have you visit me in New York, all three of you," Sharon told her.

Oddly enough, her nephew Gregory was most impressed after she went to sleep. Her cell phone went off and Simon answered it. "Sure, Jay, I'll tell her you called. She'll get back to you tomorrow, I'm sure. Tell Bee we said hello," he said before signing off.

"Umm, I wasn't trying to eavesdrop, but Jay and Bee, was that as in Jay-Z and Beyoncé?"

Simon smiled. "Producers know everyone, Gregory. There aren't too many celebs she doesn't know."

"Wow. Aunt Sharon is a big baller," he said with a chuckle. Simon had to correct him on that point.

"Actually, your aunt is a shot caller. She runs things," Simon said, unconsciously pulling her closer to his side.

Sara was concerned about getting Sharon to bed. "I hate to wake her up, she looks so comfortable," she fretted.

Simon scooped her up in his arms and easily carried her up the stairs. After he deposited her on the bed, Angela said she would get her undressed. Simon took one last look at Sharon before leaving the room. He bent over and whispered goodnight and went to press a soft kiss on her lips. She responded at once, murmuring his name and winding her arms around his neck. The kiss went from an innocent and chaste goodnight to something very personal and erotic and Simon pulled away as gently as he could. Incredibly, she was still sleeping soundly. Angela was watching with amused admiration, muttering "You go, girl," under her breath.

She closed the door behind Simon and while she was helping Angela out of her shorts and knit top, she had to comment. "Girl, I don't know where you found him, but you really picked a winner."

৪৩০৪

The next morning, Sharon slept until the ungodly hour of nine. She never slept that late, not even on weekends. She was always up and about by six, seven at the very latest. But the summer air coming in the open windows, coupled with the sinful comfort of her bed had made her sleep deeper and longer than she had since who knows when. She lay in bed, trying to recall when and how she'd gotten in the bed and for the life of her, she couldn't remember. She got up, took a quick shower and dressed in jeans and a tee shirt, ready to help Sara with the preparations for the reunion. She tapped on Simon's door and was disappointed to find that he was up and gone, his bed neatly made. She went down to the kitchen, where she found her mother, but no Simon.

"Good-morning, Momma," she said, kissing her mother on the cheek. "Where is everybody?"

"Everyone's out and about," her mother said. "Angela went to Wal-Mart to pick up a few things and the kids went with her. And Simon is out with your father taking a look at the farm."

The Wal-Mart was in the next town, so it would be a while before their return. And who knows how long it would take Daddy to show off the farm; once he got started talking about it, he could go on and on. She was distracted from her thoughts by her mother offering to make her breakfast.

"Oh, I can do that," Sharon said. She got herself a couple of pieces of toast and some bacon left over from the family's early meal and poured a cup of coffee from the still warm pot. She sat down at the kitchen table where Sara was busy making notes and checking lists. "So, Momma, what can I do to help?"

Sara didn't even raise her head from her tasks. "Not a thing, baby. You and Simon just enjoy yourselves while you're here."

"No, Momma, I want to do something productive," Sharon protested. "That's why I came early, so I could help get things prepared."

"Don't be silly, child, I have it all under control. Everything is all taken care of, so you don't have to do a thing," Sara said. "By the way, honey, your Simon is a very nice young man. I can see why you're so taken with him. He's made quite an impression on your father, too. How long have you been dating?"

Sharon spent the next thirty minutes or so answering every question under the sun about Simon, thanking the heavens that they'd spent so much time learning about each other. Her mother would have made an excellent agent for the secret police before the fall of the USSR, she thought. After she collected every bit of data with the exception of his shoe size and his Social Security number, Sara seemed satisfied. She sat back in her chair, smiled benignly at Sharon and stacked her lists and notes neatly.

"Well, honey, you've done very well," she said, approvingly. "He seems like a wonderful man and it's obvious he cares for you very much. She looked at her wristwatch and abruptly rose from the table. "I have some last-minute errands to run, so you and Simon just relax and take it easy. I'll see you later," she said, cheerily and was gone before Sharon could volunteer to run errands with her. She sat at the table by herself, rearranging the toast crumbs on her plate with her index finger.

So much for that, she thought. *Nothing seems to change around here, no matter what I do.*

She washed her plate and coffee cup out, and walked out onto the back porch. She was relieved beyond measure to see Simon returning to the house and she ran to meet him. She threw her arms around him and when he bent to kiss her, she returned it with all the love she was feeling. Simon might not share the mad passion she felt for him, but he always knew what she needed.

"Now that's a good morning," he told her, kissing her forehead and the top of her head.

"Now it is," Sharon said, wistfully. "I overslept and everyone has taken off and Momma won't let me help her do anything, so here we are."

Simon looked down at her and hugged her even tighter. He laughed at the look on her face when he gave her butt a good squeeze. "Well, if she doesn't want any help, let's go play."

"You know what? That's a wonderful idea," she agreed. "Let's hit it."

“☘”

ಬಂಛ

Despite her nagging angst, Sharon had a wonderful day with Simon. They drove all around Mason Corners and had the incredible burgers at Diane's Café for lunch. Sharon also took him to visit Miss Lit, the town eccentric. She was well into her eighties and still sharp as a tack. She was delighted to see Sharon, because they had been special friends when Sharon was a little girl. When there was no one else to pay attention to her, Miss Lit was always there for her. She and her sisters had once had tea with Miss Lit at her house, but unbeknownst to her family, Sharon had formed a close friendship with the gracious lady.

Miss Lit flirted boldly with Simon and looked the couple over with avid interest. "You two are a beautiful pair," she said, archly. She turned to Simon and fixed him with her unwavering eye. "You made a very wise choice, young man. I hope you realize what riches lay ahead of you."

Sharon wanted to sink through the porch floor with embarrassment, but Simon just smiled and took the old lady's hand, bowing over it and giving her a kiss. He whispered in her ear, "You're invited to the wedding, Miss Lit. In fact, any time you want to come to New York to visit us, let us know and we'll send you a ticket."

She smiled in delight and patted his cheek. "Oh thank you, son, but I'd rather have my memories of the city. So much has changed there I don't think it would be as enjoyable to me. Did you know I was once a dancer in New York City?"

She regaled them with stories of her heyday on the stage until Sharon thought they should leave for fear they would tire her out. By the time they reached the Johnson farm there was still no sight of anyone so Sharon decided to make dinner. Simon volunteered to chop, slice and dice and they talked as they worked. "Nothing's changed, Simon. They were all pretty excited about *you*," she said, drolly. "It seems like I've finally accomplished something worthwhile as far as my family is concerned, I landed a man." She stirred the white sauce for the macaroni and cheese and brooded for a moment, and then she got mad. "I came early so I could help, so Momma wouldn't be overworked and she won't let me do anything. Basically I'm back to being the invisible child," she said, bitterly.

While she assembled the macaroni and cheese in the baking pan, Simon gently pointed out that she needed to sit her mother down and have a talk with her. "Shay, you need to communicate with her. Your mother loves you and so does your dad. He questioned me for two solid hours to make sure I was the right kind of man for you. I had the feeling that if he didn't like what

I had to say he was going to feed me into a hay baler," he said with a mock shudder.

"Wood chipper," she said with a smile.

"Excuse me?"

"He doesn't have a baler, but he does have a wood chipper. He'd have dropped you in that," she informed him.

"That's good to know," Simon said with a burst of laughter. "At least I know how I'm gonna go if I mess over you."

Sharon turned around and flashed him a brilliant smile. "That'll never happen because you'd never, ever do that to me," she said, confidently.

The table was set and dinner was ready when the Johnsons finally came home. Angela and the children were exhausted after chasing all over Wal-Mart for all the items on the long list Sara had given them. John was just tired after his usual hard day of work and was thrilled that there were appetizing smells coming out of the kitchen. Sara looked overheated and tired from doing all the errands she insisted she could do by herself and she was frankly amazed to see what awaited her.

"What in the world is this?" She sounded dazed.

"Dinner, Momma, just some short ribs, greens, fried corn, macaroni and cheese, cole slaw, tomato and cucumber salad and hot water corn bread. As soon as you freshen up it's ready."

"Did Deborah send this over?" Deborah was the one sister out of The Biddies who was tolerable in terms of personality and she was the best cook.

Before Sharon could get huffy, Simon quickly informed her mother that Sharon had prepared the meal. Sara raised both eyebrows up to her hairline, but she went to wash up without another word. Soon they were all seated around the big dining room table and Simon said grace. Everyone dug in with great appetite and as usual there was total silence around the table while Sharon's dinner disappeared at an alarming rate. Sara finally gathered her wits enough to tell her how good everything was.

"But how did you learn to cook like this? Who taught you?" she asked in bewilderment.

Sharon looked at Simon before answering. "I learned from watching you, Momma. I saw how you made things and I do it the same way. I've been cooking for as long as I can remember, which you and Daddy might have known if you'd ever come to visit me. I'd have been happy to cook Sunday dinner for you any time." She suddenly found she couldn't quite trust her voice, but she turned to her father and told him there was dessert.

"I made you a cake, Daddy. May we be excused? I'm a little tired," she said. And with that, she and Simon left the table, taking their empty plates into the kitchen.

EIGHT

S *imon knew Sharon was upset, but it was time she took matters into her own hands.* At this point, all he could do was offer her comfort, not advice. He could sense the love her parents had for her, but somehow, they weren't connecting. Some synapses just weren't firing on both their parts and he couldn't be the agent of change for their relationship. Sharon wouldn't appreciate his interference and he had a deep intuition that told him that if he did try to dabble in it, the results wouldn't be as true. Right now, all he could do was hold her, which he did, with her cuddled into his side as they sat on the porch swing. They didn't talk; he just held her and kissed her hairline and cheek every so often. She just sighed and let him.

He smiled, thinking about the words he'd exchanged with Miss Lit. She was absolutely correct about his future. He could see nothing but riches ahead of him because he'd decided to propose to Sharon as soon as they got home. He'd even gone so far as to pick out a ring with a big honking stone that stopped just short of being grossly ostentatious. He figured it was the biggest stone Sharon would tolerate; she wasn't one to flash a lot of bling-bling, despite the company she kept. He just wanted her to have something elegant and splendid, something just like her. She sighed softly and finally raised her head from his shoulder.

"Okay, I've sniveled enough," she said, resolutely. "I'm a grown woman and I need to stop acting like a neurotic teenager. It's time I had a little talk with my parents."

Suddenly the screen door opened and her mother stepped out onto the porch, followed by her father. "I couldn't agree with you more. We need to talk, Sharon."

ഇറയ

After Simon tactfully excused himself and went into the house, Sharon found herself ensconced between her parents. The porch swing was just big enough to hold all three of them, but she found a warm comfort in being squashed between their bodies. She laughed when she saw that her father was still holding a dessert plate with a big piece of cake on it. "Is that for me, Daddy, or are you having seconds?"

Jack laughed with her. "It's mine and don't you touch it," he said, taking a big forkful. "How in the world did you remember that checkerboard cake was my favorite dessert, sweetheart? And how did you learn how to make it so well?"

She shrugged. "Come on, Daddy, I did grow up here, even if you don't seem to realize it. Of course I know it's your favorite, I watched Momma make it often enough."

"Yes, but mine isn't nearly as good as yours. And what do you mean we didn't realize you were here? How could we not know you were a part of this family?" Sara asked, indignantly.

Sharon watched the fireflies dancing around before she spoke. "I never felt like part of the family. I was the oddball, the goofy little bookworm, the one people made fun of. The Biddies started calling me Jackie and you didn't do anything to stop them," she said slowly. "Why didn't you ever make them stop making fun of my teeth?"

Jack frowned. "What do you mean? They called you Jackie because you looked so much like me, sugar, that's all."

She rolled her eyes and told them how she'd overheard her aunts talking about her huge teeth and told them what Jackie really meant. It was the first time she'd seen her parents really angry over anything to do with her and the sight was quite alarming.

Sara was sputtering with rage and used a word Sharon had never heard escape her Christian lips. "Jack, I swear if those cows weren't your blood kin I'd go blast a hole in them. I had no idea that's why they called you Jackie, Sharon. If I'd known that, I would've made them stop in a heartbeat, you can believe that. But that's not the only issue, and I think you know it. I've never shown you how much you meant to me, and I didn't realize it until recently," Sara said, sadly. "But you were such an easy child to raise. It was almost like you were raising yourself. Sometimes your father and I just didn't know what to do with you, Sharon."

"What do you mean, Momma?" It was the first time she'd ever heard such an admission from her mother.

"Candace was the oldest and the only child for eight years, Sharon. When you came along, you were so different from Candace it was more than night and day, it was like a whole different experience in having a child. Did you know you walked when you were eight months old?"

Sharon shook her head. "Don't most babies walk about that time?"

"Not usually. It's more like ten months or older. Candace didn't walk until she was almost a year old. But you were sitting on a blanket on the floor and there was something that attracted your attention and you just got up and walked over to get it. You had never been on the floor before, mind you. Johnson girls aren't much for crawling," she said with a soft chuckle. "You were usually being carried around by me or your daddy or Candace and this was the first time I'd put you on the floor. You didn't hold onto anything, you didn't wobble or anything, you just got up and walked like you'd been doing it all your life. From that moment I knew you were different."

"Different how? I think a lot of babies who have an older sibling to imitate do things faster than normal," Sharon offered.

Jack laughed heartily. "Baby, you did everything faster than normal. Tell her about the time she talked, Sara."

Sara joined in her husband's laughter. "One morning I went in to get you from your crib. You were about a year old, and I said 'Good-morning, baby. Are you ready for breakfast?' And you said, 'Good-morning, Mommy. Yes, I want oatmeal and a round egg and toast, please.' You called poached eggs 'round eggs' when you were little," she said, fondly.

Jack put his arm around Sharon and laughed some more. "Sara came running downstairs hollering about 'The baby can talk, Jack, she can talk!' I didn't believe her until you talked to me. You looked at me with those big ol' eyes of yours and said "Good-morning, Daddy. I want my breakfast, please."

"You never said Ma-ma or Da-da, you just started talking in complete sentences," Sara said in wonderment. "You were the most intelligent, independent child I'd ever seen in my life. I was so scared we were going to ruin you I didn't know what to do," she admitted.

"*Ruin* me? Ruin me how, Momma?"

"You were so much smarter than any of us we weren't sure what to do with you. You could count to one hundred; you could say your ABCs and sing nursery rhymes before you were two. You could read by the time you were three. And I swear you potty-trained yourself." Sara shook her head in remembrance. "One day you brought me a clean diaper and said you needed to put it on. So from then on it was training pants. You never had an accident either."

Sharon looked from one parent to the other; clearly skeptical of the story she was hearing. Jack held his hand up as if in testimony. "One night I heard a little shuffling noise in the hall and I thought we had mice. Then I heard the toilet flush, and the water running in the bathroom. You knew how to use the little steps Sara kept under the bathroom sink to reach the taps and you were washing your hands when I came to investigate. You had taken yourself to the bathroom and washed your hands in the middle of the night, Sharon, and you were just a bitty little thing. There wasn't anything you couldn't do for yourself."

"You know they wanted to put you ahead in school," Sara said. "They had tested your IQ and it was so high they wanted to skip you ahead a few grades but we didn't think that was the best thing for you. You were so quiet and shy we thought that being with older students would make you even more withdrawn. You were the child who never did anything wrong. You were quiet and obedient and you never gave us a moment's trouble, which is why I guess you felt like we didn't give you enough attention," she said with a sigh.

"Candace and Debra were always fighting about something, and Angela, well I know I spoiled her a little but she was my last baby. And then there you were. You were too good to be true and we took it for granted. We weren't deliberately trying to leave you out, sweetie; we just never had to worry about you. The only thing we worried about was making sure you could get away from the farm and use that brain of yours."

Sharon rubbed her forehead. "Is that why you didn't want me to major in agriculture?"

Jack nodded his head. "That's right, baby. You could have been a doctor, a lawyer, a rocket scientist or anything else you wanted, there was no reason for you to stay around here."

"But I wanted to stay here, Daddy. What's wrong with agricultural science as a field? You make it sound like farming is a jail sentence instead of an honorable lifestyle. And if you felt like that, why didn't you say so instead of making me feel like I was useless? I took that scholarship to Howard because I finally gave up trying to get your attention and approval."

"I'm so sorry you felt like that," Sara said. Sharon could see the tears in her mother's eyes and hugged her tightly.

"Oh, Momma, don't cry! I don't want to make you feel bad, I just never understood why you treated me so differently than the other girls," she said, urgently.

Jack handed his wife a handkerchief and patted Sharon on the knee. "We treated you differently because you *were* different. You were an unusual child, Sharon and we probably didn't do things right, but we did them with love. You were just so easy to love and so easy to take care of, I guess you didn't get as much attention as the others. You should have been more of a brat like Debra and Angela, you'd have gotten lots of attention," he said with his usual dry wit. "Do you know you're the only child we never had to spank? We never had to punish you for anything, Sharon."

Sharon's head was reeling from what she was hearing. "But Daddy, you never came to visit me, not once. Not on parent's weekends, not once when I was in grad school and certainly not since I've been in New York. And yet you sent me that letter, Momma, which made it seem like I was neglecting you. I'm the one who comes home twice a year and that letter made it seem like you hadn't seen me in years. Why did you do that?"

To her shock, Sara gave an embarrassed little laugh. "I was just on a roll that day. I wrote all four of you on the same day and I was so fired up with the other three you got the brunt of it too. I'm sorry, baby. And we haven't been to visit you because, well, we didn't want to embarrass you. We knew you didn't want a couple of country bumpkins coming to the city to look like tourists and get in your way."

Sharon shrieked, which made both her parents jump. "What a terrible thing to say! I love you and I'm so proud of you, I have pictures of you all over my apartment and my office and you think I'd be ashamed of you if you came to New York? I can't believe you'd think so little of me, Momma! And that goes for you, too, Daddy. I even bought you matching outfits so you'd look cute when you came. Shame on you," she scolded, but she had put her arms through theirs while she was saying it.

"I can't believe we wasted all this time," Sharon said. "You could have been coming up to see me and having a good old time. Are you going to come now?"

Sara laughed softly. "I think we'll be up there real soon. Looks like we're going to be planning a wedding," she said in a teasing voice.

Suddenly Sharon felt dizzy. She'd gotten so caught up in unraveling a lifetime of miscommunications with her parents she forgot why Simon was there. As long as she was being honest with her feelings, she had to be honest about that too. Her father excused himself, saying there had better be some checkerboard cake left or someone was going to answer for it, leaving Sharon and Sara in the porch swing. Sharon scooted closer to her mother and took her hand in hers. "Momma, about that wedding," she began, "there isn't going to be one."

ജ⁊ങ

Sharon had unburdened herself to her mother and told her that she and Simon were friends and co-workers and the whole thing about him being her boyfriend was something he'd concocted to make her trip home easier. To Sharon's relief and surprise, her mother laughed, loud and hearty.

"Well, honey, I'm so sorry you thought you had to do this, but trust me when I tell you, that man is not your friend. He's as crazy about you as you are about him. Just be honest with him about your feelings and you'll see what I mean. That man is in love with you, Sharon."

Sharon was stunned by what she was hearing and for one wild moment she allowed herself to hope that her mother was right. "I wish you were right,

Momma, but really, we're just friends. Really *good* friends, but *just* friends. I've known him for over two years and he's never once made a pass at me of any kind. We work really well together and he's just about the greatest guy I've ever known, with the exception of Daddy, but he's not in love with me. He's just trying to be protective of me, like he would for his sisters," she said.

Sara put her arms around Sharon and hugged her hard. It was a beautiful moment for her; it was the first time in her memory that she knew something her daughter didn't. There were times, even with a big-shot New York television producer, that Momma knew best.

NINE

*T*he next day, which was the day before the reunion, Sharon was so busy she didn't have time to ponder her situation with Simon. Sara was more than happy to wake her up at the crack of dawn. "You wanted to help, remember? Well, I've got plenty of work for you, sugar. Get dressed and let's get going."

By the time the rest of the family made it downstairs for breakfast, Sharon had made a huge coffeecake, a big open faced Italian-style omelet with diced onion, red and green peppers, bacon, ham, cheese and potatoes, biscuits and toast. She had also started eggs and potatoes boiling for the potato salad and was already chopping up onions and celery. Simon offered to set the table but Sara wouldn't hear of it. "You can go help Jack, son. I know he has a list a mile long and those sorry brothers-in-law of his won't be here any time soon."

Simon couldn't resist kissing Sharon on the back of her neck and whispering "Be careful what you wish for. You clear the air and now you're the chief slicer, dicer and bottle washer," he whispered. He knew all about their conversation because after her long talk with her parents she'd had a long talk with him. They'd gone to the kitchen and talked while they shared a big piece of lemon cake, since the checkerboard cake was history. She had confided that her father had probably hidden the rest of it. "Even Daddy couldn't eat that much at once, although that theory has yet to be tested. I'll make him another one tomorrow."

She had poured her heart out, all except for the part about her being in love with him. It was hard to keep the information to herself, but she didn't want to ruin the rest of their time together by making an admission he couldn't reciprocate. That didn't stop her from getting another sizzling goodnight kiss, though. They kissed in the kitchen, licking the frosting off each other's lips. They kissed in the living room as they turned off the lights. They kissed at the bottom of the stairs, in the middle of the stairs and at the top of the stairs and one more quick one at the door of Sharon's room. She'd floated into bed that night, while Angela laughed at her. The last thing Sharon heard before she drifted off to sleep was something about no tacky bridesmaids' dresses. Angela insisted on picking them out, or some such thing.

Now she was so busy she didn't have time to ponder her situation. She made potato salad, fruit salad, cole slaw, macaroni salad and three bean salad. She also made another checkerboard cake, a pound cake and dozens of cookies. True, she did have help as her nephew Gregory proved quite adept at peeling potatoes and fruit. But even with help, the sheer volume of the dishes she was making was tiring. It was okay, though because for the first time in a long time she felt like a part of the family, a real integral part of the Johnson clan.

She was tired, though, no getting around it. By the time she finally left the kitchen she was ready to swear off cooking forever. She had no idea what Simon had been doing all day, other than toiling away with her father and his brothers-in-law. She and her mother and Angela were handling the inside; the outside details were up to the men. She did manage to take a long, luxurious bubble bath in the big claw-foot tub before dinner. She wasn't sure what they were having for dinner, nor did she really care. All she wanted was a long nap. A long nap with Simon was just what she craved, to be perfectly honest. She wanted to go to sleep in his arms and wake up there every morning for the rest of her life. She was crazy with longing for him and she didn't know how she was going to stand not having him in her life. But as soon as the reunion was over, that's the way it was going to be. Momma might think she knew what was going on in Simon's heart, but Sharon couldn't allow herself to believe it.

She finally forced herself to get out of the bathtub and patted herself dry with a big fluffy towel. She put on her favorite summer robe, tied it at the waist and opened the door to find Simon emerging from the other bathroom clad only in jeans. His bare chest was slightly damp and he'd obviously just gotten out of the shower. They both froze, staring at each other with wondering eyes. It was the first time she'd seen him without a shirt and the sight of his hard, sculpted physique sent a hot thrill through her like a bolt of lightning.

"Simon," she breathed.

"I had to take a quick shower," he said. "I had to knock the funk off before dinner; your father worked me like a Mississippi field hand today."

Sharon nodded mutely; she wasn't really listening to him. Suddenly two big tears formed in her eyes and she couldn't seem to keep them from rolling down her face. Simon was at her side in two long steps.

"What's the matter, Shay? Why are you crying, baby?"

He put his arms around her and she gladly rested her face against the unfamiliar warmth of his chest, rubbing her cheek against his smooth skin. She was so engrossed in the new sensation he had to call her name again. "Shay, baby, what is it?"

"I'm sorry," she said in a tear-choked whisper. "I know you were only trying to help me and you did, you really did. But I crossed the line, Simon and I'm really sorry."

They were still in the hallway where anyone could walk up on them. Simon took her hand and led her into the bedroom she was sharing with Angela. He sat her down on her bed and sat down next to her, still keeping his arms around her. "You're not making any sense, Shay. What line are you talking about?" His voice was soft and sexy and the sound of it made two more tears followed the first ones.

She wiped them away roughly and took a deep breath as she turned to face him. "I crossed the line of friendship, Simon. I'm in love with you."

She opened her mouth to say something else but the words were stopped by Simon's mouth as he kissed away whatever else she was about to say. When they finally broke the kiss, he smiled down at her and said, "I've been in love with you for two years, Shay. Two years," he whispered before taking her lips again. They kissed long and hard before breaking apart. Sharon looked at him with starry eyes and a pounding heart.

"You love me? Are you sure?"

Simon brushed her hair away from her face and cupped it in his warm hands. "I love you more than my next breath, Shay. I've always loved you and I always will. I can't ask you to marry me, though."

Sharon felt like her heart was being crushed by a sledge hammer. "Why not?"

"Because the ring is in New York. It's not finished yet and when I ask you to be mine for the rest of your life I want to put it on your finger."

Sharon reached over and grabbed his chiseled pec, giving it a twist. Simon looked horrified. "Oww! What was that for?" he demanded.

"For scaring the life out of me! Talking about you couldn't ask me to marry you, are you crazy?" Her face suddenly burst into a smile of pure happiness. "You love me! You really do! And I love you, with all my heart," she vowed.

"Y'all better get some clothes on and get down to dinner. You can sing the Barney song to each other later, but right now I suggest Mr. Simon get some clothes on or Daddy will be up here with a shotgun," drawled Angela from the doorway.

Simon was on his feet and out the door in a nanosecond. "I saw that wood chipper, Shay. I'm not taking any chances."

Sharon ran to Angela and grabbed her hands. "Angie, I'm getting married!"

"And what else is new? Did you think I didn't know that?"

Sharon was too busy dancing around her sister to notice that Angela was laughing at her. "Well, *I* didn't know! He loves me! He loves me!"

Angela smiled at her fondly. "We all do, you idiot. Get some clothes on so we can eat. Everybody's waiting for you."

For some reason they were the sweetest words Sharon had ever heard.

NINE

*T*he reunion was everything Sara had hoped it would be and more. When she found out why her despicable sisters-in-law called Sharon 'Jackie' it just gave her more ammunition to use to extract revenge on the women for the way they had treated Candace. They had deliberately made Candace believe that Jack wasn't her father, that she'd been fathered by his brother, Robert. When Sharon was told of their perfidy she was a more than willing accomplice in handing out some long overdue justice, Johnson girls style. And even better than the look on The Biddies' faces when Sara and Jack told them off for old and new regarding the true origins of Sharon's hated nickname was the fact that everyone at the gathering said that Sharon could bake better than any of them. That was the blow that brought them to their knees, that and the fact that Sara had exposed them for the lying snoops they were.

For Sharon the weekend was sheer bliss. She was with her sisters again, the first time they'd all been together in years. She had a new understanding and respect for her parents and was more assured than ever of their love and her place in their hearts. And best of all, she had found the love she thought would evade her forever. The thought of spending the rest of her life with Simon was so exciting she found herself staring at him at odd moments, just looking at him and basking in his love. When she could pry herself away from her nieces, that is. Jack knew lust when he saw it and regardless of the fact that he could also see love, there was nothing happening with his daughter before the wedding, at least not in his house. So he paid his nieces to trail Sharon around and whenever it looked like something really interesting was about to happen with Simon, one or the other would materialize and break up the moment. Sharon was so happy she couldn't have cared less about her niece's blocking; she thought it was funny and endearing because it made her feel cherished, both by her daddy and her man.

And they figured out a way to circumvent scrutiny by calling each other on their cell phones so they could have long, sexy conversations while everyone else was asleep. "I love you, Simon. I love you, and I can't wait to get home so I can have my way with you," she cooed. It was late Saturday night and they would be leaving the next afternoon, after the festivities were over.

"I love you, Shay and you're not going to have to wait until we get home. I plan to make love to you in every state we go through until we're back in New York," he growled, softly. After a pause, he said "Uh, Shay, I gotta go. Jack wants to have a talk with me."

"Don't go in the barn, that's where the wood chipper is," Sharon said, cheerfully.

She went down the hall to her parents' bedroom and found Candace, Debra and Angela waiting for her. "It took you long enough! Do you ever get tired of talking dirty to that man?" That came from Debra.

Sharon laughed and winked at Debra and told her to hush. "You're gonna shock Momma."

Sara rolled her eyes. "If I was the type to get shocked easily I wouldn't have four of you," she reminded her.

All of them burst into laughter. They laughed, talked, brushed each other's hair and made plans until the hour got very, very late. It took several pointed reminders from Jack that he'd like to occupy his bed with his wife before the sisters finally took their leave. It was a time they would never forget, a time they would try to recreate as often as possible in the coming years because no matter how far away they lived, no matter how different their lifestyles, one thing was certain. Wherever their hearts were, that was home.

EPILOGUE

I still can't believe you're having your wedding here. Of all the places in the world, why here?" Sara was still perplexed by her daughter's choice of a nuptial site.

"Momma, destination weddings are the big thing. You watch E! TV, you know what I mean. You pick a place and all your family and friends come there and you have a big party. Everyone is going to have a ball, just wait and see," Sharon said, confidently.

"But having the wedding at the farm? Won't they think it's strange?"

"Nope, not at all. And if they do, they're not really my friends anyway, so to heck with them. Besides, it'll do Mason Corners some good to have a few new faces in town," she joked.

It was the May after the reunion and Simon and Sharon were getting married on her parent's farm over the Memorial Day weekend. The guest list included everyone from Miss Lit to Jay-Z and the town was buzzing about who might show up. Sharon couldn't have cared less about all the buzz; she was too thrilled about taking her vows with the man she adored. The man, who, strange as it once seemed, loved her madly. Chloe and Angela were her maid and matron of honor and the other Johnson girls, including Jacquelin and Sarafina, were her bridesmaids, along with Simon's lovely sisters. The flowers were in bloom, the farm looked its absolute best and the food would be way beyond compare as her dear friend Bobby Flay was catering the affair. That fact alone ticked off The Biddies to no end until Sharon asked them to bake her wedding cake. Then they got on board with a vengeance, vowing that she would have the most spectacular cake in the history of weddings. They meant it, too; since the reunion the animosity was gone with one notable exception and even she had learned to chill. It was going to be an outdoor ceremony that was spiritual, festive and highly original, just like the couple being joined.

"Just think, Momma; last May you sent out that come-or-else edict and this May I'm getting married!"

"But whoever heard of wearing a Vera Wang gown in a field in South Carolina?" Sara said, with wonder in her voice.

"Momma, this time last year you had no idea who Vera Wang was, so that just goes to show you, all things are possible. With the Johnson girls you just have to expect the unexpected and be happy."

Her mother smiled and they hugged each other tightly. "That's all I ever wanted for all my girls."

To My Readers,

Thanks for going with me on another adventure. This is the culmination of years of friendship and support. Janice Sims was such a friend and influence to me when I started my writing career and we have wanted to do a project together for a long time. I'm so blessed and thankful for her friendship and support, and for bringing me this opportunity.

Thanks again for all your prayers and support during the last months; I can honestly say that you keeping me lifted up in prayer is what got me here.

Stay blessed!
Melanie

About

MOMMA'S BABY, DADDY'S MAYBE

by
Janice Sims

ONE

C *andace Johnson-Bates opened her eyes.* She squinted at the alarm clock on the bedside table: six-fifteen A.M. *What the...*she still had an hour to sleep! Then, she felt a hand on her hip. She was lying on her right side with her back to her husband, Greg. Shortly after feeling his hand on her hip, she felt something else on her butt. Okay, she got the picture now. They'd been married for fifteen years and Greg still had not given up the perpetual hope of a quick one before work. Sometimes she wished he *would* abandon the thought. Other times she was an enthusiastic participant.

Turning to face him, she smiled. "Don't you have to be downtown by eight?"

"That's why I woke you early." He gave her a crooked smile.

That smile had been known to be a precursor to pregnancy. She threw a leg across his hip. "I'm off the pill," she reminded him. She had begun having symptoms like severe headaches, hot flashes, and irritability. Figuring forty-one was a bit too young to be premenopausal, she stopped taking them.

Greg wrapped her in his muscular arms. Those muscles had been hardened by sweat equity. He was a builder and had worked in construction for twenty years before starting his own business. "Don't worry, I'll pull out in time," he said, with a note of pleading.

Candace laughed. "The last time you said that, I got pregnant with Jacquelin."

Greg sighed. "I liked it much better when you were on the pill."

"I'm sure you did," Candace said, icily. Men were such whiners when something was an inconvenience for them. She'd been on the pill for more than ten years. He could at least show some compassion for her. Have some sense of fairness. Why should she always be the one to accommodate *him*?

She pushed out of his arms, got up and went to get a condom from the medicine cabinet. Greg lay in bed watching the undulation of her shapely hips. She was wearing a skimpy nightie that left little to the imagination. He couldn't help it: he was turned on even more than he had been before. After three children she looked sexier today than she had when they were first wed. Marriage suited Candace. She seemed to thrive on the everyday running of the household. Their house was immaculate. The kids were happy and healthy. *He* adored her. Even her job as an interior decorator was executed with such aplomb that he could only marvel at her abilities.

She returned with the condom and noticed the lascivious look in his eyes. Not even her apparent irritation at his selfish disregard for her feelings had killed his ardor.

She threw him the condom and jumped on top of him. "You'll put that on or there will be no lovin' this morning, big boy."

He put it on.

ᐁᑎᑐ

By the time the kids came down for breakfast, Candace had scrambled eggs and cooked turkey sausage links. Gregory Junior walked into the kitchen looking bright-eyed and ready to take on his day. He was already six feet at fourteen. Candace knew he would reach or exceed his father's six-foot-four before he was finished growing. Lanky and good-looking with a gorgeous smile augmented by dimples, he had on his customary school wardrobe of jeans, athletic shoes, and a tee shirt with his high school's mascot emblazoned across the chest.

He walked over and gave her a perfunctory hug. "Mornin', Mommy."No matter how she tried she couldn't get him to stop calling her Mommy. Try Mom, or Mother she coaxed him, but he would not budge.

"Morning, Gregory," she murmured happily as she folded the scrambled eggs onto a platter and handed it to him. "Sleep well?"

Taking the platter, Gregory laughed shortly. "How can anyone sleep when Sarafina snores like a buzz saw right next door? Mommy, really, you need to take her to the doctor for a check-up. That girl's got adenoids the size of grapefruits."

Gregory loved anything pertaining to science. Knowing him, he'd looked up adenoids just to make certain he was using the correct term. He was kind of anal retentive that way. *But*, Candace silently admitted, *he inherited that tendency from me.*

"Don't pick on your sister," she admonished him as Sarafina, her twelve-year-old, was turning the corner, yawning widely. "Good morning," Sarafina said, mournfully.

Candace smiled. The child barely looked awake. Her big brown eyes were drooping and her attempt at dressing might have been deemed eclectic if not for the fact that she had on two different shoes. *That settles it*, Candace thought, *she's going to the eye doctor as soon as I can make an appointment.* Candace had suspected Sarafina might be having trouble with her eyesight for some time now. Occasionally, she could not distinguish between certain colors that were similar. This morning, she was wearing a pale pink sneaker and a pale lavender sneaker. Sarafina loved soft, feminine colors. Her bedroom was decorated in pastel shades. And a day didn't go by that she didn't wear something that was pink, her signature color.

She went and hugged her mother. Candace enfolded her in her arms and kissed the top of her head while she still could. She supposed that if she had wanted shorter children she shouldn't have married such a tall man. Fortunately, Sarafina stood four inches less than her five-eight. But in a few years she had no doubt she'd be towering over her like her older brother.

"How're you feeling, sweetie?" she asked.

Sarafina moaned. If Gregory's mood could be described as enthusiastically cheerful, then his sister's was closer to somber. Not a morning person, her energy didn't kick in until around noon. Unfortunately, school started at nine.

"I woke myself up snoring," she complained.

"Told ya!" Gregory offered from his place at the table. He was busy buttering toast and wolfing it down generously slathered with grape jelly as quickly as he could get it ready. She wondered where all the calories he consumed went. If her metabolism were that efficient she could stop worrying about what she ate.

"Sounds like you might be going to see the doctor soon, sweetie," Candace told her. "For that and your eyesight. You're wearing two different colored shoes."

Mouth wide with astonishment, Sarafina looked at her feet. "Oh, I'm so glad you didn't let me go to school like this!" She turned and ran from the room.

"You could have claimed it's a new fad," her mother called to her retreating back.

Gregory laughed, then addressed his mother with, "Hey, Mommy, where's Dad? Isn't he up yet?"

"He had an early appointment," Candace told him. She sat down across from him and put scrambled eggs and a couple of sausage links on her plate. "He'll be home before seven tonight, though. So, we will have family night as usual."

Every Friday night, they either went out for a movie or rented one and enjoyed it in the entertainment room that Greg had insisted on including in the floor plan of their Charleston, South Carolina home when he'd built it five years ago. Patterned after a movie theater with a screen nearly the size of screens found in commercial theaters at any mall in the United States, it had theater seating for twelve, and enough electronic equipment to make Steven Spielberg envious. Greg was hooked on electronics.

Before the movie, the kids could help themselves to popcorn, candies, and cold drinks—treats they did not get during the school week.

"Cool," said Gregory as he snapped a sausage in two with his strong teeth. "I hope it's an action/adventure, and not one of those romantic movies the girls got to choose last week."

"Don't worry," said Candace. "This week, it's men's choice."

Gregory grinned at that, knowing he and his dad shared the same tastes in films.

"All right!" Gregory crowed happily. "A Samuel L. Jackson movie, it is."

Jacquelin, Candace's youngest at nine, strode into the kitchen looking immaculate in her school uniform of a plaid skirt, white short-sleeved blouse with a Peter Pan collar, white knee socks, a dark blue cardigan with her school's insignia on it, and black Mary Janes. Her long, curly black hair was in a ponytail, and Candace noticed that, like her brother, she was raring to go. Her bright black eyes fairly danced. "Momma, do you know what today is?"

She said this while bending down to plant a kiss on her mother's cheek.

Candace beamed at her. "No, baby, what's special about today?"

Of course, Candace knew exactly to what her youngest was referring: Today, there would be an announcement about who would represent her school at a countywide spelling bee. Jacquelin was hoping to be one of the chosen few.

Jacquelin, grinning happily, sat down at the table and began putting food on her plate. "You don't fool me, you know!"

"How can we *not* know?" Gregory asked around a wad of food. "You haven't talked about anything but the spelling bee for what seems like forever!"

Jacquelin leveled a look of resignation at her brother, and sighed pityingly. "I don't expect you to understand. All you care about is science. But those of us who love words and how they work get a certain enjoyment from the competition."

"Mommy, are you sure she's only nine, and she's not some small-sized grown person masquerading as a nine-year-old? Listen to how she talks, it's spooky!"

Candace could only laugh. She loved mornings with her children. It was always surprising and supremely entertaining. She wiped a tear from the corner of her eye. "You're right, Jacquelin," she admitted. "I haven't forgotten, and I'm keeping my fingers crossed for you."

"Not just your fingers," Jacquelin insisted eagerly. "Cross everything! I really want this!"

"Want what?" Sarafina asked, coming back into the room.

Candace glanced down. Sarafina now had on both pink sneakers.

"To participate in the spelling bee," Jacquelin told her.

Sarafina went and hugged Jacquelin. Candace was gratified that her daughters got along so well, although they were known to gang up on their brother. But, then, Gregory was often the one who antagonized them into joining forces against him.

Sarafina sat down and helped herself to the food. She smiled at Jacquelin. "Don't give it another thought, little sis, I have a good feeling about this."

"Thanks, Sara." Jacquelin smiled her pleasure and tucked into her breakfast with gusto. She always called Sarafina Sara, after their grandmother, whom they both adored. Candace thought that was ironic because she'd intentionally tacked on the 'fina' to Sarafina's name so that no one would refer to her as Sara. Greg had insisted on giving their firstborn daughter Candace's mother's name, Sara. Candace had been willing to use Sara but not to use it alone and they'd compromised with Sarafina. To this day, Greg did not know why Candace had been reluctant to name their daughter simply 'Sara' because she hadn't confided in him.

One day, she thought, *I'll tell him everything.*

She sat back and enjoyed the sight of her children interacting with one another. Her day may yet prove to be unbearable, but for now she was at peace.

ဆာလ

Three hundred miles away in the tiny town of Mason Corners, South Carolina, Sara Johnson sat at her kitchen table as well, but she wasn't having breakfast. She and her husband, Jack, had eaten hours ago. He was somewhere in the south forty right now overseeing the harvesting of a bountiful watermelon crop. May was a busy month for melon growers.

Sara had golden brown skin with deep red undertones, a handsome face with crinkles around her light brown eyes, a well-shaped nose and a full mouth. She'd never cut her naturally wavy black hair and now, salt-and-pepper, it hung past her waist. She usually wore it twisted at the back of her neck. Today, she just didn't have the energy to put it up so it hung down her back. She wasn't suffering from a physical ailment. For a woman approaching sixty, she was in excellent health. No, today she had a malaise of the spirit because she had to do something she didn't want to do: Write her eldest daughter, Candace, and *tell* her about herself!

Not that she was the type of woman who shrank from the truth. She was simply more comfortable telling someone what she thought of them face to face, not via the United States Postal Service. She and Jack were computer literate, but it was her opinion that an e-mail was too impersonal when you were getting ready to enrage somebody.

Therefore, she sat at the big oak table in her spacious farm kitchen with her best stationery before her and a well-balanced pen, and poured out her heart to Candace:

> *Dear Candace,*
>
> *It's May. I didn't hold my breath in expectation of your bringing our grandchildren to see us on the anniversary of Our Lord's resurrection.*
>
> *When I phoned and invited you all to Easter dinner, I knew you would come up with a whopper of an excuse not to. And I know I'm not going to see you on Mother's Day, either. You will send the usual dozen roses and a gift certificate from some over-priced department store that I would never set foot in—or maybe you won't this year after you read this letter—because I'm about to be brutally honest about a subject that's been on my mind for some time now: Your neglect of your father and me.*
>
> *Whether you realize it or not, Candace, you haven't been home in over three years. I could probably understand that if you lived in Timbuktu, but you live three hundred miles away! Your father and I have been to Charleston at least twice a year to see you, Greg, and our grandchildren. But it's as if you're ashamed to bring your family to see us anymore! Is Mason Corners too 'country' for you? Is our house not fine enough? Has your father or, more than likely, I done something to offend you?*
>
> *Don't try to deny that your affection for me—I can't speak for your father—hasn't lessened over the years because I know it has. Whenever I look into your eyes it's like I'm looking into the eyes of a stranger. You may say that I'm just getting old and it's my imagination but ask yourself why you haven't been to Mason Corners in such a long time?*
>
> *Can you honestly say you've simply been too busy to make the trip?*
>
> *Whatever your reason is: I want you to be able to tell me to my face when you come to the family reunion that's going to be hosted*

here at the farm from Friday, August 17th through Sunday, August 19th.

Don't give me any excuses. You've got three months to rearrange your schedule. Be here, or don't even bother coming to my funeral when I die. I mean that.

Your loving mother,
Sara Johnson

P.S. Give my love to Greg and the children.

After finishing, Sara carefully folded the letter, placed it in a business size envelope and sealed it. She set it aside, a grim expression on her face. Knowing Candace, she wasn't going to like it one bit! But desperate times called for desperate measures. Sara was not getting any younger, and she had to know why Candace had emotionally pulled away from her over the years. What's more, she had three other letters to write. Letters her remaining daughters, Sharon, Angela and Debra were not going to find to their liking, either.

She sighed and reached for a fresh sheet of paper. Best to get it over with.

TWO

A *fast-paced, dissonant hip-hop song blared from the speakers in the club.* Angela strutted onto the long, narrow runway of a stage that was mere inches from the drunken, raucous patrons, some of whom were shouting come-ons and waving damp bills, hoping to lure her a little closer.

She was a better than average dancer. Her movements, while sensual, were also smooth and artful. She knew no one in here cared that she could actually dance, all they wanted her to do was gyrate in front of them as scantily clad as the law allowed, making certain to shake certain parts of her anatomy. But, it paid the bills. And big, muscular bouncers were stationed around the room in order to protect her if a patron became too consumed with lust. So, it was safer than some places she'd worked.

A tall, brown-skinned girl with a fit, voluptuous body, Angela had legs like a dancer's and a shapely backside that the men enjoyed zeroing in on. But it was her breasts that they couldn't keep their eyes off. Not as huge as some of the other girls' breasts, they were nonetheless perfectly formed golden pillows of paradise that gleamed with promise. Many a patron wanted to get his hands on them. The rules, however, were no touching, or nudity.

Still, the occasional Don Quixote, who dreamed the impossible dream, found himself at the foot of the stage shouting, "Take it off, sweetheart. Let me see those babies!" Tonight, it was a short, good-looking college kid with a twenty-dollar bill held aloft. "Come on, sugar, take it off! It's my birthday!"

Angela executed a smart turn and sultrily reached behind her as if she were about to snap open the clasp of her skimpy bra, then she shook her generously endowed gluteus maximus which caused the audience to erupt in rapturous applause.

She spun around, smiling at the college boy, then pranced over to him, did a full split right next to him and let him put the twenty in the waistband of her g-string. He tried to touch her breasts and she responded by slapping his hand away and laughing.

He laughed good-naturedly and stepped away from the stage. His buddies congratulated his bravery with high fives and slurry comments like, "Way to go, dude. You almost touched them. Man, they're awesome. They defy gravity!"

Angela came out of the split, crawled a few feet, giving the audience a prized view of her backside, and pulled herself up using the pole. She slithered up the pole in a slow, sensuous movement with it strategically positioned between her legs. Her finale was a heated, arousing dance with the pole. The pole was not simply a device. It was her partner. She made every man in the place wish he were that pole instead of a poor schmuck sitting in a darkened club. When she bent all the way backward, her crotch pressing gently against the pole, the audience sighed as if from sexual satisfaction.

They got up and applauded when she finished and began walking from the stage. Dollar bills, and some larger denominations, were tossed onstage. She turned around to collect them and to blow kisses to her appreciative fans.

A minute or so later, she strode into the girls' dressing room and made her way to the back of the room to her locker where she started peeling off the sweaty bra and g-string.

"It just gets better and better, doesn't it?" Sandy Patterson asked, grinning at her. Sandy was a short, buxom blonde with dark roots in her Dolly Parton hair. She claimed she was twenty-one but Angela knew she was only seventeen. She'd seen her driver's license when Sandy had crashed on her couch one night after they'd partied together.

But this was Miami where youth was a commodity everybody was buying. It was where kids like Sandy went looking to strike it rich using that commodity but, more often than not, were met with bitter disappointment.

Between the two of them, youth not withstanding, Sandy was the veteran. She'd been dancing at Benny's for six months. Angela had only been working there for three.

"I warmed them up for you," Angela said, grinning back.

"Okay," Sandy said, turning to leave. "Wanna grab something to eat after I'm done?"

"Sorry, but I've got to go home and study," Angela said, regrettably.

Sandy beamed at her. She really was a pretty girl when her face wasn't hidden by thick stage make-up as it was now. "Good for you," she said, as she left.

Angela watched as Sandy crossed the threshold and disappeared in the darkness of the corridor. Sighing, she finished undressing, grabbed her robe and slipped into it.

Just as she tied the belt around her waist, a large dark brown hand slammed her locker shut and Terry Christmas—not his real name, she didn't know his real name—came around the locker and looked her up and down as if she were something good to eat. "Hey, Angel Girl, there's a big spender out there who wants to spend his money on *you* tonight. You game?"

Terry was the owner's brother. Angela wasn't sure if Benny Christmas, not his real name, either, knew that his brother was a part-time pimp, but she knew Terry had convinced a few of the other girls to barter more than their looks in exchange for easy cash. She'd overheard them bragging about the money and deriding the johns, some of whom had been too drunk to actually have sex with them. They'd counted themselves lucky to have scored a few hundred dollars for doing nothing more than letting the johns rub up against them.

Angela gave him her pat answer. "My name is *Angela*. And I ain't no prostitute."

And Terry gave her his: "You just ain't hungry enough yet."

He smiled down at her, looking like a cobra in his slick black leather ensemble.

Turning to leave, he tossed over his shoulder, "The guy wanted to give you five big ones just for sittin' on his lap. He looks like he's pushing sixty. He would have passed out before he got it up." His expression said she'd passed on a good thing.

Angela cut him with her eyes. "Then why don't *you* sit on his lap?"

"He don't go that way," was Terry's reply. He grinned at her, showing all of his big, yellow-stained teeth. Taking the ever-present plastic toothpick from his shirt pocket, he clamped it between his lips and sauntered out.

Angela was going to shower before leaving, but after talking to him, all she wanted to do was get out of there as soon as possible. She doffed the robe and quickly dressed in jeans, shirt and athletic shoes. All around her, the sounds of the other girls yammering, the fainter echo of the bass from the sound system in the club, and the steady stream of people passing in the adjacent corridor, jarred her nerves.

Grabbing her tote, she made sure the locker was secured, and then pushed her way out of the crowded dressing room. "Hey, bitch, watch where you're going," grumbled Betty Neale when Angela accidentally brushed her arm on the way out.

Betty was always itching for a fight, and had the scars to prove it. One slashed its way across her chest. Another ran from her elbow to her wrist on her left arm, the one Angela had inadvertently touched.

Angela was younger, taller, and possibly stronger than Betty. But she knew Betty carried a knife, if not a gun, and she didn't want to tangle with her. "My bad, Betty," she said. "Just tryin' to get out of here before Terry comes back."

In spite of her attitude, Betty disliked Terry's trying to turn them all into prostitutes as much as Angela did. Her scowl softened. "Oh, okay, kid, go on."

"'Night," Angela said.

"Yeah, you too," Betty said, gruffly. She pursed her lips, rubbed the tip of her nose and finished getting into her costume. She was on right after Sandy.

In the warm, moist air outside, Angela's nose immediately stopped up. Lord, her sinuses bothered her more since she'd moved to Florida than at any other time in her life. She'd thought South Carolina had hot weather, but Florida was a muggy swamp compared to South Carolina. How she wished, now, that she was back home in Mason Corners. But until she could go home in style, she wasn't going back. She'd promised that she would not go back home a failure, which was what she considered herself.

Her eyes darting about the pitch-black parking lot, she looked for any movement. It appeared as if the parking lot was empty except for her, but she'd been surprised by ardent admirers more than once. They waited for her to come to her car, then they came out of the shadows and propositioned her if they were honorable. If they weren't, they simply pounced. One of the bouncers had had to come to her rescue the first week she'd danced here. Her attacker had her pinned to the hood of her car before the bouncer had pulled him off of her.

The club's owner had not wanted to involve the police. It was bad for business when the patrons heard sirens. He'd wound up choosing to ban the guy from the club. Angela had spotted him again less than a week later. She'd started carrying mace in her purse after that.

She made it to her car without incident, locked herself in and quickly turned the key in the ignition. Backing out of the parking space, she nearly hit a patron as he staggered to his car. She blew the horn. He shouted an obscenity, and she sped off.

Tears moistened her eyes, and she blinked them away. She was twenty-five years old. It wasn't as if she was a dumb woman. She had graduated from high school, and had an associate's degree from a community college. Up until last year, she'd been doing well keeping the books for her family's business which was a large farm in Mason Corners, South Carolina. She'd been dating a nice guy: Padraic Monaghan. Padraic owned a farm in Mason Corners, as well. He grew organic vegetables. They were all the rage among the health-conscious. Padraic was full of exciting ideas when it came to the future of farming. And he was successful, something not a lot of farmers could boast.

Angela had foolishly felt as if she would be settling if she accepted Padraic's proposal of marriage. She'd never lived anywhere except Mason Corners. She was the youngest of four sisters. The other three had gone out into the world and become successes. Angela thought she would be shortchanging herself if she didn't live away from home at least once in her life. She wanted to make it on her own without help from anyone. Not her parents, or Padraic, or even her big sister, Candace, who was under the impression that *she'd* raised her.

The thought of Candace made her smile. Just that morning Candace had phoned her, complaining that she hadn't seen her in over a year. "Come home," Candace had begged. "I'll send you the money. You can fly into Charleston, and I'll drive you home."

"Really?" Angela had chided her big sister. "You, who haven't been home in ages yourself? You'd actually venture into little old Mason Corners for *me*?"

"I see you've been talking to Momma," Candace said, testily. "Okay, so I haven't been to Mason Corners. Momma and Daddy come here all the time. There's no need for me to go home."

"They do not come to your house all the time," Angela corrected her. "They come when they can no longer bear being separated from their grandchildren because their mother won't bring them to Mason Corners. They're getting old, Candace. You ought to be ashamed of yourself."

"You got that verbatim from Momma, didn't you?"

"So what if I did? I agree with her. You know, I don't think I would be here in Miami if I didn't think that somewhere out in the great big world there was someplace better than Mason Corners, too. So, I understand where you're coming from."

"You went to South Beach in hopes of being discovered," Candace reminded her.

"It was a pipe dream," Angela admitted. "Pretty girls are a dime a dozen down here. And they're all younger than I am. I'm an old hag compared to them. I made a mistake, Candace. I should have married Padraic and had babies. Instead I'm stuck here trying to prove to myself that I wasn't a complete idiot for coming in the first place, and I'm losing the battle!"

Candace laughed. "Then swallow your pride and come home. I'll send you the money."

"I'll come home when I can afford the plane fare." Angela was adamant. "I have my pride, you know."

"I hear Padraic has a new girlfriend."

"Really?" Angela cried, fear seizing her.

"No, but that proves you're still in love with that man. He's not going to wait forever, little sister."

"I didn't ask him to wait for me."

"But you hoped he would."

"Yes, I did," Angela said, sighing loudly. "Can we change the subject?"

"Daddy's growing organic corn for a company that makes organic snacks," Candace told her.

"Ooh," said Angela excitedly. "That's good business sense. And Padraic doesn't grow corn, so no competition there. I'm glad Daddy finally took my advice. I told him he should turn that fallow field into an organic plot. The soil is perfect for it."

"You know," Candace said. "You're definitely a farmer's daughter."

"So are you!"

"Yes, but you'd never know by looking at me."

"Life in the big city has changed you, huh? That, and being married to a rich man."

Candace laughed. "Charleston is not considered a big city by those of us who live here. It's a wonderful town. The perfect place to live, and raise your family. It's everything good about the South. And I'm not married to a rich man. We're just *comfortable*."

"Comfortably *rich*," Angela countered. "You live in a mansion. Your kids go to private schools, and you change cars like you change your underwear."

"Girl, you ought to quit!"

"I ain't hatin'," Angela assured her. "I'm happy for you. I just hope you don't forget the *poor* people, like you've forgotten where you come from."

"I'm going now," Candace said, sharply. "It's obvious Momma has brainwashed you."

"I love you," Angela said quickly before Candace could hang up.

"I love you, too," Candace told her, a smile evident in her tone. "But if I wanted a sermon, I could have phoned Momma."

She hung up then.

Angela turned down N. Miami Avenue in Little Haiti now. A few blocks later, she was at her apartment building. It was three A.M. by then. She felt like a hunted animal as she got out of her car, looking all around her in the deep shadows, hoping no one was lurking in them, and ran up the steps to her second floor apartment.

Safely inside, she threw all five bolts, and hooked the security chain. Not that it would do much good if anyone really wanted to get in. Her apartment had been broken into twice since she'd lived here. Luckily she'd been out both times. The police had not found the culprits nor recovered any of her stolen property either time.

Walking farther into her thrift-store-furnished but neat apartment, she switched on a table lamp and tossed her tote bag onto the couch. Sitting down, she picked up the remote and turned on the TV. She always had it tuned to the Sci-fi channel.

An episode of the old Twilight Zone was on. Leaning forward, she picked up the day's mail. She had tossed it earlier onto the coffee table before leaving for work.

Riffling through it, she found bills, bills, and more bills. Plus, offers for credit cards. Because of her stellar credit rating she was pre-approved for all of them. "Lucky me," she said sarcastically.

"Mmm, here's something interesting." She turned over the thick, business size envelope. She smiled when she recognized her mother's big, bold cursive writing. Her mother, Sara, was from the old school of handwriting when the teacher sent students to the board to practice proper cursive writing over and over again until their penmanship improved. Her mother had lovely handwriting.

She carefully opened the envelope and began to read:

Dear Angela,

I'm going to be frank with you: I'm worried about your living down there in Miami. My apologies to the lovely state of Florida and Miami, but it was insane for you to move down there where crime is rampant and there's absolutely no one that you can depend on in case of an emergency."

"Go on, Momma, don't worry about hurting my feelings," Angela mumbled.

"What's more," the letter continued. *"You turned down a perfectly good marriage proposal from the most eligible bachelor in the county. Women are all over that boy like ants at a picnic! He still comes by to sit and chat. I'm no fool, I know he comes by to hear tidbits about your wonderful life in Miami. He still loves you, Angela. Now, I'm not telling you this to make you feel guilty about your choices in life. No, that would be too easy. I'm writing to tell you that you have the chance to salvage something good. You may not value a man like Padraic right now but believe you me a few years from now, when you're finally tired of the high life in Miami, you're going to wish you had a Padraic to come home to!*

We are hosting the family reunion here at the farm this year. The dates will be from Friday the 17th until Sunday the 19th. I expect you to be here, baby girl. Be here. I don't care if you have to hitchhike, but come home. Okay, I don't want you to hitchhike. That was just me being facetious. Enclosed is a money order for 300.00. That

should be enough to get you here. If you want to go back to Miami,
you'll have to do it on your own dime.
With warmest regards,
Your loving mother,
Sara Johnson

P.S. Your daddy is going organic. Padraic talked him into it.
"It was my idea!" Angela cried, laughing.

THREE

C *an I be of service?"* asked the saleswoman in a low, velvety voice.
Greg had been trying to decide between the deep jewel-toned ruby teddy and the green one. He knew from experience that Candace looked good in both colors. He was imagining her in the red one when the saleswoman interrupted his thoughts.

Glancing at her he realized she was new here. He was a regular customer at this lingerie shop. Privately owned, he liked it better than the chain store in the mall where there were racks and racks of cloned items. He liked the idea of Candace wearing something that not every other woman on the planet was wearing.

"Thank you, no," he said, pleasantly, and peered down at the red teddy once more.

The woman, a young, attractive sister with long, wavy auburn hair and a drop-dead figure did not move away. She stood next to him, one long leg slightly in front of the other and her shapely breasts thrust forward in a provocative bid to make him take a second look at what she had to offer.

Greg smiled as he turned and held up both teddies for her perusal. "My wife looks gorgeous in anything. I think I'll take both."

Undaunted, the saleswoman smiled up at him. She had noticed his wedding ring moments before she'd approached him. In fact, if she hadn't spied the ring, she would not have been so eager to offer her assistance. Married men, especially handsome, prosperous married men like this guy, were her preference. He was wearing a Rolex. She could spot one at forty paces. Not the flashy kind that entertainers wore but a more understated model, the sort of watch that shouted, "I'm rich and I really don't care if anyone else knows it." That was confidence! She was drawn to men who were sure of their place in the world, and didn't mind sharing a bit of it with a grateful woman.

"Are you sure you don't want to look a while longer?" she asked as she gracefully stepped forward and took the teddies from his hand, making certain that their hands touched and, in a calculated move, that the back of his hand grazed her breast.

She looked up at him expectantly, a smile curving her generous mouth.

"I'm sure," Greg said. His smile was cordial, but didn't give her any hint that he was interested in more from her than what she had to offer as a saleswoman: to ring up his purchases as quickly as possible.

She knew her assessment of him was on the money when he said, "I'd appreciate it if you could get me out of here as fast as you can. I'm meeting my wife for lunch."

She automatically glanced at her watch. It was almost eleven-forty. "Of course, sir."

He gave her his American Express card. She billed his account, and had his purchases in a box in under five minutes. "May I say, sir, that your wife is a lucky woman?" she said as she handed him the box, now inside of a plastic shopping bag.

"I'm the lucky one," he assured her as he accepted the bag. But before he left he said, "And may I say that you're a very attractive woman and you're selling yourself short when you flirt with married men."

She blushed. "I hope I haven't offended you, Mr. Bates. My supervisor would be very upset if she found out I'd offended one of our customers."

"No offense," Greg told her. "Just a word of advice: When I come in here, I know exactly what I want to buy for my wife. All I need you to do is ring up my purchases."

A few feet away, two other saleswomen were watching from the doorway of one of the dressing rooms. "That'll teach her to flirt with the customers," said a tall, slim woman with blond hair.

The other woman giggled softly. "I could have warned her about Mr. Bates, but I thought the experience would be more instructive."

"It was for you when he set *you* straight!" her friend said, laughing quietly.

"Don't remind me. I still blush every time I have to ring him up."

The saleswoman who had just rung up Greg's purchases smiled gratefully. "I'll remember that, Mr. Bates."

"Thank you, I'd appreciate it," Greg said without a trace of animosity. He smiled at her again before departing. "Hope you have a nice day."

She smiled, still embarrassed. "You, too, sir."

When the door of the shop closed behind him, the other two saleswomen rushed over to tell her of the rite of passage they'd just put her through, that of the faithful husband.

"You're not going to find many like him," the blonde said, solemnly.

"Nah," agreed the brunette. "Most of the men who shop in here will flirt outrageously. They think it magnifies their manliness or something. Sharpens their teeth. We put up with it as a matter of course. But Mr. Bates has no interest in flirting. All he wants to do is pick up something sexy for his wife and get home to her as quickly as possible."

"Has she ever been in?" the new saleswoman asked, curious.

"Not once," said the blonde. "But ain't she a lucky woman?"

The new girl nodded and sighed wistfully. "That was the best-looking man I've seen in a very long time."

"Amen!" agreed the blonde. "He's got Denzel beat."

"Why is it that every time a white woman compares a black man to a movie star she has to bring up Denzel?" asked the new girl. "There are other black actors, you know."

"Yeah, but everybody compares them to Denzel anyway," the blonde said, defending herself. "I was just going for the top."

"She's got you there," said the brunette, smirking.

The sole sister in the room laughed. "I've got to introduce you witches to Terrance Howard, Boris Kodjoe, Blair Underwood, Idris Elba, L.L. Cool J, and Larenz Tate."

"You forgot Jamie Foxx," said the blonde. "I'm not blind to good looking black men, you know. I've dated a few."

"Who hasn't?" joked the brunette.

Their supervisor, a thin redhead in her fifties came out of her office, and all three of them immediately jerked to attention and faked being busy at some task or other.

"But Mr. Bates has all of them beat," the blonde whispered to her co-workers as they went in different directions.

The other two women tried to contain their laughter as they hurried off.

As Greg walked to his car, his mind was on Candace and how strangely she'd been behaving lately. Normally a person who was extremely attentive to him and the children, he'd caught her daydreaming on numerous occasions.

Last night, as they were getting ready to retire, he was already in bed waiting for her and she was at the foot of the bed applying body lotion like she did every night before climbing into bed, he'd asked her how Sarafina's eye exam had gone that day.

He'd had to repeat his question before she'd come out of her trance. Then she'd given him a rundown of Sarafina's appointment with the eye doctor.

Sarafina had astigmatism. She would require glasses and she was not at all happy about.

She'd pleaded with the doctor to prescribe contact lenses instead. However the optometrist said he recommended glasses to begin with. But when she got a bit older and her eyes had time to strengthen he would substitute the glasses with contacts.

"She pouted all the way home," Candace said, back to her old self.

Greg had suggested lunch today because he wanted to talk with her without the children around. He wanted to know what was preoccupying her. He didn't for one minute think it was another man. Candace, like him, was completely faithful. But it might have something to do with her health. She was notoriously close-mouthed when she knew something would upset him or the children. Knowing she was seriously ill would definitely cause him to panic. But, no matter what it was, he would feel better knowing. They would face it together as they faced everything together.

He backed the SUV out of the parking space, laughing softly, remembering how that saleswoman had flirted with him. If she had only known where his mind had been; firmly on his wife, she wouldn't have wasted her time.

Women flirted with him often for some reason that was completely unfathomable to him. Sure, he wasn't bad looking and he was in shape due to hard work, but lots of guys could say the same thing. He didn't flatter himself by thinking that he was such a hunk every woman wanted him, but he was aware when they were interested. He hadn't wanted his shopping experience marred by a saleswoman mooning over him, so he'd spoken up and told her what was what. Otherwise, he would have ignored it.

He would not have been in the lingerie shop if not for an agreement he'd made with Candace at the beginning of their marriage: He'd noticed that she preferred comfort to sexiness when it came to bedtime apparel. She had a drawer full of pajamas and, God forbid, flannel nightgowns for winter nights!

Even though when he met Candace she was twenty-five and already a formidable businesswoman as head of her own up-and-coming design firm, he'd learned that while the outside might look metropolitan and totally put together, on the inside she was still that shy country girl who'd lived in a small town all her life. He'd been her only lover. Ever. So, it was up to him to school her in the seductive arts. One thing he had to teach her was that men enjoyed seeing their wives in sexy lingerie.

She told him, "Well, if you'll buy it, I'll wear it."

That was good enough for him. Now, every few months, he would go to his favorite lingerie shop and choose something sexy for her to wear. It had gotten so that he enjoyed imagining how she would look in it, and out of it. Part of the pleasure of seeing her in it was anticipating taking it off.

Candace was waiting for Greg at a bistro downtown. It was a lovely June day and the restaurant was within walking distance of her building, so she'd chosen to get a little exercise.

In his absence, she took the opportunity to read her mother's letter again. She'd had it in her purse for two weeks now. She was afraid to leave it at home for fear that Greg might find it and read it. She was not ready to share it with him. Not that there was anything in it that incriminated *her*. On the contrary, it painted her mother in a very negative light.

How could she accuse her of being ashamed to come to Mason Corners? She was nothing of the sort! Mason Corners was a charming farm community. Its Main Street was among the most picturesque in South Carolina: beautifully landscaped businesses and an old-fashioned courthouse with a statue of a southern officer on horseback, his sword pointing skyward. It might be a lightning hazard, but it certainly wasn't an eyesore! Some of her fondest memories were of walking to town with her sisters to go to the movies on a Saturday afternoon. She had been the oldest and was responsible for her younger sisters' welfare, something she took seriously. But they'd had plenty of fun, too. Laughing, and eating too much popcorn, sitting in the balcony and throwing stuff on the kids below them in the theater, flirting with the boys. Walking home with Miss Lit, the town eccentric who always had her shopping cart laden with junk she'd picked up along the way. Some people thought she was the town's shame, but the Johnson girls thought she was fascinating. Besides, she was the only adult they ran into in town who spoke to them as though they had brains in their heads, and were not simply mindless children to be patronized and ultimately ignored.

Miss Lit had even invited them to her house once. They had honestly expected it to be a pigsty since she was such an avid junk collector, but it had a neatly manicured yard and was the cutest little house set back in the woods that they'd ever seen.

She served them tea and cookies on her porch, and Candace would never forget how Miss Lit held her pinky in the air as she sipped her tea, and regaled them with stories of her life as a dancer on the stage in New York City back in the forties. That lady was one of her best memories of Mason Corners.

How could her mother say she disliked her hometown? She loved it!

Back in the day, the only stores on Main Street were a hardware store, a feed store (had to have one of those in a farming community), a drugstore, a grocery store and a movie theater. These days downtown was practically burgeoning with antique stores, a movie theater with two sides so they could show two movies at once. Candace bet it had been a big deal when the proprietor renovated the theater. There were still no fast food restaurants, though. If you didn't want to cook, there was only one restaurant in town: Diane's Cafe. But they had a great chef, and the burgers were to die for.

She was still looking down at the letter when Greg cleared his throat.

He'd been standing there for several seconds before interrupting her. She was so preoccupied she hadn't noticed he'd come in. He kissed her on the cheek before sitting down across from her at the tiny, round, white-clothed table. "What's that you're reading?"

Candace's big brown eyes met his. One of the things she loved about Greg was his willingness to be honest with her even to his detriment. When he was wrong, his pride might dictate deception, but his sense of honesty always won over pride.

She couldn't sit there and lie to him. Therefore she handed him the letter and said, "It's from Momma. Go ahead, read it."

So, he did.

Candace sat quietly. She sipped her water while he read. She accepted the menus the waiter brought to them while he read. A layer of perspiration formed above her top lip while he read.

Finally, he looked up. His hazel eyes held sympathy in their depths. Candace was surprised to see it. She was hoping for indignation. She wanted him to be as upset by her mother's accusations as she had been. To see how ridiculous they were.

She tossed her long black hair—which was so much like her mother's— behind her and her eyes became fierce. She knew she was in for a fight. "I suppose you think she has a point?"

"I've also been wondering what's been going on between you and Miss Sara all these years," he said, his voice low yet completely audible because he'd enunciated every word so perfectly.

He went on before she could speak. "Whenever you mention your father, it's with love and affection. He's a hero in your eyes. But your mother is not given the same respect. You don't say things about her in front of the kids, but you've always given me the impression that Miss Sara is not the kind, thoughtful woman I've come to know. Did she abuse you physically or verbally when you were growing up?"

Candace's eyes widened with shock and amazement. "No, of course not!"

"Emotional abuse?"

"She was a good mother, Greg!"

"Then, what did she do?"

"She didn't do anything," she replied with vehemence.

"She must have done something," he insisted. "I've seen you looking at her with a disgusted expression on your face more than once. Are you ashamed of her because she's a plainspoken woman with simple tastes? That can't be it. You're not a snob." He seemed to be reasoning with himself. Tossing out options and, based on what he knew about Candace, dismissing them with rapidity. "So, your folks are farmers. That's nothing to be ashamed of. If not for farmers, we'd all starve. It's a noble profession. I've seen the way you react to Mason Corners when we go there. It's not the place that you have a problem with. It's something concerning your mother. I just can't imagine what Miss Sara could have done to alienate you."

"Alienate me?" Candace asked, truly horrified to hear those words come out of her husband's mouth. "I *do* love my mother, Greg!"

"I'm sure you do," he said, calmly. "But do you *like* her?"

His last comment gave her pause. She couldn't speak. It was as though her thought processes had become so jumbled she couldn't come up with a proper response.

He seemed unaware of her mental anguish because he continued. "She's right about our not having been in Mason Corners for over three years. I think the kids need to visit more often. They'll be missing out if they don't get to know their grandparents in their own environment. Besides, you know how interested Gregory is in everything related to science and how the world works. He loves the farm, and the girls need to realize that life is not all about a big house, private schools and shopping. We're running the risk of spoiling them, Candace, even though that's the farthest thing from our minds, I'm sure."

Candace sat there watching his lips move but hearing only every other word he said. Her mind was stuck on his last question, the one she'd clearly heard: But, do you *like* her?

Suddenly, she started talking. And it was Greg's turn to sit quietly.

"When I was seven, my daddy's momma died. I remember the day of the funeral was a *long* one. It seemed like we spent hours at the church, and then at the graveyard. Then, finally, we all wound up at our house where they gathered to eat and talk about Grandma. I have mental images of people in dark clothing. Women bending down to hug me, their bosoms powdered, and the powder getting up my nose and making me sneeze. There were people everywhere. Later on, after a lot of the guests had gone and there was just family around, I conked out on the settee in the living room. Momma and some of the other ladies were in the kitchen cleaning up. I was awakened by the sound of voices. Three of my aunts, my daddy's sisters, had come into the living room and were talking. 'She looks just like Robert,' one of them said. 'Y'all know that's Robert's child. Look at that chin. Look at that nose. She's every spit of Robert.' I pretended to be asleep because I wanted to hear more. Why did they think I looked like Uncle Robert, Daddy's brother? Well, my patience was rewarded because Aunt Ruth said, 'Sara might have *Jack* fooled, but she doesn't fool *us*. Candace is not Jack's child.'

"I lay there, holding my breath, and willing myself not to cry because those words were hurtful, so hurtful. My momma had been with Uncle Robert and gotten pregnant with me, and then tricked my Daddy into believing I was really his child? Even to a seven year-old that was as plain as you could get, Greg. But, still, I refused to believe it. My momma would have told me if it were really true! I tried to forget it, but I couldn't. The aunts wouldn't let me. Over the years, I overheard them talking about it again, and again. I finally realized that my overhearing them wasn't an accident. They wanted me to overhear. Why else would they run the risk of talking about it when I was in the house, or even somewhere nearby? They were evil, my aunts. Momma used to joke about all five of them hating her guts for taking Daddy away from them, but I never took her seriously. She was serious, Greg. They truly detested her, and they got at her through me."

After she finished, Greg reached across the table and clasped her hands in both of his. He looked deeply into her eyes. "Then you see what you've done, right?"

She was dumbfounded. "What have I done?"

He smiled at her. "You've allowed your aunts' hatred, their lies, because I know they're lies, to color your opinion of your mother. And you've never given her the chance to defend herself. You can't let this go on any longer, Candace. You've got to confront the aunts, you and your mother. Get it out in the open. They've driven a wedge between you and Miss Sara with their lies."

Candace mustered up a smile. "I know you love me, Greg, and you have my best interests at heart. But you've seen Uncle Robert. You know how much he and Daddy look alike. What if it's true?"

"It's not true, baby," Greg said, adamant. "You know your mother. If it were true she would have told you years ago. She's not the type of woman to live with a lie. I don't believe she would deceive your father. If it's true, then your father has known about it all these years. And if it's true, your mother had a damn good reason for marrying your father instead of your Uncle Robert. If it's true, it was definitely a mutual decision."

Candace sat, nodding in agreement. "Yeah, I can believe that. If it's true, maybe they both decided it was best I didn't know. I should let it go."

Greg shook his head in the negative. "You can't do that. You've already been affected by your aunts' constant negative bombardment. You've got to tell your parents you've heard the rumors, and listen to their side of the story."

"I don't know if I can do that. I couldn't bear to see the hurt on their faces," she said.

"And I can't bear the way you look at your mother sometimes," Greg told her. "Apparently, from what she said in her letter, she's noticed. Clear the air, Candace."

Tears ran down Candace's cheeks. "Yeah, you're right. I guess we should plan to be at the reunion."

Greg squeezed her hands reassuringly. "It'll be a reunion to remember." He smiled at her. Candace's smile was tremulous at best.

FOUR

A *nother night and another performance that left Angela wondering* *what she was doing shaking her rump in a place like Benny's.* The words 'pride before a fall' kept running through her mind as she stood in front of her locker changing into street togs.

It was pride that was preventing her from packing up and going back to South Carolina. What would she say to her family? *I tried living on my own, and I hated it. Can I move back in with you?*

Her parents deserved their solitude. They'd raised four children. Given them every advantage and, what was more important, had instilled in them a solid work ethic and the ability to make good decisions.

Her sister, Candace, a successful interior decorator, was deliriously in love with her husband and the mother of three. Her sister, Debra, was a casting director out in Hollywood. She was also happily married. No children yet, but she bet that she and Juan enjoyed working toward becoming parents.

Last, but certainly not least, her sister, Sharon, produced a popular talk show in New York City. Sharon wasn't married yet, either, but she was sure she didn't have any trouble meeting eligible men.

Angela hadn't had a date since moving to Miami. The main reason was she was leery of the men she ran into. She supposed if she was going to hang out at strip clubs she shouldn't expect to meet the cream of society.

She also worked part-time at a Hooter's, but she figured she'd be fired from that particular location soon because the manager loathed women who looked over twenty-one. It was no reflection on the chain of restaurants itself. She was sure all of their managers weren't worshippers of women with youth and taut boobs like Hollis Carrey seemed to be.

Unlucky for her, the men who came into Hooter's were usually family men or senior citizens. She held out little hope of meeting anyone there with whom she might have something in common.

That left the community college where she was taking a course in accounting. The only people she met there were other women trying to add another skill to their résumés or retirees who were bored with retirement and took college course after college course, hoping to keep their minds young and resilient.

"Admit it, girl," she said under her breath as she stepped into a pair of high-heeled mules. "You don't really want to meet anybody. All you want to do is go back home and have Padraic take one look at you and say he forgives you for running out on him and he still wants to marry you."

"Talkin' to yourself again?" asked Terry, looking especially slimy tonight in a leather jacket and pants in a fake Python print. Even his lid, a cowboy hat, was covered in the print. Angela wondered where he bought his clothes, Pimps-R-Us? The man was a walking anachronism.

"It's better than what you do by *yourself*," she returned.

Terry threw his head back in laughter. When he straightened up, he regarded her with a merry expression in his eyes. "I like you, Angel Girl, that's why I keep giving you a chance to improve your financial status."

"Did that hurt your brain?" Angela asked, innocently.

"What?"

"Coming up with the term, 'financial status'?"

"I'm smarter than you think," he said, not really getting her sarcasm. A sociopath, he could fathom nothing except what furthered his own interests. His eyes glittered as he continued to look her up and down. "I know, for example, that you and that little country-fried chick, Sandy, are tight. She's going to let a gentleman show her the town tonight and they need a friend to go along. He's got a friend. Everything will be real *friendly*."

Angela's eyes narrowed menacingly. She wanted to kick him in the balls, knee him in the face while he was doubled over, and then kick him in the gut while he was writhing on the floor. Doing violence to Terry Christmas would have made her very happy at that moment.

He'd convinced Sandy Patterson to sell herself. Seventeen year-old Sandy!

She grabbed her shoulder bag and slammed the locker shut. Turning on her heels, she said, "Where is she?"

Terry slithered past her. "They're waiting in his limo."

Angela followed him. They left the building by the side door. A large black Town Car was sitting in the alley with its motor running. The windows were tinted. Angela couldn't tell if there were three people inside, as Terry had said, or if there were more. She had a sinking, sick feeling in the pit of her stomach. Her fight-or-flight response was at full alert, and she was definitely leaning toward flight.

But Sandy was in that car, and she wasn't leaving without Sandy.

She began walking toward the car, and Terry stepped in front of her, leaned in and warned, "Now don't make a scene, Angel Girl. Play nice and you could come out of this smelling like a rose."

His breath smelled like whiskey, the peppermint he'd devoured to conceal its scent, and gum disease. Angela wrinkled her nose and tried to look composed even though she was a bundle of nerves. "Okay, don't sweat it."

He grinned and stepped aside. "That's a good girl."

He stepped up to the idling car and tapped on the back window. The window slid down, revealing the weathered face of a man with gray eyes and thick steel gray hair combed away from his angular face. Expensively dressed, a large gold and diamond ring glinted on his left hand.

His gaze roamed the length of Angela's body. He smiled when he got to her face. "The full package," he said, appreciatively. "I must have missed your performance, sweetheart. Maybe you can give me a private show, huh?"

He was so confident of her answer he didn't wait for a reply. To his driver, he said, "Please get out and help the lady in, Max."

Max, to Angela's surprise, was a giant black guy with a shaved head. He wore the dark suit of a chauffeur complete with the cap pulled down low on his forehead. She could have sworn she heard him sigh with resignation when he took her by the arm and helped her into the back of the car. Maybe his conscience bothered him whenever he had to drive his boss around with a pair of prostitutes in the car.

In the back of the car, a set of seats faced each other. On the one whose back was to the driver, Sandy sat beside another man who looked like he was two decades younger than his companion. His brown hair was curly and short. When she got in he looked at her with disdain. Angela gave him an equally withering look. He wasn't the only one who would rather be someplace else at that moment.

Sandy smiled nervously at Angela. "Hey, Angela, Terry talked you into coming along, huh?"

"Something like that," Angela said, keeping her voice light.

"Take us home," the gray-haired guy instructed the driver.

The big car was in motion now. Angela sat back on the seat and the gray-haired guy immediately placed his hand on her upper thigh. Angela smiled at him and removed his hand. "Let's not get ahead of ourselves. There are no freebies, boys. You touch the goods, you pay."

The gray-haired guy laughed, reached into his coat pocket, retrieved his wallet, withdrew a hundred-dollar bill and pressed it into her palm. "Is that enough for a squeeze?"

Angela took the hundred, smiled brightly, and put it deeply in her cleavage. "It's a start, baby." She pouted prettily. "I can't call you baby all night. You two boys got names?"

"Just call us Butch and Sundance," the gray-haired guy told her, moving closer to her on the seat. "I'm Butch, and he's Sundance."

"You're a fan of westerns, I see," Angela said. "Okay, Butch. Shall we discuss business before we get where we're going?" She didn't wait for his permission.

"I don't do anything for less than five-hundred. And since Sandy, here, is under eighteen she goes for a thousand."

She got exactly the reaction she was hoping for. Butch's eyes bugged out and he shouted, "What?! She's twenty-one. She told us she was twenty-one."

"Sandy tends to lie about her age. It's the only way she can work at a place like Benny's. A girl has to eat."

Angela wasn't sure, but she thought she heard the driver laughing under his breath.

"If you don't believe me, take a look at her driver's license."

Sandy, looking relieved, handed her driver's license to Butch. He switched on an overhead light and carefully perused the license. Handing it back to her, he barked at the driver, "Max, pull over at the next well-lit place. These ladies are getting out of the car."

"Celebrating your divorce from Mom by picking up a couple of strippers was a dumb idea, anyway," the younger guy spoke up.

Angela looked insulted. "Strippers! I'll have you know that nudity's forbidden at Benny's. We don't show any more skin than you would see at the beach!"

She pulled the C-note from between her breasts and tossed it into Butch's lap.

"Actually, if you'd have Max drive us back to the club, I'd appreciate it. My car is parked there."

"Max, you heard the lady," Butch said, smiling now. He gave Angela another appreciative once-over. "*You're* not seventeen, are you?"

Angela's smile was brilliant. "No, honey. I'm not for sale, either."

"But you got into my car," he reminded her with a hopeful lilt to his voice.

"To save *her* from herself," Angela said, looking irritably at Sandy.

Ashamed of her behavior, Sandy lowered her gaze. "I'm sorry, Angela. My rent's past due."

"I would have helped you with your rent," Angela said. Though, God knows where she would have gotten the money. "Terry doesn't care about you. All he wants is his cut." She turned to Butch. "I bet he got *his* before he'd even introduce you to Sandy, didn't he?"

"Two hundred bucks," Butch confirmed.

He went into his wallet and withdrew five hundred dollars. "Here," he said, handing it to Sandy. "Will this cover your rent?"

Sandy hesitated. "I can't take that."

"Oh," said Butch. "Would you rather have sex with Sundance for it?"

"Leave me out of it," Sundance cried. "None of this was my idea."

Sandy shook her head in the negative. "No, sir."

Butch placed the money in her hand. "Then, take it. And please, try to find a job elsewhere. A man can't go to a strip joint and pick up a loose woman anymore. What is this world coming to?"

"What, indeed?" said Angela.

Butch eyed her skeptically then burst out laughing. They all joined in.

Butch had to wipe a tear from the corner of his gray eyes. "I may regret this," he said, going into his wallet a third time and withdrawing a business card. "But here, take my card. If you girls want a legitimate job, call me. I own a chain of restaurants."

Angela took the card. "Thank you. And I'm sorry about your divorce."

"So am I," Butch said. "I'm still in love with her."

"Dad, I didn't know that," Sundance said. He reached over and grabbed his father's hand and squeezed it. "Don't worry, big guy, we'll get through this together."

Max pulled into the parking lot of Benny's. "We're here, ladies," he announced.

He got out and held the door open for Angela and Sandy.

Angela winked at him as she got out. "Thanks."

"My pleasure," he said.

He quickly got back into the car and sped off.

Angela grabbed Sandy by the arm. "Come on, I'm following you home before you get into anymore trouble."

They lived in the same section of town, only a few blocks apart.

"My car's in the shop," Sandy said. "That's another reason I was in that car tonight."

Angela was busy getting her keys out of her shoulder bag. "Okay, I'll drive you home. I want to talk to you about something anyway."

"Oh, please, Angela, don't get on my case about what I did. I know it was a stupid thing to do, and it'll never happen again."

When they were in the car and Angela had locked the doors, she started the battered Ford Escort and backed out of the parking space. "I'm not your momma. I'm not going to tell you how to live your life. I know you don't want to go back home because your stepfather is a creep. But maybe you could try to find another job. I'd feel a whole lot better when I'm gone knowing that you're not still working at Benny's."

"You're leavin'?" Sandy cried, her high-pitched southern-accented voice grating in the confines of the Escort. "Why? Did you find a better place to work?"

Angela realized that Sandy's world was so limited; it never occurred to her that when she said she was leaving, she meant the state, not just Benny's. But then, in Sandy's world girls rarely left Benny's unless they'd found a better place to work. Or, in some cases, a man to take care of them. Angela had heard stories about college girls who danced to pay their tuition and went on to graduate from college and join the ranks of the legitimate workforce. But after months of working at two different places she had yet to meet the mythological creature.

"No, I'm going back home to South Carolina."She had made up her mind somewhere between here and Butch's limousine. She realized when she had gotten into the car that she was taking her life into her hands. Girls disappeared after getting into cars with strange men. She and Sandy could have wound up statistics somewhere along A1A.Two more dead women that no one could identify right away because there would have been no identification on their bodies. In her absence her worried folks would launch a search that would end with the news of her murder. Her mother would then have a heart attack and her father would surely die of a *broken* heart. He loved his wife and his children more than he loved his own life.

"I thought you weren't going back home until you could go in style," Sandy reminded her. "Stay, Angela. Maybe we can move in together and cut bills that way. I have my own place, you have yours. But if we shared, that'd cut things in half right there!"

There was a note of desperation in Sandy's voice. Angela knew why. The kid didn't have anyone else. Her sorry boyfriend had left her for a better meal ticket. The other dancers ostracized her because she was so young. They hated being reminded of where they'd come from. Some of them had started as young as Sandy, and had not been able to pull themselves up. Ten years later they were still dancing and pretending that their big chance was right around the corner. And the fact was: time was catching up with them. They were sagging in places the patrons enjoyed ogling and Benny took great pleasure in firing those who didn't continue to attract the steady patrons. His livelihood depended on repeat business.

"This is a dead-end job, Sandy," Angela said, softly.

"I'm not judging anybody, but my parents didn't raise me to prance around onstage half-naked for drunken men. They would be devastated if they knew. Heck, they would be disappointed if they knew what I have to wear for my job at Hooter's. I've been lying to them for over a year."

"My mama doesn't know what I do for a living either," Sandy confessed.

"Speaking of your mama," Angela said. "Did you ever tell her what your stepfather used to do to you?"

Sandy was silent for a couple of minutes. Angela regretted asking the question. But what if her mother didn't know what a jerk her husband was? What kind of mother would side with a molester against her own daughter?

"I'm afraid to tell her."

"Why?"

"Because she might think I led him on. Mama ain't had good luck with men. She ain't pretty. I mean, she is to me because she's my mama and I love her. But she's real insecure about her looks."

Angela wondered if Sandy's mother might actually be relieved that her beautiful daughter was out of the house. But, still, a mother's first responsibility was to her child. If Sandy's mother knew that her husband had been trying to have sex with her daughter, she would put him out and welcome Sandy back home. No other scenario made sense.

"What have you got to lose, Sandy? You're living on your own, anyway. If you tell her what your stepfather tried, how many times he forced himself on you, maybe she would believe you and get rid of him. You could go back home, finish high school, and have someone to support you while you learned a trade or went to college."

Sandy sighed. "I'm almost eighteen anyway," she said, resignedly. "I would be out of the house soon, no matter what I did, or didn't do. I just hope he doesn't start messin' with Katie."

Katie was her eight-year-old sister.

"That's another reason to go back and tell your mother what happened to you, to protect Katie."

Sandy suddenly got defensive. "Oh, what do you care, Angela? You're going back home to your big farm and your great big boyfriend with his own place. What do you know about anything? Everybody has always loved *you*. Lovin' parents, and lovin' sisters, and a lovin' man. You had it made. I can't understand why you ever came to Florida in the first place!"

For the life of her, Angela couldn't either.

She didn't say that to Sandy, though. Sandy had a right to her anger. She was scared and didn't see a way out. She felt helpless and hopeless. Sandy's circumstances weren't entirely of her own making. Being underage, with no skills, put her in an untenable situation. Because she was trying to stay out of the system, and stay on her own without her mother finding out where she was, she had to work at jobs that paid her under the table. And those jobs were often found on the edges of respectability.

"I'll stay with you until August," Angela said. "We'll move in together and we'll both use this business card Butch gave us, and see if he was sincere when he offered us jobs. It's the middle of June now. In a month and a half, you should have a new job and another roommate, and then I'm moving on."

Sandy's voice cracked when she said, "Thanks, Angela. You're a true friend."

In the darkness of the Escort, Angela rolled her eyes. True friend or not, she was getting out of this city in August. Not even her fondness for Sandy was going to keep her there a day longer than August 1. Her sinuses were killing her now. In August she wouldn't be able to breathe through her nose. Some good South Carolina air was just what the doctor ordered. Anyway, that's what she told herself. She refused to admit that the lure of home had anything to do with seeing Padraic Monaghan again.

FIVE

S *chool was out for the summer.*
Candace was glad she had some leeway that allowed her the option of working from home. Her routine changed only a little. She still got up at seven-fifteen, made breakfast, and sat down at the table with Greg and the kids. But after breakfast Greg went to work, she went into her home office, and the kids were left to their own devices.

Gregory spent an inordinate amount of time in his room on the computer. The parental controls were set, however, Candace started limiting his time to three hours a day on the computer just to encourage his doing something else.

Jacquelin, who had come in second in the spelling bee, could be found with her nose in a book. Old-fashioned, she preferred books to computers. She said they let her imagination soar.

Sarafina was the most easily bored. She neither loved working on the computer nor reading for long amounts of time. So, Candace often caught her chatting on the phone with friends or in front of the TV.

After the second week of summer vacation, Candace offered to take them on a trip. She made the suggestion one Saturday morning while they were all at the table. Greg, who was reading the paper, looked up. "Where will you go?" he asked.

Candace smiled encouragingly at her children. "We could go to a museum, or to the zoo, or to the aquarium. Anywhere you want to go, as long as it's not too far to venture for a day trip."

"I want to go to the botanical gardens," said Jacquelin. "I love flowers and plants, and it'll be cool there."

"I would rather go to a museum," Sarafina said, disagreeing with Jacquelin. "I should learn as much as I can about art. I'm taking Art History next semester."

"You can learn about art from a book," Gregory said. "I'd rather go to the botanical gardens. At least there you get the chance to be around something that's living and breathing."

"Plants don't breathe, stupid-head," Sarafina said with a laugh.

"No, but they help *us* breathe better," Gregory informed her. "If not for trees and plants the oxygen level on this planet would be greatly diminished."

"You sound like you got that straight from a book," Sarafina accused him.

"I did!" Gregory told her proudly. "Just like you can find everything you need to know about art from a book."

Sarafina turned to her mother for support. "Momma, isn't it better to see the actual work of art rather than look at it in a book?"

"Yes, it is," Candace said at once.

"You can go both places," Greg suggested. "Your Mom can take you one day, and I'll take a day off and go with you another day. Toss a coin to see what you'll do first."

"That sounds reasonable," Candace said, grateful that argument was over with.

"I'll get a coin," Gregory said, rising.

"No, *I'll* get a coin," Sarafina cried, getting to her feet. Mouth fixed in a stubborn expression, she glared at her brother. "You'll cheat."

"I..." Gregory began.

The doorbell rang and disrupted his train of thought.

"I'll get it," he said eagerly.

Candace quickly pushed her chair back and stood. "No, since you're all finished eating, you can go make your beds."

At the front door, she called, "Who is it?"

"It's your mother and father, open up!" came Sara's boisterous voice.

Candace was so surprised that her hands trembled as she disengaged the lock and swung the door open. Sure enough, her parents stood on the portico looking hale and hearty in jeans, denim shirts and white athletic shoes.

Her mother had the questionable habit of dressing herself and her father in matching outfits whenever they came to 'the city' as they called Charleston. They either looked like the farmers they were in their jeans and denim shirts or tourists in colorful Hawaiian shirts and shorts. It was a good thing both of them still had nice legs.

Her father hugged her and placed a kiss on her forehead.

Her mother squeezed her so tightly she was afraid she'd crack a rib.

While she was hugging her mother, Candace sneaked a peek outside. They'd driven the double-cab pick-up. The bed of it was probably loaded down with watermelons and vegetables, some of which her dear mother had probably already shelled, blanched or frozen for her. She suspected her mother didn't think she knew how to properly preserve vegetables either by 'canning' them: putting them up in Mason jars and storing them in the pantry, or by blanching them: boiling them a short time, draining them, and storing them in plastic bags in the freezer. Candace knew how to do both. But if her mother wanted to save her the time and effort, she wasn't going to discourage her.

The rest of the family rushed into the foyer.

Greg shut the front door while the kids enthusiastically hugged their grandparents. Her parents were in heaven giving and receiving affection. It made Candace's heart glad to see them together.

Greg shook his father-in-law's hand, and kissed his mother-in-law on the cheek. "Aw, come here, boy," Sara said and hugged him tightly.

Greg grinned. He loved Sara and her warm heart. He'd loved her from the first time they'd met when Candace had finally taken him home to meet her and Jack.

Sara had taken one look at him and said, "Marry this one, Candace. He'll give you strong, healthy children."

"Momma, he's not a horse!" Candace had protested.

Her mother boldly felt Greg's bulging biceps. "I bet he's as strong as one," she'd declared.

Greg still laughed whenever he thought about it.

As they all moved toward the kitchen, Candace said, "Well, this is a lovely surprise. Why didn't you let us know you were coming?"

"It wouldn't have been a surprise if we'd done that," said Jack. Sarafina had her arm about his waist, and Jacquelin was in his arms with her own wrapped around his neck and her cheek pressed to his.

Candace didn't know how he could move with them attached to him like that but he had always been a robust man. From the expression on his face, he was thoroughly enjoying himself.

Gregory, who rarely displayed affection to anyone in public, had his arm draped about his grandmother's shoulders. "Grandma, I'm taller than you now," he said, smiling triumphantly down at her.

"It was just a matter of time," Sara said, sagely. She looked over at her daughter. "And the reason Jack and I are here is this: We've come to take your children back home with us for a visit. Jack's finished with the harvest. He doesn't start planting again for a while, and we've got two bedrooms that are just sitting empty."

The kids immediately started talking excitedly at once.

"Oh, Momma, can we?" Sarafina pleaded.

"Yes, oh, Momma, Daddy, let us go stay with Grandma and Grandpa for a while. It's never boring on the farm," Jacquelin cried, her tone more pleading than her sister's.

Gregory took a different tack. "If you let us go, you and Dad would be alone in the house. You could walk around naked if you wanted to."

"Boy, where'd you ever get an idea like that?" Candace exclaimed, aghast.

"I'm fourteen, Momma, and I'm not blind. You and Dad can't keep your eyes off each other. It's embarrassing for us kids to have to watch. If we're out of the house you two can look at each other that way all you want and we'd never know about it."

Sara and Jack started laughing first and then everyone else broke into laughter.

"Oh, please," Candace begged her parents. "Take him with you!"

The kids started jumping up and down and cheering. Their mother interrupted them with, "Go finish your chores. Then get dressed."

Candace and Greg led Sara and Jack into the kitchen where they could talk in private. Sara and Jack made themselves comfortable at the table.

"Can I make you something to eat?" Candace offered.

Sara and Jack both shook their heads, no. "We had a big breakfast at a Denny's less than two hours ago," Sara said. "I could use a cup of coffee, though."

"Me, too," said Jack.

Candace busied herself retrieving mugs and filling them with the coffee left in the carafe. Sara took the opportunity to observe her eldest daughter. She looked good. Rested, healthy. And she still hadn't cut her hair. Sara was glad. One of the few things her daughters inherited from her was her long, wavy hair. They were all tall, like their father, and their skin tones fell somewhere between hers and Jack's. Of all her daughters she thought Candace favored her the most, and had more of her personality.

She wondered if that was why Candace resented her.

No daughter wanted to turn into her mother. Sara remembered how vehemently she had resisted becoming like her own mother. But, no matter how hard she tried, as she aged, she'd acquired some of the physical characteristics of her mother, and even some of her mannerisms. Now, whenever she looked in the mirror she saw the face of her mother looking back at her. And she was okay with it. She missed her mother.

"Your father told me that I need to apologize to you for the tone of my letter," Sara said to Candace once Candace had sat down. She looked her in the eyes. "I didn't mean to upset you, but I've been heartsick wondering what I've done to make you pull away from me emotionally."

Candace started to deny that there was any emotional detachment on her part, but thought better of it. She wanted to talk about it now that her mother was sitting across from her, but she didn't want the kids to come in and overhear what she had to say so she turned to Greg and said, "Sweetie, would you go tell the kids they can start packing their bags for their stay with their grandparents? That should keep them busy while we talk."

"Sure," said Greg, rising.

"And hurry back," Candace added.

Greg smiled. She wanted him there for support. For a moment, he'd thought that she might want *him* out of the room for her conversation with her parents, as well.

Sara's stomach muscles constricted nervously. This must be serious if Candace didn't want the kids to hear, but needed Greg by her side when she said it. Jack squeezed her shoulder reassuringly, and she turned to smile up at him.

Candace didn't miss the gesture. Her dad had always been by her mother's side, come hell or high water. He was the most faithful person she knew. Could he be such a faithful person that he'd marry a woman who'd had a child for his own brother and then turn around and raise that child as his own? She knew he was selfless enough to do it.

But was it a fact, or a piece of fiction created by The Biddies, her cantankerous aunts?

After Greg's return, Candace told her parents everything from the first time she had overheard her aunts discussing her questionable paternity, to the last time.

Sara could not sit still while she related the entire sordid tale. She gasped with consternation. Her golden brown face was a mass of frowns. She sighed loudly in frustration. All the while, Jack kept a hand at the small of her back and whispered, "Be calm, sweetheart. Be calm."

"Greg believes that I've let their gossip color my opinion of you, Momma. He thinks that maybe I've come to believe the rumors even though I haven't actively accepted them as fact. He says if I didn't, I would not behave the way that I do when I see you."

Sara was at last free to speak. She took a deep breath and exhaled. Looking at Greg, she said, "You're a very perceptive man. I knew Candace's respect for me was at an all-time low but I didn't know what I could have done to deserve her low opinion of me."

"Momma, I never..." Candace began. She was going to say she had never stopped loving her mother, and she never wanted to believe what her aunts had said about her.

Sara raised a hand, stopping her. "Honey, I know you love me. But because of that dark cloud of suspicion hanging over me, you couldn't fully respect me."

She looked at Jack, and he instinctively picked up where she'd left off. "My sisters never liked your mother because she, as you know, is not one to bite her tongue. We grew up neighbors and she managed to alienate every last one of my sisters in one way or another. Plus, they hated her for taking me away from them. After our parents died, I was the one who ran the farm. They depended on me for everything."

"It was more like they *demanded* that you do everything *for* them," Sara said. "Lazy, all of them! They were going to work you to death. And you were so easy-going and the youngest boy, to boot, that you simply let them run over you."

"Your mother went out with your Uncle Robert a few times," her father said, picking up the story.

"But he was too trifling for me," Sara put in. "Even when I was a young girl I could never abide a man who didn't know his own mind, and Robert was wishy-washy. Your father was younger, but so much more mature than Robert. So I told Robert I couldn't see him anymore, and I started seeing your father."

"In secret," said Jack with a smile. "Robert was heartbroken when Sara told him she didn't want to see him any longer. In order not to hurt his feelings further, Sara and I met without anyone else knowing for months before we told anybody we were dating."

"Then," Sara said with a soft sigh, "I got pregnant with you and that's when we told everybody we were getting married."

"It did seem," said Jack, "that Sara had just stopped dating Robert and had taken up with me. So, I'm sure my sisters thought that."

"And when you were born only six months after the wedding, well then those wicked witches put two and two together and came up with the crazy notion that I'd gotten pregnant with Robert's child and had tricked *Jack* into marrying me!"

"But you're definitely my child, Candace," Jack said.

Sara laughed. "Whose else could you be? I was a virgin before your father. Your Uncle Robert tried to get fresh and I gave him a black eye. He's lucky he got off that easily!"

Candace and Greg were smiling happily.

"I told you it was a lie," said Greg.

Tears sprang to Candace's eyes when she realized how harshly she had judged her mother.

"I should have come to you years ago," she told her. "Can you ever forgive me?"

Sara's eyes were misty too. She hugged Candace tightly. "I understand, baby. You didn't want to say anything because you didn't want to hurt my feelings. But you should have said something, anyway. It would have saved you a lot of doubt. And because of it those aunts of yours have gotten away with their malicious gossip all these years."

"You never heard the rumors?" Candace said, incredulously.

Sara released her. Her gaze was steely when she said, "No. They knew better than to let me hear what they were saying behind my back. But you just wait. They're going to pay for what they did to you, an innocent child. That was pure evil, Candace. They caused you pain. They made you doubt your own mother. I suppose if they couldn't get at me directly, they decided to get at me through you. But they're not going to get away with it."

"Momma," said Candace, worried about that calculating expression in her mother's big brown eyes. "They're in their fifties and sixties. They've probably forgotten all about it. What are you planning to do?"

"Don't you worry, baby," said Sara. "The less you know, the better. It'll save you from being prosecuted right alongside your momma."

Later that night, after the kids and Candace's parents had gone to bed, she and Greg sat in the living room on the couch with the lights down low, and music playing softly on the stereo in the background.

Greg was content with Candace in his arms. He was elated by the prospect of having her all to himself for a while.

Tomorrow morning, Sara and Jack would get on the road with the second seat in their double-cab pick-up truck loaded with their grandchildren, leaving him and Candace to find some way to fill up the lonely hours without Gregory, Sarafina, and Jacquelin.

"Are you going to miss the kids?" he asked Candace now.

Candace nuzzled his neck. "What kids?"

Greg laughed softly and kissed her, which led to their hurrying to the bedroom where they started getting in shape for the marathon love-making sessions they were going to engage in once the kids were out of the house.

SIX

*B*utch's name was really Andrea, pronounced An-dray-uh, Donatelli and he owned five Italian restaurants in and around Miami.

When Angela phoned him, he made good on his offer of a job. He told her that she and Sandy could come to his main restaurant in Miami Beach where he would conduct the interviews himself.

Three days later, the two of them sat in his spacious office in the upscale restaurant.

They were dressed conservatively. Angela had no way of knowing what sort of establishment Donatelli's was before coming so she had suggested they wear black skirts whose hems fell just above their knees, with white blouses and black pumps.

She'd even convinced Sandy to leave her Dolly Parton hair at home and the girl had pulled her long, thick, blond hair into a bun. Angela had also put her hair up.

Andrea Donatelli smiled appreciatively when he walked into the office and found them waiting for him. He wore a dark summer suit, with a white silk shirt open at the collar, and Italian loafers.

In daylight, his gray eyes were even lighter than they had appeared three nights ago.

Sandy and Angela got to their feet.

He waved them back down. "Sit, relax." He sat on the corner of the desk a few feet in front of them. Smiling at Angela, he said, "You look like a schoolteacher in that outfit." He regarded Sandy. "And you look like a high school student."

Sandy's hand shook as she smoothed a strand of hair away from her face. "We can dress differently if you like."

Andrea saw how much this opportunity meant to both of them. It had taken guts for them to take his suggestion of 'finding work elsewhere' seriously. "You look fine, Sandy."

Sandy visibly relaxed.

Angela had had a small smile on her face ever since he'd come into the office, he noticed. The young girl, Sandy, was so nervous she was trembling, but Angela seemed not in the least intimidated. He liked that.

"Tell me a little about your educational background, Sandy."

Sandy cleared her throat. "Well, I finished the eleventh grade and I'd begun my senior year when I had to leave home."

"You had to leave home?"

"Tell him the truth," Angela coaxed her.

"My stepfather started getting more interested in me than he should have been."

Andrea frowned, but recovered quickly. The girl didn't need his sympathy, she needed a job. He'd been lucky. He'd inherited his first restaurant from his parents. It had been a small family restaurant that had remained such for forty years. He'd dreamed big and expanded on the foundation his parents had laid. Now, Donatelli's was the premier Italian restaurant chain in South Florida. He believed in giving people an opportunity to improve themselves as long as they were willing to work hard.

"Have you ever worked as a waitress?" he asked Sandy.

"I worked at McDonald's for a year," she offered hopefully.

"That'll do," said Andrea. "We'll teach you everything you need to know. When will you turn eighteen?"

"In two months," Sandy answered.

"That's good." He smiled. "You'll work as a trainee until then. Your hours will be around thirty per week until you turn eighteen. Then we'll increase them to forty or more. But, don't worry." He smiled at Angela. "I know a girl has to eat, so I'll make sure you can pay your bills while working as a trainee."

To be certain Angela was aware that only Sandy would be working as a trainee, he added, "Now, as for you, Angela, what is your educational background?"

"Well, I'm twenty-five, so I've been out of high school for over seven years. I have an associate's degree in business from a community college and I'm nearly finished taking a course in accounting."

"Ah," said Andrea thoughtfully. "You may qualify for our management program. We have a written test to determine if you qualify. Would you like to take it?"

Angela was flattered that he thought she might be a candidate for their management program. However, she wanted to be honest with him. "Mr. Donatelli, I'm not going to stay in Miami past August. I'm going back home. I simply wanted to see Sandy settled before I left. I'd like to be able to quit working at Benny's, but if you don't want to hire someone for only a few weeks, I'd understand. I'm just here to support Sandy."

Sandy cried, "Oh, please, Mr. Donatelli, can't she work as a waitress or in the kitchen for that long?"

"I see," said Andrea gravely. He pursed his lips, thinking. Then he said, "Sandy, would you excuse us for a few minutes?"

Sandy looked desperately at Angela, afraid that the interview was going badly.

Angela simply smiled at her. "Go on, powder your nose while we talk."

Sandy reluctantly left the room, looking back at Angela with a worried expression as she did so.

"Angela," Andrea said once they were alone. "You've been honest with me. I'm going to be honest with you: I haven't been able to get you off my mind since we met." He paused, perhaps waiting for Angela's reaction to his declaration. Angela did not lower her gaze from his eyes. She liked him. But she loved Padraic. There was no contest.

She went into her shoulder bag and withdrew a snapshot of her and Padraic. It had been taken at the county fair two years ago. They'd been very much in love then, and the photo had captured their emotions quite nicely.

She handed it to Andrea. "That's Padraic Monaghan. He's the only man I've ever loved and I foolishly left him in pursuit of a dream." She grimaced. "No, not a dream, a fantasy. I came to Miami under the misconception that I could be a model at my advanced age."   She laughed.

Andrea didn't. "You're a beautiful woman. I don't think your dream was ill conceived at all. I know some people in the industry. I could introduce you..."

"No!" Angela cried, laughing softly. "Don't lay temptation at my feet. I know what I want out of life now, and that's to go back home, marry Padraic and spend the rest of my life being a farmer, just like my parents. It took leaving home for me to realize that."

Andrea was shaking his head with regret. "How will they be able to keep you down on the farm when you've seen Miami?" He gave her back the snapshot.

Angela smiled sweetly at him.

She knew the saying.

"Believe me, it won't be hard to do. I've had my fill of the big city."

"And you will have fantastic tales to tell your grandchildren someday."

"Will I be telling them about this kind Italian gentleman who rescued me and Sandy from that den of iniquity, Benny's?" she asked, hopefully.

"Yes," said Andrea. "You will. You're both hired. You can wait tables for six weeks."

"Thank you," Angela said, quietly.

Andrea shrugged off her thanks. He grasped one of her hands in both his, and bent his head to kiss the top of it. "Padraic is a lucky man."

⁖⁃⁗

Padraic pulled his boots off in the mud room, walked into the kitchen, and went straight to the refrigerator for a glass of water. After he'd quenched his thirst, he put a frozen dinner in the microwave and went to take a shower while it cooked.

As he lathered up, his mind went to Angela as it was wont to do about ten times a day. The ache in his heart felt like it would never heal over. Day by day, he knew it was mending but he envisioned the hole as a crater that would take eons to fill in.

His friends said that to forget one woman, you needed to get involved with another one. Padraic had taken their advice. Three months after Angela's departure he'd gone out with Shana Anderson. Shana was a wonderful woman. She was smart, attractive, funny, and adventurous. He'd taken her out in his boat on their first date, and she'd gotten a kick out of it.

Plus, Shana was a second grade teacher. Padraic was attracted to women who loved children because he wanted children someday. He wanted to raise them in the country, and watch where life took them from there.

Shana should have been the ideal woman for him. Instead, there had been no spark between them. He'd asked her out two more times just to see if their first date had been a fluke. Still, being with Shana was about as exciting as watching plants grow without the miracle of time-lapse photography. In fact, he'd done some work in the greenhouse following each date and had found that infinitely more stimulating.

He had to tell Shana it wouldn't work. He felt like a heel when he'd seen the hurt and disappointment on her face. He assured her that the fault lay with him, not her. She was a remarkable woman.

She knew about Angela and him. He'd only lived in Mason Corners for a few years, but this was Angela's hometown. She and Shana had gone to the same high school, attended the same church, so it was understandable that they knew each other.

"You're not over Angela yet," Shana had told him when he'd broken it off with her. "I should have known you were on the rebound."

She'd been a perfect lady about it. She'd even kissed him on the cheek, and said, "Call me if you ever get her out of your system."

That had been more than nine months ago, and he hadn't phoned her yet.

Padraic dried off, hung up his towel, and strode into the bedroom from the bath.

Six-three and over two hundred pounds, he kept in shape most days by working from sun-up to sunset. He also enjoyed running every couple of days, and staggering weight-lifting on the days he didn't run. Staying in shape, he believed, was to his advantage.

You had to expend energy to gain energy.

Since Angela had left him, he'd started exercising more vigorously. It helped to keep his mind off her. Nothing he did to forget her was foolproof, though.

After pulling on a pair of briefs he reached for a clean tee shirt. The phone rang. He didn't like answering the phone at suppertime, so he ignored it while he pulled on the tee shirt. Usually, it was no one but somebody trying to sell him something, anyway.

This time, someone was leaving a message. He could hear the voice on the answering machine in the living room from here.

Was that...?

It couldn't be! He quickly went to the nightstand and picked up the handset.

"Angela?"

Angela was so intent on leaving a cheery message that when he picked up the receiver and started talking, she went silent. It had taken all day long for her to get up the courage to phone and when his machine had switched on she'd been relieved she wouldn't have to speak directly to him. Now that he was there her words had frozen in her throat.

"Angela, I know you're there. I can hear you breathing, more like hyperventilating," Padraic said, laughing softly.

Since she wasn't forthcoming, he started talking. "I miss you. A day doesn't go by that I don't wish you were here. I don't care if I *am* sounding foolish, and you only called to say hello, and nothing more. You didn't let me have my say before you left, so as long as you're on the line, I'm going to have it now. You didn't have to *quit* me to go after your dreams, Angela. I would have gladly supported you, no matter how long it took. Oh, hell, that's a lie. I probably would have put my foot down at a whole year without you if I'd known you'd be gone this long. But you didn't even give me the chance to be magnanimous. That sucks. What also sucks, kinda, is the fact that I haven't been able to get over you. I went out with Shana Anderson..."

"Shana!"

"So, you've found your voice."

"I didn't know you were attracted to Shana."

"I wasn't attracted to Shana while you were here. I had no reason to give her a second glance. But when you left, I had every right to date anybody I wanted to."

Angela was sitting on the bed with her back against the headboard and her legs stretched out. "I haven't dated *anybody* since I've been here."

"If you had let me finish my sentence, I would have told you that nothing happened between me and Shana."

Angela was hugely relieved. "I know I don't have any right to be happy about that, but I am."

Padraic laughed shortly. "Why doesn't that surprise me? So, what's up? Why did you phone after over a year of silence?"

"I wanted to tell you I'll be home in August."

"Yeah," Padraic said, casually. "I heard about the family reunion. I still go by to see your parents. And your dad finally took your advice and is doing a little organic farming. He wanted to know everything about it, and I was happy to tell him."

"Thanks, Padraic, that was very sweet of you."

"I thought they'd be my in-laws by now." His tone was not accusatory. It was almost wistful. Angela could imagine his handsome dark brown face crinkling in a smile. He had a smile that instantly melted her.

"Padraic, I can't ask you to take me back. I've done things since I've been gone that I'm ashamed of."

"But you said you haven't dated anyone."

"I haven't. I haven't allowed any other man to touch me, Padraic. But when my money ran out, I did something desperate. Something you'd never imagine I would do."

"You posed nude?" His tone held a little surprise, but was nonjudgmental.

"No, I danced at a strip club." She held her breath, waiting for his reaction.

"Baby, I've been to strip clubs. All essential parts are covered on the girls, and the men who go to them can't touch them, or they'll be thrown out. Was that the kind of place where you worked?"

She exhaled sharply. "When did you go to strip clubs?" she asked, a little miffed.

"Stay on the subject," Padraic said, laughing. "It was before I met you, and it was only twice. Those places depress me. Now, answer my question."

"Yes, that's exactly the kind of place Benny's was. You're right, they're depressing."

"You said 'worked'," Padraic said. "You're not working there anymore?"

"No, I'm working at a restaurant now."

She told him everything. How she'd been rejected by practically every modeling agency in greater Miami. How things had gotten so bad, she'd walked into a strip joint and auditioned for the owner (this was before Benny's), and had been hired on the spot to go on that night. But the owner had developed a thing for her and she'd had to leave because he kept coming on to her. At least at Benny's the owner, Benny Christmas, (not really his name) didn't try to take her to bed. But his brother *did* try to turn her into a prostitute. Anyway, she and Sandy weren't working there anymore.

And she was coming home in August.

She sighed when she was through. "I was a fool to leave you, Padraic."

"No, you weren't," he said, surprising her. "You had to get it out of your system. That desire to be more than you thought you were. You always did have a problem believing how wonderful you were. I'd tell you that I thought you were beautiful and you'd say, 'No, I'm not!' Your dad would compliment you on the fine job you did on keeping the farm's books, and you'd say, 'Oh, anybody could do that!'   Well, you were wrong for always making yourself smaller than you were, Angela. If there's one lesson I hope you've learned since you've been away it's that you're a survivor, and you can do anything you set your mind to. Because, you can."

Angela was crying. She tried to do it silently, but Padraic heard her soft sniffles.

"Don't cry, Angel Girl, just come on home to me."

Angel Girl was Padraic's special name for her. That's why it had rankled every time that snake, Terry Christmas, had called her that.

She cried even harder.

"You can't forgive me that easily," she protested through her tears. "I insist that you think about it and when I see you in August, you can tell me what your decision is."

"Angela," Padraic began.

"No," Angela said, fiercely. "I've been through a life-changing experience, Padraic. I know what I want now. I'm not confused anymore. I want you to be that sure about me. I left you once. That's not easy to forget. What's going to keep me from doing it again? *I'm* sure I won't. But you need the time to come to that conclusion, too."

"I don't want to waste anymore time," Padraic told her, his voice filled with longing. "I can be in Miami by tomorrow night."

Angela was tempted to tell him to hop the next plane going south.

But that wouldn't solve anything. She had damaged the trust they'd formerly enjoyed as a couple. While she didn't want any other options, and knew Padraic was the man for her, he deserved the time to weigh his options.

"I'll be home by August 2nd," Angela said quietly. "That's under six weeks from now. You can tell me whether or not you still want me then, not before. Please, Padraic. Do this for me."

"Help you punish yourself, in other words?" he said, cynically. "Because that's what you're doing. You can't believe that I love you so much; I can't bear to be without you one second longer. You have to beat yourself up for a while. Wonder if I'll change my mind between now and August 2nd." He paused. The silence grew. After two minutes he said, "So be it!" And hung up.

Angela slowly placed the receiver in its cradle. Then she turned out the light, curled up on her pillow and closed her eyes.

He was angry now but one day he would be grateful he hadn't welcomed her back with open arms, and had taken the time to think it through.

Then why were tears rolling down her cheeks?

Was it possible that she thought she'd once again made a bad decision?

Maybe she should have graciously accepted his forgiveness, and worried about the consequences later. But she'd given up on taking the easy way out. She wanted to do the right thing now. No matter how hard it was to do.

SEVEN

*T**his is where your granddaddy grew up, remember?"* Sara said to the children as she turned onto the paved drive that led to the Johnson homestead. They still had a quarter of a mile to go before they reached the farmhouse.

On both sides, whitewashed fences ran the length of the road. A field of corn was on the right and a field of watermelons, on the left. The children were peering out the window with expectant faces as the truck drove past.

"Uncle Robert never married, Grandma?" Sarafina asked, her voice full of sympathy for her elderly uncle.

"No, he says he never found the right woman," Sara said. She drove into the yard.

Robert's Doberman came running from around the house, barking and growling and baring his teeth. The girls cried out in fear.

As the only male along for the trip Gregory had his pride to protect, therefore his façade remained placidly calm.

"Does he bite?" Jacquelin asked, worriedly.

Sara laughed. "Only his food. Emmett is eighty-four in dog years. Can either of you tell me how many years that is in human years?"

"I can," said Gregory. "Seven goes into eighty-four twelve times. So Emmett is twelve years old."

"Very good," their grandmother said, smiling. "Can't let your math skills go to rot just because you're out of school for the summer."

After she'd parked and turned off the ignition, she said, "Let me get out first since Emmett doesn't know you all well. The last time you were here, you were much younger."

She stepped down from the cab of the truck. She was wearing jeans and a tee shirt that read, "GRANDMAS SPOIL 'EM THEN SEND 'EM HOME." Her brown leather cowboy boots were so comfortable from repeated use that they felt like bedroom slippers on her feet, and she'd put her hair in a bun.

Emmett stopped barking once he recognized her scent. Wagging his tail, he ambled over to her and licked her out-held hand.

"Good boy," said Sara, soothingly.

Looking back at the children in the truck, she said, "Come on out and, one by one, let Emmett get your smell."

Gregory got out first. Sara let Emmett walk over to Gregory and sniff him. Emmett whined and looked back at Sara.

"That's my grandson, Emmett," Sara said. "Y'all are going to be friends."

Gregory held out his hand to Emmett and the dog sniffed it, but didn't lick it.

Gregory smiled. The dog hadn't bitten him. He figured that was a good sign.

The girls were reluctant to get out of the truck.

"We'll just wait for you in here, Grandma," Sarafina said warily, speaking for both her and Jacquelin.

"Nonsense, child," Sara coaxed her. "You have nothing to be afraid of, and you need to learn how to deal with strange dogs. The skill may come in handy one day."

Sarafina, always willing to learn a new skill, slowly opened the door and climbed out of the cab, with Jacquelin attached to her. Jacquelin had a death grip on her right wrist.

The sisters got out and stiffly stood next to the truck.

Sara spoke to Emmett. "Now, Emmett, these are my granddaughters. I don't want you to so much as growl at them. They're a little nervous around big dogs like you."

Emmett approached the girls as if he was as wary of them as they were of him. The girls were wearing shorts, tee shirts and sneakers. Emmett paused at Jacquelin's leg and sniffed her. Jacquelin grew tense, but didn't panic. Emmett licked her knee.

"See?" said Sara encouragingly. "He likes you!"

"Or he's seeing how you taste," quipped Gregory.

Jacquelin jumped about six inches off the ground, and Emmett took off running. The last thing they saw of him was his hind end disappearing around the corner of the barn. The kids laughed uproariously, and Sara shook her head in amazement.

"Okay, that concludes my lesson in dog-handling for the day. Shall we go see what your great uncle is up to?" Then, she bellowed, "Robert! Get out here. I brought my grandchildren for a visit!"

ഇൗൽ

It was a Saturday afternoon and after eating lunch, Robert was sitting in front of the TV enjoying an old western starring Sidney Poitier and Harry Belafonte. He didn't know the name of it. A lot of things had escaped his memory over the years, but that didn't detract from his pleasure. Now, who was calling his name?

He pushed himself up; his muscles feeling a bit stiff after having sat down for so long, and went to the door. He recognized Jack's old pick-up right away. It wasn't the new double-cab he'd recently bought, but the one Sara liked to tool around in.

His heart flipped over in his chest. That hellion was here alone? He had to squint to try and clear his vision. Where were his glasses? Oh, yeah, he'd left them on the hall table.

He doubled back, retrieved his glasses, and put them on. That was better.

Sara and the kids were on the porch by now.

Sara stood there with her hands on her hips, glaring at him through the screen door.

"Where are your manners?" she asked, indignantly.

"Where is your *husband*?"

"He's home, where I left him. The kids and I came over to say hello to you, and you're gonna make us stand on the porch to do it?"

"Yeah, that's about the size of it." He opened the door and stepped onto the porch. He was about the same height as Jack, but where Jack still had some heft to him, Robert was thinner than was good for him. *That*, Sara thought, *is because he doesn't have a good woman to take care of him.*

Robert had also gotten pretty cantankerous over the years. After years of being ruled by his headstrong sisters, he'd put his foot down and kicked all of them out. *Well, okay*, Sara thought. *Three of the biddies actually found somebody foolish enough to marry them. He only had to kick out two.*

Robert smiled down at the children. When he smiled, his eyes lit up and Sara could almost see the old Robert somewhere in there.

"Are these Candace's children?" he asked, delighted.

The kids who had good hearts, all of them, and sincerely took pleasure in meeting their relatives, happily cried, "Hello, Uncle Robert!"

Robert actually laughed. "I can't believe how much you all favor your mother when she was your ages." He regarded Gregory. "Except for you, of course. You look like your Grandpa Jack when he was a young man."

Totally ignoring Sara, he said. "Come on in, children, and tell your Uncle Robert all about yourselves. What grades are you in? What are your favorite subjects? Do you like lemonade? I just made a pitcher. Come on back to the kitchen. Don't mind the mess. I'm a confirmed bachelor and who cares about a little mess, anyway?"

Smiling, Sara followed them into the small, but well-maintained farmhouse. Robert might not care about picking up behind himself on a daily basis, but he took pride in his family home and property. He hadn't let it go to seed as his sisters had predicted he would upon their eviction from it.

The sisters still tried to exact their influence over their brother. None of them lived very far away and they were known to drive by the property when they knew he was working and leave covered dishes on the porch, or effusive notes. Sara only knew about it because Robert had confided in Jack, the only sibling he still spoke to.

She could guess why the sisters: Ruby, Beatrice, Esther, Deborah, and Ruth were making conciliatory gestures. Robert had never married and the property was worth a mint. He was going to die someday, and he had no heirs. The Biddies wanted to be remembered in his will.

Their parents had left the property to their sons, alone, with the stipulation that should the daughters never marry they would have an equal share in the farm's profits. If they married, they gave up that share.

Going by the letter of the will, Robert asked his two remaining single sisters to vacate the premises. He was more than happy to send them their share of the profits every month. And they were obliged to work in order to meet the rest of their living expenses, a bonus that Robert appreciated because when they were living on the farm they didn't deign to do any of the chores, saying housework was the limit of a woman's responsibilities.

That's one of the things Sara used to ride the sisters about. Especially when they were younger, she argued, they should have learned all they could about running the farm. They should have gotten in the field right alongside Robert. She did with Jack.

Because they hadn't supported him, Robert was bitter now.

Robert was pouring lemonade into glasses and talking animatedly with the kids when Sara walked into the big, old-fashioned kitchen.

"Have y'all ever seen a piglet?" she heard him ask them.

The children had inquisitive expressions on their faces.

"Is that like a miniature pig?" Sarafina asked, confused.

Robert laughed. "Exactly. It's what you call the offspring of pigs, their babies. If you want to see one with your own eyes, just step out the back door and walk down to the pigpen. One of the sows gave birth to four less than a week ago."

The kids gulped down their lemonade in anticipation of going to see the piglets.

"Thanks, Uncle Robert!" each of them said before hurrying out the back door.

Robert looked at Sara. "Okay, what are you doing here? I know you didn't just decide to bring Candace's kids over for a visit, like you said. Out with it."

Sara picked up the other glass he'd taken from the cabinet and held it underneath the pitcher he held in his hand.

"I may need a drink before beginning."

He poured her a glass of the tart, sweet lemonade, and then they sat at the table facing each other. "According to your sisters," Sara said, "those kids out there are your grandchildren."

Robert, who was an old hand at intrigue, his sisters' favorite sport, did not bat an eye. He sat quietly while Sara told him the whole story.

He agreed that his sisters' actions had been malicious and meant to malign Sara and, inadvertently, him. "They didn't bother trying to get proof that what they believed was true. They went ahead with their campaign of sowing doubt in a little girl's mind." He shook his head sadly. "I was beginning to mellow toward them after a few years of not seeing them twenty-four-hours a day. Now, you tell me this and I realize I was right to put them out. Did they not have *any* idea what they were doing to Candace?" His tone was disbelieving.

"Jack says they probably were under the impression that you and I had just broken up when *he* and I announced our engagement. And then Candace came along so early after the wedding."

"But you and I never..."

"I know that!" Sara cried.

She calmed down. "Now, when I say I want them to pay for what they did, I don't mean I'm going to poison them or even embarrass them in front of the entire community. No, what *we* are going to do will be subtle, and will be kept all in the family."

"We!" Robert cried.

"Yes, I'm going to need your help in order for this to work," Sara explained. Robert frowned, trying to think of a way out. Sara held his gaze with the intensity of her own. "You know they deserve it."

Robert sighed. "I can't argue with that. Okay, I'm in."

ᎦᏍᏇ

"Why should we trust you to build our dream house?" Mark Christian asked Greg as he sat forward in the chair across from Greg's desk, a smirk on his tanned face.

It was Friday. Greg had graciously agreed to see Christian even though he had been half an hour late for their appointment. A stickler for promptness, Greg had been slightly irritated. But he'd been in such a good mood lately he'd let it ride.

Barry Stephens, one of the architects on Greg's in-house architectural team, had told him he and Christian had gone to college together. Christian wanted Barry to design his home and since Barry worked for Greg's firm, Bates Professional Builders, Christian wanted to personally meet the owner.

"I'm sorry," said Greg. "I was under the impression that Barry had already given you our credentials."

He smiled. "All right, let's see: we have more than twenty years of experience building in and around Charleston. We use only quality products and experienced sub-contractors. We have a large lot inventory, so you have plenty to choose from. Of course you know about our in-house architectural team. Barry leads it. We also have in-house financing, which over the years has proved to be advantageous for our clients. We stay on the cutting edge of new designs in the industry, so if there is a better way to build, we know about it, and are experts in it. We believe in keeping the environment clean, so we're considered 'green' builders, that is, we don't leave anything behind on a site that would contaminate it. We also believe in saving energy so your home will be built with the best insulation, the best windows, heating and air conditioning equipment so that you know your house will not only be beautiful, comfortable, but will not make you go broke paying your utility bills.

"Last, but not least, we're bound by a specific code of ethics. We will not give you bogus quotes. We will deliver when we say we will deliver, and therefore you're assured the best quality, the best warranties, and the highest standards for safety."

"Wow, I'm impressed," said Mark Christian, sincerely. He looked embarrassed. "You're right, Barry did tell us about your firm. I just had to meet you. Laura, that's my wife, and I aren't exactly millionaires. This is a huge investment for us. We had to be sure. Feel safe in your hands. You understand?"

Greg nodded. "Of course I do. We've built a lot of homes and the concerns you have were expressed by every one of our clients. Plus, I remember when my wife and I bought our first house. It's a stressful undertaking."

Mark sighed and shook his head in agreement. "I think I've had more sleepless nights than any other time of my life."

"Well, we'll try to make this as painless an experience as possible," Greg assured him, rising.

Mark got up and shook his hand. "Thank you so much for seeing me."

"It was my pleasure. If you have any further questions, please give me a holler."

"Thank you, I will," said Mark.

He left the office, softly closing the door behind him.

Greg sat back down and picked up the phone. Excitement coursed through him. He dialed Candace's cell phone number and patiently waited for her to pick up.

It was now after five, and if he knew her, she was either in the supermarket picking up something for dinner, or already on the way home from the office.

"Salmon or steak?" she asked when she answered.

"Salmon," said Greg. "I don't want anything to weigh me down tonight."

Candace, wearing a pale yellow skirt suit and a white silk sleeveless blouse, was walking down the produce aisle of her favorite supermarket. Her long legs, bare and moisturized so that her skin fairly gleamed with good health, were displayed to their best advantage in the short skirt, and she wore white leather strappy sandals with the outfit. Her gait was sexy and confident.

An African American gentleman in his early thirties was squeezing honeydew melons as she passed. His eyes raked over her. He almost knocked over the pile of melons as he abruptly turned to follow her with his eyes.

Candace noticed him, but pretended she hadn't. "You must think that there will be dessert after dinner," Candace teasingly said to Greg.

"I'm counting on it," Greg told her. He loosened his tie and put his feet up on the desk, getting comfortable. "I want you in the bedroom, the pool, *and* the hot tub."

"You certainly have gotten adventurous since the kids have been with my parents," Candace said, smiling.

"I can't help it. You know I've never been able to get enough of you. We haven't had this much time together since we were first married. I'm enjoying myself!"

"Me, too," Candace said.

"I should say so," Greg said. He laughed softly. "That move you threw on me last night should go in a special addendum to the Kama Sutra. Other couples all over the world should be able to enjoy it."

Candace laughed delightedly. "You know I'm in the supermarket and I can't speak freely, so stop that. I'll see you soon."

"I'll cook tonight," Greg said. "I want you well-rested."

"Deal!" Candace accepted his offer in a heartbeat. "I'll soak in the tub while you prepare dinner."

"The tub's big enough for two, you know."

"I'm hanging up now. You've got me blushing like a fool."

And she promptly did so.

On his end, Greg laughed and hung up too. He got to his feet, grabbed his briefcase, took a quick glance at his watch, saw that it was five-thirty-five, and hurried out.

He beat Candace home by three minutes. When she walked into the kitchen from the garage door entrance he was standing in the middle of the room without a stitch of clothing on.

Candace stood there with her mouth open. Two filled-to-the-brim grocery bags were in her arms. Greg went and took the bags from her, calmly set them on the counter, then began putting the groceries away as if he were not doing it all stark naked.

"Not that I'm complaining, mind you," said his flabbergasted wife. "But I don't believe The Naked Chef really gets naked to cook."

There were only a few items that might spoil if not refrigerated. Greg quickly put them away. Finished, he turned and smiled at Candace. "I don't plan on cooking while I'm naked. I just felt like having dessert before dinner tonight."

There was such a lascivious look in his eyes that Candace burst out laughing and fled, her heels clicking rapidly on the tile floor.

Greg, barefoot, and therefore blessed with better traction, caught her with little difficulty. He picked her up and carried her the rest of the way to the bedroom.

In the bedroom, Candace pleaded to be allowed to shower first. "I feel grungy," she said. Greg disagreed. His nostrils flared as he inhaled her special fragrance.

He'd always found her scent tantamount to an aphrodisiac.

Candace knew her protests had fallen on deaf ears when his mouth descended on the side of her neck and he began kissing her, and relishing every kiss. Smacking, even.

She giggled throughout the onslaught, and only stopped after he'd peeled every item of clothing off her body. The expression in his eyes then told her he meant business. And she was in trouble, *big* trouble.

She fell backward onto the bed and her husband gave her such pleasure that she wound up sighing like a well-fed kitty.

An hour later, they lay gazing into each other's eyes.

"Do you know that I think you get more desirable with each passing year?" Greg said softly.

Candace traced his strong jaw line with a finger. Smiling, she said, "Good, because I feel the same way about you."

Greg placed a hand on her flat stomach. He looked serious all of a sudden.

"Sweetheart, let's have another baby."

Candace sat up in bed. She stared at him. "This is a conspiracy, isn't it?"

Greg was baffled. "I don't know what you mean."

"First my parents conveniently come to collect the kids, then you and I are at it like rabbits, and then you say you want to have another baby."

She sounded perfectly logical. But Greg continued to look at her with a vacant expression on his face.

"Don't look at me like that. You know my parents; they love babies. I wouldn't put it past them to have planned this from the beginning. 'You know', Momma probably said to Daddy, 'Jacquelin is nine years old, and Candace is still young enough to have another baby. Why don't we keep the kids for a couple of weeks and see what happens?'

"And you!" she continued. "You have always been a sucker for a baby. Unlike some dads, you love taking care of your children. You even enjoy the dirty work."

"Well," said Greg, "I don't really enjoy changing the diapers with poop in them, but I see it as a normal part of fatherhood, so I gladly do it."

"I know!" Candace exclaimed. She scooted over to the side of the bed, and swung her legs down. Rising, she added. "I know that about you. If it were up to you, we'd have six kids."

"I was an only child. I was lonely," Greg said in his defense.

He climbed out of bed, too. "We're still young, baby, and Jacquelin deserves to be a big sister to someone just like Sarafina and Gregory."

"But where will it end?" Candace wondered. "When the child you want gets to be Jacquelin's age, will you want another? I'll probably be in my early fifties then. The mommy bank will be closed!"

Greg laughed and then abruptly stopped when Candace glowered at him.

He went to her and grasped her by the shoulders. Peering intently into her eyes, he said, "Look at me."

Candace was reluctant to look him in the eye because Greg could be powerfully persuasive when he wanted to be, and he wanted another child. She felt it in her loins.

She could swear that when Greg was trying to get her pregnant, his lovemaking *felt* different than it usually did and for the past two weeks, since the kids had been away, he had been giving it that extra oomph. It wasn't that he wasn't always a good lover, because he was. She simply knew instinctively when he was in a 'let's divide some cells and make another living being' mode. After all, she'd observed his behavior on three other occasions.

"No!" she said emphatically, pushing out of his embrace and walking away. "I like our life just the way it is now, Greg. Gregory just entered high school, Sarafina is in middle school, and Jacquelin's in elementary school.

We've got all the bases covered. I don't need one in nursery school, or daycare. I've finally got my business going exactly the way I want it. My body has come back from my last pregnancy after *years* of trying to get it back in shape."

"You're beautiful when you're pregnant," Greg said.

She believed him. There was no doubt, from his passionate love-making, to the manner in which his eyes followed her when she was pregnant, that Greg truly found her irresistible when she was in that state. But when was she supposed to have a life of her own?

"I love you, Greg. I love our children," she said softly. "I'm a sucker for a baby, too. But when I gave birth to Jacquelin you agreed that she would be our last. I took you at your word. Are you taking it back now?"

Greg turned away, his fingers pressed to his forehead in frustration. "I meant it then. I truly did. But we have so much to give another child, Candace. I didn't just come up with this request off the top of my head. I've given it some thought. I'm not going to pressure you. This will be the last time I'm going to bring it up. But think about this, please: Gregory's fourteen, and Sarafina's twelve. In under six years they will both be out of the house. Jacquelin will be the only child living at home then. She's going to need companionship. If we have another child within the next year or two, she will have a brother or a sister at home with her until she goes away to college. Then, when she goes to college, we will have one more at home. That child will have three older siblings like your sister, Angela, did. Do you think she suffered because you, Sharon and Debra were years older than she was? No, she didn't. You told me that you felt like you practically raised her because you were fifteen when she was born. And you've also said that she's close to Sharon and Debra. Let's go for four, Candace. Then, we'll quit. Just think about it."

Candace was too angry to answer him. She turned and walked away from him, went into the adjacent bathroom, and slammed the door behind her.

Greg sighed. "You can give me your answer later!" he called after her.

EIGHT

*T*he shade-tree mechanic who was repairing Sandy's car said it needed a new engine and gave her an astronomical estimate. When Sandy told him she couldn't afford his price and was coming to pick it up, he held it hostage for a ransom of three hundred dollars. He said she owed him that much for the time he'd spent diagnosing the problem.

"Let him keep it," Angela suggested one day in late-July as they were driving to work in her trusty Ford. "I'll sign over the Escort to you. It's not pretty, but it runs well enough to get you back and forth to work."

Sandy, who felt that Angela had been too generous to her already, protested. "It's a heck of a lot nicer than my old rust bucket, but how will you get to South Carolina?"

"I'm either flying or catching a bus," Angela said, turning down Biscayne Boulevard. "If you want the Escort, you'll have to switch over your insurance from the Mustang to it. But that shouldn't be much of a hassle."

Sandy winced. "I never got insurance."

Angela didn't express surprise. She imagined there were lots of people driving around Miami in uninsured cars and, even scarier, without the benefit of a driver's license.

"Okay, but if I'm going to sign the Escort over to you, you're going to have to get insurance. You can get the most basic coverage. It's inexpensive, and at least you'll be protected if you're involved in an accident."

"Okay," said Sandy.

Angela briefly glanced at the girl who looked like an entirely different person since she'd been working at Donatelli's. She was wearing very little makeup these days, and she had gone back to her original hair color, brown.

"I'm leaving in a week's time," Angela reminded her.

"I'll get on the ball," Sandy promised. "I swear, as soon as you sign the car over to me, I'll go to the nearest insurance agency and get coverage."

"Good, because all I need to do is sign the title. I'll have to leave the rest of it up to you. Once you have the title, you need to get a tag. You'll have to apply at the Department of Motor Vehicles for that."

"I can handle it," Sandy assured her with a grin. "Thanks for the car!"

"I believe you can," Angela said, seriously. "You're doing so well at the restaurant. You've made new friends. You've already lined up another roommate. Yeah, I think you can handle it."

Sandy smiled, happy with her accomplishments. "You know what? I think I *will* go see my mom in a couple of months and tell her exactly what her husband did to me. It might not solve anything, but it'll be off *my* chest. She needs to know. Even if she doesn't put him out after I have my say, she will have enough doubt in her mind to convince her to watch him around Katie."

"Good for you."

Angela turned into the parking garage across the street from Donatelli's. After parking, she regarded Sandy. "You're gonna be okay, kiddo."

Sandy impulsively hugged her. "I'm gonna miss you so much!" They drew apart. "I've never had a friend like you, Angela. You did all this for me and never expected anything in return."

"You're wrong," Angela said, her voice cracking from emotion. "I do expect something from you: I expect you to be happy."

₭℟

The July sun's rays relentlessly beat down on Padraic as he worked in the hay field along with several other men. Baling hay was grueling work, but there was no way around the process, especially if you advertised that your hay was organically grown and harvested by hand. You had to be able to back up those claims.

Exactly what was the market for organically grown and harvested hay? Padraic had been surprised at the number of people who had placed huge orders: a media mogul from Atlanta who raised race horses. He would not give his horses anything but the best.

A movie star in Beverly Hills, California who kept a prize Hereford bull in her stable because it had sentimental value. It had once belonged to her late husband who was a rancher in Montana. She thought feeding the bull organic hay would extend its life.

Padraic felt honor bound to give them their money's worth. So, if it took a little sweat to provide it, he was okay with that.

Besides, when he was out here with the sun baking him, thoughts of Angela only crept in about five times a day as opposed to more than ten times a day when he was doing less strenuous work.

He was still angry with her. She had nerve, phoning him like that, giving him hope then snatching it away by imposing conditions on him.

She'd phoned again at least twice a week since then, and he'd let the machine get it. He feared he'd say something he would later regret if he spoke to her.

He was letting her stew.

If she wanted his answer when she got home in August, then he wasn't going to give it to her until they were standing in front of one another.

Lately, when she phoned, her tone sounded increasingly desperate. He didn't revel in her pain. He ached every time he listened to her messages. But if there was one thing he knew about Angela, it was that she sincerely wanted to suffer for what she perceived as her abandonment of him.

He'd already tried to make it easy on her.

Easy wasn't going to cut it anymore. When she came home to him they had to be on an equal footing. Sure, she had messed up but she was paying for it. And after much deliberation, he would forgive her.

The fact that he'd already forgiven her would have to remain his secret.

By his refusal to speak to her until she came home, he was simply giving her what she wanted.

ഇൽ

Angela was in agony, the soul-searing kind. Today was Tuesday, August 1. In less than ten minutes she would be boarding the plane for South Carolina, and Padraic had not returned any of her messages.

She regretted that the final message she'd left had a fatalistic tone: "Padraic," she'd said as his machine recorded her voice. "By your silence I'm left with only one conclusion: That you haven't forgiven me and you're too much of a gentleman to pick up because you think you might say something awful to me. You never were any good at being rude to anybody. We're similar in that respect. Daddy used to say that we were both so sweet-natured that when we married we would undoubtedly be taken advantage of by everybody; would never accumulate great wealth because we would give our money away. But that we would have very happy children because nothing, and no one, would ever take precedence over them."

She had to stifle a sniffle at the end.

"You're my dream guy, Padraic, and it took leaving you behind to make me realize that. I'm sorry I hurt you. And if we should run into each other in Mason Corners I hope we can be civil to each other. I'll always love you."

She'd hung up after that.

Now, as she boarded the plane, her limbs felt weighed down with lethargy. Depression, dark and venomous, had descended upon her spirit. How would she be able to live in Mason Corners, with the imminent danger of running into Padraic, lurking behind every street corner?

She settled into her seat on the plane. Her seatmate was an attractive Hispanic in his late twenties. She murmured hello. He returned her greeting, his dark eyes revealing a keen interest in conversation.

"Do you fly often?" he asked.

"Not if I can help it," she said honestly. Her eyes were watery, and she knew it.

Thinking about Padraic had made her tear-up.

"Are you all right?" he asked, concerned.

She shook her head in the positive. "Yes, I'm fine. Allergies."

He smiled, understanding immediately. "Ah, yes. I have them too. I have to take a daily antihistamine."

"Where are you headed?" Angela asked. This wasn't a non-stop flight.

"Charleston," he said, smiling. "A new job. You?"

"Charleston, too, but from there I have a five-hour drive to my hometown."

"You couldn't get a flight that came closer to your hometown?"

"No, but I don't mind the drive. My sister lives in Charleston, and I'll visit her before getting on the road."

"Rental car, huh?"

"Yes."

"Why were you in Miami, on business?"

Angela supposed her sleeveless A-line summer dress in pale green linen and sandals in practically the same shade did make her look like a businesswoman donning something comfortable for her flight home.

She laughed softly. "No, I was in Miami trying to 'find' myself." His dark brown eyes were merry. "Did you?"

"Yes, yes I did."

ℝ℞

"No more cars?" Angela cried, trying to keep her voice down. "But I've got to get to Mason Corners tonight!"

The African American woman behind the desk at the rental car agency looked extremely sympathetic to her plight, but offered no solution. "August is a big month for vacations, ma'am. Families are going to reunions.

Families are going on vacation. Couples honeymooning. Charleston welcomes a lot of tourists this time of year. I'm so sorry."

Angela sighed tiredly. She had already tried the other car rental agency, and they could *possibly* accommodate her sometime tomorrow. She didn't want to stay over.

She hated to have to phone Candace. She was probably at work this time of day: 2:15 in the afternoon. Plus there was the fact that the last time she'd spoken with her eldest sister she had let slip that she and Greg were silently feuding. Greg wanted to have another baby and Candace had issues. While he was being gracious and had not brought up the subject again, Candace was being bull-headed and was giving him the cold shoulder.

Angela didn't want to get in the middle of that.

So, she'd planned to rent a car and drive to Mason Corners herself even though Candace had offered to drive her.

She grudgingly moved aside to let someone else hear the disappointing news that there weren't any more cars available. "Thanks, anyway," she said to the woman.

"There's always the Greyhound bus station," the woman said, helpfully.

Angela hadn't been on a bus in years. She wasn't averse to giving it another try, though. "Where *is* the bus station?"

"Get a taxi and the driver'll take you directly there," was the woman's suggestion.

Angela did just that.

Twenty-five minutes later, she was buying a one-way ticket to Mason Corners.

The ticket agent looked at her with a huge grin on his face. "Nobody has bought a ticket to Mason Corners in a *long* time."

"I guess not," Angela said with a laugh. "Mason Corners doesn't have a bus station."

"Don't worry, sugar, the driver makes exceptions for small towns like that. He'll drop you off somewhere like a courthouse or a supermarket."

"Are you sure?" Angela asked. "I don't have any desire to go on to North Carolina."

The ticket agent laughed even harder as he handed her the ticket and her change. "I'm sure. We haven't kidnapped a passenger yet."

A little later, Angela once again settled into a seat on a public transportation conveyance. This time, however, the seats were bigger, the air smelled like Lysol and somebody's lunch of fried chicken in a paper bag. As she remembered, the combination of grease and paper had a distinct odor. Instead of turning her stomach, it reminded her that she hadn't eaten in hours.

She found the source of the smell in the seat right next to her. An elderly African American woman in a flowery sundress and orthopedic shoes smiled at her. "Are you hungry, sweetie? I fried this chicken myself this morning."

She held the bag open, encouraging Angela to take a piece.

Angela didn't think twice, she reached in and grabbed a drumstick. "Thank you."

The woman smiled and helped herself to a thigh. They ate companionably for several minutes. The chicken was delicious. Not too salty, and with just the right amount of spices, sweet and fiery, added.

Like her mother, this woman had obviously spent years perfecting her fried chicken recipe. "This is the best chicken I've had since I left home," Angela said, expertly nibbling around the bone to get the last morsels of meat and crispy coating.

"Where are you from?" asked the saint with the chicken.

"Mason Corners."

Her light brown eyes twinkled in her chubby face. "Darlin' I know Mason Corners like the back of my hand. I'm going there myself to see my sister, Literary."

"Did you say, Literary?" Angela thought her hunger might be making her delirious.

The woman laughed shortly. "I know it's a strange name. Our parents were strange people. They were from Harlem. She taught school, and he was a writer of some note. They named my older sister, Literary because they wanted her to love books. They named me Kithara because they wanted me to love music. A kithara is a large lyre, a musical instrument something like a guitar that was used by the ancient Greeks. I told you they were strange. Anyway, their naming us the way they did didn't work. Literary became a musician, and I became an English teacher."

Angela finished eating while Kithara was speaking. Seeing she was finished, Kithara offered her a napkin and another piece of chicken.

Angela modestly turned it down. "I don't want to eat all of your dinner."

"Sweetie, I have half a chicken in this bag. I can't eat all of it. I'd better not be full when I get to Lit's because she will be highly upset if I don't partake of the meal she's probably fixin' right now. That woman loves to cook."

"If this chicken is any indication," Angela told her. "So do you."

Kithara laughed softly. "Yes, I do. I cooked for my husband for fifty years. I cooked for my children fewer years because they left home after high school. A couple went to college, and the remaining boy went into the military. They all have big families of their own now. My husband, Milton, died last year."

"Oh, I'm so sorry," Angela said, sympathetically.

Kithara smiled wistfully. "We are powerless against death. That's a lesson you learn if you keep living. But, then, we are powerless against being born into this world too. I think we should simply have faith that in being born, and in dying, God knows what he's doing." She frowned suddenly. "What's your name, sugar?"

Angela was embarrassed. Here she was eating Kithara's chicken, and she hadn't even introduced herself. "Angela," she said softly. "Angela Johnson."

"Do you have three sisters by the names of Debra, Candace, and Sharon?"

Angela's eyes stretched with surprise. "Yes, I do!"

"My sister adores you girls. She told me about you. When you were children, you used to walk to town every Saturday. Lit lives just outside of town. But she loves to walk and collect things. She told me that not many townsfolk take kindly to the fact that she pushes an old grocery cart through town loaded with what some people think of as junk. But you girls would always engage her in the most interesting conversations. Your parents, she said, must be special people to have raised such self-possessing little girls."

"You're talking about Miss Lit," Angela cried happily. "We loved her! How is she doing?"

Smiling contentedly, Kithara said, "Literary is doing well for an eighty-year-old. She still walks everyday to keep her limbs loose, and she still has all her faculties, thank God. I'll be staying with her for a month. You must come by for a visit. I'll make tea cakes and we'll sit on the porch and drink tea and gossip."

"I'd love that," said Angela. And meant it.

More than six hours later, Angela and Kithara were walking into the Winn Dixie, one of the supermarkets in Mason Corners. Angela waited with Kithara at the service desk while she placed a phone call to her sister, Literary, telling her she had arrived.

"It'll be a few minutes," Kithara reported after putting down the receiver. "Lit has to run across the street and get her neighbor to come for me"

It was almost eleven P.M., but the Winn Dixie stayed open until midnight.

"Aren't you going to phone your folks and ask them to come for you?"

"I didn't tell anyone I was coming home," Angela told her. "I planned on driving straight from Charleston, but there were no rental cars available. I wanted to surprise them. But now I suppose the surprise is going to be spoiled. I'll have to phone somebody." She fleetingly thought of Padraic. He probably wasn't in bed yet.

Her parents went to bed at nine o'clock. They retired early and rose early. She was reluctant to interrupt their slumber.

"Here goes," she said, stepping up to the counter and picking up the receiver. As she dialed, a Winn Dixie worker announced on the P. A. system, "Shoppers, don't forget to pick up some WD brand pork chops for your barbecue this weekend. We have them on sale tonight for 2.99 per pound. Stock up while you can!"

Padraic's phone was ringing.

Angela's stomach muscles clenched with nervousness.

"Hello?" He sounded sleepy. She'd awakened him after all.

"Padraic, it's Angela."

"Angela, I'm in bed. If I'd looked at my caller ID, I wouldn't have answered."

Her heart felt as if it had just plummeted to the pit of her stomach. Tears came to her eyes. Padraic truly didn't want to see her anymore. Her hand trembled as she went to hang up the receiver.

Kithara had been watching her face. She'd seen it crumble. She'd seen the pain that had appeared in her eyes and she'd become instantly incensed at the person on the other end of the line for making a sweet girl like Angela look so defeated and hopeless.

"Look here," she said after taking the receiver, "I don't know who you are, but this child has been on a Greyhound bus for over six hours. She's exhausted, and you're going to come down here and pick her up, right now!"

Padraic had sat straight up in bed at the sound of someone else's voice.

"Who are you?" he asked the strange woman, none too nicely.

"Who I am doesn't matter. Angela has been traveling all day. You just said something that devastated her. I hope my sister has come and picked me up before you get here because I might be tempted to say something equally cruel to you once you get here. We're at the Winn Dixie. Now, are you coming or not?"

Padraic was out of bed in a split second. "I'm on the way," he told the stern woman on the phone. "Tell her I'll be right there." He was stumbling over his words. "And tell her I love her!"

"You tell her!" said Kithara, and hung up. To Angela, she said, "He's on his way."

Angela felt like such a fool standing at the service desk in Winn Dixie wiping her eyes with the back of her hand.

Kithara beamed at the woman behind the service desk. "Thank you, darlin', for letting us use the phone. God'll bless you for that. Do you have any tissues for my friend?"

The woman, a tall redhead, produced a box of Kleenex. She put it on the counter.

"Help yourself."

"Thank you," Angela told her before blowing her nose.

"Rough day, huh?" the woman asked with a tired sigh of her own.

"I've had better," Angela confirmed.

"Look on the bright side. The day's almost over," she returned with a smile.

A customer stepped up to the service desk and Angela and Kithara moved aside to let the woman do her job.

"If the mosquitoes weren't so bad, we could sit outside and wait for our rides," Kithara said. She smiled at Angela as they began walking toward the exit, carrying their bags. Angela had a suitcase, a heavy suit bag, plus a tote bag and her shoulder bag. Even if she'd wanted to walk home, which was a mile away, she wouldn't have been able to with such a burden. Kithara, who apparently traveled light, had only a small suitcase and her purse.

৪০৫৪

Kithara didn't know why, but she felt it was important that she not give Angela the message from the startled man on the phone. He'd said to tell her that he loved her. Well, judging by Angela's reaction, she didn't know he loved her.

Kithara felt it was best if he told her himself. It wouldn't be half as wonderful coming from a third party.

Kithara's ride arrived first.

A short black gentleman with white hair walked through the electric doors, and upon seeing Kithara, cried, "Baby girl! You're like a cool drink of water for a dying man."

He and Kithara hugged. Then Kithara introduced him to Angela. "Honey, this is Matt Hempstead, he and Literary have been neighbors for a lot of years. Matt, this is Angela Johnson."

"One of Jack Johnson's daughters?" Matt asked, smiling at Angela.

"Yes sir," said Angela.

He enthusiastically pumped her hand. "I've known your daddy a long time. Fine man. It's a pleasure to meet you, Angela."

Angela was surprised that she didn't know Matt Hempstead. But she supposed she couldn't possibly know everybody in Mason Corners, which had a population of 3768 the last time she had checked. Besides, Mr. Hempstead was definitely closer to her father's generation. He had to be seventy-five, or older.

Kithara had said she was sixty-eight, so she supposed that did make her a girl when compared to her eighty-year-old sister and Mr. Hempstead.

"It's a pleasure to meet you, too," Angela said with sincerity. "I'll have to tell my dad I ran into you."

"Do that," said Matt Hempstead, pleasantly.

He grinned down at Kithara. "Give me that suitcase, gal, and let's go. Lit will be wondering what's keeping us."

Kithara gave Angela a brief hug. "Take care of yourself now. And don't forget you promised to come for a visit."

"I won't," Angela promised. "You made that bus ride a memorable experience for me."

"Ditto," said Kithara.

And she and Matt Hempstead hurried off, both of them spry for their ages.

Angela was still smiling when a deep, masculine voice said from behind her, "Angel Girl, is that really you?"

She spun around to find Padraic standing there with a sad aspect in his eyes, and his hand held out to her in a plaintive gesture. "I'm so sorry, baby. If I had known you were in town and that phone call wasn't like all the rest, designed to drive me nuts, I would never have said what I did."

He had Angela at the words, Angel Girl. The rest had barely been heard.

She *flew* into his open arms.

Padraic picked her up and held her tightly against him. He thanked God she was back in his arms. He hadn't realized, sincerely and truly, how much he'd missed her until this moment. And now his emotions were so overpowering that he felt tears prick the backs of his eyes. He'd known that he had missed her, but until now he hadn't known that he'd *needed* her. When you live your life day to day, as he did, in hard physical labor, you work until you drop and then go home, go to bed, and then, in the morning, you start all over again. What had been missing was the reason for all that hard work, and his reason was Angela. She was the only woman he'd ever wanted to spend the rest of his life with.

He set her back on the floor, then they were kissing, and his life-support seemed to magically have been switched back on. This was what had been missing. This energy. This intense feeling of rightness. This meeting of two souls that belonged together.

Now he knew why it would never have worked with Shana Anderson.

She wasn't Angela.

Some part of Angela's thoughts were telling her this was wrong, kissing Padraic in the middle of Winn Dixie, but she figured this came under 'pardonable sins.' Besides, if happiness were legal tender on the world market, she would be a very rich woman.

Padraic loved her.

If that wasn't worth celebrating, what was?

When they finally parted, he gazed down at her with such tenderness, that her heart turned over with pure joy. "Let's get you home," he said softly.

Padraic took the heavy suitcase and the overstuffed suit bag, while she picked up the lighter bags. He reached back for her with his free hand. She took it, sighed contentedly, and said, "I love you, Padraic."

"Prove it by marrying me as soon as possible," was his reply.

"Okay," she said. And it was as simple as that. Sometimes life handed you lemonade.

NINE

A *fter writing letters to all four of her daughters and mailing a bundle of flyers about the upcoming reunion to family members from Alabama to Alaska, Sara found herself composing yet another letter.*

This one was addressed to a Mr. Robert Johnson who lived on Route 7. She took special care to make certain that every word in it was legible. When she'd finished writing it she sealed it, put the proper addresses on it, and as a final touch she lightly spritzed it with her favorite cologne.

Angela, who had been home nearly a week, walked into the kitchen and found her mother sitting at the table, spraying cologne on the letter.

It was nearly eleven on this Saturday morning, and her dad had taken the kids with him to the farmer's market where they were going to hawk late-season watermelons.

She sat down across from her mother and regarded her with questioning eyes. "Why are you putting your favorite perfume on that letter?"

Sara, looking very summery in a sleeveless pastel pink cotton blouse and a pair of cropped pants in turquoise, smiled up at her. "Just setting a trap."

"What kind of trap?"

"For your aunts."

Angela deftly reached across the table and snared the letter. After seeing her uncle's name and address on it, she narrowed her eyes at her mother. "Maybe you ought to explain what's going on before I come to the conclusion that you're cheating on Daddy with Uncle Robert."

Sara smiled triumphantly. "It'll do the trick, then."

"What'll do the trick? Start making sense, woman!"

Sara laughed shortly, and told her youngest daughter exactly what she had planned for the first day of the reunion. When she was done, she looked at Angela, trying to gauge her reaction to her plot.

Angela humphed. "After what they did, they deserve it. What can I do to help?"

Delighted to have another accomplice, Sara said, "Well, when your daddy gets back from the market, you can follow me over to Robert's place and leave my pick-up parked in his yard."

"Another bit of illusion?" Angela deduced.

"The more physical evidence, the better to convict me," said her devious mother.

Angela shook her head in wonder. "And I thought I met conniving people while working at a strip club."

She had told her parents how she'd earned a living in Miami. They had surprised her by not expressing disappointment in her. On the contrary, they had expressed relief at her coming out of the experience with a lesson learned, physically unharmed, and her mental health intact.

They were simply grateful to have her back home in one piece.

Sara laughed at her comment. "Honey, those aunts of yours are so devious and cunning they could put the deadliest mastermind criminals to shame. Let's be grateful that they didn't use their formidable skills for evil on a global scale, and concentrated on the local population."

Angela laughed. "Isn't there anything positive you can say about your sisters-in-law?"

"They're demons in the kitchen," Sara said. "And as far as I know, they've never poisoned anybody."

Angela laughed harder. "Their children turned out fine."

"Yes, because the aunts who were fortunate enough to marry found exceptional men to mate with. Their DNA was diluted, therefore the children were saved."

Angela got up from the table. "There's no winning an argument with you when it's The Biddies we're discussing. You've had too many years of warring with them. Do you think that after your stunt, you will be able to live in peace after all these years?"

"That depends on how they take the joke," her mother reasoned. "If not, we'll go to our graves disliking one another."

"You don't seem to care which way it goes," Angela observed.

Her mother shrugged. "I'll be the same old Sara no matter what."

Later that afternoon, Sara phoned Candace to ask if the children could stay with them until after the reunion.

Candace had been expecting the call. Her mother had phoned twice before with, "The children would like to stay another week, sweetie. Is it all right with you and Greg?"

Candace had given her permission both times. Today, however, she called her mother on the mat with, "Momma, are you keeping my children to insure that Greg and I will come to the reunion? You know, kidnapping is a federal offense."

Her mother had laughed at her assertion. "Darlin' child, I know you're coming to the reunion because you've said you'll be here. That's good enough for me. The children and your daddy and I are having a good time together, that's all. Today, they went to the farmer's market with him."

"Watermelons?" Candace guessed.

"Yeah, they sell really well this time of year. It's so hot, and everybody's having weekend get-togethers. Nothing is as refreshing as an ice-cold piece of melon."

"Don't I know it," Candace agreed. "I just cut the last one you all brought us when you came to kidnap our children."

"Do we have your permission?" her mother asked. She wisely ignored that last crack.

"Okay," said Candace, sighing with frustration. "But next year there will be no renegotiating. We miss them!"

"Oh, Darlin' I know you miss them. They miss you, too. Imagine what it's going to be like when you're reunited at the reunion."

Greg walked into the kitchen at that moment, and Candace mouthed, "Momma."

He nodded, acknowledging the communication that had passed between them.

"All right, Momma. Give everybody our love."

"Will do, sweetie. Kiss Greg for me."

Candace didn't think that was going to happen anytime soon. But she promised to do it, nonetheless. "Okay. Bye!"

Greg had gone to the refrigerator and gotten a pint of bottled water while she wrapped up her conversation with her mother. He looked at her now. "How is everybody?"

Candace, who had been in the garden when the phone rang, felt sweaty and grimy in her sleeveless polo shirt, shorts and gardening clogs.

Greg had also been doing yard work, but he fairly glowed with good health. Yes, he was perspiring but on him, it looked good.

She hated being this attracted to the traitor. He'd promised her Jacquelin would be their last child, and now he'd changed his mind.

"Candace?" he said softly.

Candace frowned and turned away. She was irritated with herself for losing her train of thought. He'd asked her how everyone was doing in Mason Corners, hadn't he? "Momma phoned to see if the kids could stay until after the reunion."

"That's over a week from now!"

She nodded. Her eyes held a hopeful aspect in them. Would Greg be so upset by her mother's proposal that he would get in the car and go pick up their children?

With the children here as a buffer between them, she would not feel his emotional appeal as intensely. Ever since he had brought up the subject of having another child, she had been in mental turmoil over her objections to it. Sure, he'd said he would not bring up the subject again, and he hadn't. But that didn't mean she was immune to his desires. They had been in love for so long that his desires were communicated to her over the airwaves, it seemed. He wanted another child. And no amount of silence between them was going to change that fact.

"I know," Candace said to his protest. "I told her okay, but if you're not fine with it I'll get on the phone now and tell her we'll come pick up the kids."

Greg's first instinct was to say, yeah, let's do it. However, when he thought about it, he knew that having the children here would only extend the miasma he and Candace found themselves in. An unwholesome atmosphere had settled over them. She'd pulled away from him in a way she'd never done before. He had disappointed her when he'd broken his promise that he would be satisfied with three children.

But he'd said he wouldn't broach the subject again, and he hadn't. Why wasn't she happy with that? No, she wanted him to squirm. She wanted him to feel bad for wanting another child, and he wasn't going to go there. There was nothing wrong with wanting to have another child with the woman he loved. He was not going to apologize for it!

"Mmm," he said thoughtfully as he peered into her upturned face. "Maybe they *should* stay a little longer. We'll be going there soon, anyway. As long as they're having fun."

Candace looked piqued and turned away. "Okay, then," she said, calmly. Calmer than she really felt, he bet. Her long ponytail swished as she almost violently turned back around to regard him. "I guess I'll get back to my gardening."

Greg watched her shapely hips move in those shorts. Her long, gorgeous legs were calling to him. He wanted her. They hadn't made love in over two weeks.

She wanted him, too. He'd seen the way she'd looked at him not five minutes ago. Her passion matched his, always had. Why was she so stubborn?

"Candace?" He set the bottle of water on the counter and walked toward her.

She gracefully pivoted to face him. "Yes?"

He took off his sleeveless tee shirt and turned around. "I think I was bitten by a wasp or something. Would you take a look for me?"

Candace's concern instantly kicked in. She went closer, her gentle fingers touching his broad back. "Where?"

Greg inwardly shivered at the slightest touch from her. He could have sworn she had felt it, too. "On my right shoulder?"

Candace squinted. She didn't see a thing. No reddening of his skin nor any telltale puffiness that would surely be there if he'd been bitten by an insect.

"I don't see anything," she reported.

She placed a kiss in the middle of his back. "There, that's better."

Greg closed his eyes and exhaled softly. Sensual pleasure suffused him.

Candace wrapped her arms around his waist from behind and laid her cheek on his back. "I've missed you so much."

Greg didn't move. He let her embrace him. He reveled in it. "I haven't been anywhere," he said, his tone tender.

He felt her tears on his skin when she started to cry. He turned and pulled her against his chest. Looking deeply into her eyes, he said, "I can't help wanting more children with you. I won't say I'm sorry for feeling that way, because I'm not. But I'm happy with what we have, here and now, and I'm not going to dwell on it if we never have another child. The time I have with you is too precious for regrets."

Candace blinked back her tears. "Do you know how hard it is for me to deny you anything that you want with all your heart? It's tearing me up inside!"

"I'm sorry, baby, so sorry." Greg found himself saying the very words he'd vowed he would not say. However, now that he had heard her side of the conflict, he knew that he had caused her pain. It didn't matter that it had never been his intention to do so. He would move heaven and earth to give her whatever she wanted. Why had it not occurred to him that she felt the same way and would feel pressured to deliver when he expressly wished for something that was within her abilities to give him?

It would be eating him up inside, too, if he had been unable to give her her heart's desire.

He kissed her forehead repeatedly. "I'm such a stupid-head."

Candace laughed. That was Sarafina's favorite insult to her brother.

She kissed his chin. "No, you're not. You just love babies."

Greg took advantage of her lips' close proximity to his and bent his head to kiss her. They both sighed with the sheer pleasure of finally locking lips again.

Throughout their marriage, as both of them would attest, their love had ebbed and flowed. Sometimes life felt downright *routine* what with taking care of the kids and working everyday. They almost felt as if they were roommates working toward a common purpose, the kids' well-being. At other times, like now, they were so deeply in love that their passion threatened to consume them. In and out of love, there was invariably a deep respect for one another. Respect sustained them in times when the passion ebbed. And an abiding love underneath the surface always brought them back to moments like this, when passion burned.

They could not get to the bedroom fast enough.

Later, their passion spent for the moment, they slept in each other's arms.

ଔଔ

The week the reunion was set to begin Sara was so busy taking care of last-minute details like making sure the rental company brought the tent in time and properly set it up; and touching bases with the men, all relatives, who were in charge of the gas grills and the jumbo frying vats they'd be frying fish in on the first day of the festivities, that she had little time to wonder if her efforts to ensnare The Biddies was actually working or not.

Therefore, she would have been pleased to find out that three days after she mailed the letter to Robert, his sister, Beatrice, went to his house and knocked on his door. When there was no answer, and she could hear music playing inside, she guessed that Robert was just being his usual ornery self, and ignoring her.

A tall, gaunt woman in her early fifties, she wore a long tunic over an even longer skirt, and flats. Holding the tuna casserole in both hands after balancing it in one in order to knock on the door (she didn't know why Robert wouldn't invest in a doorbell); she set the casserole on the slat-back rocker on the porch.

Mumbling to herself, she walked back down the steps, and headed to her car. Emmett half-heartedly growled at her. Already irritated, she growled back at him, sending him scurrying under the house, which sat high off the ground. He peered out at her from his safe hidey-hole.

Smiling with satisfaction, she continued to her car. Why was she wasting her time coming out here with food for Robert? He didn't appreciate it. However, he did leave the clean dishes on the porch after he was finished with them. She supposed in a way that amounted to communication. He *could* toss the casseroles into the yard for Emmett.

When she got to her car, she stared at the pick-up truck she'd parked directly behind. If she didn't know better, she'd think it belonged to that busybody, Sara. It looked just like the blue Ford she drove.

Having never noticed the tag number of the truck Sara drove, she had no way of corroborating that this truck was one and the same. Anyway, why would Sara's truck be parked in Robert's yard?

She glanced around a moment or two looking at the yard, which was neat, trying to find some sign that Robert was letting things go. He wasn't. It probably gave him great pleasure to prove them wrong. They'd cast aspersions on his good character when he had forced them out of his life, saying the place would go to ruin without them to take care of it. Beatrice was woman enough to admit she had been wrong.

Of course, since he wouldn't talk to them, she would not get the opportunity to tell him that. While her other sisters still carried a grudge, she had grown up. She sincerely wanted to make peace.

Her gaze lit on something she hadn't notice when she'd driven in, her mind had been so focused on that unidentified pick-up truck: Robert hadn't come outside to retrieve his mail yet. The red flag was still raised on the battered silver mailbox.

She could at least walk over there and get his mail for him, and leave it beside the casserole in the rocking chair on the porch.

When she had the mail in her hands, she made a conscious effort not to look down at it. It wasn't her business who was sending Robert mail. However, the scent of cologne wafted up and she could not help inhaling it. Surely Robert didn't subscribe to women's magazines. Then why was that scent so prevalent? In fact, there were no magazines in the bundle of mail in her hand.

Now, her curiosity was piqued. A quick shuffle through the letters wouldn't hurt. What if Robert was seeing someone? It wasn't too late for him to become romantically involved with a nice woman. He was only in his early sixties, and he enjoyed relative good health. He was too thin, but what were you to do when he wouldn't eat enough to keep weight on him?

He probably found eating alone depressing. Someone to eat with could very well boost his appetite.

Beatrice riffled through the mail as she walked to the house.

Finally, here was the culprit, a personal letter, quite thick, written on nice stationery. She was smiling until she noted the handwriting. There was no mistaking that particular cursive writing. She'd been seeing it for the past forty odd years. It belonged to her sister-in-law, and she only had one sister-in-law, Sara.

She paused in her tracks. Even if she had been mistaken about the handwriting, Sara had put her return address on the envelope. Now, why would Sara send a perfumed letter to her brother-in-law? It made no sense.

Maybe as she was sealing the envelope, cologne had spilled on it. No, there would be a stain on the envelope and it was pristine, not a mark on it except for the postmark.

She sniffed the envelope. That was definitely Sara's scent. The woman hadn't changed colognes since she'd been married to Jack. Some expensive French perfume, Chanel something. She'd heard Sara say that Jack only bought it for her on very special occasions, like their anniversary. Jack was a farmer, and they were frugal by nature. He didn't have to be, though, because his farm was extremely profitable and then there was the thousand acres. His girls were going to have to split it when he and Sara died.

There were no sons to leave the land to.

Beatrice got hold of herself. No use crying over spilled milk. Her parents had not seen fit to leave part of the property to their five daughters. They figured it would be the sons who would run the place, and it would be the sons who left behind more Johnson male heirs to inherit in perpetuity. The joke was on them.

Jack had no sons, only four daughters. And Robert didn't have any children at all, that she knew of.

Men like him could have a few outside children that nobody in the family knew existed. Some part of her *wished* that he did have a son he could leave the farm to.

Her son, nor any of the sons belonging to her sisters, had expressed any interest in running the family farm. As for Jack's daughters, all of them, except for the youngest who had just returned from Miami, were spread out over the United States. She couldn't imagine any of them coming back home to run the family farm.

When Robert died, the old Johnson farm would probably be sold.

She hated to admit it, but one thing that evil troll, Sara, had been right about was that she and her sisters should have shown more of an interest in the farm while they had the chance. Instead of burning their bridges behind them, perhaps one of their sons would have been close to his Uncle Robert and been prepped to step in his shoes one day. But it was too late now.

Almost as if she were having an out-of-body experience, Beatrice slipped Sara's letter into the deep pocket of her skirt, and put the remaining mail next to the casserole in the rocker.

She turned and hurried to her car.

When she was behind the wheel, she felt as if the letter were burning a hole in her pocket. Guilt and excitement coursed through her.

She started the car and backed out of the driveway.

TEN

*W*hy are you steaming it open?" cried Ruth. "Rip that sucker, and let's get on with the show. Let's see what Miss Sara said in her love letter to Robert."

Beatrice carefully held the letter in the vapor coming from the teapot. "I'm going to put the letter back in his mailbox, remember? I can't just rip it open."

"You're all going to hell for this," Esther said. She'd gone and gotten herself saved. Now, she was constantly predicting they'd all go to hell for one sin or another.

"Not if we find out something really juicy about Sara," Ruby said, almost licking her lips in anticipation. "She's the one who'll be going to hell."

All of the sisters favored each other. They were tall, trim women in their fifties or early sixties, with medium brown skin and hair styles ranging from braids to a long weave, or two. Except for Deborah whose husband was also a wonderful cook. They competed in the kitchen, making delicious dishes that they also consumed. She now tipped the scales at two-hundred pounds. Not surprisingly, she was the most good-natured of her sisters. She told them on a regular basis that if they would eat something a bit more substantial than salads they wouldn't be so angry all the time.

Deborah didn't offer any comment. She simply sat and watched and nibbled on a blueberry muffin. They were gathered at her house. She'd made the muffins especially for them and none of them had touched one yet.

Beatrice removed the letter from the stream of steam and shook it delicately. Then she went and sat down at the kitchen table across from

Deborah who was the only sister sitting at that moment. The rest hovered over her shoulder, hoping to read whatever was in the letter as soon as she pulled it from the envelope.

She gingerly peeled the flap away from the envelope. This done, she shook the letter out onto the tabletop, and picked it up.

Spreading its folds flat, she read:

Dearest Robert,

I can't live with a lie any longer. I'm going to tell Jack that Candace is your child and divorce him. Enough sneaking around, I want to declare to the world that I love you and I want to be with you. Jack will just have to live with it. And after all this time, Candace deserves to know who her real father is. I'm going to tell him at the reunion. All of his family will be around him. It should be easier for him to bear with them there.

Yours now and forever,
Sara

"How thoughtful of her," said Ruth dryly. "To wait and tell him when he's surrounded by his loved ones."

Laughing with utter delight, Ruby said, "We were right all these years! I can't believe we were right." She shook her head in amazement.

"I can't either," said Deborah. "I never believed Robert was Candace's father. I just went along with you witches."

"Then what are you doing here?" asked Ruby, testily.

"This is my house. You invited yourselves. You're my sisters, what was I going to do, tell you not to come?"

"Your house is centrally located," Beatrice said by way of an explanation. She looked down at the letter almost sadly. "As thick as the envelope was, I thought there would be more. She used thick stationery."

"You want more?" cried Esther. "Isn't that enough? Sara is getting ready to break our brother's heart. We've got to do something!"

"Exactly what do you suggest?" asked Ruby.

"I don't know," Esther said. "I need to pray about it. Why don't we all hold hands and ask the Lord to give us strength?"

"Are you forgetting that we're gathered here in order to find incriminating evidence on Sara so that we can stick it to her?" asked Ruth. "I don't think God is going to put His blessing on that!"

"Will you all just sit down and stop yelling?" Deborah asked, calmly.

The standing sisters each pulled out a chair and sat down. The five of them looked from one to the other, expecting an idea to materialize out of thin air, perhaps.

Esther bowed her head and closed her eyes.

Her sisters looked away, giving her a modicum of privacy to commune with God. They remained silent, blowing air between their lips intermittently.

After about five minutes, Esther raised her head and smiled at them. "I think we ought to ignore it, and simply be there to support Jack after Sara plunges the knife in his heart."

"I agree with that," Deborah said at once. "What else can we do? Get to the reunion early, pull Jack aside and show him the letter?"

"That's precisely what we should do!" Ruby exclaimed, her eyes glittering with malice. "Sara and Robert, who have obviously been carrying on an affair for I don't know how long, don't deserve our consideration. You heard what she said in her letter, 'Enough sneaking around.' They should be made to pay for what they've done to poor Jack. Let's give him the option of putting her out of the house instead of waiting and giving her the chance to break him. Jack is the one we should be concerned about."

"Jack and *Candace*," Deborah said, quietly. "I've always felt bad for letting her hear us talking about Sara and Robert. Even if it is true, it was a mean-spirited thing to do. If we had a problem with Sara, we should have targeted Sara, not a child. I hope she doesn't remember any of it."

"Of course, she doesn't," Ruby said. "She was a child back then. How much do you remember from *your* childhood?"

"Now, be honest," Esther said. "The last time one of us said something in Candace's hearing she must have been around twelve or thirteen. I think she remembers. Is she close to any of us? No. There's a reason for that. We should be on our knees asking God to forgive us for what we did, right after we ask *her* to forgive us."

"You mean you want us to apologize to Candace?" Ruth asked, surprised.

"Yes," said Esther.

"But what if she doesn't remember anything?" Ruth wondered. "We'd be apologizing for nothing. No, I won't apologize. I suggest we forget about it. She probably has."

"Anyway," said Ruby. "It's true, so we don't need to apologize for anything."

"Keep thinking that way," Esther warned. "As if you don't have to atone for the bad things you've done in the past. She was a child, and what we did could have negatively affected her. We won't know until we talk to her about it."

"Candace is forty-one years old. She's got a gorgeous husband and three beautiful children. She doesn't seem as if she's suffered any to me!" Ruby said angrily. "You and Deborah are a couple of softies. You've changed over the years. No matter what, we were sisters and we always stuck together. We used to have so much fun together. Now, all we do is argue."

"I'm leaning toward Deborah and Esther," Beatrice said, softly. "I think there has already been enough bad blood between members of this family. A family reunion is about togetherness, not divisiveness. What's going on with Sara and Jack and Robert is tragic, but it's their business. I think we should stay out of it, and support Jack later on."

Deborah smiled. "That's three against two. Then, the verdict is, we stay out of it."

"I don't have to listen to you witches," Ruby yelled as she got up so abruptly that she pushed the table forward and almost upended her chair. "I'm going to tell Jack about that letter, and you can't stop me."

She eyed the letter in Beatrice's hand.

Beatrice firmly held onto the letter. "I won't give you this letter, Ruby."

Ruby grabbed her purse from the countertop and rushed out the backdoor, slamming it behind her.

"Hey!" cried Ruth, running after her. "I came with you. Wait up!"

The three remaining sisters sat around the kitchen table with tired expressions on their faces. "I'm too old for all this drama," said Deborah. She reached for another blueberry muffin. "Will you two skinny Minnies eat something?"

Beatrice smiled, picked up a muffin, bit into it and pronounced it, "Delicious."

Esther also partook. "I'm ravenous. I haven't eaten anything all day."

"Esther," Deborah said. "It's after four in the afternoon. You'd better eat two."

∽∾

Early on the morning of August 17th, family members began arriving at the farm.

They came in economy cars, vans, SUVs, RVs, pick-up trucks and pick-up trucks with trailers attached. They came singly, or with families comprised of numerous siblings, the largest of which was a family of ten from Mobile, Alabama.

By seven o'clock in the morning, Sara had the men out in front of the huge royal blue tent frying fish for the crowd.

Jack pulled her aside and joked, "All we need now is for Jesus to come and do a repeat of the miracle of the loaves and fishes."

"Just don't ask him to turn the water into wine," Sara said. "I think some of the cousins brought enough for everybody."

She gestured toward a RV parked on the grass a few yards from the tent. Two male cousins in their twenties were laboring under the weight of a keg of beer. They got it to ground and then one of them tapped it, and filled a tall clear plastic cup with the brew.

"It's a little too early for spirits, don't you think?" said Sara, hoping Jack would take the hint and go speak with the early drinkers.

He did. "Excuse me," he said, as he sauntered over to them.

Sara watched as he approached them, and soon had them laughing about something or other. They were putting the keg back into the RV inside of five minutes.

Sara turned away from the scene, and spotted Candace and Greg walking across the grass. Candace had on a white summer dress with purple orchids on it, a pair of low-heeled, comfortable natural-toned leather sandals, and a white floppy hat.

Greg was wearing a pair of his favorite worn jeans, a purple polo shirt that displayed his arm and chest muscles to perfection and athletic shoes. Sara smiled. Her daughter certainly had married a fine, strapping boy. She'd liked him from the start.

She hugged both of them. "You two look well-rested. Are you sure you want to take the children back home with you? We have excellent *schools* around here."

"I want my children, and I want them now!" Candace said, laughing as she looked around what looked like fair grounds. "Where are they?"

"They went to Winn Dixie with Angela and Padraic to pick up the ice I ordered."

Candace pursed her lips. "You've been working my poor children to death, haven't you?"

"Yes," Sara said, unashamed. "And they've loved every minute of it."

They began walking back to the house. "You and Greg are staying at the house, right?"

"Well, we did get a room at a bed and breakfast," Greg said. "Because we figured you'd be booked up."

"I was young once," Sara told her son-in-law. "If you and Candace want your privacy, just say so."

"We want our privacy, Momma Sara."

A grin split Sara's pleasant face. "There you go! Glad to hear it." Her eyes fairly sparkled with good humor. "Debra and Juan and Sharon and Simon are staying at the house, so we have plenty of company."

Upon hearing her sister Sharon had brought a man with her, Candace expressed delight. "Sharon's seeing someone special?"

"From the looks of things I'd say they're in love," Sara said. "I'm hoping for a wedding very soon."

"Momma, you won't scare the poor man off!" Candace said, firmly.

Sara appealed to Greg. "Darlin' did I scare you when we first met?"

"A little," Greg admitted. "Then you tried to stuff an entire pie down my gullet, and I warmed to you."

"See, Candace," Sara said. "I'm a pussycat."

When they got to the house, Candace and Greg sat on the porch while Sara went inside to see how the women were coming along with the side dishes that would be served later today. The men were barbecuing pork ribs, chicken, and thick sausages. The women were preparing vast amounts of garden salad, potato salad, baked beans, and macaroni and cheese. Sara's stove had a double oven, and the refrigerator would not be out of place in any restaurant, it was so huge. She was used to feeding crowds.

She had left the desserts up to The Biddies who were bakers nonpareil. She hadn't been exaggerating when she'd said that they were demons in the kitchen. They could definitely burn. Besides, they loved the accolades they received when people bit into their delectable pound cakes, pies and cobblers.

Padraic and Angela pulled into the yard in his big truck, the children riding on the back amid piles of crushed ice in huge plastic bags. Candace and Greg were instantly out of their chairs and hurrying down the porch's steps when they saw their children.

The children, in their excitement, leaped from the back of the truck like tough country children, Candace noted. They'd been on the farm for six weeks, and they were so self-assured, glowing with health, and (if her eyes were not deceiving her) had each grown taller since she'd last seen them.

She hugged each of them in turn. Jacquelin, first, who ran into her arms so roughly that she almost knocked her over. She kissed the top of her youngest child's head. Jacquelin had her arms wrapped around her waist.

She gazed up at her mother with love. "Momma, I missed you so much. I like the farm, but I don't think I want to be away from you for this long ever again!"

"All right, baby, you don't have to," Candace assured her tenderly.

Sarafina was less dramatic, but no less happy to see her.

"I missed you, too. But I'm glad you and Daddy let us come. I learned a lot, and I met kids who don't live like us. It was an enlightening experience. We've got a lot to be grateful for, Momma. But we must never forget that the reason we're put on this earth is to help others."

Her Sarafina: always profound. "No, sweetie, we must never forget that."

Gregory simply hugged her tightly. When he peered down into her upturned face, she expected him to refer to her in a more mature fashion, given his edifying experience here on the farm. But he grinned at her and said, "Mommy, you're a sight for sore eyes." Then he kissed her cheek, something he'd stopped doing when he was around five years old.

Soon after that, they ran to help Angela and Padraic take the ice through the backdoor to store in the big freezer in the kitchen.

Candace turned to Greg. "Okay, one more. But after that, you and I have got to discuss the dreaded V-word. I'm not going back on the pill."

Greg picked her up and spun her around. "Vasectomy. See, I said it!"

As far as he was concerned, a vasectomy was worth the price of another child.

Candace, however, wasn't convinced of his veracity.

"Let's see how enthusiastic you are when you get on the operating table."

The rest of the day, they mingled with relatives and the occasional ex-schoolmate who showed up when he or she heard about the reunion. All of the Johnson girls had made many friends while in school, and since the reunion was being held in August, a summer month, some of them were also home to see family, so they dropped by.

Not long after she and Greg had gotten there, Debra came back from showing her husband around town. Candace had seen pictures of the two of them together, but she had never met Juan. A Mexican American, his skin was as dark as Debra's and he wore his dark brown hair in a conservative cut. He and Debra made a lovely couple, and Candace told them that. That is, after she had hugged her sister and had successfully fought back tears. Greg and Juan shook hands and immediately began talking to each other as if they were old friends.

Candace pulled Debra aside. "Girl, you look good. Healthy, fit. Juan must be doing something right!"

Debra grinned. "I could say the same for you. Here you are the oldest of the Johnson girls and you look like the youngest. I've missed you so much. You
and Greg are an inspiration to me. You know that, don't you?"

Their conversation was interrupted by a yell from Angela. "Ladies, look who I was finally able to track down!"

Sharon came running to embrace her sisters. All four of them were together now. Candace was certain that every last one of them would remember this day differently, but as for her, she felt complete once more.

She had been six when Debra was born, nine when Sharon came along and nearly sixteen when her parents sprang baby, Angela, on them. She had practically raised these girls. She'd changed all of their diapers, combed their hair, read them stories.

They had cried on her shoulder when princes turned out to be frogs.

She'd consoled them through crises, big and small.

No wonder she felt almost like a mother to them.

Now, she looked at them. They were women, beautiful, accomplished women!

They wound up in a group hug. "I'm so proud of all of you!" Candace cried happily as she kissed their cheeks. "The Johnson girls are all grown up."

Momentarily, they parted and regarded each other. "Can we talk about those Mafioso tactics Momma used in those letters she wrote us?" Sharon joked.

To which her sisters burst out laughing and shared the contents of their individual letters. When they had each revealed the good, the bad and the ugly their mother had pointed out in her letters to them, Candace said, "Well, mission accomplished. Call Sara Johnson what you will, but she achieves what she sets out to do."

"Our mother, the efficiency expert," Angela said.

"The miracle worker," Sharon offered.

"The terminator!" Debra said, laughing.

ELEVEN

*J**ack!" Jack was making his way across the deep front yard with three restaurant-size pans of food.* His destination was the open-air tent where tables were set up for the evening meal.

He didn't have to turn around to know that it was his sister, Ruby, addressing him. And he had a pretty good idea as to why she'd come looking for him.

"Ruby, these pans are heavy, and Sara's in a state. If I don't get them out to the tent soon, it's my butt."

Ruby walked around him and lifted the aluminum-foil covered pan on top, making his burden lighter. "No problem. I'll walk with you."

"Thanks," Jack said.

They fell into step beside one another.

"What can I help you with?" he asked, pleasantly.

It was a lovely evening. The heat had subsided, and there was a gentle breeze. Jack enjoyed the sight of children ripping and running, and grown folks either standing near the tent, or sitting in lawn chairs of various shapes and sizes.

It had been a wonderful first day of the reunion. A day he would remember when he recalled the halcyon days of his past.

He smiled down at his sister. "Cat got your tongue?"

Ruby had been trying to form the words in her mind. It wasn't that she hadn't given much thought as to how she would approach Jack. She'd thought of little else the past three days. But now that she was here she realized that she didn't want to hurt Jack. He was the purest soul she knew.

And while she hated Sara and Robert for what they were doing behind his back, she hesitated to tell Jack about it.

"Jack, if you knew somebody was cheating on someone you loved would you tell him or her about it, or keep it to yourself?"

Jack didn't have to ponder the question. "I've always make it a point to stay out of other people's personal business, Ruby. No, I wouldn't tell my friend his wife was cheating on him. No matter how close you are to someone, you can't truly know what's going on in his marriage. I had a friend once who was beating his wife in secret. I didn't know about it until he got arrested and phoned me to post bail for him. I was so shocked, I let him stay in jail. He never spoke to me again. But that's okay. His wife left him, and I hear she's doing fine now. Why? Do you know someone in the family who's cheating? If so, don't tell me about it. Please. The last thing I want to hear on a fine day like this is bad news."

"That's a fine position to take!" Ruby said. "You can't help if you don't get involved."

They were at the tent now and she marched inside, deposited the pan on one of the long tables and walked back out, her bottom lip protruding. Jack, who was just going inside the tent with his pan smiled at her. "Ruby, don't 'out' anyone here today. If somebody's cheating, you can wait until after the reunion to spill the beans, can't you? As a favor to me?"

Ruby narrowed her eyes at him. "Jack, you are just too oblivious to what's going on around you to live!" After that, she stormed out.

Jack could barely contain his laughter. One sister foiled.

He wondered which of them would approach him next.

He didn't have long to wonder because by the time he had walked back to the house, Beatrice was waiting for him outside the backdoor.

"Hey, baby brother," she said, smiling, her tone friendly.

Jack returned her smile. "Beatrice, it's good to see you. Are the kids coming?"

Beatrice's children, a son and a daughter both lived out of state.

"Yeah, they'll be here tomorrow more than likely. They had to work."

The reunion was being held from Friday through Sunday. Most of those who couldn't get time off from work on this day would be arriving the next day.

"Good, good," said Jack.

Beatrice stepped forward, placing her hand gently upon his arm. "Jack, has Ruby or Ruth spoken to you about anything important today?"

Jack rubbed his chin. "Ruby said something about somebody being cheated on, but I couldn't make head nor tail of what she was getting at. I told her that if anybody was cheating I didn't want to hear about."

Beatrice looked so relieved that Jack nearly burst out laughing. What was up with his sisters? Did they have a bet on as to which of them would give him the bad news first? "Why? Is something the matter?"

"No, no!" cried Beatrice. "Good. I'd avoid both Ruth and Ruby if I were you." She sighed. "Well, I'd better go. I have cakes and pies to deliver to the tent before dinner starts."

Then she said something Jack hadn't heard from her since they were kids. "I love you, baby brother."

Slightly stunned, Jack nevertheless smiled. "I love you, too, Beatrice."

Her eyes were misty as she departed.

Jack sniffed back a tear or two, himself, before entering the kitchen. This was not going as he and Sara and Robert had expected it to. They had assumed the sisters would form a united front against Sara and gleefully expose her as the cheating wife she appeared to be. But it seemed, to him, that there were two camps, and one was decidedly less vengeful than the other.

Interesting.

Meanwhile, across the grounds, Robert was sitting outside on the steps of a RV with one of his cousins shooting the bull and enjoying a beer or three when Esther walked up to him and knocked his can of beer out of his hand.

Robert got to his feet and glaring at her, cried, "Woman have you lost your mind?"

"No, I haven't," yelled Esther. Remembering that she was a Christian woman she apologized to the startled cousin. "Excuse me, Jacob, but this brother of mine and I need to have a word in private."

"I'm not going anywhere with you," Robert declared.

"You're not, huh?" Esther said. "Oh, you don't care if I put your business in the streets?"

Robert was obstinate. He stood with his arms akimbo, meeting her gaze with no fear in his whatsoever.

Esther humphed. She tiptoed and whispered in his ear, "I know you're Candace's father."

"Excuse us for a minute, Jacob," Robert hurriedly said, grabbing Esther painfully by the arm and leading her away from the RV.

The muscles in Esther's legs were complaining by the time he paused in his tracks.

"Okay, so you know," he said, a bit breathlessly. "Sara and I are trying to handle it so that nobody gets hurt. You stay out of it! If Jack or Candace finds out from anyone other than me or Sara it could be bad, real bad."

Esther laughed. She stared up at Robert as if he were one step from the loony bin.

"There is no way that you and Sara are going to prevent Jack from being hurt, you fool! He loves that woman. Why? We have never been able to understand, but he does. He loves her! Now, what *you're* going to do is quit her. Quit her and never have anything else to do with her. You two are too old to be running away together. This ain't no romance novel for senior citizens!"

"I'll never give her up!" Robert said, vehemently. His thin face was a mass of frowns. "And you and the other Biddies had better stay out of it if you know what's good for you. That's my final warning."

"You don't scare me, you randy old coot!"

"I know that son of yours is out of work again," Robert said, plotting. "And I could give him a job. I could very well make him my heir if he showed an aptitude for farming and had any interest in hard work."

That gave Esther pause. It was true. Her son, Teddy, had been fired from yet another high-level job. It wasn't that the boy was dumb. He simply did not work well with others. He was too independent. If he saw that something could be done more efficiently his way, he did it, no matter what company policy dictated. He was too smart for his own good. Two college degrees and he wasn't using either of them.

A farmer was an independent thinker. Nobody was the boss of him. And Teddy enjoyed working outdoors. Maybe farming would be an excellent choice for him.

The carrot Robert was holding in front of her was tempting.

But, she wasn't biting.

"No, Robert! Teddy will just have to make a way for himself. I love Jack, and I'm fighting for him. You and Sara have to call it quits, or else!"

"Or else what?" asked Sara, her tone laced with humor.

Esther spun around to find Sara, Jack, Candace, her husband, Greg, and her sisters walking toward them. She couldn't have been more shocked if aliens had landed in the field close by and started disembarking.

"Cousin Jacob came running to the house saying you two were fighting," Jack explained. "Said you'd knocked a can of beer out of Robert's hand and had demanded to speak to him alone or there would be hell to pay. Then, he dragged you off."

Esther couldn't very well say Jacob was full of beans because she was guilty of everything he'd reported to them. She was, frankly, speechless. She was grateful when Beatrice and Deborah came to stand on either side of her, offering what comfort they could, given the present situation.

It was Beatrice who spoke first. "Okay, I think we all heard enough to know that the pretense is up." She turned to Robert. "Robert, I stole a letter that Sara wrote to you from your mailbox." Twisting around, she regarded Sara. "Sara, you know what was in the letter since you wrote it." Then it was

Candace's turn. "Candace, I'm sorry that you had to hear this in this manner. I'm also sorry that we were so jealous of Sara back in the day that we resorted to saying evil things about her when you, an innocent child, was within hearing distance. We had no proof that you were actually Robert's child. We assumed it because you were born only six months after Jack's and Sara's marriage. The possibility existed that you *could* be. Sara had dated Robert not long before the wedding, after all. But, even if we had irrefutable proof, it was still a vicious thing to do to a child. I hope you can find it in your heart to forgive us someday."

Candace stepped forward and opened her arms to her Aunt Beatrice. Beatrice eagerly accepted the proffered hug. When they parted, Candace said, "I do forgive you, Aunt Beatrice. You've admitted what you did, and now I think that we should move forward and stop being a family divided by misplaced hatred." She smiled at all five of her aunts in turn. "Momma and Uncle Robert were never intimate. They told me that themselves."

"I wouldn't touch that woman with a ten-foot pole," Robert said with a laugh.

"You'd never get the chance!" Sara returned with alacrity.

Candace laughed. "Okay, I think we have that settled. There was nothing romantic going on between Momma and Uncle Robert. But, apparently, there was something very romantic going on between Momma and Daddy before the wedding."

"We were young and in love," Jack said, winking at Sara.

"And frisky as all get-out," Sara added.

"So, you see," Candace continued, her cheeks hot from embarrassment due to her mother's last comment, "I was born early because Momma and Daddy got busy when they should have waited until *after* the wedding."

"What about that letter!" Ruby demanded to know. She moved around those blocking her way and went to stand in front of Sara, her eyes full of malice.

"It was bait to trap you," Sara said, a smile on her lips. "That and my truck parked in front of Robert's house. All I wanted was for you all to confess to what you'd done to Candace, and to my reputation."

"Mine, too!" Robert spoke up.

"I've got my pound of flesh," Sara said, peaceably. "Everything is out in the open. Candace and I are closer than we've ever been thanks to the fact that she finally told me what was bothering her. Because of you, she'd begun to think less of me. You all achieved that with your *amusing* banter around impressionable ears. She grew up wondering if Jack was really her father, or if her Uncle Robert was. A child needs to feel safe and secure about her parents. You stole that from her. But since Candace is willing to forgive you, so am I."

All the fight went out of Ruby. "I spent more than forty years hating you. It ain't going to be easy to give that up."

"Life ain't easy," said Sara, cheerfully.

Ruby laughed in spite of herself. She turned and rapidly walked away. Waving her hand at all of them in a dismissive gesture, she said in parting, "Oh, heck, this is too much for me to take in one day. Y'all enjoy the reunion. I'm going home."

"Anybody else want to leave?" Sara asked.

"Not me," said Deborah stepping in front of Candace with outstretched arms. "I'm sorry, baby."

Candace hugged her tightly. "Thanks, Aunt Deborah."

"Me, too," said Esther.

Candace hugged her, as well.

Ruth ambled slowly toward Candace. Tears were in her eyes. "If I had known how much my words would hurt you, I would never have said them."

She sobbed in Candace's arms.

The next day, Robert got the chance to speak with Teddy.

It was midday when Teddy arrived in a sweet ride, a bright red Mini Cooper convertible trimmed in white. He'd driven alone from Atlanta.

Robert was in the backyard draining water off the melted ice in a huge cooler. Bossy Sara had given him the assignment. He had to remember to stay out of her field of vision if he didn't want to be put to work.

"Uncle Robert," Teddy said as he entered the backyard. "How are you? I haven't seen you in nearly two years."

Robert looked up. The boy had braids in his hair, was wearing a baseball jersey, and baggy britches. His white athletic shoes were so immaculate they almost hurt his eyes to look at them. Robert's first thought was, *That ain't no farmer.*

He had to give the boy credit for not being soft, though. He obviously didn't mind sweating. He didn't appear to have any excess flesh on him. Although, who could really tell what was underneath with how baggy young folks wore their clothing nowadays?

His face was lean and hungry-looking. His eyes were serious, even though he was trying to appear all sunshine and light. Robert didn't miss anything when he had his glasses on. And, he did.

He finished draining the cooler.

Teddy was used to his taciturn manner. Robert had a reputation for speaking very little, but when he spoke it behooved you to listen. So, Teddy patiently waited.

"Grab this here cooler and take it inside," said Robert.

Teddy did as he was told.

When they got inside, Robert ordered him to fill the cooler with soft drinks of various flavors. Then he told him to cover them with ice. This done, he grasped one handle of the six foot cooler and told Teddy to grab the other.

As they walked out the door and toward the royal blue tent, Robert said, "I hear that you got fired from another job. Is that true?"

"Yes, sir," Teddy said, his voice sounding neither offended nor self-pitying. He was simply stating a fact.

His uncle respected him for that.

"You own that car you drove up in?"

"Me and the bank," said Teddy.

"Well, then, it's the bank's," said Robert, astutely.

Teddy didn't deny it. He was in hock up to his ears. In the city, appearances meant everything. So what if you went home to peanut butter and jelly sandwiches for dinner every night? You drove a fine automobile, and that's what counted.

He wished he could leave all that behind and live a simpler life, a debt-free life. If that were really possible in the twenty-first century. He'd read somewhere that the average tax paying American was at least twenty thousand dollars in the hole. That was about the amount he owed the credit card companies.

After they had delivered the cooler to the tent, Robert said, "Walk with me, I want to talk with you about something."

Biting his bottom lip, betraying the fact that his uncle intimidated him, Teddy said, "All right. What do you want to talk about?"

Robert walked slowly. Teddy, who did practically everything swiftly, had to adjust his pace to his uncle's. He peered closely at the old guy as they walked. He was thinner than he remembered. His hair was a bit grayer too. But he sensed that his spirit was still as strong and stubborn as it had always been. He'd admired his Uncle Robert all his life.

"You remember working in melons when you were a teenager?" Robert asked.

"Yes, sir." He'd been young, strong and full of energy back then. He and the guys in the field had been so fit that they'd tossed the huge watermelons to each other when Uncle Robert wasn't looking. If a melon slipped and fell, the cost was taken out of their paychecks. Uncle Robert knew how to squeeze a dollar until it screamed. Now, Teddy knew that his uncle had had to keep an eye on the bottom line because profits were hard to come by when you ran a farm. That's another reason he admired his uncle, farming was worthwhile work. He didn't derive much pleasure from the business world. He had a degree in economics, and a degree in accounting. Heavy, that's what they called him in high school and in college. Meaning he learned easily and retained the information with little effort.

Everything came easily to him, it seems. Maybe that's why he didn't appreciate it.

Maybe if he were immersed in something challenging, got out of his element, was made to call upon his reserves of strength and resiliency he knew he possessed deep down, way down, inside then maybe he'd finally feel some satisfaction and be able to live a rich, purposeful life.

"You planning on going back to Atlanta?"

"I gave up my apartment. I'm kinda living out of my car now."

"You can't live on your parents, son. It ain't right and it affords you little dignity."

Truer words were never spoken, Teddy thought. "I don't plan to, sir."

"You can come work for me," his uncle suggested. "You would live on the farm and I would require a one-year contract. That means you would have to work for me for an entire year before you could quit."

"A contract, sir?"

Robert turned and offered him his hand to shake. "This is my contract."

Teddy shook on it.

They continued their trek. "We get up at four o'clock every morning."

"Then I'd better set my alarm clock," said Teddy, smiling.

☙☣

Saturday night was talent night for the kids.

The men built a stage underneath the open-air tent, and rows of chairs were lined up in front of it. Parents had coached their children for months. Although everyone was encouraged to participate just for the fun of it, a hundred dollars went to the act that received the most applause. Immediate family: mother, father, sisters and brothers were barred from applauding.

A hawk-eyed aunt was in charge of making sure that the immediate family adhered to the rule.

Eight acts performed. They sang, danced, recited poems and enacted scenes from plays. One child performed a gymnastics routine.

Candace and Greg were surprised when their children took the stage.

Sara was sitting with them in the audience. "I would have told you, but they wanted it to be a surprise. We've been working on the act ever since they got here."

Candace was tense. She knew the kids enjoyed singing along to iTunes on their iPod players but they hadn't shown any talent for it. They sang loudly and off key. Of course, they heard her singing around the house all the time. And, no doubt, her mother had told them that she and her sisters had won this competition several times over the years.

She clasped Greg's hand nervously as the music began to play. She immediately recognized it as Otis Redding's version of *Shake*. Sam Cooke wrote it, but she loved Otis' version best.

Gregory stood in the middle, his sisters flanking him. Where her mother had managed to find sixties-era clothing for all of them, Candace had no idea, but Gregory was wearing a Nehru jacket, slacks that tapered at the ankle and pointy-toed black leather shoes while the girls were wearing flowery blouses, mini skirts and white go-go boots.

The girls were all legs, looking like colts up there.

"Shake!" Gregory began in a gravelly voice reminiscent of Otis'.

His left leg was wriggling rhythmically with the music, otherwise he stayed in one position. However the girls shimmied and dipped, their long legs and slim hips doing things Candace had no idea they could do, or had any business doing!

By the time Gregory got to, "Let your backbone slip..." the audience was on its feet applauding and shouting accolades.

Candace couldn't believe her eyes or her ears; her children were good, really good.

"Oh, Lord," Greg murmured. "Next thing you know, one of them will be auditioning for *American Idol*."

Behind them Angela had two fingers between her lips, whistling for all she was worth.

Sara turned around. "Louder, Angela!"

It was okay for Angela to show her support because she was not the kids' mother.

Sharon and Debra stood up too, shouting at the top of their lungs, "Encore, encore!"

The emcee for the night, Padraic, went to the stage when they were done. "The judges have decreed that by your applause you've chosen Gregory, Sarafina and Jacquelin Bates as the winners of tonight's competition. Congrats, kids!"

More applause.

Candace was grateful that the judges were elderly members of the family whose opinions no one would impugn. Her kids had won fairly.

She watched as the kids went back onstage to receive congratulations, and their prize. She had no doubt that Sarafina would make certain that it would be equally divided between them, to the penny.

She smiled happily.

Their children were the next generation.

She felt certain that they were all in good hands.

Later, when the reunion attendees had left for the night, and the children were in bed, the adults sat on the screened-in porch listening to rhythm and blues, drinking wine or beer, and chatting.

They sat around on overstuffed chaise lounges and comfortable sofas. Candace sat on a chair while Greg sat at her feet.

"This has been nice, Momma," Candace told Sara. "I'm glad you threatened me with ostracism and made me come."

Everybody laughed. Sara laughed loudest.

"The talent show reminded me of when you girls used to perform together," she said wistfully. "My favorites were the gospel songs you harmonized to. Do you think you could do one now for your old mother?"

"It's been years since I sang in front of anybody," Candace said self-consciously.

"You sing at home all the time." Greg had to put his two-cent's worth in.

"Oh, come on, Candace," Angela encouraged her. "None of us have been onstage in years. Give it a shot."

"I'm willing if you all are," said Sharon. She and Simon were sharing a loveseat. Candace had noticed the way they looked at each other and thought it wouldn't be long before they'd be making an announcement.

"So am I," Debra said. "Let's try *It Won't Be Very Long*. I used to love that one."

"Oh, I don't know," Candace said, still unconvinced.

"Well, we won't be able to do it without you," Angela said. "You led every song we ever sang." She looked at Sharon and Debra. "Didn't she? Acting like she was our momma, or something. She was the bossiest big sister ever."

"Now the truth comes out," said Greg. He gently squeezed Candace's hand.

Candace pretended to take umbrage with Angela's comments. "Bossy? I couldn't help it if you three were hard-headed and I had to get dogmatic on your behinds. When Momma left me in charge I took it seriously. If Sara Johnson said, 'jump!' you asked, 'how high!'"

"I wasn't that bad," Sara said, laughing.

Her daughters all looked at one another.

In unison, they cried, "Yes, you were!"

"But it was good that you were tough, Momma," Candace told her. "It taught us to be independent and hard-working."

"And to never take any crap from anybody," Sharon said.

"And to be honest with ourselves, most of all," Angela said. "Because if you'll lie to yourself, you'll lie to anybody."

"True, true," said Candace, getting to her feet. "So, come on, sisters. Let's sing this song for the woman who made us the women we are."

The four of them stood in a semi-circle and cleared their throats. Then, Candace, her voice clear and full, began to sing: "Well, you know it won't be very long..."

Her sisters' voices blended together to produce a sound so beautiful to her ears that she was almost struck speechless, but she rallied and continued. "You know it won't be very long till we meet him in the sky..."

They moved closer together, their arms draped around each others' waists, and they brought it on home in honor of their mother who was crying her eyes out.

The End

Dear Reader,

I have three brothers and a sister. Over the years we've talked about how our mother raised us. Love was always present in our household, but regardless of that each and every one of us perceived our mother differently. I was amazed by this and thought that exploring that theme: how each child perceived her mother, the most important figure in her life, would be a good topic for an anthology. I hope you've enjoyed reading the entire book, and that it reminded you of your mother and your siblings. Thanks to our publisher, Toni Child, for letting us run with this project. And thanks to Melanie Schuster and Maxine Thompson for contributing stories to it.

Janice Sims
http://www.janicesims.com
Jani569432@aol.com
Post Office Box 811
Mascotte, FL 34753-0811

About The Author

Janice Sims is the author of 14 novels and has had stories included in 9 anthologies. She is a best-selling, award-winning author who is always looking to improve upon her skills as a writer. She writes in the romance, suspense, mainstream, and paranormal genres and, lately, she's been working on a mystery series.

Janice lives in Central Florida with her husband and daughter.

More From Dream Books

From Crack Addict To Pastor
a true story by Karen Sills
ISBN 0-9770936-3-8

Pastor Karen Sills describes her years of substance abuse in this dramatized rendition of her life. She gives detailed accounts of how drug addiction impacted her and the lives of the people she loves dearly. Through this book she shows just how merciful God is. And because of His mercy and grace, she is delivered from prostitution, lesbianism, imprisonment and drug addiction.

Perfect Love
a novel by Arsoleen Woolcock
ISBN 0-9770936-4-6

Breanna's one dream is to find that special love by a man who's as wonderful as her father. But the secret that has been hidden for years surfaces likely to destroy her dreams of forever after in a Perfect Love.

The Homecoming (Mt. Hope Series Book #1)
a novel by Angela Santana
ISBN 0-9770936-7-0

Tragedy turns to blessing when a despondent, desperate young pioneer woman finds herself alone and in crisis in an unfamiliar place. Faced with a decision she never thought she'd have to make, she learns that God's grace is not just sufficient but abounding, and that all things work together for good if only she can learn to trust...

Victory Day By Day
by Dr. Arlene H. Churn
ISBN 0-9770936-8-9

Victory Day By Day is a personal collection of affirmations for achieving and living a victorious life through the spoken word. It is meant to increase the faith of the reader and to fortify them with vocal power over life's daily adversities and challenges. Victory is achieved gradually, day by day, and each victory will lead to spiritual growth with unlimited possibilities. Keep VICTORY IN YOUR VIEW

Call toll free: 1-877-209-5200 to order by phone or use this coupon to order by mail.

Name_____

Address_____

City_____State_____Zip_____

Please send me the books I have checked below.

___**Perfect Love**
a novel by Arsoleen Woolcock
ISBN 0-9770936-4-6
$13.99 USA $21.99 CAN

___**From Crack Addict To Pastor**
a true story by Karen Sills
ISBN 0-9770936-3-8
$12.00 USA $19.00 CAN

___**The Homecoming**
Angela Santana
ISBN 0-9770936-7-0
$13.99 USA $21.99 CAN

___**Victory Day By Day**
by Rev. Dr. Arlene H. Churn
ISBN 0-9770936-8-9
$6.99 USA $10.99 CAN

I am enclosing $_____

Plus postage & handling $_____

Total amount enclosed $_____

*Add $2.65 for the first book and $.60 for each additional book. Send Money Order. (No Cash, C.O.D. or Personal Checks) to Dreams Publishing Co. P.O. Box 4731, Rocky Mount, NC 27801.

Price and Numbers subject to change without notice. All orders subject to availability.

Check out: www.DreamsPublishing.com

The Dilemma's Series by Reign

Book #1

Book #2

The Dilemma's Series are stories base around Ivy Jones-Miller, Sheena Daniels, Miranda Jones and Jade Sanders. Each woman tackle trials and tribulations and winning against all odds though their faith in God and love and devotion of friendship. Books In The Dilemma Series: "Ivy's Dilemma (Thy Will Be Done)" published 2005 "Jade's Dilemma (Lead Us Not Into Temptation)" published 2006 and "Sheena's Dilemma (It's Better To Marry Than to Burn) not yet published.

Call toll free: 1-877-209-5200 to order by phone or use this coupon to order by mail.

Name_____

Address_____

City_____State_____Zip_____

Please send me the books I have checked below.

    ___**Ivy's Dilemma – Thy Will Be Done**
       ISBN 0-9770936-0-3
       $12.00 USA $19.00 CAN

    ___**Jade's Dilemma – Lead Us Not Into Temptation**
       ISBN 0-9770936-5-4
       $12.00 USA $19.00 CAN

I am enclosing $_____
Plus postage & handling $_____
Total amount enclosed $_____

*Add $2.65 for the first book and $.60 for each additional book. Send Money Order. (No Cash, C.O.D. or Personal Checks) to Dreams Publishing Co. P.O. Box 4731, Rocky Mount, NC 27801.
Price and Numbers subject to change without notice. All orders subject to availability.

Help Me With The 90%

By Kevin & Laura Hinnant

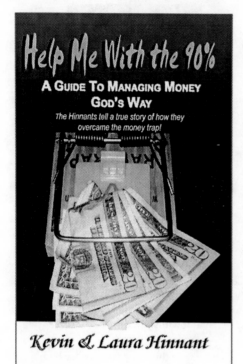

Do you or someone you know live from paycheck to two days before the next paycheck? If so, that spirit of bondage can be broken once and for all. Help Me With The 90% will teach you to manage and control your money God's way.

Don't stay ensnared by The D.E.B.T. (The Devils Elaborate Bondage Trap")

ISBN 0-9770936-9-7
Price $9.99 USA $14.99 CAN

🔊 **WORLD WIDE ARTIST** is an internet radio station with a different kind of format. Though traditionally we broadcast Book Club Discussions, Gospel Music and Talk shows, we are different because the audience can participate during live broadcasting using toll free numbers or by communicating through the Chat room.

TUNE IN AND SEE THE DIFFERENCE!

www.worldwideartist.net

Printed in the United States
99497LV00010B/173/A